MW00586313

THE LOST WORLD OF KHARAMU

ROBERT J. STAVA

SEVERED PRESS
HOBART TASMANIA

THE LOST WORLD OF KHARAMU

Copyright © 2018 ROBERT J. STAVA
Copyright © 2018 by Severed Press

WWW.SEVEREDPRESS.COM

All rights reserved. No part of this book may be
reproduced or transmitted in any form or by any
electronic or mechanical means, including
photocopying, recording or by any information and
retrieval system, without the written permission of
the publisher and author, except where permitted by law.
This novel is a work of fiction. Names,
characters, places and incidents are the product of
the author's imagination, or are used fictitiously.
Any resemblance to actual events, locales or persons,
living or dead, is purely coincidental.

ISBN: 978-1-925711-88-2

All rights reserved.

Dedicated to Arthur Conan Doyle,
whose 'Lost World' spawned generations of fantastic tales of men
and dinosaurs, and Edgar Rice Burroughs, who directly inspired
this author's career.

THE LOST WORLD
OF
KHARAMU

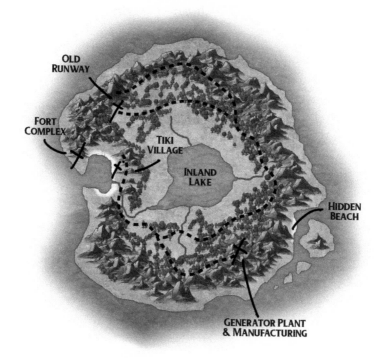

OLD
RUNWAY

FORT
COMPLEX

TIKI
VILLAGE

INLAND
LAKE

HIDDEN
BEACH

GENERATOR PLANT
& MANUFACTURING

PRELUDE

The clearing in the jungle had the muted, expectant air of a trap.

Both men instinctively sensed it; the vestigial, primitive part of the brain that hundreds of generations of civilization could not eradicate was immediately alert and sending up red flags as they stood at the edge of the dense vegetation, observing. The outward signs were unmistakable as well – the lack of any bird chatter, the broken branches, the tattered fiber optic cable that was dug up out of the loamy soil and chewed. Only the insects seemed unbothered by whatever menace might lurk nearby.

Chen Lee felt his pulse quicken, inwardly cursing his supervisor. Even the Plant Biology teams were always supposed to be a minimal of three, but in the last two weeks 'temporary' budget cuts had been creeping in everywhere. Today it was just himself and one guard, a stocky Malaysian named Paul Cham.

Lee was one of those careful, methodical workers that didn't like being rushed, and that his super had been badgering him all morning with extra duties hadn't helped. Neither had Cham's constant smiling and talking. It was almost as irritating as the gnats and mosquitoes.

Now this.

The change order to get a set of new brilliantly colored 'Vitae Eternus' plants set up had come just after five a.m. The third time this week. Someone – or something – was tearing them up.

Lee did not understand what was doing it – the glade he was now looking at was at least a mile outside the nearest containment perimeter and he wasn't aware of anything else on the island sizable enough to do this much damage, let alone *why*.

It wasn't even his usual sector – Team Beta covered this particular area. His assignments were always at the north end of the island.

Away from the dinosaurs.

Lee was strictly a plant man. Animals, reptiles, even other humans made him uncomfortable. There had been rumors (ones he made a point of ignoring) that several people – perhaps *deliberately* – had been killed by the creatures. But those kinds of fears were insidious.

They had a way of nibbling at you, distracting from the work at hand.

Plants!

Nearby was one of the tiny marker flags, lying broken next to a fern.

Who had left that out? The sight of it was irritating to him - Lee was meticulous about such things. If a guest found a *flag*, of all things, it would ruin the whole vacation! Could it have been one of the dinosaurs? That seemed ludicrous. More likely it was one of the monkey species rumored to be on the island, brought over by European explorers centuries ago.

He shifted his weight. The satchel looped over his shoulder was chafing him through his work shirt, as was the tool belt around his waist. He guessed the temperature must be close to a hundred, the humidity nearly so. The air had the cloying smell of vegetation, rot . . . and something else. Something unpleasant that reminded him of snakes.

Screw the company, he thought, *they should have paid him better for his skills and knowledge. Now there were too many weird things happening. And the budget cuts weren't a good sign.* His supervisor, Mr. Tsou, was acting increasingly irrational. Lee had a cousin in Taipei that had emailed him the other day about a new pharmaceutical company that was hiring. . . and he was now positive that odd plant he'd stumbled upon days ago, a strange-looking thing (unlike the bogus 'eternal life' species he was currently planting in key locations) was the one the German Pharmaceutical company had been looking for. With it's odd, radiant flowers and thick, veined leaves that issued a milky sap when torn, he found it simultaneously captivating and repulsive. That and the fact he'd only seen two of them so far. Which was quite odd for such an environment.

It would be worth millions. He could retire a rich man! Open his own company in the United States!

He looked up and saw with a start that the Malaysian was no longer smiling. Cham's round eyes were narrow and alert, his nostrils flared. Under the camo cap a trickle of sweat ran down one temple. The surplus Chinese-built AK-47 with a 30-round banana clip held at an upward angle.

Lee stared at the cart with its three brightly colored plants. They were a customized hybrid of *bromeliad*, with flowers reminiscent of a sunburst.

Five more minutes and I'll be done. Five minutes and I can take my lunch break, damn what Mr. Tsou tells me or not! In weeks this will all be ancient history!

Still, he hesitated.

Cham signaled him to wait. They sat like that for a good five minutes, while Lee's bent legs throbbed and ached from crouching. Then a warbled bird cry from above the tree they were next to – an octopus branched Alexandrian laurel – broke the tension. Another bird answered, and Cham relaxed slightly. He nodded toward the clearing and raised his automatic rifle.

Lee stood and stretched, his knee caps cracking, then stepped into the clearing.

Almost immediately something burst through the bushes to his left and he shrieked.

Just slightly taller than him and covered in bright-colored feathers, striped along the sides with a russet crest on top, was a fearsome-looking lizard with glaring eyes and a leering mouth filled with pointed teeth. It looked like a lunatic hybrid of reptile and bird, its long forearms flared with a fan of feathers along the outer edge and its long tail rigidly pointed upward.

Deinonychus antirrhopus.

Or 'terrible claw'.

Also known in the employee guidebook as 'velociraptor'.

Lee stumbled backward, pulling the unpotted plant to his chest. His heart hammered as adrenaline flashed through his body. Outside of dummy training he'd never seen one up close. He had no idea how utterly terrifying the things were. And the smell: a combination of metallic, reptilian odor and rotting meat. He was sharply aware of the atavistic centers of his nervous system all but exploding with revulsion.

The raptor hissed and corkscrewed its head.

Cham didn't hesitate. Flicking the safety, he let out a short burst that pulverized the raptor's head, then pumped two rounds into the thing's chest. The creature stumbled, its tail flicked left and right then fell over. A second later its back arched up in a dying reflex, air escaping out of its open jaws, before collapsing a final time.

Lee straightened up, barely registering the wet streak along the inside of his pants where his bladder had let go. Cordite cloyed the air, along with the ringing silence that follows a sudden burst of gunfire.

Blood leaked out of the ruin of the raptor's face.

Lee let out a reflexive laugh, sounding more like a bark.

"Well, that was close!" he said, too loudly. His voice died in his throat as he realized Cham had disappeared.

Just like that.

A rustle came from behind him, and a moment later a coconut-sized object came tumbling out of the brush, landing near Lee's foot.

He looked down, not wanting to see, but unable to stop himself.

The Malaysian's head lay on its side, thick lips drawn in a rictus of agony, the eyes glazing.

Lee stepped backwards as another nightmare emerged from the leaves. He desperately wanted to run, but as death approached him with stealthy footsteps, his own refused to obey. He hugged the plant tighter, realizing in his last moments the absurdity of dying holding of all things a plant he detested – a fake of no real value.

No, no please!

A scream cut through the air and was cut off as blood sprayed upwards, fanning the lower branches of the tree in crimson.

Inches from his glazing eyes, the veiny leaves of a mysterious plant had a drop of blood on it.

After a brief gurgle, the glade was quiet again.

PALISADES CLIFFS, HUDSON VALLEY

"This really isn't a good time, Jeff," Grant Taylan said, dangling a hundred and fifty feet up along the cliffs overlooking the Hudson River. He was still trying to process what he had been looking at in the narrow cave revealed by the rockslide a week previous. He should have known better than to take the call then, but he'd just hooked himself up to the rappelling harness again and there was something exhilarating about the day that eclipsed his judgement; a brilliant mid-summer afternoon in the Hudson Valley, the river and wooded hills a dramatic study in patchwork shadows cast by the mountainous clouds scattered across the sky. The vast expanse of open vista was enough to make one's heart skip a beat: an agoraphobics' nightmare or a landscape artist's fantasy.

"Oh, come on, Grant, did you read the brochure or not?"

If Grant had a hand free, he would have smacked his forehead with it. A roughly handsome man, average in build and his chin stubbled with a couple day's growth, he might be the type one would dismiss as a reasonable catalogue model if not for the eyes. They were brown, intense - almost hurt-looking, and had a way of riveting one's attention, but only after they finally stopped wandering and zeroed in on you.

That was when one realized how incredibly charismatic was the personality behind them.

Grant Taylan, the 34-year-old whose climbing boots were planted on the cliff-face while one muscled arm gripped one of the two belaying ropes, wasn't just some eye-candy for middle-aged housewives, however. He was *Doctor* Grant Taylan, an expert paleontologist and archeologist with the American Museum of Natural History – AMNH – and recently reduced to adjunct professor at Columbia's Lamont campus after a recent incident involving the assistant dean (and his nemesis) there, Doctor Karl Zweig.

He was known informally in certain circles as 'The Bone Hunter', due to his ruthless pursuit of criminals stealing and trading dinosaur remains in the grey and black markets. Having seen many of his own digs looted over the years, Taylan wasn't much concerned with splitting hairs when it came to stealing remains for profit, though some of deeper pockets (including legitimate museums) weren't keen on him poking around their storage rooms or examining their books too closely.

4

The brochure – folded and jammed haphazardly into his left cargo shorts pocket – was the one that had landed a day earlier on his desk via a FedEx package, a brochure that at first glance he'd dismissed as an elaborate joke.

An *expensive* elaborate joke, from the quality of the printing and custom size, which he later noted was of Golden Ratio proportions.

On the cover was arguably some of the most realistic CG dinosaur art he'd ever seen, featuring a trio of feathered Utahraptor's leaping through the air at a 1950s movie star man with a bolt-action rifle, with the horrified brunette (in full make-up) on the ground clutching his leg, her requisite torn blouse revealing ample cleavage all but bursting out of her bra. In the background was the usual primordial jungle-swamp, with grazing sauropods and soaring pterodactyls.

It was a mailer for the latest in 'Themed Vacations', though not the typical shlock targeting the brainless Disney masses, in Taylan's opinion. This was more a mash-up of high-quality art and classic graphic design geared toward the elite rich.

In stylized type across the top it read:

"The Lost World of Kharamu".

Below it, the script tagline read: *For those who dare.*

What Taylan couldn't fathom was why Jeff Doyle, a college class-mate from Harvard he hadn't spoken to in years, had sent him the thing in the first place. They weren't particularly close – Doyle was a happy-go-lucky rich kid who had drifted into real-estate after college, and Taylan was currently on precarious financial footing at best. His latest funding had been pulled (AMNH was in rough shape these days, even without the meddling of his nemesis), he was pretty much an outcast by his peers at Lamont and besides, even on a good day, paleontologists were seldom known for being flush.

So, after signing the NDA he'd glanced at it, dismissed it as a lark, and with his usual single-mindedness, geared up to check out the tip he'd gotten from a friend at the NY State Parks & Recreation department about some unusual things that were revealed by the recent rockslide along the cliffs. Which led him to dangling off a cliff just opposite the river from the riverside village of Wyvern Falls.

"Sorry Jeff, I didn't really get a chance just yet. Can I call you back?" A warning beep on the smartphone showed another call coming in.

From his mother.

"Well, I was kind of hoping you'd—"

Squeezing his eyes shut, Taylan tapped the screen with his thumb.

"Grant?" asked his mother, presumably from her home in Cleveland.

"Mom, really not a good time."

A cluck on the other end of the line. "It's *never* a good time for you, son."

Taylan shifted in his harness, so he was just by the overhang opposite where he'd seen the falcon's nest earlier. The crevice formed by the rockslide kept the worst of the wind out of the phone, so he could hear better.

"Okay," he relented. "Can you make it quick? I'm hanging in a—"

"Yen sent us another letter. She still wants us to return the gifts she gave us from last Christmas. Including the smoked salmon!"

"Seriously? She asked for the salmon back . . . from *last year?*"

"*Seriously.* Should I tell her to go to the town dump?"

Taylan squeezed his eyes shut even more. His ex – an exotic Vietnamese art gallery owner who had gone psycho after their break-up two months previous – had been escalating her revenge tactics in recent weeks.

Now she was writing letters to his parents? Who else?

". . . and your sister as well – she's gotten *three* letters! Demanding Aaron's birthday toys be returned! And what's this about a bill for a cancelled wedding? Did you really tell Yen you were going to *marry* her!?"

"No, no, of course not. It's a misunderstanding. Look, I have to . . ."

"Son, you and I are going to have a sit-down talk about this! Your father would be horrified if he were still here!"

Again, if Taylan had had a free hand, he would have smacked his head with it. "Mom, I'll put in a call to the police. The restraining order was very specific. Ring you right back. Bye."

". . . Peyton's boat is on its way to pick you up right now," came Doyle's voice again, in mid-sentence.

"*Peyton who?*" Taylan shot back, somewhat absently. He was focusing again at the crevice in the rock. If what he had found in there was what he thought it was, it would rewrite the whole narrative of human civilization, astrobiology *and* dinosaurs.

Not to mention his career.

"Um, as in Allen Peyton III, the multi-billionaire financier," Doyle replied. "He's one of the investors behind the 'Lost World' themed vacation? The Chinese have developed this whole thing. He wants to know it's legit through and through. He wants a team of experts for the trial run. That's where you come in, old man."

Taylan grit his teeth. Doyle's insistence on calling him 'old man' – even though Taylan was only three months older – had been one of those irritating affectations that had started their freshman year. Every time Doyle said it Taylan wanted to strangle him.

He was about to say as much when a sharp tug on the rappelling line distracted him.

Any further conversation was cut off by a second tug, this one jolting him hard enough that the smartphone flipped out of his hand. He glanced down briefly as the thing described a sickening tumble, dropping hundreds of feet into the trees below.

A voice spoke from above.

"Well, hello down there, Doctor Taylan."

There was no mistaking the thick Russian accent.

Igor Gorimov.

Not good, Taylan knew. When you're dangling on a rope on a very dangerous cliff, the last person in the world you'd want standing at the top holding it was Igor.

A lower to mid-level smuggler who had been operating out of Brighton Beach since the early 90s, Gorimov had become a thorn in Taylan's side when he'd gravitated to the illegal fossils trafficking market a few years ago, procuring rare specimens for discriminating private collectors with deep pockets. It wasn't only that Taylan was professionally outraged at what Gorimov did, on a personal level it simply pissed him off. Even more personally, when several key specimens from a rare dig Taylan himself had been working on – a collection of *Tarbosaurus bataar* skeletons that included soft tissue samples - Gorimov confiscated *en route* from the dig site near the Nemegt Formation, a fruitful expanse of Late Cretaceous sandstone and mudstone in southern Mongolia. Taylan had tracked down the remains back to New York, where Gorimov had arranged a private sale with a wealthy collector for what was later revealed to be somewhere in the 4.5-million-dollar range. Had the sale gone through, not only would the specimens been lost, so would their scientific value as they were processed for display and critical provenance information destroyed.

But once again, despite being caught dead to rights, Gorimov had slipped through the wheels of justice and was a free man. A few years previous, in a rare moment of face-to-face confrontation (at a run-down bar outside of Butte, Montana), when asked how he kept avoiding hard time he'd told Taylan; "In Russia I had to deal with KGB. Compared to that, U.S. police and FBI are pussies."

Taylan was convinced it was really because Gorimov was coated in some sort of invisible grease.

"What can I do you for, Igor?" Taylan shouted up. He could make out two other figures on either side of him. Vlad and Oleg, his strong-arms. Or as Taylan thought of them as: 'The Impalers'. Like some sadistic heavy metal duo. Not that Gorimov was any weakling. Taylan bet the stocky, shaven-headed Russian could crack walnuts with his hands.

"Oh, I could think of a couple things," Gorimov replied, pronouncing it 'thinks' as usual. "Starting with the few million dollars you cost me when you tipped off the Port Authority about the merchandise I was importing."

"They were *Tarbosaurus bataar* skeletons, Igor, the ones you stole from my dig."

"Not 'stole'. *Redirected.*"

Taylan was all but snarling. "Right. Just like the money would be *redirected* into your bank account. It was illegal. Period. That's the way it works."

"Yes, well what it was business you shouldn't have stuck your fucking nose in, smart guy. What happened to the container?"

"Someplace where it can easily be returned to the rightful owners, last I checked." Taylan glanced around quickly. About twenty feet to his left was the outcropping with the falcon's nest. To the right was a broad stretch of vertical rock, offering no footholds larger than what would accommodate a mouse. A few feet below him was the crevice from the rockslide, but he wasn't sure what good it would do him even if he got there, with his phone smashed to pieces on the rocks below. The rock slide had destroyed a section of the cliffs roughly thirty feet across, but below the outcropping to the left were a series of staggered ledges and trees. The doubled climbing ropes were 200' long, which meant he could drop to within fifty feet of . . .

Another sharp tug grabbed his attention.

"You might wish to think about telling me where to find it," Gorimov said. There was a bright glint as the sunlight reflected off the gold tooth in his grin and the ring in his ear. "Looks to me like a long way down, Taylan. As you know: it's not the fall, it's that sudden stop at the bottom that hurts like hell."

Taylan thought quickly. "No. And if you kill me, you'll never see your money."

A sharp laugh came down from above. "Maybe I don't care so much about money anymore. Maybe what I care about is watching you shit your pants!"

The rappelling lines swung back and forth. Taylan had to work his feet fast to avoid twisting and getting slammed into the cliff face.

"Screw you!" he yelled, realizing they were already past negotiating.

Gorimov wasn't just nuts, he was insane. And a sadist to boot.

"Having fun yet?" Gorimov shouted on the third pass.

"All kinds!" Taylan yelled back. He was trying to time the release so that his momentum would at least swing him toward the partial slope where the trees were. It would still mean a fifty-yard tumble to the bottom after he got to the end of the rope, but it was better than the alternative.

In one regard Gorimov was completely wrong about him: when it came to these situations, Taylan was pretty much fearless. That was due primarily to one traumatic childhood event at age 13 - the death of his father during a fluke storm on Lake Erie during a regatta.

They'd been sailing Lightnings when the squall hit. The small sailboats had become scattered as the race quickly dissolved from an elegant formation to a chaotic 'every man for himself' free-for-all. The speed at which a storm could whip up on the shallow Great Lake was breathtaking – the flat surface morphed into 6-foot rollers, huge thunderclouds had issued diabolical forks of lightning everywhere at once. Hell had arrived out of nowhere.

At first it seemed manageable – they'd gotten down the fore sail and reefed in the main, securing everything as the squall hit. Then – ironically - lightning struck their little boat. His father had died instantly of heart failure, it was later determined. Taylan was catapulted out of the small cockpit, unconscious, tethered by the safety line attached to his lifejacket. He'd vaguely remembered coming to and seeing the open-mouthed corpse of his father tangled in the main halyard, the horrifying sense of loss and tragedy, the overwhelming feeling of being an insignificant mote helpless at the merciless wrath of nature. Then nothing until he'd awoken days later in a hospital bed.

Some people would have been psychologically devastated by such an event. With Taylan, the effect had been opposite: it had stripped him of any illusions about life and his ego. From that day forward, he wasn't afraid of death, he was only afraid of not *living*.

A piercing screech and swooping sound over his shoulder distracted him, causing him to lose his footing and take a heart-stopping swing out into thin air. It took a moment to register he'd just been attacked by a very large peregrine falcon.

The nest! Of course!

The bird squawked as it reversed and took another swipe at him, it's claws narrowly missing his eyes and tearing open his left shoulder. He instinctively swiped at it with his left hand and instantly dropped a dozen feet down, stopping with a bone-jarring hitch as the safety lock caught. He spun and slammed his shoulder into the rock face.

"Ha-ha! Look at big-mouth scientist now! Bird got your tongue yet?" Gorimov taunted.

"It's 'cat', asshole!" Taylan shot back, narrowly avoiding another dive bomb attack from the falcon. He swung out again in a dizzying arc, legs flailing, nylon ropes now twisting and putting him a sickening spin. If he hit the cliff the wrong way, he could easily shatter his skull.

Picked the wrong day not to wear a helmet, he thought, as he swung back in to the right.

He twisted his hips in the same direction the rope was, legs up, taking the worst of the impact with his boots. Still, he slammed into the rock face with his shoulder again a moment later, hard enough to make his teeth clack. Loose sandstone rocks flew and tumbled away.

Risking a glance up he saw something he liked even less. Vlad and Oleg were handling the ropes. Gorimov was standing between them, holding a large military knife in his hand.

It would only take him seconds to cut through the nylon rope.

Scrabbling to stop his momentum, he angled his body sideways so he was perpendicular to the cliff, then with a few running steps pushed himself off in the same direction he was being swung. For a crazy second, he saw the falcon coming in straight at his head, talons first, then he released the lock and was dropping in a heart-stopping arc, his weight and descent causing him to swing out like an ungainly Spider-man. His brimmed hat snapped off and sailed away. The bird overshot him, screeching, talons clutching at empty air where his head was a second before.

Thirty, forty, fifty feet. His climbing gloves smoldered from the friction.

Taylan bared his teeth and prepared for the worst.

The ragged trees were zooming up toward him at an alarming rate. He forced his legs to stop pinwheeling and put his feet together.

Almost . . .

Then came the sickening jolt that was every climber's worst feeling – the first line had been cut, the sudden slack accelerating his descent. He tried to slow himself but a moment later the second line was cut, and he was free falling.

The wind roared in his ears.

It's too far, he had time to think, then: *I'm dead* as he tucked his chin in.

Not yet! said a voice in his ear. His father's.

Then he was crashing through leaves and branches.

It was like being beaten with a hundred switches and bats. A tree limb banged his head hard enough to make him see stars, then he ricocheted off the trunk and was falling again with thirty feet of open air to a pile of boulders and rubble.

Taylan's eyes went wide.

How exactly his lines got tangled in the branches of the tree he never found out.

Ten feet above the largest boulder he felt a tremendous bone-wrenching yank on his harness. The nylon ropes were static lines and didn't have a lot of play in them, which also saved him from more severe injury.

Taylan landed hard enough on his back to knock the wind out of him.

He lay there, stunned, staring up at three hundred feet of cliff face, bruised and bleeding, but miraculously still alive. Something coming down from the sky caught his attention. For a few seconds, he thought it was the damned falcon coming at him. A painful cough exited his throat as his lungs kick-started themselves again. Even so, he managed a lopsided grin: it was his hat. It fluttered down and landed a few feet away.

He stared up at the sky, savoring the incredible rush of realizing he was still alive; the sky impossibly blue for a moment, the fantastic shapes of the clouds overhead amazing. Then life reasserted itself. His head was throbbing, his entire body felt like he had the shit kicked out of him. Several times.

He blinked slowly, eyeing the detritus of leaves and dust still coming down after his fall. The cliff face of the Palisades looked a mile high from this angle.

I survived that, he thought. *I was way up there, now I'm down here, alive. How ridiculous is that?*

Then he remembered Igor and his two sidekicks were still at the top.

Wincing, Taylan forced himself to stand up. Some of his ribs were bruised, maybe even cracked, but nothing seemed broken. He staggered over to where his hat lay and crouching down painfully, picked it up. It was bleached from the sun across many continents and fraying on the edges, and now sported a sharp nick where the falcon had snipped at it.

A battered old veteran, he mused.

Then he spotted his smartphone nearby. The face was cracked, but it too appeared to have survived.

The conversation he'd had on it with Doyle felt like it had been hours ago.

What the hell had that been about a boat picking me up?

From where he was standing the ground sloped about twenty yards down through trees and brush to a rocky shoreline. Almost right on cue he heard the burble of an outboard motor approaching. Through the trees, he saw a Zodiac inflatable launch swinging in, while further out was a large, sleek-looking motor yacht easing to a stop.

He looked up toward the top of the cliff but there was no sign of the Russians. If they were coming down to follow up on their handy work, he didn't want to be around. Knowing Igor, there were probably more than just the three of them.

How the hell did a promising day go to hell so quickly?

He scheduled to meet with an old professor and mentor of his – Dr. Lee Snyder - in lower Manhattan for dinner down at Fraunces Tavern. He was looking forward to them having a few chuckles over this latest adventure. And getting his opinion on what he'd just found up on the cliff face.

Dropping the phone in his pocket, he made his way toward the shore.

As it turned out, the day was just beginning. The only dinner he would have that night would be somewhere over the Atlantic Ocean.

"Fucking shit!" Oleg cursed an hour later as they stood near the spot Taylan had landed. "We'll never find the bastard now."

Gorimov ignored him. Oleg was useful when it came to dirty work, but he was also an unrelenting naysayer who always dwelt on the negative side of everything. "Oleg Eyore-ski" was his nickname for him. Vlad at least kept his mouth shut and seemed to enjoy his work. Oleg could be a real pain. Some days Gorimov wondered if it might just be easier to put a bullet into the man's skull and put them both out of his misery.

Not today, though. There was work to do. If there was one thing Gorimov knew about success, it was that it sometimes required patience and determination. And *thoroughness*.

Little thieves are hanged, but great ones escape, his father used to say, usually while using his leather belt to make his point.

Something caught his eye. It was a folded bit of paper that looked like a brochure, just visible between two rocks. Bending over he picked it up and unfolded it. A moment later he smiled.

Oleg came up alongside him, shaking his head. "He's probably back in New York, already, getting ready to leave the country. We should have just cut the lines immediately and killed him. This sucks. We'll never find him."

Gorimov's free hand fingered the grip of the pistol holstered at his hip.

Maybe I should end this now.

Instead he looked up at the sky and smiled.

"Shut up. I know that yacht. Don't you worry, my *eyore-ski*. We find Taylan, no problem."

OF COURSE, YOU CAN, MR. TAYLAN!

"Seriously? The Russians tried to kill you? That is so awesome! You're always my 'go-to' man when it comes to excitement!" Doyle was saying on the phone to Taylan, who was recuperating in the forward stateroom of the yacht.

He'd forgotten how much he'd hated Doyle back in college, but now it was coming back to him in spades: a bullet-pointed checklist in bold type. Son of a wealthy real estate developer from Montclair, New Jersey, Doyle had drifted through college with the privileged nonchalance and uncanny luck only the very wealthy seem to stumble into.

For Taylan, every course and class were a battle, in part due to his innate inability to accept rigid norms or anything at face value. It was as if he was born with an automatic *question everything* switch that was set off by any imposition of proven facts, dogmas or even theories. Not that he wouldn't ever come around to agreeing with it, it was simply that he had to bang it around, smack it a few times or kick it across the floor to see if it held up; it was his way of *understanding* things.

Doyle seldom had any question marks in his head, unless it was attached to matters of drinking, parties or where to go skiing on winter break. What Taylan found utterly confounding was how Doyle continuously *got away with it.*

Such as his present circumstance.

Filling him in on the first part of the call, Doyle mentioned he'd worked a few low-action real estate jobs in the area until six months prior, when a distant cousin of his had hooked him up with Allen Peyton III, a money management success story whose current net worth was estimated around 4.5 billion dollars. Doyle wasn't doing much more than pushing paper around his cubicle at Peyton Financial Management's midtown office, making a half-hearted attempt at appearing to be useful, when word got around the water cooler Peyton was nosing around for specialists in the dinosaur business.

For a change, Doyle found one of the few things he excelled at – social networking – making himself useful at PFM.

"That's when your name came up, pal," Doyle said, "which landed me in the big guy's office."

"Terrific," Taylan replied, sitting (and feeling somewhat ridiculous) in the lush bathrobe they'd provided him with. A middle-aged Chinese woman had whisked away his soiled clothes after the yacht's medical officer had seen to the worse of Taylan's injuries, including a butterfly bandage for the shoulder. The cabin he was sitting in was one of those sleek, luxurious, and utterly tasteless ones typically seen in high-end yachting magazines.

"I figured you'd appreciate it, especially after Peyton looked into your current financial situation."

Taylan stiffened. Despite being a tenured professor, anyone poking around in his private business (particularly when it came to money) instantly made him bristle. He was just about to hang up, nail down the skipper and demand he be let off on the nearest dock – clothing be damned – when Doyle said something that got his attention.

". . . would give your school a grant of 1.2 million dollars, to be used specifically for *your* research."

"*What?*"

"Peyton Financial would give you a grant, of 1.2 million—"

"I got that part, Doyle. Why the hell would they do that?"

"In exchange for your services. Mr. Peyton wishes to engage you as a consultant for this new venture he's involved in: *The Lost World of Kharamu.*"

"The 'Disney Dinosaur park' brochure you sent me?" Taylan was getting a sinking feeling in the pit of his stomach with this one. He was always suspicious of anyone with the number of zeroes attached to people with Peyton's net worth. "I don't have time for this, Jeff."

"Pretty, wild, isn't it?" Doyle went on, unfazed. "Mr. Peyton is one of the primary investors of MuTron International. The thing is, it's a Chinese venture and he doesn't have unconditional confidence in their company and the scientists behind it. That's why he's bringing in his own independent experts for the trial run. And naturally I thought of you, bud, us Harvard boys—"

"*Trial run? Scientists?* What in the hell are you talking about, Doyle?"

"Dude, *didn't you read the brochure?*"

Taylan rolled his eyes. If Doyle called him 'Dude' or 'Bud' one more time, he was sure he would discover a way to reach through the phone and strangle him with both hands.

"I've kind of had a busy day here," he replied.

"Oh yeah, I almost forgot about the Russians! Anyhow, the beta test adventure run is next week. Mr. Peyton has requested you and two other dino scientists you know to join him, all-expenses paid, right now so we can—"

Taylan held up his hand to the empty cabin. "Wait a minute, what 'beta test run adventure'?"

"Dude, you need to get your head out of the dark ages and get with it! Themed vacations are the latest thing, and this one is the ultimate! A 1950s expedition to a remote island where you get to fight – and kill – real dinosaurs! How cool is that!?"

"Doyle, what exactly do you mean by 'real dinosaurs'? That's not possible."

"Oh, it is *now*. The Chinese have been working on it for two decades, now they've really done it! T-rex, raptors, the whole fucking Jurassic Park thing, dude. It's a total reality!"

Taylan stood up and glanced out the cabin windows. The yacht was just passing the Route 9 bridge over Spuyten Duyvil.

"A *total reality*," he said to himself, trying to wrap his head around this concept. There had been a lot of talk about it - it was every Paleontologists' wet dream since the early 1990s when Michael Crichton made the concept seem remotely possible. Recently, the legendary paleontologist Jack Horner had predicted they were already 50 percent there, with scientists having already modified chicken DNA to revert some parts back to their dinosaur ancestors. That was just early stage tinkering – it was still a hell of a leap between getting a toothed mouth to appear on a chicken embryo to generating a full-blown, chomping-stomping T-Rex.

"Man, you are going to love this one, you signed the NDA, right? Of course you did, the FedEx delivery man couldn't have left you the package without it! The letter inside should have explained everything."

Taylan rubbed the bridge of his nose. He vaguely remembered that part, but it didn't stick out at the time. He was often called to sign for sensitive materials. But the letter? He'd only glanced at it, figuring on going through it later today. He was preoccupied with the climb and what his contact at the Parks Department workers had claimed seeing on the cliff after the rockfall.

"Maybe you can refresh my memory, Jeff."

"Jeez," Doyle replied, unable to mask his disappointment. "I hand you a request to attend the coolest thing on the planet – especially for guys like you – and you didn't *read* it? That hurts, dude. That really hurts!"

Taylan didn't even consider breathing a word of what he had really been up to that day – he wouldn't trust Doyle with his laundry list let alone a major scientific discovery – but he also couldn't deny that he *was* curious.

If the Chinese had really come up with some way to genetically engineer dinosaurs, that most definitely qualified as *major*.

"Get to the point, Jeff. And where the hell is this boat heading right now?"

There was silence on the other end. When Doyle spoke again, it was a few degrees less friendly. Which made Taylan suspect much of his 'easy-going-dude' shtick was just that.

"Okay, pal, here's the deal . . ."

NATURAL HISTORY MUSEUM, KENSINGTON, LONDON

"You can find her in the Dinosaur Exhibit Hall, ground floor, blue zone, to the left and the front of the building and toward the back of the room, sir," the woman at the check-in told Taylan after he'd arrived at the Natural History Museum.

He was still jet-lagged from the red-eye flight from JFK to Heathrow, but two cups of harsh English coffee had brought him somewhat to his senses. He had to remember to insist on 'black' after the waiter had plopped a milk-muddled cup in front of him at the hotel restaurant.

At least the breakfast had been good – those hefty English breakfast sausages he could never get in the States along with scrambled eggs, navy beans and juice. The toast, as always, confounded him. He never grasped the British obsession with burnt, white toast.

The Victorian industriousness of Hintz Hall never failed to impress him. From the third-floor balcony one had the best vantage point. The light brown and Prussian-blue tiling, combined with the intricately detailed galleries, iron ceiling arches and glass roof panels set an austere yet magical atmosphere from another era. It was as if the architects had specifically designed the space to pique one's curiosity. From his seat at the top of the stair landing on the opposite side of the hall, the casually posed statue of Charles Darwin seemed inclined to agree.

The statue of 'Dippy', the Diplodocus skeleton that had greeted schoolkids for generations, however, had been given the boot. In its place was hanging a skeleton of a great blue whale.

Maybe dinosaurs just aren't that interesting to kids anymore, he thought, in the current climate of global warming, mass extinctions and Jihad terrorists. *But that wasn't true either – there's all sorts of dino theme parks opening, like that one in Japan and that company in Australia.*

And now the 'Lost World of Kharamu'. The ultimate rich man's cosplay. Terrific.

He still hadn't had time to find something to wear other than his climbing khakis in the whirlwind of the trip, though they'd at least been cleaned, pressed and the torn shoulder mended by someone on the ship's crew. With the Russians still hot on his tail, his new 'benefactor' had decided it too risky to return to his house. After a career of last-minute trips to remote locations, Taylan had a habit of keeping his passport on him.

The customs agent had looked at him skeptically when he'd shown up at security with nothing more than a toiletry bag (purchased at one of the Duty-Free shops). But after he produced his First-class ticket, the woman's whole attitude had done an about-face.

The whole set-up sounded off the charts as far as Taylan was concerned, but for the moment he'd gone along with it, despite the bad taste it was leaving in his mouth. According to Doyle, two other scientists had been approached and turned Peyton down. Not one to take no for an answer, now he was using Taylan to convince them otherwise, knowing full well Taylan's weak spot. Despite the amount of credibility he'd brought with him to the college, his curriculum was on the verge of being 'phased out' thanks to the incessant back-stabbing by the assistant dean and shriveling budgets at the American Museum of Natural History. After months of inquiries, Taylan was discovering something else about the current 'please-like-me' education climate: anyone with so much as a whiff of bad news about them – God forbid, a sexual misconduct allegation - were tainted goods.

A hefty grant would quickly flip that around.

Still, if Peyton thought he would be another lackey on his payroll, the billionaire was in for a surprise. Taylan already had a good idea why the two scientists in question – Australian Paleontologist Dr. Audrey Adams and Indian Dinosaur Systemologist Dr. Roma Banaji - had turned down the opportunity. The former was way too independent and temperamental to get involved with the likes of Peyton, the latter, though Taylan knew of her through reputation only, most likely considered herself too prestigious to soil her reputation with an American billionaire financier. Sugar Daddys were a double-edged sword in the world of science and academia: they could both save your ass and tarnish your credibility depending on their reputation.

His first objective, according to Doyle, was to convince Dr. Adams to sign on to this adventure.

"And how exactly do you expect me to do that?" Taylan had asked en route to JFK.

"Seriously?" Doyle had shot back, "Did *Senor Studmeister* actually just ask me that question? The same *hombre* who charmed his way past the garter belts of Professor Amanda Roberts, she of the mouth-watering *bodacious tatas*? The uncrackable Ice Queen herself? Tell me I'm hearing things!"

Taylan had grunted and rolled his eyes.

The only thing you're hearing, you shmuck, is the crude, beer-toasted thoughts of a fuckwit who never outgrew college.

Aloud he couldn't resist throwing a barb: "Why doesn't Mr. Peyton drop in and charm her himself?" He already knew the answer to that – Taylan knew the volatile Audrey Adams quite well, in fact. After several mercurial and argumentative dates, he'd stood up and walked out on her in a restaurant in the East Village two years previous.

There'd been a hesitation on the other end while Doyle formulated a response.

16

"Well-l-l," Doyle finally said, before stuffily adding, "Mr. Peyton doesn't get along well with the independent types. Strategically, it was decided you would be better situated to attain a desirable result."

More like he doesn't like women with brains and spines to go with them.

Instead he'd replied: "You want me to fly over there? Fine. But don't expect anything. Our last meeting didn't exactly end on good terms."

"No results, no funding. The big guy was clear on that. Got it?" Doyle had responded, then hung up.

"Fucking desk-jockey!" Taylan muttered to the phone. He was about to chuck it across the cabin, then remembered it was his own.

Instead he'd made a call to his old professor to take a raincheck on dinner.

Now here he was, in the same building as Audrey Adams. How bad a grudge would she carry after two years? She'd been badgering him unrelentingly since that night of the Halloween Parade at a Thai restaurant in Midtown Manhattan when, in the middle of a sentence, he'd simply stood up, dropped a couple twenties on the table and walked out.

She'd called a few times after that – to give him a piece of her mind – but he'd never responded.

The Dinosaur exhibit hall had changed around since the last time he'd visited, he noted with envy. The animatronic exhibits had been updated to reflect the newer evidence supporting feathers on certain species (particularly raptors) and the walkway was now punched up to make the dinosaurs more engaging – or alarming, as it were. Toward the far end a temporary augmented reality installation was set up, which was where Audrey Adams would be. The travelling exhibit had been her brainchild.

A series of dramatically designed banners were hung from the ceiling, depicting 'realistic' dinosaurs in action. The last banner had a larger-than-life Audrey Adams featured in it, flashing a charming smile and decked out in what Taylan thought of as an 'Australian Dino-hunter adventure costume". The front buttons were down to reveal just enough cleavage to get the boys' hormones jumping without being too *risqué*.

He had to admit she looked terrific.

Still, Taylan wondered if she would still prove to be the bundle of contradictions to him she'd been in the past; a woman he was simultaneously attracted to and driven to the brink of screaming in frustration around. The chemistry between them was undeniably unstable, but from the very first time he had been at a loss as to why, exactly. Part of it was her uncanny ability to push his buttons, he supposed, as if whenever in his proximity her fingers couldn't resist poking and prodding his emotional aggravation points whether or not she wanted to. And no matter what he ever said to her, it was invariably the absolute *wrong* thing, inciting her to flare up like an accidentally lit Roman candle.

It didn't help he found her oddly attractive. Though of average height, she had pronounced features (particularly her cheekbones), long tawny blonde hair that seemed untamable and the most unique aquamarine blue eyes he'd ever seen. They had a way of drawing you in like a magnet. It was the mouth, however, that really got him. Finely drawn in a way that suggested a strong line of blue-blood somewhere in her family tree. Along with her strong, even teeth, he found her mouth inexplicably erotic. Until she talked. Much of the time the scathing Australian slang that came out of it would make a sailor blush. He'd seen her reduce more than one ignorant student (or colleague) to tears, particularly if she caught any whiff of arrogance about them.

Just to be safe he'd popped a couple aspirin before taking the tube over to Kensington.

As he stood there before the entrance of the installation a group of Asian students shuffled past him, one of them knocking into him somewhat rudely.

"Hey!" he said, half turning. He thought there was something odd about them, but he was distracted by the voice coming out of the mini-theater.

Her voice.

Clenching his teeth, Taylan stepped forward.

Like ripping off a band-aid, pal, he thought. *Get it over, fast.*

". . . imagine, if you would, stepping right out from this moment into the bright, humid weather of a day in the Cretaceous Era!" Audrey was saying as Taylan entered. There were roughly fifteen school kids ranging from eight to twelve, along with two adult chaperones. The circular chamber was roughly twenty feet in diameter, arching up to a dome perhaps 12 feet high. It was made of a seamless curved surface marred only by the entrance door and the required FIRE EXIT sign at the back. At the moment, it was a neutral grey, giving off a diffuse illumination.

A giant LED screen, Taylan thought. *Brilliant.* Looking carefully, he could see there *were* seams, but it took a discerning eye to spot them.

The chamber floor was set up with tropical plants, ground and rocks, simulating a patch of prehistoric world. Audrey stood toward the back, a laser pointer/remote in one hand, dressed in the same get-up advertising on her promotional materials.

She glanced at him as he entered, eyes flaring briefly, but like a true professional continued her introductions without a hiccup. Even as she spoke the temperature in the room seemed to go up several degrees and the pungent aroma of outdoor jungle tickled his nostrils. Hidden fans kicked in and a slight breeze moved around the space.

Quite the hi-tech simulator, Taylan mused, with a touch of admiration.

The dome lighting dimmed.

"Imagine a world . . . if you will," Audrey continued, drawing out the words to build anticipation, "filled with creatures . . . like this!"

There was a collective gasp as the walls seemed to melt away and it was as if they were transported back in time to the earth as it was 140 million years ago. They were on the edge of a primeval forest, not far from a large body of water. A small group of titanosaurs – *Argentinosaurus*, Taylan guessed – were nearby; chunkier versions of the *Diplodocus* (like Dippy) with broader heads. Across an azure sky with mountainous cumulus clouds flew groups of pterosaurs the size of WWII fighter planes. Herds of bullet-headed *Pachycephelasaurus* and *Hydrosaurus'* roamed with ambling *Stegosaurus* and *Triceratops*. Here and there tiny raptors darted, while giant insects buzzed the air around them. Even the sound was completely 3-Dimensional and so finely tuned everything from the distant cries to nearby chomps were crystal clear.

Taylan realized the installation was set on motion plates that vibrated as the larger sauropods drew closer.

One student let out a cry as one titanosaur approached them, casting the group in shadow as it towered over them. Even Taylan had to force himself not to flinch as the thing's massive foot came down as if to squash them flat, then landed a yard past the perimeter of their little room – there was even an accompanying breeze of air and the faintest whiff of leathery hide, like that of an elephant. At least half the students cringed and cowed down as the thing continued past them, it's counterbalancing tail arcing through the air with enough force to topple a building. A quarter-sized version - a calf – followed in its footsteps.

Taylan had to admit the production values were top notch, worthy of any latest Hollywood effects studio he'd seen. They'd even gotten the proto-feathers along the neck right.

One of the school girls let out a scream as a hissing roar came out of the left side of the room. All heads turned to see a mottle-skinned tyrannosaur come charging out of the woods like an onrushing locomotive, the rusty covering of feathers along its upper back and neck making it somehow even more terrifying than its usual movie representations: it evoked a giant, diabolically homicidal bird on a rampage.

This time several kids collapsed to the floor as the thing came right at them, the simulated ground shaking violently. Just as it seemed like it was about to land right in the middle of the room and tear the lot of them to shreds, it bounded nimbly past and sunk its teeth into the back of the sauropod calf's leg.

A moment later it was joined by a second, smaller *Tyrannosaurus rex* (whom Taylan pegged as the male) that feinted in from the opposite side. The young titanosaur trumpeted in pain. Even as the first one tore off a gory chunk of flesh and tendon, however, the second miscalculated and got the full impact of the mother sauropod's massive tail, sending it tumbling and rolling away with half its rib cage staved in.

The injured titanosaur twisted about, collapsing on its maimed leg, but before the *T. rex* could strike again a trio of *Triceratops* came stampeding through, the one in the center impaling the large predator in the belly with its two massive horns. Two of the kids fainted as the belly was torn open, spilling its insides out. The *T. rex* let out a wet roar that sounded more like an enraged alligator, then collapsed.

Several *Triceratops* thundered past and continued on, skirting the pack of smaller, feathered raptors that were already running over to feed on the fresh corpses.

The school kids were spared further horror as the screen faded to grey. Both chaperones were pasty-faced.

". . . so, you see, the Cretaceous Era wasn't some storybook funland, but a dynamic – often brutal – world. And it was like that for millions and millions of years!"

Even as the teachers tended to the fallen students, one neatly dressed Asian-esque boy looked up at Audrey and said, "But it's not the Jurassic Era, like the movie. The dinosaurs you showed were, shall I say, 'highly imaginative!'. Derived from pure speculation. And the plants were all wrong, I Googled it while the simulator was running. I've already posted my review on *Snapchat* and *Yelp*."

Another student, a ten-year old girl who looked minted out of a private boarding school, added in, "I thought it was overly stressful. I'm, afraid I can't 'like' this event and I might even suffer from residual trauma. My parents won't be pleased."

A third boy, with an unruly mess of ginger hair also chimed in: "I bet all that CG was outsourced to a Chinese effects studio – you really should support local sustainable businesses you know!"

Audrey blinked rapidly several times. For a moment, Taylan though she would swat all three of them with the controller. She fished up a brittle smile regardless.

"Well, thank-you for coming, I hope you, er, enjoyed the presentation!"

As the students filed out one little girl, cute as a button with little pigtails and oversized glasses stepped over and in a quiet, proper voice said, "I wanted you to know, Dr. Adams, that I really enjoyed the entire presentation."

She turned to go then paused, her face turning rueful, "But I'm afraid I still must report you to the NSPCC."

The room empty, Audrey turned to Taylan as if just realizing he was there.

"Oh, great," she said, her azure eyes turning stony. "As if my day hadn't hit the bottom of the crap barrel already. I suppose you've shown up just to gloat over my humiliation! Those little shits, have they any idea the work that went into this? *Any!?*"

"Well . . . the skin markings were a bit 'over imaginative'," he said, one eye squinting. "They actually approved this for kids?"

Lips compressing into a thin line, she stepped over and swatted him on the head.

"Well, not exactly *this* version. The directors said *drama! Excitement! Hollywood-quality effects!* I raised 500 hundred pounds on Kickstarter, worked my bloody arse off for six months on all this . . . 'Report me to the NSPCC?' That little bitch! I'll be ruined!"

This time she threw the remote. It bounced off the wall and landed in one of the plants.

"For whatever it's worth, I thought it was impressive," Taylan added.

Audrey folded her arms, her expression smoldering. "*Impressive* doesn't cut it these days, in case you haven't noticed, Grant. This is the kick-off presentation for the whole tour. I'll have to redo the whole bloody thing!"

Her eyes narrowed, "Besides, what the hell *are* you doing here? Come all the way to London to apologize, finally? There's a Thai restaurant just down the street, if you want a rematch."

"Actually, I'm here to talk you into going with me to a little island in the South China Sea."

"Oh God, don't tell me. That overstuffed goat's penis, *Peyton*?"

Taylan laughed, "Yeah, that's the one. Goat's penis or not, it appears he's onto something."

"I wouldn't touch anything 'he's onto' with a ten-foot pole. One of his show ponies swung by here last week with all sorts of cash and promises. Not the full quid, Peyton, from the cut of it. Don't tell me he's convinced you? Made you an offer too good to be true?"

"You could say that," Taylan said, musing how Audrey could go from talking near perfect school English to a pronounced Aussie accent at the drop of a hat. "But think about it; if this MuTron International *has* cracked the DNA code, it'd be a shot to see living, breathing dinosaurs first hand. Surely that beats the pants off any computer simulation?"

"Good God, come off it, Grant, *seriously?*"

Taylan put on his best smile. "Seriously."

For a split second, he saw her expression soften; a brief glimpse of the little girl behind the tough façade that *wanted* to believe. Then, just like that, it vanished.

"Tough bit, Grant. I've got too much time and effort invested in this project legitimately – no way would I risk it all on a rich man's fucking lark! Besides, after the way you walked out on me in New York it'll be a cold day in hell before I go anywhere with you." She bent to pick up the remote, her face growing hard. "Good luck. Send me a post card."

Taylan was about to respond when there came some sort of disturbance outside. There were sharp words, the shout of an angry man with an Asian accent, followed by a muffled pop. A moment later the door slammed open and three Vietnamese men in business suits and sunglasses filed in. The first thing Taylan noticed were the machineguns in their hands.

How on earth . . . ?

Then it hit him: *Yen.*

Did she put a contract out on him? She wasn't that crazy, was she?

There was no time to ask. Fortunately, Audrey was quick on her feet. Even as the guns came up, she thumbed a button on the remote and the room exploded into color, this time with a half-dozen of brightly feathered *Utahraptors* charging at them.

Gunfire erupted.

Taylan and Audrey leapt toward the rear exit door.

Even as the curved screen exploded in glass fragments they tumbled through the metal door, Taylan thinking to kick it shut behind him. A hail of bullets thumped into it a moment later. He spotted a chair nearby and grabbing it, jammed it up under the door bar.

"Come on!" he shouted, dragging her by the arm.

"Let go of me!" she protested.

"No!" he replied.

The exhibit space had erupted in chaos, with people running every which way. Taylan pulled Audrey down to an intersecting hallway where a bunch of confused foreigners were trying to figure out which way to go. He plowed through them as more bullets flew overhead, whickering off a primate skeleton hanging from the ceiling, causing it to drop one arm and swing down precariously.

"Exit?" Taylan shouted, to no-one in particular. A wide-eyed Korean man in front of him pointed a shaky finger down the hall to his left. Two of the

Vietnamese hit-men disguised as students popped out. Oddly, Taylan recognized them – Yen's brothers.

I thought she said they were commandos, not contract killers!

"Tuan? Lanh?" he said.

Both brothers raised their guns, their faces expressionless except for the eyes. Acting on instinct, Taylan leapt up and grabbed the bottom of the promotional banner overhead and yanked. It landed on top of them (along with another primate skeleton for good measure). Without waiting to see what happened next, Taylan grabbed Audrey's arm and took off toward the west exit, which opened onto Queen's Gate, if he recalled correctly.

They bolted out into the Wildlife Garden courtyard, made a wrong turn and ran over the wooden bridge on the lily pond. Even as they were halfway across Taylan sensed something was amiss. They came to a jolting stop as he blocked her with his arm.

Something out of place.

Then he saw it; the irregularity of a shape camouflaged in the tree overlooking the pond. Sunlight glinted dully off painted metal. Simultaneously he dove forward, pulling Audrey with him.

There came a dull *thud* as the crossbow bolt embedded itself in the wood rail where he had been standing a moment before.

Christ!

They landed on the other side, then cut right on the path leading to the west gatehouse. Three figures were just coming out of the doors of the museum behind them.

"Quick!" Taylan said.

Sirens already approached from the distance.

"Who the hell are they?" Audrey yelled.

"No time," he said.

Audrey stopped dead in her tracks, hands on hips. "I'm not going anywhere until you tell me!"

"A bunch of men hell bent on killing me. And you too by association. Come on!"

"*No*," she said, firmly.

"Suit yourself," he said, and ran.

She looked back and spotted the suited men running at them, raising their guns again. There came the hornets' whine of bullets around them.

"Shit!" she said and took off after Taylan.

She caught up with him on the sidewalk on Queen's Gate where an elderly man in a bowler was just entering one of the new TX4 black taxi cabs, giving instructions to the driver. There were no other cabs in sight. Just as he was pulling the door closed, Taylan grabbed it, throwing Audrey unceremoniously into the back seat and jumping in after her.

"Pardon me!" the man exclaimed as Taylan slammed the door shut.

"Sorry, it's an emergency," Taylan said, as usual not raising his voice. He leaned over through the partition at the driver, a middle-aged Chinese man with a shaved head and round face like a Buddhist monk. The man was heavy-set and looked like he'd been shoe-horned into the driver's seat.

"'ey, wot?" the driver said, looked back at Taylan as if only mildly surprised. The plastic encased license on the dash Identified him as 'Paul Chan'.

"Get us the hell out of here," Taylan snapped, pulling out a twenty-pound note and tossing it onto the driver's lap.

"Now, oi believe that gentl'man—"

Chan cut himself off as a bullet hit the side window, spidering the glass.

He jammed the gas pedal and the taxi shot forward, causing Taylan to tumble backward right into Audrey's lap. The car took off southbound toward Cromwell Road, but they hadn't gotten a hundred feet when a black Saab came careening around the corner and right at them into oncoming traffic. One of the Vietnamese was hanging out the passenger window with a submachine gun – Taylan thought it might be a Pindad PM2 - but even as he sprayed fire at them the taxi driver cut a hard right, fishtailing the taxi over the center divider. Taylan rolled over into the old man's lap, who gave him a mildly perturbed look as he raised his cane out of the way.

Chan corrected the spin with the practiced ease of a racecar driver and accelerated back up Queen's Gate, deftly weaving between slower moving traffic.

"Bloody git's got heck-uva punch under the hood, eh?" he said out of the side of his mouth, his Cockney accent incomprehensible to Taylan's ears. Taylan straightened himself up in the back seat, brows furrowed as he tried to reconcile what was coming out of the driver's mouth with his zen-like face.

"Ahhh, Mitsubishi engine, one-five-o horsepower, you see, five-speed fuel injection!" he added proudly, giving the dashboard a quick pat for good measure.

"I thought they weren't available in our country," the old man said, speaking up for the first time. He sounded vaguely annoyed.

"Typically, ain't, guvnor, but oi got connections, see!" He grabbed the steering wheel with both hands and frowned as the traffic picked up density. Behind them came the squeal of tires, horns blaring, more shots and people screaming.

"I thought the new traffic zones cleaned up the traffic here in London," Taylan said, realizing he hadn't been in London for years.

The driver made a combined chuckle/snort. "Hah, that's a bit pony, mate! Worked for about six months, right? Then people just started paying up an' hell, everythin's jammed up again! Still a fucken' mess, eh?"

Spotting an opening on the divider where there were no trees or parked bikes, he jumped over into oncoming traffic for a few car-lengths, then jumped back over to the right lane again.

"Didn' mention where you're off to?" he asked.

Taylan hadn't thought of that, he was just focused on escaping. "Anywhere near Bloomsbury would be good. Look, can you shake these guys? They mean business. If you haven't noticed."

"Sure thing, mate, soon as I drop me preferred passenger here at Albert Hall, he was in first, you know?"

All three of them in the back seat banged their heads on the ceiling of the cab as they landed off the divider. Despite the situation, the driver seemed as calm as if he was involved in deadly car chases every day.

"What the mayor needs is a good kick up the bottle, yeah? Straighten 'im right out! And don't get me rolling on the whole 'Brexit' thing, like the whole country's gone Chicken Oriental, right? Any inkling what the socio-political ramifications are, not to mention how it will make financial markets more sensitive to the vulnerabilities of the 19-nation eurozone? Of course not! Then a bunch of foreigners showin' up, act like they own the place, an' that's where the trouble starts! Move to Rome, better try acting a little Roman, or get the fuck out, I say! Bloody mess!"

Taylan recovered himself enough to lean forward, "What in the hell are you talking about?"

"The man has a point, Grant," Audrey piped up. "Not to mention that the right-wingers are having a field day."

As the taxi swerved around the corner a mother and carriage seemed to materialize out of nowhere. The driver slammed on the brakes and put the car into a sideways skid, missing her by a hair, even as the pursuing car did an almost identical maneuver on the other side of her. Taylan had a brief impression of a pretty face going white as a sheet, then their back window shattered as bullets sprayed across it.

Despite an alarmed look, the old man tapped his cane on the front seat and said politely, "That's my stop coming up, you know."

"Afraid we may have to loop back around," the driver said, as he righted the skid and accelerated down A315. In a deft maneuver, he drove around the opposite side the other car was skidding in, distracting the other driver enough that the black sedan slammed into the side of a double-decker tourist bus.

After a block, Audrey asked, "Did we lose them?"

Taylan glanced back through the shattered remains of the rear window and replied, "Yes, wait, no. Shit. They're coming."

"What's the safest place to go?" Audrey said.

"Buckingham Palace?" the old man offered.

"Good thinking - plenty of guards: surely they wouldn't try anything there!"

The driver shook his head. "'fraid not, ma'am. Big event with *Raksha Bandhan* going on there today! Place'll be mobbed with Hindus all bonding and affectionate-like!"

"Dear God!" the old man said.

"No - dear *Vishnu*, I'd say!" the driver shot back, laughing. "Or *Parvati* if you 'ave to be technically correct! Best we head up to Piccadilly, oi think, skirt Trafalgar Square and zip up the Strand, if that works for you? Should be able to shake 'em in Piccadilly. Bitch with all the bloody vendors and tourists, right?"

They raced down the road and into the Knightsbridge tunnel, plunging them into momentary gloom.

The driver flicked the headlights on and asked, "What's their beef with you, mate? They look an awful lot like Asian Mafia!"

"Yes, what exactly *is* their beef? Just who the bloody hell are those nuts!?" Audrey chimed in, glaring at Taylan.

Rubbing the bridge of his nose, Taylan muttered something under his breath.

"Sorry, what was that?" Audrey asked, her tone going sharp.

"*Commandos*. Vietnamese commandos."

"Oh, Vietnamese commandos, I see! And why on earth would they be trying to kill us? Mind illuminating us on the subject?"

"Yes, do tell," urged the old man.

"A woman I used to date. At least two of them are her brothers," Taylan replied, looking straight ahead.

There was a space as Audrey digested this. From the flushed color on her face, it didn't appear to be going down well. The horn of an oncoming car blared in protest as they momentarily swerved over the meridian as they banked toward the up ramp. Finally, she said, incredulously, "You mean I've just probably had my whole fucking professional career destroyed because of an *ex-girlfriend of yours!? What the bloody hell did you do to her?"

"Nothing."

"*Nothing*!? People don't generally come after you with submachine guns and try to kill you in a public museum over 'nothing'!"

Taylan rubbed his forehead. "Yes, well, she apparently got it in her head that I would marry her. Hell, we weren't even engaged. She went a little psycho. Look, I had no idea things would go this far. I had a restraining order against her back in New York."

"Oh, that's wonderful!" Audrey snapped at him. "I guess they didn't get the memo over here across the pond. Any bright ideas what to do next, short of getting us all killed?"

From the front seat, the driver let out a low whistle, "Oof! 'ell hath no fury like a woman, scorned, wot?"

"Or the rest of the family, apparently," the old man added, dryly.

Audrey leaned forward. "Driver, as soon as we reach Piccadilly Circus pull over. I'm getting out."

"I'll second that!" the old man added.

Chan did a quick shake of the head. "Luv to oblige you, miss, but it looks like they're on our tail again!"

Audrey and Taylan looked backward and saw not one, but two black sedans in hot pursuit, gaining on them.

"Can't you go any faster?" she asked.

"Hold on," the driver said, upshifting as the ramp straightened out and they shot out into the August sunshine. The taxi went momentarily airborne before landing hard enough to bottom out the suspension. To the left of them were indistinguishable blocks of 19th century limestone row buildings, soot-stained from decades of pollution, while to their right sprawled the vast expanse of Green Park.

The second car – an Audi – swerved out into oncoming traffic and after narrowly missing a bus, came up hot on their right quarter. More bullets plunked into the taxi chassis. The driver swerved them over the divider and clipped the Audi on the fender, then bumped back to avoid an oncoming car. Pedestrians scattered. From further back came the flashing lights and sirens of the metropolitan police.

The driver kept them an elusive target by irregularly swerving, though as they burst into Piccadilly Circus he veered right onto the sidewalks, horn blaring. They went around the Shaftesbury monument, nearly running over several shoppers coming out of Lillywhites sportswear. Swerving left to avoid the underground entrance stair, he skidded into a hard-right turn before heading southbound down Haymarket. Here three lanes opened into a one-way street and Chan could accelerate around several ungainly busses.

25

Further discussion went on hold as they ran an erratic cat-and-mouse race down Haymarket. Nearing Pall Mall, however, the Saab went on to the right sidewalk – nearly killing several pedestrians – and shot ahead of them. When they came close to the intersection one of the gunman leaned out the left window, trying to fire back at them.

Chan snarled and floored the taxi, ramming into the back end of the other car.

It was just enough to put the Saab into a spin – and then get rammed by a metropolitan police car as they skidded into the intersection. There was the screech of tires skidding and muffled crump of metal and plastic imploding.

Chan righted their spin and they tore off down Pall Mall toward Trafalgar Square, the second car still in hot pursuit.

Hammering on the car horn, the taxi zipped narrowly through the bollards – banging one in the process - and past the front steps of the National Gallery, sending more pedestrians fleeing and pigeons exploding into the air.

"What's with the horse skeleton?" Audrey said as they zipped past the fourth plinth.

"Some bleedin' Kraut artist, oi think!" Chan responded, "Better than that god awful blue cockerel they had before! Can you believe people actually get paid to come up with such shite!?"

Taylan was still struggling to make out what the man was saying – he could only pick out every third or fourth word, at the same time trying to think of a way out of their predicament. Something was nagging at him . . . a memory from years back when he'd gotten lost sightseeing along the banks of the Thames . . .

Christ! Would the damned driver ever shut up?

More bullets and the front passenger window shattered, with Chan letting out a grunt as a bullet hit his shoulder.

"Barmy, I've been hit!" he yelled. Blood splattered across the inside windshield.

They skidded then straightened out again as they rocketed across the intersection at Duncannon in a surreal 'Warner Brothers' moment where they impossibly flew between cars coming in opposite directions with uncanny timing. The Audi pursuing them wasn't quite so lucky – it ricocheted off one of the passing vehicle and skidded into a t-shirt kiosk, sending clothes flying in all directions.

It bought them some time, however, as they merged onto the Strand and eastward.

"How bad?" Taylan asked, leaning forward. The driver was clenching his teeth but managing to keep both hands on the wheel.

"Hurts like a Berkshire's hunt! Better think up something soon, 'fraid!"

Taylan glanced back. The Audi had righted itself and was pulling out after them.

Think, dammit!

Something about a walkway . . . the Hanseatic walkway. He remembered: an odd little street called 'Allhallows Lane'.

Yes. It might just work.

"Look, Paul," he said, "slow down just enough to let them close in on us at the next turn. You're going to make a hard right on Allhallows, then slam on the brakes and wedge the taxi to the left when we get to the bottom of the stair – but we'll need them right on our tail. Can you manage that?"

The driver nodded, sweat already pouring down his forehead.

A moment later they fishtailed into a sharp right turn and shot down the narrow street, which was little more than a cobblestone alleyway. Looking around, Taylan saw there was an umbrella in the front passenger seat.

"I'll need that," he said, grabbing it.

There was a screech of tires as the Audi followed them down the short lane. At the end, the view opened to the Thames River.

Taylan leaned half out the shattered rear window and as they neared the end of the lane snapped the umbrella open and hurled it backward at their pursuer.

It was just enough.

He saw the one gunner already leaning out the passenger window, the snarling expression of Tuan behind the wheel turning into an 'o' of surprise, then Taylan was hurled forward and half into the front seat as the cabbie slammed on the brakes. The taxi fishtailed and stopped.

The Vietnamese couldn't have stopped if they wanted to. Tires screamed on the wet cobblestones. With the taxi stopped at an angle, the other car shot up the short flight of steps and hitting the low restraining wall, catapulted up into the air and did an ungainly backflip out into the river.

A moment later came a heavy splash.

Taylan put together a make-shift compress on the driver's shoulder and after deciding the wound wasn't life threatening, instructed him to sit tight until they could summon an ambulance.

"Are you all right?" Audrey asked the old man, who sat shell-shocked in the corner of the backseat, unblinking.

"Yes, I believe so," he said, avoiding her gaze. "Was that a public lavatory we passed on the way down? I'm afraid I may have had a little accident."

A minute later Taylan clambered up the stairs. The bottom of the Audi's chassis was still afloat, though even as he watched, it tilted and submerged into the muddy water. Along the Thames it was a brilliant summer afternoon, just another day in London if one ignored the sinking car and several Police launches already on their way.

"Good Christ," Audrey said, stepping up next to him. "I'm going to absolutely kill you for this! Then revive you so I can kill you twice!"

Taylan snorted. He was looking at the bubbles breaking the surface around the car. "You'll have to take a number."

"What do you mean?" she asked. Behind them came several blinking lights as the police cars came down the lane.

He nodded toward the sinking boat. "Those guys are commandos. We may not be through with them just yet."

Not to mention the Russians, he thought.

"We? There is no *we*, Grant Taylan," she snapped back. "There's absolutely no way in bloody hell I'm going with you on some asinine billionaire's fantasy quest!"

Taylan turned and looked her in the eye, "Really?"

ISLAND OF KHARAMU: WEDNESDAY, 1500 HOURS.

"I saw it again! The ghost of the Japanese soldier!" Wang Chan said in a harsh whisper. "This is a terrible omen!"

"Ah, you and your omens! There are no such things!" replied his friend, Tao Dong, rolling his eyes comically. "*Fèihuà!*": Bullshit!

The two young men were standing outside on one of the half-concealed observation platforms on the dizzying cliffs overlooking the small bay. The platform, near two of the WWII anti-aircraft gun emplacements, was at one of the highest points on the north arm of the bay, and one of the few places they had access to and could smoke without being caught. Not that it was a huge deal – most the programmers did, even their supervisor, Zhang Chuanzhou, though both Wang and Tao hated him. Zhang was Cantonese while they were both Mandarin.

Nor could the two young men be more unalike. Wang Chan, stocky-built with a wrestler's physique and broad, serious features, was both dourly pragmatic and by his friend's estimate, ridiculously superstitious. Fierce-eyed, his face by default seemed to always be set in a scowl. Tao Dong, on the other hand, was taller and something of a goof. Deceptively bored-looking with strong eyebrows and narrow eyeglasses, he possessed an uncanny talent for pulling out-of-the-box solutions out of thin air and had an irrepressible sense of humor that tended to put his friend's teeth on edge.

Both had been discreetly culled two years previous from the top of their class at Peking University by a recruiter from MuTron International in a way that at first had them suspicious they were being pulled into some secret government program. Both were relieved and alarmed that they were being sent to an inhospitable island in the South China Sea.

The pay was exceptional, though, and in short order they acclimated to their new accommodations, which if isolated, were at least first-rate. Their chief complaint was the scarcity of women, which was about one to every three men. Most of them seemed to be with the scientist and maintenance staff, neither which seemed interested in computer programmers.

Wang and Tao's jobs mainly consisted of IT work, making sure the servers and systems were functioning properly. They also had to repair and maintain workstations, routers, etc. Due to the unusual electromagnetic properties of much of the island, which was a long dormant volcano, Wi-Fi systems were unreliable, and everything had to be hard-wired with heavily insulated fiber optic cable as a back-up.

Neither had personally seen the dinosaurs on the island except on the surveillance cameras (and numerous scale gift-shop prototypes surrounding their workstations), as they were located outside the immediate areas. Most of the operations staff had only restricted access to the complexes around the bay and all the staff were kept rigorously compartmentalized. Indoor access to any of the breeding and DNA labs was highly controlled due to the risk of contamination and viruses. During the Second World War, the island had been developed into a secret operations base by the Japanese, creating a honeycomb of complexes including a naval gun battery overlooking the harbor and a submarine pen on the seaward side of the cliffs that had incorporated the naturally existing caves there.

Situated in the northwest coast of the island, the steep-sided bay was too small to accommodate anything more than a medium-sized freighter, which was one of the main reasons it was ultimately abandoned as a sea-base. Roughly fifteen by twelve miles in size, the island had risen out of the ocean somewhere between 35-40 million years ago, and now featured heavily jungled cliffs rising as high as 4,500 feet. The interior flattened out into a shallow basin with a large lake a mile and a half across at its widest.

One complex on the leeward side of the cliffs included a large underground aircraft hangar which had been converted into an all-purpose storage warehouse, though it still housed the decaying relics of two Japanese WWII aircraft: a Kawasaki Ki-61 'Tony' and a rare twin-engine Mitsubishi Ki-67 'Hiryu', both of which were in the process of being sold (illegally) to private collectors. A runway had been built out from the landward side of the cliffs, which had now been refashioned into a helipad.

It was in the hangar a month previous that Wang Chan had claimed he'd first seen the ghost, while retrieving one of the new workstations off a newly arrived shipping pallet for the DNA sequencing lab. A major thunderstorm had just passed, the lights in the hangar turned low to save on electricity – a new policy that had been put in place nine weeks previous – and looking over from the pallet of computers Wang had glanced over and seen a pale face peering at him from the shadowy cockpit of the Ki-67 just visible over the stacks of boxes. It appeared to be an older face, which was odd, as Wang had rarely seen anyone over 30 on the staff. Stranger still was the tattered, old-fashioned khaki WWII Japanese soldier's cap with the side flaps.

The event was quite upsetting to him: raised in the communist education system he was explicitly taught his entire life there was no such thing as ghosts or supernatural phenomena: the world was an entirely explainable place, governed by science and reason. Yet he had thousands of years of his culture's mysticism in his DNA.

The large box with the XRP workstation he had been loading onto the cart had almost dropped on his foot. When Wang looked up again the cockpit was empty, though he hadn't heard a sound.

That's impossible. That rusted old plane would make a racket if a real person moved around in there!

Though spooked, he'd dismissed it as a hallucination due to lack of sleep - they regularly worked 17-18-hour days at that point - until a couple weeks later, when he'd seen the ghost in one of the abandoned tunnels near the IT lab. Such areas were typically blocked off by a steel mesh wall and gate. Just at the edge of the pool of light he'd seen it: the Japanese soldier in the WWII uniform, this time staring straight at him, he would swear, with a cold-blooded look of death.

Wang had closed his eyes and counted to three. When he opened them again, the apparition had vanished. His grandmother had a reputation for seeing ghosts; she always avoided graveyards or any place where violent deaths had occurred like the plague, and was prone to getting physically ill near such places. She claimed it was ever since her first husband died, during the Second World War.

He'd dismissed it as the superstitious ramblings of an old woman.

Now here he was seeing one himself.

Impossible! There is no such thing!

A colleague of his who worked security systems said there had been several instances of tripped sensors over the past year that couldn't be explained, which had initially been put down as equipment bugs, but even the security teams were a little spooked.

Then last night, Wang had awoken from a nightmarish dream. He'd been running around the Forbidden City naked, being chased by an enraged pack of *Deinonychus* – feathered versions of the *Velociraptor's* of Crichton's Jurassic Park. He realized he had to pee terribly. The low-ceilinged dorm room was bathed in the twilight glow of the dimmed nightlights as he'd tiptoed to the door to use the hallway bathroom, but froze when he saw the figure standing in the gloom of the hall.

The ghost.

It was as if it was just standing there, it's back to him. *Listening.*

He knew it could hear him, his heart pounding in his ears. With that came another cold certainty: the ghost was in some fashion connected to him, had singled him out personally for some unknown purpose. Perhaps even *drawn* to haunt him. Then it appeared to glide down the hall, disappearing down the corner. Gritting his teeth, Wang had stood there another fifteen minutes before necessity overrode fear.

As the two of them stood on the concrete observation platform, he gave Tao the abridged version of what had happened.

"Why didn't you wake me up?" Tao asked, pulling off the cigarette in his effeminate way and blowing smoke upwards. Wang suspected his friend was gay, but such things were forbidden to talk about, even here.

"And wake up the whole room? Let someone else make an ass out of themselves by ruining what little sleep we get! Or worse. That last guy, Xie, remember him?"

Tao made a wincing grin, teeth clenched comically. "Oh yeah. They fired him after two weeks. Totally cracked up. That jerk turned the whole crew into the *Walking Dead* with his all-night nightmares. And that other guy, Liu? Remember him? I swore he jerked off all night in his cot. Guy was a maniac. He lasted a whole month."

That usually got a chuckle out of Wang, but today he just scowled and stared out along the inner rim of the bay.

What if I'm going insane? he wondered. *This is how it starts!*

Below was the primitive village and dilapidated dock, looking – quite deliberately – like a set piece out of an old Hollywood movie. Most of the island's supplies were flown in by helicopter; the harbor was strictly for show.

On the steep incline to his right something dark moved in the trees. For a second he swore it was the ghost again; he imagined an (un)dead Japanese sniper with a rifle taking aim at him . . . a moment later a large bird took off into the sky.

Wang rubbed his eyes.

NO! It's not real!

"We should get back to work," he said, making a show of checking his watch. It helped him avoid the more troubling question of his eroding sanity.

One hundred yards away in the CEO's office, a major argument was happening.

Luo Pan Wei – referred to strictly by the staff as 'Mr. Luo' – was standing before his chief accountant and his technical director, in a temperature-controlled office the two latter employees would both agree had dropped a dozen digits from its usual 68° F in the last fifteen minutes.

Mr. Luo, one of the newly minted billionaires in the Chinese business world, was a 'behind-the-scenes' star of the Asian tech sector, having been the driving force and brainchild behind several highly successful business ventures in the pharmaceutical & bio-tech businesses.

Slightly built with sharp, commanding features and a fearful presence, he exuded a steely ruthlessness mixed with an eloquent charm that made it naturally difficult for many to question him. He had all the hallmarks of a born leader and it would be a small jump, say, to imagine him leading the Emperor's army to stunning victories or commanding the Ming Dynasty fleet across the oceans of the 14th century, a persona he worked tirelessly to project. The reality of his bio, however, read considerably different from the one offered in MuTron International's official marketing materials. Few knew that he had worked his way up from a poverty-stricken existence in Hong Kong, the son of a computer parts dealer and a disgraced woman of supposed royal bloodlines. Now remolded into the image of the quintessential hip, successful business leader, at 36, Mr. Luo looked like he had been born into the part.

Dressed in a tailored, sharkskin suit with handmade Berluti shoes and a Carlo Franco silk tie, Mr. Luo was giving his three chief company officers – Nancy Wú, Greg Xióng and Roger Burroughs – the kind of merciless stare that would have had less competent employees trembling in their shoes. All three were more than capable of handling their boss' verbal whippings and icy-anger, which was why they had been employed as long as they had.

The fourth key officer, Byron Farnsworth, was conspicuously absent. Farnsworth was the Programming Director in charge of designing the storylines for guest's vacations. A high-strung theme-park producer recruited out of Disney and known for his hysterical melt-downs, Farnsworth was a maverick at improvising narratives with dramatic flourishes. He was also the last person, Mr. Luo knew from experience, to have around when hard news was being meted out.

The office itself was of ultra-modern design integrated with original elements of the bunker complex. To one side of the sleek mahogany desk was a seating area with leather chairs, couch and table, behind which was an immense wall-sized aquarium with reconstituted prehistoric sea life in it including ammonites, trilobites, crinoids and sea scorpions. It lent the space an aquamarine glow, augmented by cove lighting, recessed LEDs and architect's table lamps. A bank of HD monitors lined the opposite wall, while a few modernists works of art the others. Several tropical plants were scattered about the space. The overall impression was of a hi-tech, minimalist space worthy of any Bond supervillain.

Perpendicular to Luo's desk was one of the key technical marvels of the space: an ultra-high definition 3D holographic display of the entire island. Developed by an R&D division of a South Korean technology firm, it was one of the most advanced units of its kind. The 4' x 4' table was currently set to its default full 3D realism mode, showing the entire foliage covered landscape, complete with animated proxies of dinosaurs and hovering clouds.

One other identical unit was down in the command center one floor below, though only Luo's private one had the entire data set which depending on which filters were active, his could display everything from geo-technic data, power grids, personal locations and so on. It was still in development, however, and the next upgrade promised even higher resolution and real-time data feeds.

Nancy Wú had just delivered the latest round of bad news: their government subsidies were being cut yet again due to the refocusing on defense against the Russians. Along with the latest financial projections that left little doubt that at their current burn rate, MuTron International would have zero operating funds within months if they didn't land more investment capital and successfully get the 'Lost Island of Kharamu' operational quickly.

That had been after Greg Xióng had added his latest grim report on the software issues with the mainframes and security protocol breakdowns. The latter was the more serious: Xióng was convinced there was a saboteur in their midst. Numerous cameras and relays had been damaged and several supplies from the maintenance sheds and kitchens had disappeared recently, but it was the bugs in the dinosaur fail-safe activators that had him most concerned. Missing supplies were one thing, clients getting physically harmed in anyway was a whole other.

That was why they had run the Beta X program: to work out all those bugs . . .

As the Science Group Director, Roger Burroughs was the only one with good news: four more species had cleared testing and would be available for the upcoming trial run with Peyton's group. A squat, grey-haired man with piercing, hooded eyes and the unflappable calm of a veteran battleship captain, the Oxford-schooled Burroughs had been a rogue geneticist in his native Great Britain with his unconventional approach to reconstituting extinct species. He'd been exiled to Switzerland some five years when MuTron recruited him to lead their team, offering unprecedented facilities and budget at his disposal.

"We have three potential investors arriving on Saturday," Mr. Luo said, standing in front of the panoramic picture window overlooking the island. Built with light-sensitive glass and coated with an anti-reflective coating that made it all but invisible from the outside. Like everything built in the initial complex retrofit it was executed with top-quality materials and workmanship. That was until their financial holdings tipped into the red zone these past six months. The radical drop in oil prices – one of MuTron's hidden major revenue streams, had been a contributing factor.

"There's no more room for excuses," he added. His voice was both cultured – and for the last ten minutes – steely-toned.

"I haven't made any," Nancy Wú replied, unfazed. Though slim and pretty with somewhat narrow, sharp features, her demeanor had earned her the nickname *bīng nǚwáng* or 'ice queen' amongst the staff. She was the embodiment of dread for the department heads at the weekly performance meetings.

"No, you haven't," Luo agreed. "But we may need to renegotiate several of our original contracts or get new suppliers. Stretch out payables another few weeks, at least until I get these three new investors on board. Peyton should be the main focus for now: he claims Peyton Financial may inject as much as one billion if the opportunity is right. And he was insistent about having the 'Level One' experience!" He paused, contemplating something else. "You've done a second risk assessment, yes?"

"Yes," Nancy Wú replied, forcing herself not to fan through her smart tablet – an obsessive habit of hers. Mr. Luo was exceptionally strict about such things in his presence. "Their financials look good. Our 'reluctant approach toward Western investors' strategy has worked quite well. Their CFO was keen to comply. What did you say to him?"

"Nothing you need worry about just yet," Mr. Luo said. "But he is like a *xiǎonánhái* – a little boy waiting for his candy." His icy stare switched to his technology officer again. "No mistakes this time. Yes? They want the full "Chills and Thrills' vacation, we deliver! Yes!?"

"*Shì!*" Greg Xióng snapped back, recognizing his cue, he stood to leave. Nancy Wú and Roger Burroughs joined him.

"One moment, Miss Wú," Mr. Luo said. The technical director bowed and saw himself out. Burroughs, as usual, took his time. Mr. Luo waited until the door was completely shut before continuing.

Nancy Wú forced her eyes not to flick toward the door – an escape reflex – knowing full well Mr. Luo was watching her carefully. Instead she maintained her poise, even drawing up a polite smile.

"You will hold off on your weekly financial report to the investors until Monday, is that understood?"

"But we're required to, every Friday," she answered. It was unnecessary of course, Mr. Luo knew the protocols. But appearances – and roles – had to be maintained at all costs.

"Yes, but an exception will be made, this time. Yes?"

Nancy Wú blinked, as if having difficulty comprehending such a violation of routine. She knew full well of the dire financial straits MuTron International was in. After all, she was partially responsible. The corporation was tilting toward total financial collapse. Even the government subsidies wouldn't save it.

"As you wish," she replied, standing up.

Mr. Luo let a minute drag by in uncomfortable silence as he stared at her – one of his usual domination tricks.

"I needn't remind you that your future is at stake here. If MuTron fails, I will be obliged to give *full* disclosure of everything, including my subordinate's activities."

The implicit threat was of little concern to her, however. Nancy Wú's plan was twofold: fulfill her obligation as a spy for the Chinese government by submitting her report anyway through a secret high-encryption satellite link and afterward, send a second report to MuTron's top competitor, HEIAN Data Corp. The former would ensure her family – under strict surveillance in their mainland house – would remain safe. The latter was her nest egg that would ultimately help all of them escape to the west.

"Yes." She waited, avoiding his direct gaze, prepared to stand there until Monday.

"You're dismissed, then. And please send Miss Grey up. We need to discuss our new marketing plan."

Nancy Wú had to suppress a smile. She had been having suspicions about Mr. Luo and Miss Grey for some time, and about Miss Grey's true gender identity.

Patience is a bitter plant, her mother would say, *but it has sweet fruit.*

She turned and headed to the door, her face going blank again. Mr. Luo's cameras always watched.

Almost always.

MUMBAI, INDIA, WEDNESDAY MORNING

"I *cannot* believe I'm doing this! I should have my head examined," Audrey Adams said – too loudly, as always – as she sat next to Taylan. They'd spent the past nine hours in the First-Class section of the Boeing 777, British Airways Flight 269 overnight from Heathrow to Mumbai. After a delay they'd finally exited the landing pattern and were coming in low toward Chatrapati Shivaji International Airport, the morning sunlight lending a rusty tint to the sprawling acres of shanty housing to the east. The sheer volume of the poverty-stricken slums was staggering to Taylan's eye; an unending mass of ramshackle structures stretching miles.

The other passengers pointedly ignored them, except for one German woman in the aisle next to them who had been glaring daggers at them after complaining several times to the stewardess.

"I – if you want an apology, I'll give it," Taylan replied tersely, keeping his voice low. Apologies were something he rarely, if ever, offered but after hours of incessant accusations he was willing to try anything to get Audrey off his back.

He'd taken the window seat and was peering out at the sprawling metropolis they were coming into. In all his world travels he'd seen nothing close to the sheer volume of poverty here.

"Oh! That's *lovely!* Do you think an apology will fix everything with the bloody Board of Directors at the NHM, particularly after they found out your little ex-psycho has put a contract on my head as well? That should be a delightful little meeting!"

Taylan rubbed his temples. The stale air of pressurized cabins always gave him headaches. "It wasn't my fault she thought you were my secret girlfriend, she's just . . . well, insane," he said.

Audrey put on a sarcastic smile. "Well, why don't all three of us sit down and have a little chat and straighten everything out? Then I can get onto my lovely career as a . . . oh wait a minute, I forgot, I don't *have* a fucking career anymore thanks to you and your discriminating taste in psychotic women!"

Taylan gave her a lopsided 'give me a break' grin, realizing something else: in an equally messed-up way, Audrey was *enjoying* this. She'd never admit of course, but she thrived on chaos and confrontation. Give her ten minutes alone in a room and somehow, something would break, explode or self-destruct. He also knew better than to say as much at this point; the flight had been an on/off sparring match for nearly nine hours, in between snatches of sleep.

With the bars of morning light flooding the cabin and her hair in disarray, he couldn't deny there was something undeniably attractive about Audrey. He was almost tempted to lean over and . . .

"Excuse me, I just wanted to make sure your seatbelts are properly buckled for landing," the stewardess said, leaning in. A small, young Indian woman with a British accent and a nametag identifying her as 'Asha', she'd done her best to keep their arguments to a minimum throughout the flight and looked relieved the ordeal was nearly over. If she was a little shocked at their messy, disheveled appearance, she did not indicate it.

"Yes, we're all set, thanks," Taylan replied, a little gruffly. "Any word on the weather in Mumbai for the next twenty-four hours?"

The cultured smile widened. Taylan suspected it took a lot of practice.

"Just some light rain squalls that should pass through by afternoon," she replied. "Temperature is around 36 degrees Celsius and humid, but that's normal for this time of year."

"Thanks."

Taylan rubbed the bridge of his nose and marveled at the whirlwind they'd navigated after sending their would-be assassins tumbling into the Thames.

They'd been arrested and held at the nearest police station and subsequently grilled by both MI5 *and* MI6 agents (since the contract was put out overseas) for hours until it was sorted out to their satisfaction that they were the victims and not perpetrators of domestic and international terrorism. Regardless, the solicitors from the NHM were eager to get some distance between their client and 'roughshod' foreigners, as the press was already having a field day with the fiasco.

The Telegraph and Guardian were straightforward in their coverage, but the Daily Mirror's "Cretacean Carnage!" and the Sun's "Deadly Dino Duet!" headlines already hit the stands even as the car was being fished out of the Thames. Six people were dead, including two Vietnamese, though the car had come up empty except for the driver. Paul Chan, the taxi driver, was recovering and already giving interviews, alternately being portrayed as a hero and as an accomplice.

When a messenger showed up with two first-class tickets to Mumbai, courtesy of Mr. Peyton, the authorities made it clear they thought it an excellent idea to pack up Taylan and Audrey and get them out of harm's way before anything further happened. Based on the indulgent expression frozen on the one MI6 interrogator's face when Audrey ran off about her rights and threatening to call the Australian Prime Minister and press, Taylan had to agree it was probably a good thing, too. The idea of a bunch of pissed-off, waterlogged Vietnamese commandos looking to hunt him down in the ghost-addled streets of London didn't sit too comfortably with him: high-tailing it to India seemed discretion being the better part of valor. Plus, the commotion would no doubt draw Oleg and his team like flies. He'd made a point of not mentioning a word of them to either the Brits or Audrey, which arguably had nothing to do with what happened at the NHM and would only muddy a messy situation even further.

Audrey had been furious, but not even her indomitable will could overcome the U.K. damage control machine. By that evening they found themselves with a hefty police escort being whisked off to Heathrow, ushered through a High-Security clearance customs and unceremoniously booted out of the country. It was made politely but firmly clear neither would have any need to return to the U.K. for the foreseeable future unless explicitly requested.

As the Boeing's tires touched the tarmac on Runway 1, Audrey fell into a sulk while Taylan felt his curiosity pique. He'd read several of Dr. Roma Banaji's white papers on her systemic theories of dinosaur population collapse, and like it or not, he was about to put to her a few questions that had been nagging him.

Her presentation was being given at the JW Marriott Mumbai Juhu along the ocean side of the city. The flier had been in the packet along with the plane tickets. It mentioned the event was being held in the downstairs Grand Sangam ballroom from 1-3 p.m. and would involve a catered meet-and-greet afterward.

Taylan glanced out the window as they taxied up to Terminal 2. The slums pressed right up close to the perimeter of the runway and he could only guess at the noise levels from the overhead jets in the flimsy shacks. Outside it *looked* hot and humid, the skies having turned a sultry, woolen grey since they landed.

He sat back and forced himself to be patient.

In and out. The second set of tickets had them on Cathay Pacific non-stop to Hong Kong where they would be transported to a ship – a Portuguese tramp freighter named the *Vazão* – already en route to Kharamu.

The question was if Dr. Banaji would be with them.

Exiting the plane to the terminal, the air hit them like a physical solid – after the coolness of the cabin it was like walking into a hot, moist furnace.

As they navigated the spacious new terminal with its soaring honeycomb ceilings, it occurred to Taylan it would look a little odd going through customs with nothing but the clothes on their back. Heading downstairs, they breezed past the baggage carousels on the lower level and went straight to customs.

"Anything to declare?"

The customs agent was a bored-looking, overweight Indian who, if the bags under his eyes were any indication, hadn't slept in a week. His accent was a mash-up of English and rapid-fire Marathi, which was almost unintelligible to Taylan's ears.

"Sorry?"

"Anything to declare?" the agent repeated, as if used to repeating himself. The words came out fused as one.

"Uh, no," Taylan replied.

"Business or pleasure?"

"Business." Taylan found it a little annoying how the agent looked preoccupied, not even meeting his eye with a cold glare the way most did these days. He didn't even seem interested in the visa, which was equally annoying in a way: what usually took months to process had been expedited in minutes at the Government customs at Heathrow – presumably with some wheel-greasing from Peyton Financial.

"How long will you be staying with us?" the bored custom agent said. It sounded more like *howlungwilyoobeestangwithus*? to Taylan's ears.

"Just one day. I'm here for a conference."

The agent produced his stamp and slammed it down, leaving a smudged seal in Taylan's passport that was all but illegible. Scribbling equally illegible initials and an ID #, the agent handed it back.

"Welcome to India. *Next!*"

As Taylan stepped over to wait for Audrey, he didn't notice the agent bending down and punching some keys on a smartphone.

Outside by the taxi stand a tall Sikh wearing a turban and sporting a blue-black beard pulled the vibrating phone out of his pocket and checked it. Then he reached into the backseat of the black Cadillac he was driving and grabbed a placard sign.

As they exited into the Arrivals lobby, a man – Russian-looking with blond hair, casual tropic attire and sunglasses – glanced up from where he'd been standing by the restrooms, apparently engaged in conversation on his cell phone. He raised his hand slightly and made a small wave to someone standing past the glass windows.

The Arrivals lobby was busy. The Sikh stood towering amongst a horde of suited drivers, while next to him was a very dark-skinned, Dravidian-featured man holding up the placard with block letters reading: 'Grant Taylan – Audrey Adams' written in magic marker.

"At least we won't have to hoof it," Audrey quipped as they walked up to the driver. Next to him the Sikh looked like a giant bodyguard out of a historic movie set about British Colonial India with his embroidered tunic, jeweled diadem in his turban and silk pants. His face was fierce-looking with a pronounced hook nose.

Taylan was only half-listening. Something had his antenna up, that instinctive early-warning radar that alerted him danger was in proximity. He was about to guide her past all of them and to one of the anonymous black taxis (with their odd yellow roofs) when the Sikh, as if picking up on his intention, leaned forward slightly and gesturing toward the sliding doors, said in a quiet voice, "Professor, *please*."

Despite the fearsome appearance, the urgent sincerity in the man's voice got Taylan's ear. As did avoiding the use of his name.

"Yes, of course," he replied, nudging Audrey's elbow.

"But—"

"Our ride, *honey*." Taylan cut her off, his voice terse. The driver holding the placard looked simultaneously alarmed and confused.

"Don't you—" Audrey began again, but before she could finish Taylan was already shoving her past, gripping her upper arm. The Sikh made a sweeping gesture with his massive arm and in response – no doubt due in part to the man's intimidating presence - the crowd parted to let them through.

Just as quickly they filled in again, causing the other driver to engage in a struggle to follow them.

Outside they were ushered over to a Cadillac, a gleaming brand new one. The rear door let out the weighted click only expensive cars have as he opened it for them, his movements executed with a smooth urgency that seemed odd in a man his size, which Taylan estimated at six and a half feet.

Audrey looked around the leather interior with grudging approval while Taylan leaned over to read the license in the laminated holder on the dash, the only thing which he could make out was the drivers name: 'Karam Johal'.

A moment later the driver slid into his seat and in one fluid motion, put the car in gear and took off into traffic.

At the sliding doors, the blond-haired Russian came running out, looking around wildly. A glint of metal showed briefly as his shirt hiked up, revealing the pistol concealed in his waistband. He spotted the receding taillights and punched a number in his phone.

The driver with the placard joined him a moment later, his hat askew.

The Russian shoved him toward his car and jumped in after him.

"Follow," he snapped.

As they sped down Sahar Elevated Road out of the terminal Taylan was struck by the subtle scents mingling with the 'new leather' aroma of the new car; a mix of sandalwood, jasmine, cloves and saffron, and more subtle ones he couldn't identify off-hand. Even with the air-conditioning, it was as if the complexities of Indian culture had been contained with them in what was unquestionably a luxury ride, underscored by the poverty-stricken housing they were literally driving over.

Audrey, who despite all her globe-trotting had never been to India before, was agog. For the first time in 9 hours, Taylan realized, she wasn't talking.

"You do know where we're headed . . . *Karam*?" Taylan asked.

Karam Johal glared at him in the rearview mirror, but answered equitably enough. "Yes. I'm a cousin of Dr. Banaji. Her father requested I pick you up, for your own safety." He spoke in precise British English.

"Safety?"

"Yes. We're being followed. Did you not see the Russian at the airport?"

Taylan winced.

Igor, dammit. How on earth did he get his men onto him so quickly? Or was it someone else? Another unsettled score?

"I'm afraid not," he said. "Something was off, though."

Karam grunted. He seemed to find this amusing. "Off? Yes, you could say that. Drax Kuklinsky is a real piece of work. Ex-KGB, if the rumors are true."

"Great."

This time the driver grinned. "Don't worry. Here in India there are all manner of ways to lose people."

To make his point he floored the gas and the Cadillac lunged forward, soaring onto the exit ramp to the Western Highway. "You may wish to fasten your seatbelts," he added.

Audrey turned to Taylan, eyes narrowing, "Pardon my asking, but exactly why would the Russians be following *you*?"

Here, Taylan felt he was on safer ground. "Igor Gorimov. He's a little upset over a business deal I 86'd for him."

"*How* upset?"

"Very."

"Oh, that's just lovely, isn't it? It wasn't enough to have a bunch of Viet Cong commandos try to plant us in the ground, you had to rope in the Russians just to make sure. Are you mad!?"

Taylan chuckled, staring at nothing. "*Vietnamese*, not Viet Cong. But Gorimov had it coming. He stole a bunch of remains from a dig I was working on at the Nemegt Formation in Mongolia. Three nearly complete *Tarbosaurus bataar*. The bastard was trying to sell them to a collector in New York. I tipped off the police just in time." He turned to Audrey, his lip raised in a snarl. "Those were *my* dinosaurs – or at least the Government of Mongolia's. He's a vulture. Lining his own pockets."

Audrey raised her eyebrow appraisingly, all professional interest. "Really? Three nearly complete? That's rare!"

"Tell me about it."

"Hold on," Karam said, as he put the Cadillac into a fishtail turn that led them down off the highway and into an open roadway. Glancing back Taylan saw the taxi catching up to them.

The roadway was complete chaos. There seemed to be no rhyme, reason, or any traffic laws whatsoever. Three-wheeled 'Auto Rickshaws', cars, bicycles, people where everywhere. If that wasn't enough, Karam *sped up* as they came into the mess.

Taylan gripped the back of the driver's seat with white knuckles, bracing himself as they plowed into what must be certain catastrophe.

The car swerved onto a sidewalk (if the fractured concrete could be called that) just as a hunched over woman with an overfilled shopping cart ambled into their path. Audrey was clutching the door handle with one hand and with the other Taylan's forearm, her face wide-eyed in horror. Taylan squinted and turned his head sideways, waiting for the inevitable impact.

Instead, missing the cart by inches, Karam swerved the car at the last instant. The Cadillac's creamy suspension caused the two backseat passengers to bob up and down as they bounced off the sidewalk and back onto the street, nearly sideswiping a rust-bucket delivery truck. They passed a few families sitting around in chairs and on blankets along the roadside, listening to radios or portable TVs and eating, as if enjoying a leisurely picnic.

Karam also constantly used the horn, to where it took on the cadence of a barking, haranguing dog. It seemed to only have a marginal effect, but the margin was apparently enough. The Cadillac forced its way by constant jabbing and braking through the clogged traffic, which filled in behind them. Taylan looked back and could pick out the taxi pursuing them by the Russian leaning out the passenger window.

Even as it occurred to him a person could probably run faster than any of them were driving, he saw the man already exiting the taxi. That was also when he spotted the two motorcyclists aggressively weaving their way toward them. They looked like Moto Guzzis. The drivers had flashy brand-new jackets and visored helmets.

"Karam?" he said.

"Yes, I know. Traffic is always bad this time of day!"

Taylan tapped Karam's shoulder and made an exaggerated point gesture backwards.

"Ah, I see. Hold on."

He whipped the wheel to the right and hit the gas, clipping a street vender's cart. They careened down a narrow side street for thirty yards. Taylan and Audrey got their first look at a residential neighborhood.

Up close the buildings looked even worse, water-stained and streaked with mold. Most seemed on the verge of complete collapse. Drying clothes hung over rusted railings, some housing seemed to be missing entire walls (even as they passed one concrete apartment, Taylan realized they were looking into someone's open living room with people watching television in it) while trash and filth prevailed everywhere. As far as Taylan could tell, the only exterior paints readily available in Mumbai were white or beige, though the occasional brown or faded turquoise building stood out.

Karam took a hard left and accelerated, enough that Audrey tumbled into Taylan's lap. A light ping ricocheted off the rear window, cracking it.

"I think someone just took a shot at us," Taylan said.

Grinning, Karam replied, "Yes, that is correct."

He's enjoying this, Taylan realized. Audrey sat upright, hair in tangled disarray, just as one motorcycle appeared behind them.

The motorcyclist sped up, bending down low. Karam spotted a less crowded street to their right and with a quick skid, shot down it. They were heading down a broader, open avenue with clothes and knick-knack vendors lining the streets on either side. The car skidded on a long patch of trash, whisking by a young homeless boy washing himself at the curb using a large plastic container, then Karam righted the car as they passed a series of older, colonial-style buildings.

Pedestrians seemed unfazed by the speeding juggernaut, but the motorcycle with its armed riders – the second one had quickly caught up - got their attention.

Karam was hunched over the steering wheel, glancing to his left as if searching for something.

"Ah!" he said, spinning the wheel to the left. The Cadillac sped up a ramped roadway to an overpass bridging a series of rail lines leading into a metro station. The one cyclist was speeding up on their left, leaning over and ducking his arm in a way Taylan didn't care for.

"Swerve right into him when I tell you," he barked at Karam, unbuckling himself and clambering over Audrey.

"Will do."

Taylan leaned back and tucked in his legs, putting his feet up against the door while gripping the handle. His eyes were just above the back seat, watching the cyclist close in.

I hope to hell this works, he thought as the cyclist eased his speed to come up alongside.

"Now!" he yelled.

Karam cut the wheel left, closing the distance. Taylan waited a second then, yanking the door handle, kicked the door out as hard as he could. It swung out slower than he'd hoped, but it was enough. The edge of the door caught the rider right on the leg, sending him careening off across the opposite lane and into the railing. The bike crumpled into the concrete base, sending the rider cartwheeling over the top and down onto the electric train cables. There was a bright flash and bang, but Taylan had other things to contend with.

He hadn't factored the smoothness of the leather seats. He was so keyed-up that the force of his kick shot him halfway out the door before Audrey thought to grab his shoulders. The heels of his shoes bounced off the pavement, nearly dragging him all the way out. After years of excavating, fortunately, Audrey was no slouch in the strength department. She dug her heel to the curve of the floor well and hauled back with all she had.

Taylan found his butt back on the seat, the free-swinging doors banging his knees painfully. To make matters worse, the second motorcyclist pulled in. Taylan could see the glint of teeth behind the visor and the 9mm in the gloved left hand aiming at him. The open door was probably obstructing Karam's view from the side view mirror.

"Brakes!" he yelled at Karam.

The Sikh must have jammed both feet on the pedal.

The tires screamed as the Cadillac de-accelerated, but the response was too sluggish. Braking with his foot, the cyclist nudged his Moto Guzzi deftly away from the swinging door and raised the pistol, his grin more pronounced.

Taylan felt like a sitting duck.

The distraction was enough. Taylan didn't see exactly what happened – it was way too fast – but a delivery truck had been coming in the opposite direction. One moment the motorcyclist was there, in another instant he was gone, subtracted by the truck's grill. There was a muffled crump then squeal of tires as the truck ran over the bike, mangling both as it skidded into a crash.

Once over the bridge, Audrey was able to drag Taylan into the car far enough so he could reach and close the door.

"Is the taxi still following us?" Taylan asked, buckling himself back in.

Karam made a quick study of all his rearview mirrors. "If he is, I think you convinced him to be a lot more careful about it. *Haramjada.*" He grinned again. "But we should be sure."

Once off the bridge, Karam pulled down a side street, using the same push-and-honk method to get them through the crowds. They spotted fewer of the ubiquitous black-with-yellow roof taxis, none gave any indication of following them. After a lengthy series of twists and turns they came out speeding southbound down Juhu Church Road. The neighborhood switched to 'upscale' buildings and homes. Taylan was somewhat amazed at the dizzying speed at which neighborhoods went from ramshackle shanty houses to affluent residences – zoning was apparently a foreign concept in India. Even then a new office building might be found shouldered in next to a sagging tenement.

Karam seemed only happy when he was driving the car at maximum speed. They flew down the road about half a mile, swerving expertly around other vehicles, until they came up on the gated sandstone wall of the JW Marriott. At the beachfront on the Arabian Sea, the hotel itself was a modern, ochre-colored affair accented by rich green palms and foliage.

Once in they raced up the ramp and under the second-floor Port Cochere where they screeched to a halt.

"Well that was quite interesting," Audrey said, rubbing her face with both hands. "Are taxi rides here in India always this eventful?"

Karam laughed. "Only for special visitors. But both of you should be careful. That Russian is still looking for you."

Taylan reached for his wallet, but Karam shook his head.

"Your bill is already settled. I will be back tomorrow morning to take you back to the airport. I'm quite sure you will enjoy Dr. Banaji. And her presentation. Until then, stay safe."

"You too," Taylan said, though he pitied the person who came after the Sikh. He looked powerful enough to take apart his enemies by hand.

Looking out, he saw the rain had turned into a steady drizzle.

"Anything to be concerned about?" he asked.

"It *is* monsoon season. Hopefully just a touch of rain," Karam replied.

A moment later the bellhop – a similarly dressed young man – materialized beside the Cadillac and opened the door. With him was one of the concierge, a small, striking woman dressed in a business suit with a gold nametag that said "Anika". She greeted them with a smile.

"Welcome to JW Marriott Mumbai, Dr. Taylan and Dr. Adams. No need to check in, your accommodations have already been taken care of." She rattled this off with smooth efficiency, not even glancing at their rumpled khakis and backpacks.

The bellhop extended his hand to Audrey, who took it with amused approval as she stepped out of the car. The concierge handed them two passkeys. "Your suites are on the top floor, overlooking the ocean. You may wish to freshen up and have lunch first. The Lotus Café has a full buffet. The presentation starts at one-thirty."

Taylan nodded, trying to get his bearings. The hotel looked first-rate and was behind a high-walled compound. The guards at the gates looked like ex-military, which he guessed security had been beefed up since the terrorist attacks in 2008. Rain was coming down in a gray drizzle. The heat was suffocating.

As he turned to enter the main lobby, he realized Audrey was studying him oddly.

He raised his brows in a *what?* expression.

She shook her head dismissively, "Just something the driver said. Never mind."

Taylan couldn't recall what she was referring to, only that she looked somewhat peeved.

Don't bother trying to figure it out. You'll only go insane, he decided.

Inside the broad, marble-floored lobby was an oasis of cool air and refined style. Seating areas with leather chairs, potted palms and oversized oriental rugs were neatly arranged in orderly groups; to the left was the concierge desks while to the right a hall led to a series of hotel shops. Ahead of them a set of broad steps led down to a mezzanine with some chairs and a concert grand piano with stairs leading down either side to the cavernous dining area below. Opposite was a floor-to-ceiling glass wall overlooking the landscaped gardens and pools, which led to another wall and the broad expanse of beach on the Arabian Sea.

Not a huge fan of luxury hotels, Taylan had to grudgingly admit this one looked quite impressive.

He looked down at the café, presumably the 'Lotus Café' the concierge had mentioned.

"Should we freshen up and grab some lunch?"

Audrey shouldered her back pack. "Sure. As long as we don't get in any taxis again for a spot."

"Oh, and a word of advice."

He got a raised brow in response.

"Don't drink the water, even here. Not even to brush your teeth."

DISASTER STRIKES, AGAIN

"So, to summarize, the K-T extinction that wiped out the dinosaurs, in this Paleontologist's opinion, was not the dramatic, catastrophic Hollywood-style event many would have you believe, but a complex series of related events that triggered a systemic breakdown both biological *and* psychological in dinosaur populations. Now I would be happy to answer any questions you may have."

The Grand Sangam ballroom was less than half full. On one wall, an oversize projection screen had been set up with smaller HD screens off to either side. The hushed lighting had come up and behind the lectern Dr. Roma Banaji placed her laser pointer down and put on a show of looking out confidently over the audience.

On the short side, but well proportioned, Roma Banaji was a beautiful woman and she did not try to conceal it. Her features had a royal cast to them – sharp lips with a slightly disdainful downturn at the corners, arched brows and a gracefully curved nose. The mind behind the narrow glasses was sharp, possessed an uncanny analytic capability, and had a merciless tendency to skewer anyone perceived as not taking her seriously. Rather than redress those same people, however, she was more likely to simply shut them down or ignore them altogether.

As a result, much to her family's upset, she'd had few close personal relationships and to date any potential suitors had crashed and burned messily. Her father – a successful medical doctor in Mumbai – was terrified she might be a lesbian and constantly harped onto her mother about this. He was equally horrified that his daughter had opted to pursue paleontology halfway through her schooling in England and insisted on coming back to attend Panjab University in Chandigarh to study under acclaimed Indian paleontologist Ashok Sahni. This was a topic her father was also quite verbal about to his family, usually with some variation of: "But there's *no* money in it! Who will marry a woman who studies old bones!? My daughter has gone mad!"

To this, Roma's mother (whom she took after), would usually shake her head and shoo him away. Few people would guess the two things her and her mother shared as both kept it highly concealed: an outrageous sense of humor and love of dirty jokes.

The presentation Dr. Roma Banaji had given today had lasted nearly two hours. Most of the attendees were from the University, though a few desultory members from the press had shown up to cover it, Paleontology not being a particularly popular topic in India these days. Most of the population was more preoccupied with the cash crunch. Between rampant corruption and counterfeiting, money was scarce.

There was a lengthy pause after she finished speaking in which she had the sinking feeling that *no-one* would ask any questions, then mercifully a few hands went up. She pointed to a young, hatchet-faced student near the front whose clump of unruly hair had a mind of its own.

"Yes?"

"You seem to favor the *intrinsic* as opposed to the *extrinsic* theory for K-T extinction event, doesn't the evidence at the Deccan Traps strongly suggest otherwise?"

Ah, a first-year student trying to sound smart, she thought, catching the self-satisfied smirk on his face and nod to the female student seated next to him.

She repeated the question for the audience's benefit, then clarified it. "He's referring of course, to the plateau in west-central India where a surge in volcanic activity at the end of the Cretaceous period has been potentially linked to the Yucatan meteor impact that triggered the K-T extinction."

She toyed with the finger on one hand, a subconscious gesture she did when contemplating a response.

"To answer your question, yes, I do tend to favor intrinsic theories – there's growing evidence to support them, including the collapse of so many animal and insect populations going on in the world today. I hope that would have been clear to those of you paying attention throughout the entire presentation."

A hand waving at the back of the room distracted her before she could elaborate.

"But the main problem is the *selectivity* of the mass extinction, no?" Taylan said, loud and clear enough that many heads craned around to look at him. "Why did certain species die out and others weren't affected at all?"

Dr. Banaji frowned. "Yes, well, it's certainly one of the issues we're still trying to work out."

"Because without working with living, breathing examples of dinosaurs, it's really just a lot of conjecturing, wouldn't you say?"

"I wouldn't," she replied, unable to keep the irritation out of her voice. "Next?"

"It *was* an interesting presentation, Dr. Banaji," Taylan said to her, after introducing Audrey and himself at the reception in the lobby. Outside the lower entrance the rain was now coming down in a heavy downpour.

They were standing near the reception table where the students were more focused on eating everything in sight.

"I'm glad you thought so. I think most of the students only came here today for the food. Paleontology has been on the decline here in my country. Many of the universities these days are lumping the curriculum in with geology. Can you believe that?"

"Yes, well things are tough all over," Taylan replied, sipping a paper cup of coffee. "The Museum of Natural History isn't exactly flush these days, either."

Audrey was being uncharacteristically tight-lipped, which had Taylan at something of a loss. She stood with them but was looking off into the distance, pivoting her shoulders back and forth slightly as if impatient with something.

Is she jealous? he wondered. Then he noticed the makeup she'd applied, and the way she'd done what she could with her hair. *I think she is! And where in the hell did she get make-up?*

Before he could further ponder the mysteries of a woman's cosmetics sources, his thoughts were interrupted by Dr. Banaji. She cut a striking figure with her tailored business suit and the buttoned-down blouse gave a tantalizing hint of her ample cleavage.

"Sorry?" he said.

Dr. Banaji studied him over the top of her glasses, as if reading his thoughts. She put on a professional smile. "I said: 'I would infer that you disagree with the conclusions in my presentation?'"

Taylan rubbed the bridge of his nose with his thumb and forefinger. It was a fall back gesture that back when he was a kid, his father used to joke made him look like a pint-sized Detective Colombo.

"Well, Dr. Banaji—"

"Roma, you can call me Roma, if you wish."

"Yes, er, *Roma*, your points are all well made, and fascinating," (here Audrey rolled her eyes), "but there are all sorts of holes in them."

"Such as?"

"—such as the mass marine extinctions millions of years prior to the K-T event," Audrey said pointedly, her arms now folded across her chest.

Roma gave her a quizzical glance. "I know you," she said, addressing Audrey for the first time. "You're the Australian 'Dino-hunter'. Didn't you have some sort of augmented-reality 'experience the dinosaurs' thing happening in London? How did that work out?"

Taylan had to restrain himself from smacking his forehead. He could never fathom how some women could, with laser-guided accuracy, intuitively seek out the sorest topic on another's mind and plunge a needle in it.

Audrey's jaw clenched, and for a wild moment Taylan thought she was going to cold-cock Roma and storm out. Instead he cut her off as she responded.

"Yes, well it's—"

"—on hold," Taylan interrupted. "But tell me, Roma, wouldn't it be more useful to study an actual *living* dinosaur before pouring your theory in concrete?"

Roma shook her head. "I'm afraid I don't . . . oh, *now I get it.* You two are pitching for that loony Texas billionaire. Preston? Paxton?"

"*Peyton*," Taylan corrected.

"Yes, whatever he's called. Look, Dr. Taylan, I'd already made it clear I'm not interested in soiling my reputation by signing on with a crackpot ugly-American with too much money on his hands. I have serious work to do. Good day to both of you."

"Look, Roma," Taylan said, blocking her path, "I'm—"

"Actually, let's stick with 'Dr. Banaji'."

All of Taylan's charm and force of personality came to the fore, like he'd spun an internal dial to the max. He tilted his head and looked her straight in the eye. "Fine, *Doctor Banaji.* Look, I'm not exactly a card-carrying member of

Peyton's fan club. But I am convinced this venture he's asked us to consult on just might be legit. I think it's possible that the Chinese really have created living dinosaurs on this 'Lost World of Kharamu' and if they have, I sure as hell would like to see them first-hand. Christ, the name does sound hokey, doesn't it?"

Just as abruptly, Roma's mood switched yet again. This time a trace of an amused smile touched her lips. "Yes, it really does. What are you proposing?"

Taylan smiled back. "We came here quite a way to have a few words with you. Why don't the three of us grab some tea over at the café and discuss this like the three professionals we are? From the looks of the weather outside, none of us are going anywhere anytime soon. What do you say?"

Roma didn't reply immediately. Arms crossed (and pushing her cleavage up, Taylan couldn't help but noticing), her forefinger tapped at her lower lip.

"Okay, I'll bite. I'll meet you there in fifteen minutes. I just need to collect my things."

"You were just interested in her tits!" Audrey said, after they had settled into the same table at the Lotus café they'd had lunch at earlier. Taylan was still feeling a little off from the intense and complex spices in the Indian food. He'd stuck mainly with the Tandoori chicken and lamb, skipping the fresh fruit for cooked vegetables just to be safe.

"*What?*" he shot back, nearly jumping out of his chair.

"Her *tits*. Admit it! She had to practically peel your bloody eyes off 'em!"

"Give me a break."

Audrey refused to back down. "This is just great. You mashed my career over a psycho ex-girlfriend, then dragged me down to this God-forsaken place so you can . . . what? Drool all over little Miss India's *bodacious norks?*"

This time Taylan did smack his forehead with his palm. Then the penny dropped. He gave her a squinty look.

"You're jealous! Isn't that what this is about? Good old classic school-girl competitiveness?"

Audrey's eyes flared. Before she could reply, however, they were interrupted by someone approaching their table.

"What's all this about '*bodacious norks?*'" Roma said pleasantly as she joined them.

Taylan glanced up, tea cup paused in mid-air. "You heard that?"

Roma smiled. "Clear across the room."

Audrey looked straight up at the ceiling before burying her face in her hand.

Putting his cup down, Taylan let out a laugh, "*Hmph.* Well, thanks for joining us, anyway."

A waiter materialized and poured Roma a cup of hot water. She fished a packet of Assam tea out of the caddy. After adding judicious amounts of milk and sugar, she leaned back and studied Taylan over the rim of her cup. Next to her Audrey kept her face covered.

"So, tell me, Dr. Taylan, why I should risk my reputation with Mr. Peyton's tacky investment operation for obnoxiously rich people?"

Taylan leaned back, "Oh, I can give you a list of reasons."

Twenty minutes later, Roma still didn't appear sold, but Taylan wasn't sure if due to the lack of a convincing argument on his part or simply because she was enjoying sitting here, flirting with him. He was leaning toward the latter, no doubt in some small part to wanting to make Audrey squirm.

Christ, she's a maverick at this, Taylan told himself, as Roma crossed her legs once again. *In fact, I think she's toying with both of us, just for the hell of it.*

". . . because funding isn't really a personal issue with me, per se," Roma was saying, her head slightly tilted and wearing an expression that might have added: *but you could be . . .*

Taylan glanced over at Audrey but was vaguely annoyed she didn't seem to pay any attention at all. Instead she seemed to study the landscaped gardens out back. The sky had darkened and despite the high overhead lights the café had taken on an atmosphere of cavernous gloom.

"Really?" Taylan replied, not really believing her. She'd already admitted herself that the Universities in India were closing their Paleontology courses due to lack of interest. He suspected her father's piggy bank would probably only go so far in the current recession climate.

"So, set aside the whole money issue for a moment, and look me in the eye and tell me you would pass up the opportunity to see how living, breathing dinosaurs act in their environment."

"See, that's just it, they wouldn't be—"

"We should probably think about getting out of here, soon," Audrey cut in, abruptly.

"What?" both Taylan and Roma said, nearly in unison.

"The rain, it's coming down harder. In the past half hour that garden has flooded. See? The paths are now underwater."

Roma smiled. "Oh, it's just the monsoon, it's the season. Don't worry, it'll pass quickly."

"I don't think so," Audrey replied, "I've been watching the clouds out over the ocean – they're getting darker."

Roma twisted around and did a double-take. Her second look wasn't reassuring.

Just then their waiter arrived. He was a dark-skinned man with deep set, primal features.

"I'm very sorry to interrupt, Dr. Banaji," he said, "but it appears the weather is getting much worse. I would recommend you leave immediately as there are reports of flooding."

"How bad is it?" she asked.

"Very," the waiter admitted. "There are already reports that an oil rig off the coast has collapsed. I've already called a car for you just in case."

Roma smiled. "That won't be necessary, I have a . . . what was that?"

There was a sound of muffled, staccato pops from the lobby. Followed by screams.

Both Audrey and Taylan jumped up.

"That sounded like gunfire, from the entrance," he said.

Audrey looked up at the balcony, then outside at the flooded gardens.

"This is not going to be fun," she said.

Roma stood up in alarm. She was a freshman in college when the last terrorist attack had occurred in this very hotel.

"Come on!" Taylan shouted, heading toward the back doors.

Roma looked at the flooded gardens. "Out there!?"

"Yes!"

As they ran out into the downpour, Taylan looked back to see the first Vietnamese appear at the railing.

Christ, these guys don't give up! he thought, then dragged the two women with him, just as several glass panes above exploded outward from bullets.

Outside, the water was up past their ankles, making for difficult going. The rain was like being drenched with warm bathwater. Taylan led them along the winding pathway to the upper tier of swimming pools. Fortunately, the palm trees and statues gave them plenty of cover. Just past the pools to the right was a tile-roofed cabana, which gave them a momentary respite from the rain. All three were soaked to the skin. Roma had lost both her shoes along the way.

"Any bright ideas?" Audrey asked, wiping her hair out of her eyes.

Taylan weighed up their situation. Three of the Vietnamese were fanning out from the back of the hotel, searching for them. From where they were a heavy wall of ochre sandstone topped by sculpted heads separated them from the beach. Or what had been the beach. The entire stretch was now under water, with waves breaking right up to the wall.

Then he spotted the nearby shed where the Jet Skis were stored.

Pulling Audrey to him, he pointed, "You know how to handle one of those things?"

"Happy to give it a burl!"

"Great. Help me find the keys!"

"No time for that," Audrey said, already jogging toward the shed. She went up to the nearest one – a Kawasaki Ultra 310 – and popped the hood.

Roma looked incredulously out at the rising ocean, then at the Jet Ski. "You intend to go out *there* . . . in *that*!?"

"Or you can stick around and have a chit-chat with those Vietnamese Commandos. Wouldn't recommend it though!"

"But that's insane!" Roma said. A bullet whined overhead, shattering a roof tile.

"Oh, don't get yer knickers in a knot. It's just water!"

Given something to do, Audrey was in her element. "C'mon Taylan, you and the miss take this one and I'll follow!"

Taylan jumped on, testing the throttle. At least the gas gauge read full. Audrey scooted around front, gave the gate a few hard kicks until it broke open, then popped the hood on the second Jet Ski.

"Hop on," he told Roma.

Straddling the seat behind him, she looped her arms around his waist. Thrusting his legs out in an awkward waddle, he walked the Jet Ski down the short ramp into the water. They were hit by a wave that jolted them up, then Taylan gunned the throttle and they shot out into the surf.

Visibility was bad, but as he did a half loop around he saw that Audrey was having difficulty starting the second Kawasaki. Even worse, one commando was creeping up on her flank, approaching in a half-squat with one hand holding a Glock and the other shielding his eyes.

Acting on instinct, he swung the Jet Ski back in, fishtailing as he approached the wall. A satisfying fan of water arced up and over, drenching both Audrey and the commando.

"Are you good?" he shouted at Audrey, who looked ready to kill him.

"Bloody hell!" she snapped at him.

"Skip it," Taylan said. "Jump on the back!"

She took three sloppy bounds and leapt onto the Jet Ski. Taylan raced the throttle again, sending a rooster-tail plume back over the shed, then they were off, racing through sheets of rain southward along the Arabian sea.

Taylan weighed up his options. With three people, the Jet Ski was running tail-heavy. He was also sure it wasn't particularly smart to be riding blind through a rising ocean in a full-blown monsoon. Racking his brain, Taylan vaguely recalled there was an inland lake alongside a small airport just past the main road beyond the hotel.

"Grant!" he heard Audrey shout, barely audible above the rain, waves and roar of the engine.

She reached around Roma and poked him, then jabbed her finger backward.

The message was obvious: *they're following.*

Taylan kept the Jet Ski just outside the crashing surf, the throttle opened all the way, as he looked for some sort of opening. Risking a quick glance backward, he spotted the second Kawasaki with a single rider way back, but gaining on them. Short of dumping his two passengers, there was no way he could outrun him for long.

Eyes squinted, hunkered down behind the windscreen, he tried to make out a landmark along the beach.

There it was! A breach where the storm surge had broken through to the airport!

The water was traveling over the crest of the beach and the two-lane roadway beyond in white-water rapids, before fanning off to the sides from the higher elevation of the runway tarmac.

The question was whether the roadway divider was submerged enough for them to clear or break their necks on. Abandoned cars were scattered here and there, doors swinging open and closed. As it was, Taylan wasn't much one for second-guessing. Cutting into a slow bank, he steered the Jet Ski into the center of the surge and hoped for the best.

They were halfway through when the hull hit the divider with a jaw-snapping crash and shattered the hull of the Jet Ski. The Kawasaki slewed sideways for a dozen yards before striking the slope running up to the runway and tumbling, sending all three of them flying off.

Fortunately, the frothing water cushioned the worst of it.

Taylan found himself sitting on his ass facing the storm surge, while Roma landed face down next to him. Audrey was a few feet away on her hands and knees, water sluicing around her. Even more gruesome, several dead bodies were floating past, spiraling and rolling lazily in the rapids. Taylan wondered if they had come out of the abandoned vehicles on the swamped roadway.

Out toward the ocean their closest pursuer – one commando – pulled his Jet Ski up alongside a car to steady it, then pulled out his Glock and aimed it over the hood.

Taylan was about to lunge and grab Roma and Audrey if he could, when an even louder sound came from overhead. It sounded like the chugging of the world's largest washing machine. The rain seemed to spiral in all directions and he held up an arm as an even harder wind buffeted him.

He looked up.

It was a helicopter, a Gazelle AH1 British Army surplus of all the damndest things.

The pilot swung it around in an arc over the commando, forcing him to flatten and take cover, then eased it down at the edge of the runway. The door flew open and Taylan saw a figure jump out and run toward them, sloshing through the water.

"Jeff?"

Somehow, he knew he shouldn't have been surprised, but he was.

"Hey, pal!" Doyle replied, half-covered by a poncho that the idling copter blades had whipped about his head. "We got to get out of here, pronto!" He looked over at the body of an elderly Indian man drifting past. "Yikes!" he added.

Taylan helped a sputtering Roma to her feet. "Take her!" he yelled. He ran over and grabbed Audrey by the arm and hauled her up. Over behind the car the commando was popping his head up. It was only moments before he shot at them.

"You okay?"

Audrey nodded.

"Stay low!" he shouted as they sloshed toward the helicopter in a crouched run. They clambered into the back where Roma was already seated, while Doyle climbed into the shotgun seat and strapped himself in. A bullet *tinged* off the side of the copter.

"Buckle up!" Doyle yelled.

The pilot didn't wait. In a slewed, sickening motion the copter lifted off and went down the runway at an angle. Taylan was convinced they were going to skid and crash into the tarmac. Then halfway down the copter straightened out and lifted upward into the pelting rain.

Taylan buckled himself and Audrey in, before leaning back against the padded seat, water running off his head and face. He looked up at the ceiling of the copter with his mouth open before closing his eyes in disbelief.

As they flew eastward the rain lessened in intensity, enough so that Taylan could see much of the city was already underwater.

"Good God," Audrey said, looking down at the chaos. Many of the shanty neighborhoods were submerged, with bodies floating about. Many people were huddling on rooftops or upper balconies. Some waved, others stared despondently.

"Your family down there?" Taylan asked Roma.

"No," she said. "They're all in Nagpur. But those poor people."

Taylan thought about that. And the Russians and Vietnamese down there as well. Something was nagging at him, though.

"How did you know where to find us?"

"Dude, Mr. Peyton knows where to find everyone when he wants to! Besides, who else would be insane enough to be out Jet Skiing in a monsoon? You're the man!"

Audrey rolled her eyes while Roma simply stared out the window.

"What about all those people down there?" Taylan asked.

"What about them? We're not here to save the planet, bro. I was instructed to get only yours and two premier scientists' asses out of Mumbai, monsoon or no monsoon!"

And here I was just about to forget what a complete dick you are . . . 'bro', Taylan almost said aloud. Instead, he replied: "So now where to?"

"Peyton's private jet is waiting on an airfield fifteen minutes northeast of here at Nashik. Give you a few minutes to get dried off and cleaned up. Then we'll fly you directly to Hainan Island off China from there, where a copter will take you to join a freighter en route to Kharamu. Then it's time for a whole lot of *awesome.*"

Taylan glanced over at Roma. She had an odd, flushed expression on her face. "If you want to get off at the next stop, I understand."

She let out a soft laugh.

"No, I think I'll stick along for the ride. Maybe a little distance would do me some good."

SOMEWHERE IN THE SOUTH CHINA SEA, FRIDAY, 1100 HOURS

The tramp freighter *Vazão*, for all visual purposes, was a complete rust bucket that defined a whole new wishful definition of 'seaworthy'.

That was all on the surface, however. The original ship – a WWII era AKL light freighter once used by the NOAA – was in excellent shape after a complete overhaul the year before. The 177-foot, 550-ton vessel was refitted with modern hybrid electric-diesel engines that took up a fraction of the space the originals did. Like most things on the ship, the original engine room looked as it once did, even hooked up to a bypass switch so that when visitors came down, it would clank and hammer away like the failing antique they expected, right down to the oily smoke and grease-coated surfaces. The real engines were underneath, accessed by a modern watertight crawlspace.

Likewise, the bridge, which had been reverted to its late 1940s heyday, complete with wooden wheel and brass throttle that clanged when operated. The real operating bridge was concealed down in the hold in a small but modernized compartment, complete with oversized HD monitors linked to concealed cameras on the original bridge which gave the operators the sense of the real thing.

The passenger accommodations had been restored to their early 1950s décor, including mahogany paneling, floral patterned upholstery and standing ashtrays. Period light fixtures were installed (though close scrutiny would reveal the bulbs were fitted with low energy LEDs to simulate the originals) along with framed paintings and Kodachrome prints.

Outside the ship had been cleverly 'aged' to give it that weary patina of an overused, probably unsafe vessel, the kind an unscrupulous captain would no doubt use to ferry his passengers to some dangerous destination in a remote area of the world.

Despite this, the result was a painstakingly accurate experience for visitors looking to relive the relaxed, halcyon days of freighter travel before affordable mass air travel ushered in the era of jam-packed cruise ships jazzed up with many Vegas-style entertainment events.

The Chinese military surplus Z-8 transport helicopter landed then in calm seas fifty yards off the beam of the *Vazão*, where an inflatable Zodiac took them over.

Sitting in the bow with Audrey and Roma, Taylan had to admit the whole 'shaky expedition' ship was exactly like something imagined out of an old 50s monster movie. Doyle had filled them in on the details during their leap-frog trip to get here, including how the 'expedition' would spend three nights and four days camping at the island while the 'scientist' leading the expedition would search for a legendary 'longevity plant' while encountering various dinosaur species along the way.

Of course, seeing photos and experiencing the 'real' thing were vastly different matters. Taylan couldn't help but to feel a pang of excitement at the old warhorse freighter, hove to so it drifted in the rich blue waters under a bright, azure sky.

The *Vazão* had clean, elegant lines: the bridge and superstructure set in the back half of the ship, an open deck in the fore half with a boom crane and raised forecastle.

The launch pulled up alongside where a wood-and-rope ladder had been dropped. Several unshaven crew in soiled fatigues awaited by the gunwale to assist them aboard. As they clambered up onto the deck a small group of men stood waiting for them.

"Welcome aboard! I'm Captain Gunther Steneck," a dark blond-haired man said, stepping forward. The cap and white uniform were only mildly soiled, though he had a couple weeks of beard.

A German. Of course, Taylan thought. *It's always a German captain in the movies.*

Next to him was another sailor – a sharp featured man Taylan guessed was the first mate, while behind them were half a dozen other crewmen, except for a pudgy-looking man with greying blond hair who looked about ready to burst out of his pressed white shirt and pants. He reminded Taylan of a beefy Bill Clinton in his younger days.

Captain Steneck flashed a smile of strong white teeth as he shook hands with them.

"This is my first mate, Liam Farrell, and—"

"—Roger Blodgett," the pudgy man said, pushing past the captain. He greeted them with a beaming, yet unconvincing grin, shaking each hand like a seasoned politician.

"*Oh*, hi, Doyle!" he added when he got to the last. Then spreading his arms, said, "I hope ya' ll had an excellent trip! Everyone's waiting to meet you in the main lounge at the back – I mean *aft* – of the ship. They just served lunch! Come, come!"

Ignoring the rest of the ship's crew, he led them down to the rear deck and into the aft state-room. Stepping out of the withering tropical sun into the air-conditioned interior was close to a system-shock, like walking into a freezer.

The cabin was spacious and the elegant quality of furnishings incongruous with the appearance of the rest of the ship, from what they'd seen at least. A cold buffet had been laid out on a table to one side; sandwiches, salad, a large bowl of tropical vegetables and soft drinks.

In the middle of the cabin stood a group of men and women dressed in 50s period clothes, all talking quietly, as if sharing a secret conversation. Dominating the center was a tall, beefy man with an obsessively trimmed moustache.

"They're here, Mr. Peyton!" Blodgett announced. A hush fell over the group.

"—Allen Peyton III!" the tall man spoke up abruptly, with a boisterous voice. He pushed past Blodgett and took Taylan's hand while clapping him hard on the shoulder like an old friend. "So, you're the infamous Grant Taylan! The Dino-hunter himself! Glad we could wrangle you into joining our little *adventure!* You look even more competent in person! Can't wait to hear what you think of the dinos those gooks have cooked up!"

Up close Peyton was pretty much as Taylan had anticipated: garrulous, obnoxious and reeking of some expensive aftershave. He spoke with just a trace of a Texas accent, though Taylan had heard he was from Florida. Peyton was dressed in what could only be described as '50s travel casual' – white pants, canvas deck shoes and a navy Polo shirt. The stub of an unlit cigar was clenched in his teeth.

He caught the two women staring at him and gave an 'aw shucks' shrug. "I don't really smoke 'em," he said. He leaned forward and shook Audrey's hand. "And you must be the illustrious Audrey Adams! Nice to have you aboard, ma'am!"

Audrey blinked, and said in an icy voice: "It's *Doctor* Adams, actually."

"Aw, sure!" Peyton replied, though his eyes hardened briefly. He moved on to Roma. "Ah, the wonderful doctor who's both pretty *and* an Indian! What a treat!"

Taylan sensed her stiffen up, but she maintained a pleasant demeanor. "No doubt it is, Mr. Peyton."

Peyton let out a grunt, then realized he hadn't introduced his group, all who might have been dressed up for a Universal Pictures' horror-themed costume party.

The first was Suzie Blodgett, a right-wing Republican talk-show host (and author) Taylan recognized from her TV 'news' show. An attractive woman in a late 30s 'cougar' sort of way, she had the shrewd look of veteran suburban mall-shopper. Her straight blond hair was cut in a modest attempt at a period hairstyle, while the blue eyes measuring them up over the rim of the tortoise-shell sunglasses were dark and merciless in the tropical sun. Her greeting was perfunctory and her handshake man-like. She was dressed in a floral print halter top and white pants. She also wore canvas deck shoes.

Stepping in next to her, Roger Blodgett made a show of putting his arm around his wife, who smiled stiffly. Blodgett had the smooth, effusive manner of a born yes-man, Taylan decided. It didn't take much guesswork to figure out who wore the pants in their marriage.

An elderly couple introduced as 'Mr. and Mrs. Charles Banyon' followed. The husband was a slightly overweight, white-haired man with creased features that suggested a friendly grandfather type. Except for his blue eyes, which were hard and flinty. His wife was a grey-haired doddering type, with too much jewelry and make-up. Her demeanor was tired and distracted, as if she'd just discovered she'd arrived at a party she couldn't exactly remember being invited to.

Last was a lean, dark-skinned black man with deep-set eyes and a quick, but engaging smile. He was decked out in soiled khakis and boots.

"Joseph Bello," he said, pumping Taylan's hand. There was a ready enthusiasm about him Taylan immediately warmed to.

"Nice to meet you," Taylan said, the first time he'd said that aboard the ship and meant it.

Doyle stepped up, a handful of brochures and flyers held up like some tour guide. "This is great," he said awkwardly. "What's next?"

Peyton gestured expansively toward the table. "Well, you folks help yourself to some chow, then Roger here will show you to your rooms. Later when the sun is down I can give you a tour of the ship, but right now it'll cook your nuts off!"

Taylan frowned, fixing Peyton with his intense gaze.

He had a hunch this trip was going to be even worse than he feared. *Far* worse.

Half an hour later he was just stretching out on the bed in his cabin when someone hammered on his door.

He'd barely cracked it open when Audrey pushed her way in and dropped herself in the chair near the open porthole. Before she said anything, she glanced at the porthole and back at Taylan.

"Guess I'm not the only one who thrives on fresh air."

Her eyes travelled around the room. The passenger cabins were spacious and comfortable, closer to a mid-century hotel accommodation than the compact, utilitarian quarters one would have expected. Paneling accents were in burled mahogany, the chairs done in deep sea-blue upholstery and the single bunk bed sumptuous. The colorful ocean-themed prints and nautical details (like the fish reliefs on the metal radiator grill) added a light touch to the stateroom.

Audrey was wearing only a thick terry-cloth robe and slippers – their clothes had been collected earlier by a steward while they were getting cleaned up to be laundered. Taylan was just wearing a pair of striped pajama bottoms he'd found in the bureau.

She turned her full attention on him. "I cannot believe I let you talk me into this damn trip! Bloody Peyton and his white Republican posse. If that Charles Banyon isn't a big game hunter, then I'm a Dutch uncle. And the Blodgetts?" She dropped her head in her hand in mock despair. "Ughhh!"

Taylan sat on the edge of the bunk, looking over the brochures and a printout Doyle had given him over lunch.

"Well, strange as it is, heading to an island full of dinosaurs is probably the safest place to be at this point."

Audrey toyed with the pull chain of the lamp on the table next to her. Like all things in the cabin it was bolted down. She also found her eyes drifting back to Taylan's muscled torso. Not one of those 'cut' physiques cooked up in a gym. Taylan's body was banged, bruised, and somehow *hard*. His shoulder was still bandaged where the falcon had injured him. She forced herself to focus on the lamp.

"So, this isn't some elaborate joke? You think they've really brought back *dinosaurs*?"

"Yes," Taylan said, absently. His brow had furrowed as he flipped through the printouts. It was a breakdown of the party and the respective "characters" they were supposed to be playing, each allotted a full page with an accompanying photo and 'bio'. He was horrified to see that Roma, Audrey and himself were included.

Skimming through the headers, they read in order:

1) Sir John Orville Roxton (Allen Peyton III): British Adventurer, explorer, philanthropist. Infamous member of the Royal Geographic Society.
2) Lady Olivia Roxton (Suzie Blodgett): Adventuress, aviatrix and champion equestrian: only child of the Somersbys of Northumberland.
3) Professor Edwin Challenger (Roger Blodgett), Zoologist and WWII 8th Air Force Fighter Ace, race car driver.
4) Professor Derek Summerlee (Charles Banyon): A famous Harvard scientist and expert in indigenous species and lost civilizations.
5) Mrs. Summerlee (Ethel Banyon): his wife and Art Historian.
6) Bemba (Joseph Bello): their guide.

Penciled in underneath that in neat, block handwriting someone had added:

7) Edward D. Malone (Grant Taylan): Reporter for the New York Daily Sun.
8) Gladys Hungerton (Audrey Adams): British High-Society debutante.
9) Raksha (Roma Banaji): her maid.
10) Jeff Doyle - TBD

Christ, he thought, *this is what happens when you have way too much money and time on your hands: you come up with lunatic things like this.*

He tossed the printout on the floor.

"I haven't even looked at it," Audrey said. "How bad is it?"

Taylan chuckled. "Awful. Like Doyle told us earlier, this whole 'Themed Vacation' is still in beta. Apparently, as part of the 'Adventure' each participant is allowed to pick from either a set character, or sketch out their own. The MuTron marketing team then has one of their writers work up a detailed fictional bio. It's essentially a 'Cosplay' for the very wealthy. In this case, the theme is a bunch of early 1950s adventurers – led by Peyton of course – on an expedition to a remote South Pacific Island rumored to have dinosaurs. Professor Challenger – 'Blodgett' – is the esteemed scientist searching for this wonder-plant reputed to . . . well, to whatever. I don't know who cooked up this asinine storyline, but Peyton's character is intent on retrieving one or more of the dinosaurs – dead or alive – to re-establish his disgraced title at the Royal Geographic Society. Peyton has this fixation with being a lauded hero in British Society – even sponsors a cricket team he bankrolls from the Caribbean. We just have to go along for part of it. Once we arrive we'll get a side tour of the facilities, then rejoin the 'expedition' on the main island to see how it all works. Peyton wants our take on the science behind the dinosaur development, the accuracy of their behavior and the reliability of their fail-safe measures."

"Fail-safe measures?"

"Yes. It seems the key element of the 'thrill' factor is that the dinosaurs run loose. No cages. An implanted collar device keeps them constrained to certain areas, similar to the way electrified collars for dogs work."

Audrey bent over and picked up the brochure, a slick promotional printed on a glossy stock. The graphic design was top-notch. Walking back and forth as she fanned through it, her face registered a combination of wonder, disbelief, and horror.

"Oh my God. These twits are so full of themselves! Is this what big money does to people? Makes them utterly tacky and delusional?" She paused and frowned. "They have me down as a bloody 'debutante'!? What the hell?"

When she got to Roma's profile she had to stifle a laugh. "Oh, this is rich. Doctor Banaji will blow a gasket when she reads this one!"

Audrey realized she was standing in front of Taylan and found herself hyper-aware of his proximity and blunt maleness. The man drove her nuts and yet . . .

Taylan looked up and saw it too; the odd way she was tilting her head at him, a slight flush on her cheeks, lips slightly parted. It was as if through some odd shift in reality she'd abruptly revealed herself as someone else: a sexually charged, vulnerable woman. For a wild moment, he thought she was going to slip out of her robe, bend down and kiss him.

Audrey felt like she was on the verge of falling into a trance, one where . . .

A loud bang on the door startled them out of it. Followed by several more.

Taylan shook his head, blinking, then stood and crossed the cabin while Audrey sat down on the bunk bed, her face a study in confusion.

No sooner had Taylan opened the door than Roma stormed into the room, her eyes livid. She was also in a terrycloth bathrobe, an identical brochure crumpled in one fist. She held it aloft like an incriminating piece of evidence.

"Do you believe this!" she yelled. "They cast me as a *maid*!? A MAID!? I have a fucking PhD for heaven's sakes!"

Shocked by her own profanity, Roma's hand flew to her mouth.

Audrey let out a laugh.

Taylan had his fingers to his temple. It wasn't lost on him that through a variety of twists in fate, he found himself half-naked aboard a ship with two very intelligent and attractive women wearing nothing but bathrobes. Simultaneously, another part of him realized it as well, a development not lost on either Roma nor Audrey.

"Oh!" Roma said, eyes widening. Then she glanced at Audrey sitting on the bed, "I didn't realize you two were . . .?"

Blushing, Audrey bounced out of the bed like it was electrified.

"'We . . . *we* were doing nothing of the sort!" she sputtered. She managed to appear angry and embarrassed at the same time. Realizing her comment made the situation even more awkward, she fled out of the cabin, slamming the door behind her.

A moment of silence followed.

Taylan was aware of Roma watching him, and aware of her perfume as well. Like all things Indian to him, it was exotically complex and enticing.

"What?" he said, turning to face her.

She looked down at the tent at the front of his pajamas, her lips in an amused smile. Shaking her head, she turned around and left.

Taylan looked up at the ceiling.

This was going to be even longer and more torturous than he could have imagined.

DANANG, VIETNAM, THURSDAY.

"You're absolutely *sure* you can deliver?" the man with the mousy-colored hair and tinted glasses asked. He was German, which automatically nominated him on Gorimov's shit list, and he was a shrewd bargainer, which *cemented* him on the list. He'd paid cash up front, which in Gorimov's checkbook made him stupid. That at least balanced the equation somewhat.

They were sitting at the back of one of the chic nightclubs along the Hân River – Le Bar Bak - a modern, neon trimmed affair with the requisite throb of house music, its promise of sex and illicit action all but tangible in the scented atmosphere and pulsing lights.

Gorimov preferred it as the noise levels rendered eavesdropping all but impossible and the back tables afforded both an unobstructed view of everyone coming and going in as well as an emergency exit to his back. Unlike his two grunts, who were sitting the next table over ogling the young ladies giggling at the bar, Gorimov didn't care much for the young Vietnamese girls. He could never tell if they were female or transgender. His weakness was young, blonde-haired, blue-eyed ones. The more innocent American school-girl type, the better.

He took a pull off his vodka, which was mercifully from a decent Polish bottle instead of one of the ridiculous designer rip-offs. "*Nyet problyem,*" he replied, looking the German straight in the eye.

Always look them in the eye.

The German, a trim, peckish man who spoke with the clipped enunciation of a born Prussian was Klaus Böse, a regional representative for IGF Pharmaceutical, a subdivision of D-Base Chemical. He was also a man extremely interested in a particular plant species that was rumored to have been discovered on an island in the South China Sea, a plant known for containing elevated levels of chemical known by the human ATC code L04AA109. It was also called "Shou Yuan", the longevity drug that would make Rapamycin look like a candy tablet.

On the island known as "Kharamu".

IGF had been first approached through one of the Chinese staff on the island a year previous and had been secretly negotiating since, though the strict security protocols on the island made smuggling out a sample all but impossible. For the last three months, the place had been in lockdown mode as they prepared the first trial runs for their "Dinosaur Theme Park". And now, as of this past week, their source had gone silent. Within the 'acquisitions' department of IGF, the mood had grown agitated.

IGF was interested in any genetic engineering technology they could get their hands on from MuTron, but it was secondary to the potential rewards to be reaped by cornering the market on L04AA109. So far, the plant was known only to grow on this particular island. If IGF could exclusively control it, the profits would be legendary.

The issue of how to get it out of there was solved when IGF had gotten wind of Igor Gorimov, who already had separate business requiring him to get to the island.

Böse sipped his Thai iced-tea and stared back at Gorimov unblinkingly. He tapped the bulging manila envelope in front of them. Even in the digital age, hard cash was still the best way to do business.

"Inside is also a map of the island, marking the location of the generator plants and relay towers. The generator plants have a battery back-up system good for twenty-four hours, so you'll want to knock those out as well. There are also the codes for disabling their security protocols, though I recommend you bring a hacker on your team as a backup. That should create enough chaos for you to get in, acquire the sample and get out." He tapped the envelope with his finger. "There is also an image of the longevity plant along with the GPS co-ordinates it was last seen at. The extraction should be straightforward."

Böse had made no mention of IGF's deal with their original source, who had been deemed expendable, if not already dead.

"You seem to have a lot of information about this island. You make it sound like a little child could walk in and pluck this thing out. Why not just get it yourself?"

Böse smiled. It wasn't pleasant. Gorimov knew the answer. Companies like IGF never got their hands dirty – at least not directly. Not as long as there were people like himself around to do it for them.

"It's complicated. And dangerous. We are talking about dinosaurs, living, breathing . . . eating dinosaurs. That is why you're being well compensated for your 'consulting' work. That includes not asking questions you should not, yes?"

Gorimov took a gulp of his vodka. After this operation, he would drink whatever vodka he wanted, for quite a while.

The German leaned forward, tapping the envelope again. "You will get the sample to us within the week? *Correct?*"

Gorimov grunted in reply. Böse loved ending as many sentences with the word *correct* as possible. This was their third meeting and it was all he could do not to leap across the table, seize the German's scrawny neck in his powerful hands and break it, shouting *"This is the best way to end a fucking German's life . . . correct!?"*

Böse had revealed little about himself, though Gorimov had discovered through his sources that the man had a taste for the 'Lady Boys', something that might prove useful in obtaining a little 'bonus' before their final transaction was concluded.

Gorimov took a sip of vodka and put it down on the table hard, to make his point.

"Yes, my word is good. My patience, not so much. We'll meet at the drop off next Friday, as arranged. Is that all?"

Böse studied him silently another minute. It was one of the little games that made him feel dominant, Gorimov knew. For once, however, Gorimov wasn't lying.

His patience *was* growing dangerously thin.

The silence dragged out. More tittering giggles came from the bar, where several of the girls were gathering the courage to approach their table. Finally, satisfied, Böse stood up, leaving a half-full tea on the table.

"Good," was all he said. Then swiveling on his heels, left. As he approached the door several sharp-dressed young Vietnamese men entered. With their sunglasses and aggressive demeanor, they might have passed for local *Nam Cam* thugs. The two in front looked battered and bruised, with one sporting several stitches above his eyebrow. The girls at the bar scattered like crows.

As two of the men stepped up to Gorimov's table he smiled and patted the chairs next to him.

"Hello Tuan, hello Lanh. Have a seat. The vodka is good. And we have much to catch up about!"

ISLAND OF KHARAMU, FRIDAY 0700 HOURS.

The repair teams were always supposed to be three men – two workers and one-armed guard – but today there were six. Three were guards. Some Filipino and Vietnamese ex-military had been brought over to beef up security after several workers had met with 'unfortunate accidents' and while neither group particularly favored each other, the generous pay bonuses Mr. Luo had put in their contracts had put the lid on the worst of their differences.

Even more unusual was that one of the repair personnel, Ling Heng, was the project manager for maintenance operations. Mr. Luo had insisted middle management work hands-on to address any issues. With barely twenty-four hours before the first official trial run he'd made it clear that not only would any further mishaps be met with immediate dismissal without pay, but as a further disciplinary incentive they would be sent back to the mainland for a hearing with a certain judge known for his overzealousness at being a 'soldier for the state'.

Ling was in a particularly foul mood this morning. Not just because of being forced out in the field into the sweltering environment wearing uncomfortable khakis and boots (which had already given him several painful blisters), but because of the sense of danger and vulnerability that secretly terrified him about the place. Ling was a product of the densely packed urban neighborhoods of Beijing. His comfort zone was grim concrete, jammed traffic and bicycles, smoggy skies and relentless tides of people.

Even here on Kharamu he'd sought refuge in the sanitary orderliness of his office and elaborate underground facilities, eschewing the monitored field trips around the island that were offered from time to time.

Ling was, hot, nervous, and hungry. He'd just sat down to his usual morning breakfast of rice, steamed pork bun and soy milk when the alert had come in via the pop-up on the laptop screen: 代码10 or 'CODE 10'. That meant another data failure between sectors.

Now here he was, his breakfast forgotten and cold, having to babysit his tech workers.

They were on the southeastern part of the island, just north of the old hospital complex that they'd repurposed into dinosaur breeding and husbandry facilities. They were along a path at the base of the mountainous ridgeline that sheltered the eastern coast, not far from a cascading stream that came down from the pools and caves above. Heng didn't like those caves either. When the island had first been discovered in the late 17th century, they'd been rumored to be occupied by a degenerate aboriginal race known as the *Chī mèi,* or 'Mountain Goblins'.

Another rumor had it that was where they'd found the word 'Kharamu' etched in old Chinese on one of the cave walls.

They'd arrived to find fiber optic cable torn up out of the ground in several places. After twenty minutes, the new cable was spliced in and they were filling it over, this time with a protective sheathing that would make it more difficult to unearth. The two Filipino guards were studying the perimeter, looking for clues, while the one Vietnamese guard perched on the thick branch of a nearby laurel tree, smoking a cigarette. A Type 81 assault rifle was slung from his shoulder, a razor-sharp machete at his hip.

Smoking was strictly prohibited out in the field, but it was a rule frequently broken, especially by the security staff.

Ling heard a chittering, chirpy sound off to his right where the stream was, along with the delicate pad of many little feet moving swiftly past. Along the underbrush was what appeared to be a pack of brightly colored birds – their plumage evocative of macaws – in pursuit of something along the banks of the stream. There was something unusual about their tails, he realized; they were long and banded in coloration, like a slim racoon's tail with brilliant feathers instead of fur.

Immediately the two Filipino guards swung around and crouched, weapons ready, while the Vietnamese flicked his cigarette away and jumped up to his feet in one fluid motion. The two other workers stepped backward, cautiously, as something heavier stepped through the bushes.

To their surprise a man emerged from the jungle, dressed in the tan and green livery of the MuTron field workers. He also wore gloves and had protective goggles perched atop his cap, armed with a long Commando knife at his hip and a Taser clipped to his belt. Behind him two more workers ran past, shouting, toting nets and bags.

"*Nǐ hǎo!*" he said, grinning. Then it faltered as he realized there were three automatic weapons trained on him.

The six men looked at him like some ghostly apparition. Only authorized personnel were allowed to roam freely on the island. This one looked like he was out for a Sunday stroll. And dinosaurs – even small ones – were to be strictly confined to controlled sectors.

Sensing the awkwardness of the situation, he indicated the creatures that had just run past.

"Field testing," he explained in Chinese. "*Sinosauropteryx* – new batch!"

Just as oddly, he turned around and disappeared into the brush, chasing after his colleagues.

For a moment, no one said anything, then the Vietnamese guard's attention perked up as he heard something else creeping on the opposite side of the stream.

Very carefully he eased himself down off the tree and slid into the underbrush, as stealthy as a ghost.

Ling motioned for his two co-workers to hurry, fresh sweat breaking out on his brow. He wasn't sure what unnerved him most; that the breeding labs were letting (even small) dinosaurs run loose, that the breeding staff seemed to treat this like a joke, or that something even larger seemed to be hunting them.

A couple minutes later a single shot rang out, sending half a dozen birds into the sky.

Then silence.

The two Filipino guards looked at each other. Both were ex-military and not the type easily spooked. At the same time neither seemed particularly inclined to find out what had befallen the third guard.

One looked at Ling. "Finish up," he said in Chinese. He pulled the X-5 handheld every personnel was required to carry from his hip holster and was about to call the whole incident in to his supervisor, then decided against it. There had been all sorts of breaks from protocols these past few weeks and upper management was increasingly oblivious as to the extent of it. He'd already learned the hard way speaking up only put himself in the crosshairs for blame.

Best to keep one's mouth shut.

"You're not going after him?" Ling asked.

The Filipino shook his head. "He broke protocol. Let another team find him. Our job is to get you here and back in one piece. Period!"

***

"I'm telling you, the ghost is real!" Wang Chan said. "This place is cursed!"

Tao Dong chuckled as he took another pull off his Coke. The two of them were in the cafeteria downstairs from the IT lab where they worked, grabbing a quick lunch.

"Still on that ghost shit, huh?" Tao replied, swirling his can of soda like it was a fine wine.

Wang poked at his instant noodles, preoccupied. "I did some research. This island was a Japanese base in WWII. You know who dug out all these tunnels?" Without waiting for a response, he went on: "Chinese slave labor! There were still Japanese soldiers living in the jungle here for years after the war!"

"So?"

"So? This place has all kinds of bad history. Did you know a race of cannibals were living up in the caves on the eastern side of the island when it was first discovered in the 1700s? Or that in the 1970s a German pharmaceutical company named Faber-Munchaus tried to redevelop the complexes we're in, but abandoned the project when too many people started dying mysteriously?"

Tao rolled his eyes. "You're losing it. There is no such thing as ghosts. We need to get you a new hobby, Chan. Maybe something involving women. You need to get laid."

Wang snorted. "What about you? Why don't *you* go chase a woman, huh?"

The blanched expression on his friend's face made Wang immediately regret his words. He didn't really grasp how keyed up he was until that moment. He put his bowl down.

"I'll tell you what, Dong. You and I are going to do a little recon this evening after we finish our shift. Whenever they let us go that is. I'm going to prove to you I'm not crazy, got it?"

Tao fidgeted with his glasses. His confusion over his sexual orientation was an ongoing source of guilt and shame. It had only increased with a recent encounter with the Marketing Director, Miss Grey. She'd stopped by their IT

Group with some issues she was having with her tablet and pulling up a chair next to him had asked him – quite boldly – to have a look. He was immediately aware of several things; her meticulously neat business attire, the voluptuous curve of her breasts (accented by the cut of her blazer), the vaguely pretty-yet-confident features and the unnervingly direct way she sized him up over the top of her glasses.

She was incredibly masculine and sensuously feminine at the same time. During his lunch break that day he'd run off to the bathroom and masturbated furiously, more confused than ever.

Someday, if he ever went through with his plan to go to America, he could sort it all out and explore his options. Back in China – outside certain communities in major urban areas - it would most likely get him shot.

But the truth was the mere idea of facing something truly supernatural scared the crap out of him far more than any sexual issues, something he had never hinted at to his friend. They were forbidden to discuss such things openly in China. Ever since the field trip he'd taken as a kid where they'd gone to the cemetery and he'd seen the ghastly face peering out at him from the crypt, grinning.

Underneath the table the hand in his lap was trembling.

"Maybe when this weekend is over," he heard himself saying. "We really should get as much sleep as we can until then. I already—"

"No!" Wang replied, cutting him off. "Tonight. You're coming with me!"

***

Up in his office, Luo Pan Wei threw the report down on the side table and looked at the holographic projection table again. Next to him stood Greg Xióng and another man, David Zhou, the Security Director. A thin, round-faced man with pouty lips and an almost feminine air to him, many mistook Zhou as being soft. Until they looked at his eyes, which were as cold and merciless as an executioner's. The cold charm he exuded was just that; except for the ex-military members of his staff, he was dreaded by everyone who served under him.

"*Another* member of your personnel has gone missing, Mr. Zhou!?" Mr. Luo said. "What is your *explanation*?"

David Zhou hadn't been hired for his tendency to hide behind excuses. He also – quite unusually – always took direct responsibility for anything happening on his watch, positive or negative.

"I haven't established one yet," he replied, stepping over to the High Definition 3D holographic projection of the island. "May I?"

Mr. Luo nodded.

At one end of the projection table was an elegant, wafer thin podium and keyboard. Zhou keyed in a few data filters and a series of bright red highlight zones appeared.

"All four incidents in the past week in random locations, three in areas well outside any 'asset' zones," he said, using the accepted company euphemism for 'dinosaur'. "We've conducted a dozen overlapping sweeps of the areas, but there's no evidence of asset interference with any of the staff, aside from the lab technicians who broke protocol this morning by letting a herd of new specimens

66

run loose in one of the new test area without alerting security. The new assistants from the western provinces haven't been the highest quality, and they've been disciplined."

"And the one inside the asset zone?" Mr. Luo inquired.

"An unfortunate accident," Zhou replied. "Two staff had gone in to retrieve samples from a diseased new-born sauropod, and only one had his Zecon-47 canister with him, which he dropped when they were ambushed by a predator asset."

Mr. Luo let out a thin smile. The 'Zecon-47' was essentially a chemical super-mace that all personnel were now required to carry in the field. While having no lasting side-effects, a hefty spray in the face of any attacking dinosaur would render it momentarily numb, at least long enough to beat a hasty exit. The question had been why the two guards had been so slow to respond. A young Tyrannosaur had torn the one man to pieces. The other had escaped, minus one arm. He was now recovering in the infirmary, though there was still some question if he would make it.

"I'm deeply concerned about the other three," he said. "You've mentioned before there might be a saboteur in the staff?"

"Yes," Zhou said. "But this is more like the work of a ghost assassin. The victims disappear, or at least we haven't discovered them yet except for the one Malaysian guard, and his body had been chewed up by wild boar. His remains are currently being examined by the forensics team, but nothing conclusive yet. Also, between security cams and the X-5 units, all staff were accounted for during the incidents."

Mr. Luo stood with his arms crossed, one hand fingering his chin.

"Then it must be a third-party operative running loose on the island. Find him or her, and dispose of them. Yes?"

Zhou frowned. His was a rigid disciplinarian and extremely thorough at his job, forcing his staff to accomplish results at any cost. But this one was beginning to have him spooked. He'd never seen anything like it, even in his years doing covert ops along the China-Russian border. They hadn't found any evidence of who – or what - was picking off the staff. And he didn't like the rumors coming up from the lower staff.

That they were being hunted by a *ghost*.

"Yes," Zhou replied, not bothering with any sort of excuse.

APPROACH

The dinner was one of the more torturous ones Taylan had ever been through.

It started with a cocktail hour around 5:30 at the lounge on the deck below their accommodations. On the starboard side was the bar, with tables and chairs overlooking the stern. Fortified with a whiskey on the rocks, Taylan found himself cornered on one end by Doyle and the Blodgetts, being peppered with the kind of questions that tended to put his teeth on edge.

"So, Jeff tells me you're the 'rough and tumble' sort of dinosaur guy?" Suzie Blodgett was saying, swirling her second vodka martini. The way her eyes traveled all over Taylan made him feel like he was being sized-up for the auction block. Her husband stood to her side, frowning and looking flushed.

"I do field work, if that's what you're asking," Taylan replied, his eyes focused on a point past her shoulder. The 1950s' khaki getup made him feel like he was in a Halloween skit. He was wondering how quickly he could extricate himself from this mess and just order room service. Even as a professor he dreaded mixers and parties and the inevitable brittle, phony conversations.

"I just *bet* you do," Suzie said, tilting her head back appraisingly. For a moment, he thought she was going to reach over, pull back his lips and check his teeth.

"Grant here is a regular gun-slinging cowboy!" Doyle interjected, knocking back a whiskey sour. His third, if Taylan was counting correctly. "Tell them about the time you shot those two Mexicans who were trying to kill three women paleos working a dig in Butte?" Doyle made a gun out of his free hand and mimed shooting into the floor.

"They were Yugoslavian, and I didn't shoot them," Taylan said evenly. Privately, he was calculating if he were to take Doyle by the scruff of the neck, which was the best window to chuck him overboard through.

Probably the right one, where the propellers at the stern might have a shot at chewing him up.

Just when he thought it couldn't get worse, Peyton walked up to them.

"What's this talk about shooting Mexicans?" he asked, slapping Taylan on the shoulder. "God-damn, that's about my favorite pastime! Popping wetbacks!"

Taylan was about to pivot and slug him, damn the money and everything else. Doyle must have caught the look in his eye as he slid smoothly in between them, clinking Peyton's glass with his own.

"Come on now, Mr. Peyton, you know you can't go using terms like that, you have enough litigations going on as it is!"

Doyle said it as a joke, but for a second Peyton glared with fury. Just as quickly, however, his face cleared, and he put on one of his better *aw, shucks* smiles. "Heck, you got a point there, little man," Peyton said, grabbing Doyle's shoulder and squeezing it. "Come on everyone, let's go get to our tables. I made the chef promise to put on something extra special tonight. Tomorrow, we get to see some real dinosaurs!"

He let out a forced laugh, with everyone but Taylan joining in.

As the group slid away (with Suzie Blodgett giving Taylan a blatant wink), Roma and Audrey entered the room and walked up to him.

Having apparently discovered her character's 'wealthy socialite' wardrobe, she was wearing a tight, shimmery cocktail dress and low-heeled pumps in what struck Taylan as a highly 'un-Audrey' – yet very appealing - look. She'd also put on some heavy mascara and a striking shade of lipstick that was more Bridgette Bardot than Audrey Hepburn. Roma had been forced to wear a plain white maid's uniform, but Taylan thought she made it look terrific.

"What was that all about?" Audrey asked. "Cozying up to our ugly American financer?"

Taylan grunted, "Not quite." He'd already decided Peyton and his money could take a flying fuck at a rolling donut, even if it meant the end of his career. But having come this close, there was no way he was going to pass up seeing the dinosaurs either, or at least whatever the hell the Chinese were passing off as such.

He took a long pull off his scotch, wincing as it burned down his throat.

"Looks like you weren't particularly fond of the joke," Roma added.

"*Heh*," Taylan grunted.

"I don't think a stoned hyena would laugh at them," Audrey said, signaling the bartender for a drink. With his white suit, pomaded hair and bow-tie, the elderly man behind the bar looked like he'd been tapped out of central casting.

"What may I get you, ladies?"

"Rum and tonic," Audrey said. "Make sure it's dark rum. With a lime."

Roma slid up to the bar. "A glass of white wine will do. Do you have any Sancerre?"

"On ice, yes,"

Roma let her eyes gaze around the room before she turned to Taylan. "Well, you have to admit Peyton has done pretty well for himself, no?"

Taylan took another sip. "Yeah, well that's because there aren't any limits on greed or ignorance."

After the plates were cleared, it was Joseph Bello who opened the after-dinner conversation.

"So, what's new in the world of Paleontology?" he asked, sipping his coffee.

Taylan, Roma and Audrey were grouped together with him at one end of the table while Peyton sat at the other end, regaling the Blodgetts and Banyons throughout the meal with tales - highly exaggerated ones, Taylan suspected - of his hunting exploits in Africa. He made himself out to be a mash-up of Hemmingway and John Wayne characters.

"Plenty," Taylan replied. "This past year all sorts of things have been springing up."

"Such as?"

"*Feathers*," Audrey cut in.

"Feathers?"

She perked up. "Dr. Lida Xing discovered the feathered tail of a dinosaur preserved in amber on a dig in Burma. Er, sorry, *Myanmar*. Everyone has updated their names these days. But yeah, it was one of the most perfectly preserved samples ever found. Lucky bastard! Wish I could make some breakthrough discovery like that!"

Taylan glanced at her and the drink in her hand. He'd forgotten she didn't handle her alcohol too well. The last time since their break-up he'd been around her socially had been the international Paleontology conference in Tokyo a year previous, when a bunch of them had ended up in a restaurant getting loaded on *sake*. Somehow that had resulted in Audrey attempting to swim the *hori* or moat to the East Gardens of the Imperial Palace at two in the morning, in her underwear. Taylan and another colleague ended up having to bail her out from the police station.

He plucked a dried date from the dessert tray the waiter had laid out and bit off a piece.

"They were able to determine it had a chestnut brown color, with white undersides. It was a tiny, raptor-like creature – about the size of a sparrow. But it gives us an invaluable insight as to the evolution of feathers on dinosaurs."

"So, is it true the Tyrannosaurs had feathers too?" Suzie Blodgett chimed in from the other end of the table. She'd graduated from cocktails to after-dinner liquors. Her husband, Roger, seemed to have regained some of his earlier cheer after a few rounds himself.

"It's possible, yes," Taylan replied, trying not to laugh at her obviousness. She'd completely ignored anything Audrey and Roma had said through dinner and repeatedly stole lingering glances at Taylan. "Though they were more likely 'proto-feathers'. The infants, however, may have had a soft, downy covering."

Suzie giggled. "That sounds so *cute!* A little fuzzy-wuzzy T-Rex!"

Roma rolled her eyes while Audrey sunk her forehead in her hand.

Peyton set his brandy snifter down and shot Suzie an annoyed look. "I didn't foot the bill for this adventure to collect stuffed animals," he said. "We're going there to . . ."

"—to *what?*" Audrey spoke up. "What exactly *is* this 'themed vacation' about?"

Roger Blodgett and Peyton exchanged glances. It was clear Peyton didn't like being challenged by a woman. He leaned forward with his beefy elbows on the table and flashed Audrey a trademark car-salesmen grin.

"I'm not paying you to worry about the vacation end of things, Miss Adams, your *job* is only to make sure the science behind it is valid. *Got it?*"

The table grew quiet.

For a moment, Taylan thought Audrey was going to stand up and hurl her glass down the table at Peyton's head. Bello perked up for the first time that evening, casting a watchful eye back and forth between Audrey and Peyton. Taylan's hand tightened around his coffee cup.

To his surprise, Audrey stayed silent, studying her drink moodily.

Abruptly, Peyton leaned back in his chair and grinning, raised his glass.

"Come on, folks, we're here to enjoy ourselves and have a little dino-safari! Here's to 'Lost Expeditions'!"

"Huzzah!" Roger Blodgett chimed in.

A few glasses went up in a half-hearted salute. Perhaps because at least some of the group sensed the ominous implication behind Peyton's words.

"It's quite an evening, don't you think?" Roma asked later.

Grant Taylan glanced sideways from where he was standing at the railing near the bow. The sea was calm and aside from the steady churn of the engines, it was an idyllic night in the South China Sea. Overhead the skies were a dazzling display of stars and constellations, as if the universe were putting on its most brilliant show for them. The nebulous band of the Milky Way was clearly visible, the Southern Cross hovering low on the meridian. To the south, a nearly full moon was rising just above the horizon, the salt air balmy.

Back from amidships came the glow of cabin lights while in the wake of the freighter, the roiling luminescence of phosphorescent plankton.

Taylan had been leaning on the railing, lost in thought. The hopscotch incidents that had landed him on this very spot over the past few days seemed surreal. Yet here he was. Heading to an exotic location to witness something he'd only dreamed about. With two very attractive paleontologists and a vacation group of very rich, white assholes.

"Yeah, you could say that," he said, still gazing out to sea.

Roma came up alongside him – flirtatiously close – and grasped the rail in both hands.

"And what is the illustrious Doctor Taylan thinking?"

"About how I'm the first member of my family not here in the South China Sea trying to kill somebody."

Roma tensed up. "Seriously?"

"Seriously. My great uncle was a B-25 Pilot with the 345th Bomber Group, 5th Air Force, during WWII. One of his last missions was in April of 1945 when they intercepted a Japanese Convoy somewhere in this area. His plane – nicknamed "Dirty Dora" – scored a direct hit on one of the escort destroyers, blowing it half out of the water. The survivors were either taken out by subsequent strafing passes or drowned. Hell of a thing."

"War always is," she said in a thoughtful tone. "My older brother was a soldier. Ashok."

Now it was Taylan's turn to look surprised, "Really?"

"Yes. It's the war the Western media rarely if ever talks about – along the border with Pakistan. It doesn't make for catchy news. But there's constant skirmishes, shelling, casualties. Especially in Kashmir, where he was based."

Something in her voice drew his attention. He gave her a searching look.

"He died four days ago. A group of militants attacked the base he was stationed at in Kashmir."

"Christ, I'm sorry," Taylan said.

"It's still a shock. My parents wanted me home, but I left right after the funeral services. Escaping into my work seemed like the best thing for me at the moment, and I didn't want to cancel the presentation in Mumbai. And now . . ." She let out a light, sarcastic laugh, "here I am in the middle of nowhere. Talk about escaping."

Taylan nodded. Escaping into his work was something he knew a thing or two about. He also was aware how close she was standing next to him, her upper arm brushing his.

The air was balmy, the inky depths of the sea endless. A few clouds drifted along the horizon, partially obscuring the moon.

Taylan couldn't deny a certain electric attraction to the woman next to him. She'd changed into a tailored pants and open-necked blouse that accentuated her figure. In the pale light, he could see she'd put on a trace of lipstick. The dark eyes studying him through the glasses may have had a hidden message for him . . . or not. He was never particularly good at gauging subtleties.

After a moment of quiet, broken only by the sluice of water past the hull and the methodical rumble of the engines, she sighed.

"Let's not talk about my brother, if you don't mind. Tell me about your great uncle. Why on earth was his plane called 'Dirty Dora?'"

Taylan smiled. "It's a bit of a 'dirty' story," he admitted. "Are you sure you want to hear it?"

"I always love a good dirty story, tell me."

"Well, it goes back to Australia, actually. My grandfather and the other officers in his squadron would rent a suite of apartments in Sydney, to use on the rare occasions they could get a week or two leave from combat. This was when they were still fighting in New Guinea, mind you. Anyhow, on his first leave he'd gotten word of a particular 'Sheila' – that's what they called the Aussie women – who had a reputation for screaming out the most profane obscenities while in the throes of passion, you know, particularly when she was about to reach her climax. Hence the nickname, "Dirty Dora". My great uncle, being from a conservative San Francisco family and being a young man facing death nearly every day, was naturally intrigued, particularly as the girl in question was known otherwise to be perfectly sweet and charming.

"So, through a few inquiries and a hook up at a popular place known as the Criterion Hotel, he found out firsthand that the legend was absolutely true. A few weeks later he managed to get her out to the base and show her his B-25 with her nickname newly painted on the nose, but apparently, she wasn't impressed. In fact, I believe he earned a slap upside the head for his little joke."

Roma smiled. "Cute. Not quite as dirty a story as I would have imagined."

"Well, that was one of the cleaner ones. I also heard a few ones from him he swore me to never tell my great aunt that were worthy of any XXX feature."

She looked at him curiously. "Is that what you like in women? Ones who talk dirty?"

Taylan laughed. "That sounds a little like a leading question. Is it?"

Again, he was keenly aware of her nearness, and an undeniable sensuality to her demeaner when her guard was lowered just a bit. It was also impossible to deny the moment had a certain romantic flair to it: an old steamer headed toward an island with dangerous creatures, the rising moon over a tropical sea.

She leaned forward, as if to kiss him.

"Perhaps it is," she teased.

Taylan got as far as tilting his head slightly when a woman's voice behind them broke the spell.

"Oh, there you are!"

Audrey came sauntering up along the deck, a tall glass of beer in one hand.

Taylan straightened up, teeth clenched.

Roma did a graceful half-turn, one arm resting on the rail, and said (a touch icily, Taylan thought), "How nice of you to join us!"

Audrey stepped in unceremoniously between them, a slight stagger in her step. Taylan realized she was drunk.

"God, fuck me dead, those people are utterly dreadful," Audrey said, gulping her beer with a giggle. "Peyton wouldn't stuff his gob for a minute, going off again about 'I own this' and 'I own that'! Private jets and private yachts. I think you set off his competitive bone, Grant! I may need to score a bloody keg of rum to keep myself from hosing the lot of 'em and jumping overboard! And that drippy bugger friend of yours, Doyle? He just tried to pick me up back at the bar!"

Taylan stifled a laugh. "I'm sure he was quite charming about it."

"Not after 'e looked down and saw the business end of my steak knife almost touching his privates! I had a hunch one of Peyton's goons might get a case of itchy pants. He was ogling me all over dinner!"

She turned to Roma, as if seeing her for the first time. "What do you think, Little Miss Maid? Fancy a roll in the hay with the Dino Doc here? Cuddling up for a fair suck of the sav, are ya? Careful though, his psycho exes have a way of showing up and putting you to the top of their shit – er, I mean *hit* – list! Not to mention putting your career in the potty!"

Roma stepped back, appalled.

Taylan didn't know whether to curse or laugh. Either way another part of him wanted to strangle her.

Audrey leaned over the rail and smiled, as if contemplating some inner joke.

"Maybe you shouldn't—" Roma began.

Audrey turned on her "—what!? Speak my mind? Have a fair dip in the sauce? *Ugh*, you uptight Indian Princesses are all the same!"

Roma went red. "I'll have you know I'm a doctor! I—"

"*Oooh*! A bloody doctor *are you*!?" Audrey switched the beer to her other hand, and to Taylan's horror reached over and grabbing Roma's left breast, tweaked her nipple through the blouse.

"Well, *doctor* this!"

Roma screeched and jumped back as if she'd been struck by a cattle prod. Audrey took a sloppy gulp of her beer, then tried to point it at Roma. "Oh, don't be such a prude!" she said, sloshing beer all over the front of Roma's blouse.

Eyes flaring with anger and humiliation, she stormed off down the deck in a huff.

Audrey giggled again and turned to Taylan.

"Gawd, isn't she the life of the party!" Then with a hiccup she fell forward into Taylan's arms.

"Stay still, damn you!" Taylan said as he tried to unstrap Audrey's left shoe. He'd managed to half carry, half drag her back to her cabin. The glass of beer had been chucked unceremoniously overboard en route (along with another colorful curse from Audrey), and they had been met with a bunch of forced smiles as they went past Peyton and his guests in the main lounge. Doyle was nowhere in sight.

Audrey was straddling the bunk where Taylan had dropped her. Her arms were spread-eagled, and her hair tangled around her head as if she'd just exited a tornado.

Taylan was struggling with the strap while she used her other stockinged foot to prod at his face with her toes. She started teasing her hair with one hand while giggling.

"Oh God, I do believe I may have drunk too much at dinner," she slurred, then she winked at Taylan. "Sandy is randy, but liquor is quicker!" Her toes abruptly snuck down to his crotch and gave him a playful nudge. Taylan jumped back.

"Oh, sod off, you know you still fancy me just a little bit, no?"

Taylan blushed.

Damn the woman! he thought, *how in the hell does she manage to be so desirable and such a pain in the ass at the same time!*

She wriggled her way further up onto the bed and looked at him with half-closed eyes. Drunk or not, she might have been auditioning for a late 50s oversexed French art film. Based on his earlier observation, one probably starring Bridgette Bardot.

In fact, he realized, studying her in the dim light of the cabin with the caustic reflections playing around the room, she could even pass for a young Bardot, though Audrey's face was narrower and more defined.

The moment seemed to stretch out, as if the physics of time and space had conspired to slow down and let him savor this unexpected development: half-crouched over her bunk, the smell of the sea coming through the open porthole, the lingering hint of rose perfume she had put on. Years ago, they'd never progressed past the three adversarial dates and had never gotten as far as even a kiss on any of them. This was completely unanticipated.

He wasn't sure what she was thinking, until she whispered, "Kiss me."

Taylan was in conflict - scant minutes before he had been about to do just the same thing with a different woman, and this one was clearly out of her senses. Or inhibitions, at least.

After hesitating what felt like an eternity, he felt himself succumb to his baser instinct and climbed on top of her.

He was about to kiss her hard on the lips when he realized she was out cold. A light snore escaped her mouth.

With a smile ghosting his lips, he kissed her on the forehead instead and backed away.

A minute later the cabin door closed quietly as Audrey rolled over in her sleep.

Taylan paused by Roma's door, debating whether he should bother her and apologize.

And maybe see if things might pick up where they got interrupted, you dog! Admit it!

He couldn't deny that impulse either, but then he also realized it just wasn't his style. Too much confusion and tomorrow was going to be a big day.

Tomorrow, if all went well, he was going to be seeing a living, breathing dinosaur.

Not something he wanted to be half-asleep or unfocused about.

Mere feet away, lying in her bunk, Roma stared at the book she had been reading and realized she had been staring at the same page for five minutes and not read a single word of it.

Damn that woman! she thought. *She squeezed my nipple! What in the hell was that all about!? Is that any way for a doctor to treat another?*

A small laugh escaped her lips.

I am not a prude . . . am I?

Oh God, and to think I almost kissed Grant Taylan! What was I thinking? The wine. I had three glasses of wine – that was it! Damn him too! Though he has that rugged handsome thing going . . . no, he's complete trouble. You heard Audrey. And doesn't liquor loosen the tongue and let the truth out?

She realized she was in emotional turmoil – *had been in turmoil* – with the death of her brother, Ashok, something she still wasn't ready to face or accept. The grief had been a simmering black turmoil under the lid, something that she had (so far) successfully avoided looking at too closely. She'd never been particularly close with Vani. Though only two years older he was cut from a whole different cloth than the rest of her family; quiet, reserved. Almost sullen. There'd been a falling out with her parents that had led to him joining the army years previous. Then oddly, there had been a tentative reconciliation a half year previous. He was supposed to be coming home for *Maha Shivaratri* in August.

Now the only thing arriving home would be his ashes.

So, for Roma, getting in any way tangled with anyone at this point was unquestionably a recipe for disaster.

From this moment on, you are to go back to being the consummate professional: Dr. Banaji. Nothing else!

Another few minutes passed before she realized she still hadn't read anything in her book. It was a paperback edition of "Behavioral Tendencies of Early Cretaceous Sauropods."

She dropped the book on the nightstand in frustration and pulled the sheet up to her neck, like she used to do when she was little. She listened, wondering if she might hear a footstep and knock on her door.

His footstep.

Nothing came.

KHARAMU, 23:41 HOURS

"This way!" Wang hissed, as he and Tao crept along the perimeter of the converted aircraft hangar.

Due to the newly enforced cost-cutting measures, most of the overhead lighting was off, lending the vast space a spooky, spectral appearance, like sneaking through an abandoned industrial warehouse at night. The effect was enhanced by the two WWII Japanese airplanes (now pushed off to one side), sitting on their flat tires. Next to them was a tarp-covered old dune buggy that had been left behind by the Germans – it had become a little side project with Wang who'd bribed one of the maintenance mechanics into letting him help restore it.

The rest of the space had been turned into an auxiliary bio-engineering lab with cubicles, various workstations and lab equipment (including the new 3D bio-print station) though with most of the first-wave specimens up and running it hadn't been used much in the previous three weeks.

On the opposite side by the newly replaced aluminum hangar doors was a small pool of light where the night security guards were sitting around a table playing poker and smoking. Near them was a row of motorcycles used for patrolling the island – mostly dirt bikes and ATVs, though there was one antique military cycle and sidecar. Another guard, with an assault rifle slung over his back, paced slowly back and forth by the far side of the massive doors, more interested in playing 'Hitman GO' on his handheld than anything else. His footsteps echoed through the hangar, underscored by the muted voices and card shuffling of the poker game.

The two programmers had been all nerves toward the end of their shift, convinced Mr. Tsou was creating new nonsensical tasks for them to tackle out of sheer spite. Both had carefully left their ID cards – with their embedded tracking chips (as if management thought they didn't know about them) – in their cots.

One thing Wang possessed, fortunately for both of them, was uncanny eyesight, especially in the dark. That went back to his mother's Mongolian parents, who could spot a bird miles away on the empty steppes. He expertly led them around several work benches, their crepe-soled slippers making little noise on the polished concrete, until they were at the far end of the hangar where the utility door was.

The door was a new heavy-duty fiberglass one – they'd proven much more durable (and cheaper) in the island's intense heat and humidity, with a simple push-button lock. Getting the code had been simple enough: Wang had bribed one of the security guards with a judicious amount of HD porn, a precious commodity here on the island blocked by the server's firewalls. The very same guard who was pacing by the gate, playing a bootleg game Wang had also provided.

Cupping his hand, Wang produced a tiny penlight and tapped the touch pad. A moment later came a soft *hiss* and *click* as the door opened. Beyond was a broad storage corridor with dim lights installed along the base. Once inside Wang pulled a large LED flashlight from his backpack and flicked it on. Tao did the same.

The space had originally been used as a temporary holding area for anti-aircraft ammo (and aircraft munitions) brought up from the magazine below. When the facility had first been renovated it had the original fireproof doors – all but rotted away – with the munition dollies neatly stacked against the wall. They'd been replaced by rubber-coated storage racks and all the cleaning equipment required for the hangar.

In short, it had been turned into an over-sized janitor's closet.

At the far end, however, was a smaller access tunnel that led northward past a few small bunk rooms toward the old AA and observation outposts.

They'd made it a few yards down the tunnel when from further down came the sound of something large scuffling away. Tao reached out and grabbed his friend's shoulder.

"Look, we don't *have* to do this," he whispered in Chinese. "I believe you! Let's just go back!" There was something else troubling him too, something he'd overheard being whispered in the men's showers. One of the programmers with contacts in the infirmary had heard about a couple of test groups that had been brought over from the mainland that had never been heard from again.

He realized Wang was looking back at him, one fierce eye squinting like a gangster's.

"Oh no, you're not getting off that easy! Not after all the jokes you made at my expense! You're coming if I have to drag you by the neck!"

Tao was terrified, but there was something even more frightening in his friend's demeanor and savage grin.

Forward they went.

After twenty more yards, the smooth concrete gave way to coarser, rough-hewn stone. The air was dank and reeked of mold, prompting both men to pull out paper face masks and put them on. Particularly disconcerting were the large centipedes and spiders their flashlights revealed, though fortunately they seemed inclined to slither or scurry away from their probing light beams. Past a boiler room filled with rusting pipes and machinery they found a crude barracks filled with rotting cots and shoes.

The main tunnel turned off to their right, which Wang knew from his previous explorations led to another observation post and an old naval battery overlooking the harbor. At the bend, however, was a small alcove with a rusted metal door that he'd observed earlier but didn't have the courage to explore.

It was one of those heavy steel doors set in a wall with bolts like one saw on an old ship or submarine. He saw something else that grabbed his attention: marks in the mold-coated concrete floor that suggested the door must have been opened recently.

If there were ghosts, surely, they must lurk deeper in the cave systems, he figured.

With an ear-splitting screech, he pulled down on the lever and pushed the door inward.

Flakes of rust rained down through their flashlight beams and a fist-sized, angry colored spider darted into the folds of its web where the wall met the ceiling.

Tao looked up at it in horror, but only its black-tipped forelegs remained visible. He felt his arm jerk.

"Come on! It's only a spider!" Wang hissed. "Look at this place!"

"*Only* a spider," Tao mumbled into his mask. Just the thought of it made his balls shrivel in response.

The crude tunnel had rusting electric and water conduits along the top, bearded with mold and moss. To one side were the rotting rubber soles of old Japanese military boots, most featuring colorful sprouts of fungus.

Wang ran his flashlight along the floor. The mold and debris looked disturbed, as if someone had passed through here recently. For the first time, he realized the ghost he was seeking might be more corporal than he originally thought.

After a series of dizzying branches and turns (and tunnel intersections) it became clear they were lost. Most of this network of tunnels looked identical, and it was apparent from the scuff marks they'd covered some of the same ones several times.

Finally, Wang pulled up short, playing his light down a new tunnel that went for a few yards and branched in a 'Y'.

"I thought you knew where you were going!" Tao hissed. He'd been feeling increasingly spooked. Several times he would have sworn he heard footsteps behind them.

Frustrated, Wang looked the walls up and down. Something was bothering him. Then he spotted it: a chalked 'x' on the wall about half way up on the left.

"*Hmpf*!" he grunted. "I bet no ghost left that! Come on!"

Further down on the branch to the left they found something even more macabre. The room appeared to have originally been some sort of storage locker, perhaps five feet deep and seven across. The entrance was covered by a rotting blanket that fell away in tatters when Wang tried to pull it aside.

What met their eyes was a horrifying display.

A decaying corpse was hung from the opposite wall by shackles, the remnants of the moldering jumpsuit and rotten clumps of blonde hair suggesting it might be one of the missing German pharmaceutical workers from the 1970s. Around its feet were piled a half dozen skulls along with the decaying remains of soldier's equipment – gas masks, ammo pouches, scraps of uniforms. Some of the remains looked recent.

Wang's sharp exhale came out in a huff.

Even at a glance it was apparent that the arrangement wasn't random; there was a ritualistic order to it, like some sort of altar. Even as their flashlight beams played over it, several centipedes and beetles scurried over the remains. Though the remains were long dead the fetid aroma of death and decay filled their nostrils.

"*Wǒ cào!*" Tao breathed: *Fuck me!* Then, with a slightly hysterical edge to his voice: "What in the hell is this? Chan? What is it!?"

"I have no idea, Dong," Wang replied. "But I think we better—"

The distinct sound of a footstep from the tunnel outside cut the words off in his throat.

Followed by a low snicker.

There was another footstep, then both men were blinded by a light in their eyes. Tao panicked and jumped behind Wang, grasping his shoulders.

"Well, well . . .," said a low voice. "Looks like I caught the two homo perverts red-handed!"

"Mr. Zhang?" Tao asked. It seemed inconceivable that their supervisor had followed them all this way into the catacomb of tunnels. Worse was the awful, naked feeling that his secret was out, even though nothing had happened between him and Wang.

Wang shrugged his way out of Tao's grasp, horrified. Friend or not, if something like this got back to the mainland losing his career was going to be the least of his worries – by Chinese law he was guilty until proven innocent.

"It's not what it appears!" Wang stammered, realizing he was probably just digging himself in deeper. "I came out here . . . looking for a ghost!"

"Yes, a ghost!" Tao echoed.

Their supervisor snorted. He lowered the flashlight, so they could see him outlined in the doorway. "Oh yes, a 'ghost'. Is that what I should put in my report to security? Two gay perverts sneaking around off-limits tunnels looking for 'ghosts'?"

Wang's temper got the better of him. "Wait just a second, Mr. Zhang. For starters, nothing perverted was going on here! And second, we've discovered something far worse in this . . .?"

The light reflections in Mr. Zhang's glasses made him almost diabolical. Grinning, their supervisor reached for his belt.

"Perhaps a little lesson is in order, first."

Wang was horrified. "What!? No . . .!"

His voice trailed off as a shadow appeared behind their supervisor, followed by the hideous sound of steel penetrating flesh. Mr. Zhang let out a wheezing gasp and lurched forward as seven inches of blade erupted from below his sternum. The flashlight tumbled out of his hand and sent light beams erratically in every which direction. The blade withdrew with a meaty *snick* and Zhang dropped to his knees, blood curtaining over his lower lip.

Behind him was the strangest apparition either man had either seen: a gaunt, elderly Japanese man with the remains of an old uniform tied around him in tatters like some sort of nightmare Man Friday, a bloody *Katana* sword held forward in both hands. In the elusive light, the fierce eyes of the figure glittered like a demon's.

Both men stood there, slack-jawed in shock.

Apparently judging them no immediate threat, the figure slid the sword into a lacquered sheath slung at its hip in one fluid motion, then straightening up barked one word:

"*Kia!*"

Too fast for their eyes to follow a bare foot covered in hard callouses snapped out once, twice, under each of their chins.

Wand and Tao both knew blackness.

ARRIVAL

The ship's watch had just tolled seven bells as the *Vazão* approached the harbor of Kharamu. Taylan was standing near the bow again, a fresh mug of steaming coffee in his hand, sizing up the island as they approached.

Audrey sat slumped in a deck chair nearby, nursing her hangover with a large glass of orange juice, looking like a celebrity in disguise with the over-sized sun hat and sunglasses. She'd switched her original khakis for a newer, tailor-fitted set that was apparently the wardrobe department's idea of a debutante on safari.

Roma was standing apart from Taylan, having been aloof through an awkward breakfast (in which Audrey had run through a colorful gamut of Australian swear words while hunkered over in the corner). Peyton and his group were back by the bridge, as if guarding the baggage the porters had brought up on deck.

The island was even more impressive than the brochure promised, Taylan mused. Set against the empty expanse of the South China Sea, it was a tropical mirage lifted straight from a cinematic adventure epic: ragged, jungle-infested basalt cliffs rising out of an azure ocean, the ghostly remnants of the fortifications at the top of the north arm, the dissipating mists from the morning with gossamer clouds lingering around the higher peaks.

If you were looking to sell a primeval lost world teeming with dinosaurs, this was the ticket, in spades, he decided. *Their Portuguese tramp steamer was a nice touch. The only thing missing was a race of primitive savages waiting to greet, then drug and capture us before we end being offered up to a big sacrifice on the altar of some bloodthirsty god.*

The harbor entrance was particularly dramatic. Formed by one of the lava run-offs a millennium ago, the north arm rose nearly five hundred feet out of the water while a quarter mile to the south the opposite arm was half as high. A hundred or so yards along the north coast one could just make out the natural caves that had been developed into a submarine pen during the Japanese occupation.

As they eased past the headland and entered the harbor itself Taylan could see it was somewhat small and shallow. The water was pristine down to a sandy bottom, with a dredged-out channel giving access to a rickety dock and wharf system that looked like it was a prayer away from collapse.

Beyond that was an equally rickety village, a sort of South Pacific island remnant (one would imagine) from the 1930s; a relic of some European outpost now half-forgotten and falling into decay. From behind the village the ground rose into low, jungle infested cliffs that gave way to the broad central plane of the island. Taylan could even make out a crack in the cliff face where a waterfall cascaded down.

There was a curved stretch of beach to the north where several outrigger canoes and battered fishing boats were drawn up past the high tide mark. Overlooking them was a ramshackle Kon-Tiki bar with a veranda. The only thing missing seemed to be some native dancers in grass skirts and U.S. Army nurses.

Overhead the tropical sun was bright and merciless. Taylan had found a fedora in a props locker Doyle had pointed out to him and as he stood on the bow, brim pulled low, couldn't help feeling a little ridiculous, like some sort of Indiana Jones cosplay. Even so he had to shield his eyes from the bright sparkles shooting off the water.

As the *Vazão* cut her engines and eased toward the dock, a mixed group of swarthy looking whites and New Guinea natives spread out to assist with the docking. Further back was a small Chinese woman with glasses in a white suit and tropical hat, standing with her hands clasped behind her back.

"Please tell me I didn't squeeze Miss India's nipples last night?" a quiet voice said behind Taylan's shoulder.

"Sorry. Definitely guilty, on that charge," Taylan replied, suppressing a smile.

"Oh God," Audrey sighed, knuckling her forehead under her sun hat. "I knew I should have stayed off the bloody rum and tonics. It feels like a mule kicked me in the head. Will somebody please shut off that god-awful sunlight?"

"Did you get some aspirin?"

"Dry chewed them. Don't look. This isn't going to be one of my prettiest days."

Taylan chuckled. "Well, you better pull it together. Look at all those handsome devils waiting for you on the docks."

As the ship eased in Audrey moved a little closer to Taylan.

"I really made a horse's ass out of myself, didn't I?" she asked in an uncharacteristic moment of chagrin.

Taylan said nothing.

Audrey poked him in the shoulder, "Grant?"

"Yes?"

He glanced over at her, but she wasn't looking at him, nor the dock they were coming up alongside. She was gazing up past the village, past the broken cliffs into the interior.

"I don't know what it is, but there's something I don't like about all this."

"Really? You're here to see something every paleontologist dreams of. *Dinosaurs.* On someone else's nickel, no less."

"That's not it. It's something else."

Taylan was a little surprised. The Audrey Adams he knew had to be one of the most unstoppable, unflappable humans on the planet. He was expecting a sharp-tongued quip, but none came.

"*What?*" he asked, finally.

"Just an intuition. I don't think this trip is going to end very well."

"You've been watching too many movies."

"This isn't a movie, Grant. I'm serious. There's something not right about this place."

The *Vazão* ground to a stop alongside the dock with a groan of timbers as lines were tossed and secured, accompanied by the usual chorus of shouts and commands that made every docking Taylan could remember sound like a chaotic emergency: "Secure the bow lines!" "The hawser, the *hawser*, dammit!" "Lively there! She's slipping!" along with a host of others in languages he couldn't understand.

Ten minutes later the entire party found themselves deposited on the dock with their luggage. Taylan noted that the dilapidated, sagging state of the wharf was carefully staged window-dressing. Barely visible under the sun-bleached timbers were dark-painted steel reinforcing beams, probably with spring suspension systems to give the illusion it was on the verge of collapse.

Of course, he thought, it wouldn't do to have your millionaire guests taking a dive into the drink before the adventure even got started.

They were greeted by a Chinese woman in a business suit, who politely introduced herself as "Miss Grey, Marketing Director for MuTron International" while the luggage was loaded onto an old dolly.

"Welcome to Kharamu!" Miss Grey said with a quick bow, flashing a perfect set of teeth. She had the smooth, effusive demeanor of a hotel manager. Despite the tropical heat, she was impeccably dressed and made up, yet gave off an odd, overtly sexual aura. A manicured hand shook each of theirs in turn. Her handshake lingered on Taylan's a little longer than the rest.

A hidden invitation? Taylan wondered. Then he chuckled as the penny dropped – he noted the firm grip and strong hand. The steady gaze watching him behind the heavy-rimmed, 'librarian' glasses.

Transsexual. Be willing to bet the bank on it.

"The porter's will take your belongings to the hotel." She turned to Taylan, Audrey and Roma. "I'll give you a quick tour of the village, then escort the three of you up to MuTron's facilities. Mr. Luo has been eagerly awaiting your arrival and has had a special lunch prepared for you in his offices. Mr. Peyton and his guests will get a start on their 'expedition'. You can catch up with them later this afternoon near 'camp A'."

The 'village' was pretty much as expected.

Primarily it consisted of a dirt street with a bunch of thatch-roofed buildings on either side. The one permanent structure was the Colonial-style hotel, an Art deco affair with mold-stained stucco walls, a sagging balcony and an attempt at landscaping that may have been abandoned in the mid-1950s. There was also an RX and general goods store, a souvenir shop and a café, but most of the buildings looked to be either seedy residences or for storage. Taylan couldn't quite put his finger on it, but it looked pretty much what it was: a too-well-thought out Disney theme park designed by some clever Chinese for outrageously wealthy Americans.

Either way Peyton's party seemed taken by it, looking around like a bunch of bewildered tourists. Except for Peyton – who looked annoyed. Joseph Bello was over with the dockhands, directing the loading of luggage onto a couple of early 1950s Land Rovers. Roma was engaged in a conversation with one of the dock-hands – Taylan noted with an irrational twinge of jealousy; a good-looking fellow with a few days' growth of beard. With his long eyelashes and quirky smile, he reminded him of the actor Billy Zane. Peyton was inspecting the vintage Wiley's Jeep parked in front as one of the porters manhandled some extra jerry cans onto the back. It was painted olive drab with a faded white star in a circle on the hood and a vertical bar on the back of the front seats where a .50 caliber had once been mounted. He made a short wave as Taylan looked over at him. It appeared a bunch of the deck hands would be doubling as luggage carriers.

"Nice place," Taylan said to Miss Grey. "Was any of it really here?"

"Most of it, actually," she replied. "It was apparently a workers' village originally. There were more warehouse buildings, but they were too dilapidated to save. The shops, tavern and bar have been upgraded with some modern conveniences, like indoor air, running water and upgraded, with period-appropriate furnishings."

"I guess rich folk's role-playing only goes so far?" Audrey chimed in.

Miss Grey checked to see if Peyton was out of earshot and smiled. Taylan thought he detected a hint of malice in it. Doyle had been talking privately with Peyton and had just started walking toward them.

"Well," she said, "it would be somewhat unrealistic to expect guests of our target demographic to 'rough it' the *entire* trip."

"What about out there?" Roma asked, joining them. She pointed toward the interior of the island. "I find it difficult to imagine people like the Banyons using the traditional wilderness means to go to the bathroom. Particularly in a jungle infested with dinosaurs."

Miss Grey let out a light chuckle, her mood going playful with a hint of 'just between us girls': "No, of course not! Some exceptions needed to be made for, shall we say, 'sanitary' reasons. You'll see! It's all really quite exciting! But come: lunch awaits."

Miss Grey escorted them over to an oversized golf cart-type vehicle with balloon tires and six seats in the back. A Chinese driver in MuTron livery drove them up the rutted road northward, toward the cliffs overlooking the bay. Miss Grey rode in front, with the three of them in back.

"Naturally, modern vehicles like this buggy would be kept out of sight for the duration of any scheduled 'vacation events'," Miss Grey offered, conversrtionally.

"What about in an emergency?" Taylan asked. "Do you send out a team in that old Wiley's Jeep? Or just by donkey?"

"Of course not," Miss Grey replied. "We have emergency protocols should the need arise."

"Have any arisen yet?" Roma asked.

Miss Grey gave them an enigmatic smile in response. "Ah, here we are!"

Shielded by an outcropping of rocks was a set of stainless-steel doors recessed into the cliff face. The buggy pulled to a stop and everyone clambered out. Miss Grey stepped over to the small keypad net to the frame and tapped in some numbers. The doors slid open with a pneumatic hiss.

"Please," Miss Grey said, waving them inside.

The elevator was deliciously cool after the sweltering jungle air.

Staged or not, after the rough-shod appearance of the freighter and the village, the high-tech sleekness of the elevator was a jarring reminder that the modern world still existed. The sense of motion was all but imperceptible. It wasn't until the doors opened that it was evident they'd zipped up hundreds of feet in seconds.

"Wow," Roma said as they stepped out into a broad, low-ceilinged lobby. To one side was a polished concrete and mahogany reception desk, behind which sat a pretty, fine-featured Chinese woman in a black suit. Over her shoulder a backlit "MuTron International" announced itself in sleek, boldface metallic characters across the wall. Opposite was a set of picture windows while to the right a vast dinosaur-themed mural with all species lined up like a who's who of the Cretaceous period. The space evoked the corporate lobby of a sleek, hi-tech company with discriminating, if slightly imaginative tastes.

'Wow' scarcely covers it, Taylan decided.

The lobby had originally been a gun battery overlooking the harbor. From an elevation of over 350 feet, the view was spectacular.

From here it was evident the harbor had been created by a weaker part of the island's volcanic rim, probably from the more porous rock of a secondary vent that had collapsed in the distant past. The half-eroded cliffs that rimmed the harbor were broken on the south curve by the cascading waterfall they'd seen entering. It appeared to be fed by a twisting creek that snaked through dense jungle to the central lake in the center of the island, formed in the broad basin of the volcano's crater. The lake, perhaps three miles across at its widest, was surrounded mostly by marsh and grassland, before rising to the higher peaks along the east coast of the island.

It looked every inch the exotic, danger-laden island paradise.

And something more, Taylan realized. Looking past the ship and village – which was more like a model diorama from this height – he could see slender shapes in the hazy distance of the lake moving in herd-like formations.

Those are sauropod, Taylan realized. *No shit. I'm looking at honest-to-god sauropods!*

"Crikey, it's real, isn't it?" Audrey whispered from his side.

"It certainly is," said Miss Grey quietly, from the other side. Taylan noticed she was wearing a strong perfume, but something decent, not cloying. "Those larger ones are *Brontosaurs*. We originally considered *Argentinosaurus,* but they were too big. We had to factor the limited resources of the island against the consumption rate of such large sauropods. And they *do* like to eat!"

Roma joined them, eyes as rapt as any kid at Christmas.

"Incredible," she said. "Just incredible. Are those *Iguanodons*. . .?"

"Yes. And there's plenty more," Miss Grey said. "Don't worry, you'll have an opportunity to see them up close, later. First, I believe Mr. Luo is waiting to meet you and give you a tour of the facilities. But first the ladies will need to sign the NDAs and release forms over here at our receptionist. *You*, on the other hand, have been taken care of. Ladies, if you would please. . .?"

Taylan and Audrey remained rooted to the window, however. Neither were the type to be bustled around.

"So just how does this 'vacation' work?" he asked.

"It's right there in the brochure," Miss Grey replied, a little pointedly. "Over the course of three nights the 'expedition' moves through the island in search of a 'rare plant'. It's a loosely scripted storyline with a few 'surprises' arranged to keep the excitement level up. You did read the brochure, did you—?"

"He means the dinosaurs," Audrey cut in. "How do you have a bunch of rich tourists running in the field with a bunch of deadly creatures and not have them all get killed? As in eaten? Torn to pieces?"

"Killed?" Miss Grey pursed her mouth as if the word itself was distasteful. "Of course not! We have several failsafe protocols to ensure the safety of our guests! It's all quite safe, I can promise you!"

"I bet it is," Taylan said, "I bet it is."

Audrey and Roma walked over to the desk, where Audrey gave the receptionist a brittle smile. "I hope they're paying you well," she said, scribbling her signature. The receptionist gave her an enigmatic smile in response.

Taylan turned to Miss Grey, "But this is just your first trial run, no? The one where you still have bugs to work out?"

The assured smile was back. "No Dr. Taylan, we've had several. And the only 'bugs' you'll be encountering are those dreadful ones out in the jungle, though we have very effective repellents for that!" She tipped her head and looked at him over the rim of her glasses.

"Are you ready?"

A sweeping post-modern spiral staircase led them up to Mr. Luo's offices on the floor above. Miss Grey led them into the conference room where a light breakfast buffet was laid out on the sideboard, next to the 3D holograph table. As they filed in, Mr. Luo was standing by one of the plate glass windows with his hands clasped behind his back, gazing out at the island as if deep in thought.

"Mr. Luo?" Miss Grey prompted, in a quiet voice.

"Ah, yes!" Mr. Luo said, turning around and dialing up the charm. "Welcome!" he said, smiling. "It's quite an honor to have you here. Dr. Taylan! Dr. Adams, Dr. Banaji?" He bowed to each but made no effort to shake hands.

"We have much to cover so you may join up with Mr. Peyton's 'expedition' and enjoy your taste of a "Lost World of Kharamu' vacation!"

"No rush," Audrey replied.

"We're obviously more than a little curious how it is you were able to recreate full-sized dinosaurs," Taylan said. "To the best of my knowledge, such technology was at least decades away. Miss Grey was a little elliptical when we asked her how you plan to put tourists – especially extremely wealthy ones – out in the field with them without getting anyone killed. Or eaten. Peyton talks like this is all some big game. Is it?"

Mr. Luo's smile didn't waver. "All good questions, Dr. Taylan, and I assure you, no, this is not a 'big game'. Though some might say it is the cutting-edge crossroads of entertainment and technology, which, alas, is the world we must embrace today if one wishes to succeed. And despite the thrills, it is all quite safe, I assure you. But please, help yourself to some coffee or tea if you like, and we can get started."

Instead, the three paleontologists were all drawn to the holographic projection map.

Mr. Luo looked pleased. "Quite incredible, isn't it?"

Taylan nodded. "Can't say I've ever seen anything like it on the market."

"Nor will you, not for many years at least. I had it custom built by LG Electronics."

Roma pointed to a tiny T. rex lurking by the trees, perfectly still as it appeared to watch a herd of *Hadrosaurs* feeding in the marsh near the lake. "Is that real time? Is that T-Rex really hunting?"

Mr. Luo nodded, stepping over to the control console. "Oh yes, every single dinosaur on this island has a GPS bio-feedback tracking tag embedded at the back of their neck. The actual stance is just an estimate, based on a behavior algorithm, but it gives us a reasonably good idea what they're up to, in addition to remote camera feeds."

Even as they watched the *T. rex* hologram wavered and blinked out before reappearing in a completely different stance a few seconds later. A moment later the Hadrosaurs did the same thing.

"Looks like there's some bugs," Audrey commented, lifting her sunglasses.

"Yes," Mr. Luo said, jaw tightening. "We're still dealing with lag issues, particularly with the areas relying on wireless feeds. This level of data processing is unprecedented. We recently upgraded to more powerful routers hardwired out into the field, but they're still not perfect. It's really a secondary system, regardless. Our primary system still relies on traditional security cams to monitor the dinosaur's activities. But the hologram system allows to monitor much more than just the dinosaurs!"

He flicked through commands, showing off the various layers of data: geothermal, weather, air flow.

"The hologram projects a fully integrated data-set. I can monitor in real time everything from supplies, location of staff, delivery timetables . . . it's quite considerable."

"Dedicated satellite?" Taylan asked.

"Well, we share one of the new Shijian 16's with the Chinese Government – part of our subsidy agreement."

Roma pointed to several medium sized, feathered dinosaurs hopping around the body of a young *Stegosaurus*.

"*Utahraptors*?" she asked. The coloration of several of the creatures was almost garish – Sienna brown on top, with bright blues and reds around the head and upper body.

"Yes, they scored a kill early this morning," Mr. Luo replied.

Audrey tapped her chin. "I don't understand, how do you sustain this many dinosaurs on such a small island? Also, the predator-prey ratio looks all off."

Mr. Luo smiled. "We supplant the food supply from the mainland where necessary. Plus, we anticipate a high turnover."

Roma was still focused on the simulation. "But . . . are they *really* acting like that?" One of the Utahraptors was flapping its feathered arms and doing what looked like a victory dance.

A pause. "Well, not precisely. The data feeds aren't that sophisticated. Yet. We teamed up with a computer software company – Sauropodia – that had recently developed a highly realistic dinosaur simulator based on the latest paleontology data."

"A *computer game*, in other words?" Taylan said, one eyebrow going up. He was also thinking about the predator-prey ratio.

Maybe they found a cure for the excess population problem . . .

Mr. Luo shot him a hard look. "A *simulator*. As I told you, what we do here at MuTron International is not a game." Then the high-wattage smile was back. "But you didn't travel all this way to ogle flashy graphics – you came here to see dinosaurs, no?"

"I thought you'd never ask," Audrey said, dropping her sunglasses back into place.

"Miss Grey, would you care to join us?"

"Of course!" she said, sidling up to Taylan, giving him a wink.

Taylan nodded to himself. *Oh boy.*

Mr. Luo led them out of the office and down a sloping corridor to a stairwell.

"So, I understand this place was once a Japanese base during World War II?" Taylan asked Mr. Luo as they walked.

"*Correct.* Actually, it was occupied in 1938 and initially developed as a secret base to conduct submarine operations against allied shipping, though it quickly became bypassed in both directions – first with the swift occupation of the South Pacific by the Japanese in the early stages of the war, then later as McArthur leapfrogged up to the Philippines. While the fortifications were first-rate, the harbor was inadequate for heavy shipping and as the vagaries of war went, of limited strategic value."

"And what about the German Pharmaceutical company?"

"They came here looking for a rumored miracle plant that would prolong life. When they didn't find it, they left."

"Really?" Taylan wasn't buying it. "I heard a bunch of their staff died under mysterious circumstances."

"It's a dense, tropical island in the South Pacific, Dr. Taylan. There's all sorts of ways to die in this environment: disease, dangerous plants, poisonous snakes and spiders."

"And now dinosaurs, you forgot dinosaurs," Taylan added.

"No one is getting killed by dinosaurs, here, Dr. Taylan."

"I hope not, because I have a hunch that would be very unpleasant."

Mr. Luo didn't seem amused. As they arrived at the bottom of the stairwell, they paused in front of a massive steel door. He tapped in a code on the keypad next to it. The door opened with a pneumatic hiss.

"Please," Mr. Luo said, "I promise you will find this quite interesting."

THE LOST WORLD OF KHARAMU

FIRST TASTE.

"Is the whole place this hot?" Mrs. Banyon asked, shaking her head. "It's positively awful!"

Charles Banyon gave her a withering look, "For Gods' sake, Ethel, it's no worse than our place in Florida! If it's too much, stay in the damn hotel!"

Oblivious, Mrs. Banyon produced a fan from an oversized, tropical-style carry-all and waved it across her face. Though it was well before noon, the air was hot and suffocating, particularly after the air-conditioned interior of the Land-Rover (certain levels of authenticity had been sacrificed in a nod to customer convenience).

Before they'd set off, Joseph Bello, 'Bemba' – who was also doubling as their tour guide – had jumped up on the hood of the Jeep and explained a few of the ground rules.

"As your guide, it's recommended you stay within my sight at all times," he said, in clearly enunciated English. "Just because you signed those liability wavers doesn't require you test them to the letter. Kharamu is a dangerous place . . . for many years there have been rumors about it . . . about large - once thought *extinct* – creatures roaming in its jungles. Not to mention a host of dangerous snakes, spiders . . . and if the *other* rumors are true, an aboriginal race of cannibals living in the Eastern caves!"

Mr. Banyon checked the Thompson Submachine gun slung from his shoulder. One of the fringe benefits of this particular vacation was the lack of U.S. (or any other) federal regulations when it came to automatic weapons like this. He caught Roger Blodgett's eye, "Just as long as Mr. Jungle Bunny there gets out of the way when the shooting starts, we should be fine, eh?"

Blodgett *harrumphed* and winked in return. An M-1 Carbine with a banana clip was slung over his shoulder, with a .45 automatic in a hip holster for extra measure. Between that and the machete at his other hip, he looked pretty much the overweight sales manager playing adventurer.

The three vehicles had taken the crude road that led up the low cliff in a series of switchbacks overlooking the bay, pausing at one scenic turnaround by the waterfalls for everyone to clamber out and take a group photo.

It was all but a classic Kodak moment: Peyton in the center while in full safari regalia (including the Aussie military slouch hat with the brim pinned up on one side and a puggaree band), the Blodgetts to one side and the Banyons on the other. Everyone putting on their best grins, Peyton with his arm around Suzie Blodgett's shoulder, Charles Banyon with a cigar clenched in his teeth while holding the Thompson angled up like a 30s gangster. Joseph Bello took the shot. Behind the group the roaring cascade was framed by dense jungle, a rainbow-tinged mist rising out into the late morning sun.

By all accounts it looked like a stunning start to an exciting adventure.

Then tragedy struck.

One porter had snuck off to take a leak on a precipice by the falls when one loop of hanging vines dropped and coiled around his neck, hauling him up into the branches, kicking and screaming.

Roger Blodgett swung around and raised his carbine, but Bello quickly stepped forward and knocked it upward, dropping the camera and drawing his machete. The carbine let out a single, barking shot that echoed out across the bay, followed by muffled grunts and the hideous sound of snapping bones up in the tree.

Bello sprinted to the trunk and grasping a vine with one hand, leapt up, hacking furiously.

Mrs. Banyon shrieked, while Peyton stood nearby, scowling, as if uncertain what role he should play.

Blood sprayed out from the tree and abruptly the porter half fell out of the tree, one glistening coil still wrapped around his neck and shoulder. He dangled for a moment in full view, face purpled from strangulation, then struggling to free himself, he somersaulted outward and into the falls. His trailing scream was cut short by the sound of impact, then nothing else except for the continuing roar of the cascade.

Mrs. Banyon fainted dead away.

Bello dropped down, his shirt sprayed with blood, and wiped the worst of it from his machete on a nearby fern. He glanced up at the party, eyes hard.

"Python," he said. "Better be careful when you're around trees here."

Suzie Blodgett had her fingers touching her lips, but from the excited gleam in her eye it was apparent she had enjoyed the whole spectacle.

"Oh my God, he's dead?" she asked.

Bello glanced over at the falls, then back at her. "That's a one-hundred and twenty-foot drop. He made a stupid mistake and paid for it. We'll send a recovery team over later."

Mr. Banyon, who was kneeling over his wife and fanning her back to consciousness, eyed the Zambian warily. "You're a cold-hearted son-of-a-bitch, aren't you?"

Bello replied with a frown, "I'm paid to do a job. Sometimes unpleasant things come with it. Every man here knows that. Best we load up and get a move on." He headed over to the Jeep, but Preston grabbed his arm. Bello shot him a hard look, but Peyton winked: *Good one.*

Bello pulled away and ignored him, only smiled to himself when his face was turned.

It had gone off rather well. The porter – an ex circus acrobat named Jean Luc – would be untangling himself from his harness by now and waiting eagerly until they were off again so he could enjoy a smoke. It had been a pre-scripted event, the first in many to come over the next three days designed to keep the excitement factor up for their guests. The python hadn't been real and not even a full snake. Just enough for the effects group to rig up a convincing scare.

There was a tiny burst of static in his ear followed by a woman's voice in the earpiece. It was one of Farnsworth's assistants. The audio quality of the new earbuds was so good it was as if she was standing right next to him. Bello had to resist the urge to look around.

"Mr. Farnsworth is very pleased how that went," the woman said. Bello remembered her well – a sultry Haitian woman with a French accent. Her name was Catherine. It felt oddly intimate with her sounding so close. Bello knew better than to respond, other than a quick nod that would be picked up by one of the HD video cams.

The Jeep's suspension sagged as Peyton clambered in next to him.

"Well, that was something," Peyton said, brows raised. "What's next?"

Peyton had insisted on riding shotgun the whole trip, his vintage Weatherby Mark V .460 Magnum rifle cradled across his chest. It was a rifle his grandfather had owned (so he claimed) and carried on several big-game safaris around the world. Like many things about James Peyton III, the truth was just a little less than glamorous.

For starters, the rifle had been another family's heirloom purchased at a fraction of its value from a nearly bankrupt client of Peyton's desperately trying to raise cash. And contrary to the well-polished story Peyton had repeated over the years about Clarence "Clay" Peyton being a successful Texan Oil man with frontier sensibilities and a taste for hunting, his grandfather was in fact a failed mechanic and small-time hustler with a taste for hard liquor and even harder living. He'd been found in a flophouse outside of Tallahassee, Florida, after being dead three days, left beaten and strangled. An ex-con named Rudy Capelli he'd been seen hanging with the previous week was a prime suspect, along with a hooker with the dubious named of 'Ginger Peabody', but neither was ever apprehended. When a middle-aged white-trash got offed under questionable circumstances - particularly back in the mid-50s - the local police tended not to put their sharpest investigative hats on.

Peyton began to craft his fictionalized family history not long after when he'd transferred to a high school in Jacksonville, claiming his father – who had recently run off and was working in the mid-west as a grifter hustling oil-investment schemes - was on the road 'prospecting' in their home state of Texas. When the son of a wealthy local Arlington family questioned him on it one day, Peyton, who in his Junior year was now 6'2" and serving as a running back on the Varsity football team, Peyton beat the Senior within an inch of his life.

In college Peyton learned early on one of the truths of life: if you painted yourself successful enough, along with a good dose of unflinching confidence, people had a funny way of believing it. Which led him to another truism about humanity – people *wanted* to believe it. And they gravitated toward confidence. Peyton wasn't exactly a genius, but what he did have was an aptitude for leveraging opportunity, no matter how small, along with developing a staid persona modeled after his idol, the late actor John Wayne. Right down to the one-eyed squint and slow drawl. Combining his version of good old American *frontierism* with a bit of business savvy, by the time he graduated from Pensacola University he was already working on a successful career as a loan officer with a major bank, breaking records with his ability to open new credit accounts, usually with utter disregard of the customer's ability to ever make good on their debts.

Now, nearly thirty years later, Ed Peyton – now restyled as *James Allen Peyton III* – appeared to be the poster boy of the American success story: owner of four houses – including one sprawling beach house in the British Virgin Islands – along with an investment capital firm estimated to be worth some 4.5 billion dollars, two ex-wives and a private jet.

Except for the various performance drugs and anti-depressants he'd been on for years. This weekend, however, he'd decided all that was going to end. James Allen Peyton was going clean.

Once over the crest and into the island's interior, the small convoy had followed a meandering game trail that threaded along south of the lake, which was where the party got their first good look at the dinosaurs.

Even at a distance the sauropods were impressive.

At twenty tons and seventy feet long from head to tail, they made elephants look like runts. The Brontosaurs weren't as elegant as their Diplodocus cousins, but they were certainly interesting: russet colored markings at the top of their neck and head, an array of fine dorsal spikes trailing along their spine, massive shoulders and fore legs that had a distinctive claw on the inside. They were much more deep-chested than their cousins as well, with a slender tail, unlike the chunky images made by paleontologists of years past.

The herd near the south edge of the lake wasn't huge – eight adults at a glance, with two smaller infants wandering off at a distance. A second herd could be seen way off in the distance on the northeast shore of the lake. Interspersed with the Brontosaurs was a herd of duck-billed Parasoaurolophus, mostly grazing on all fours, their long knob-ended crests bobbing up and down. Every so often one gave out a low, subsonic trumpeting sound that seemed to carry straight across the island. When they did, another would raise its head up and answer in acknowledgement, in a similar but never identical tone. To the southeast flank of the Brontosaurus herd, a group of Triceratops leisurely grazed in the tall grass, occasionally letting out low grunts as they chewed up shrubs and 'Droopy Leaf' bushes.

The Brontosaurs seemed to have their own call-and-response dialogue going on, more randomly than the duckbills. Oddly, they didn't seem overly concerned with the two younger juveniles focused on a copse of bushes near the edge of the jungle.

Overall it was a tranquil, exotic scene, resurrected from 65 million years ago.

The sublime beauty of it was apparently lost on Peyton's group, who were more interested in taking pictures of each other for the moment with the dinosaurs as a backdrop. Except for Joseph Bello, who stood leaning against the front fender of the Jeep, scanning the scene with a pair of Zeiss binoculars.

The Joseph Bello who had grown up in the steppes of Zambia was in complete awe of the dinosaurs, while the Joseph Bello who had earned his doctorate in mathematics from the University of Zambia was cataloguing and categorizing all the behaviors he was witnessing.

Bello had been offered a career in academia, but ultimately turned it down. He'd grown up in the capital city, Lusaka, but had found himself employed during his first summer break as a guide when one of the visiting professors cajoled him into assisting him on some photography excursions into the bush.

Bellow had discovered he had an aptitude and fascination with safari expeditions, and photography as well. He became something of a naturalist, going on excursions and photographing Zambia's incredible range of wildlife and landscapes, such as the breathtaking Victorian Falls.

The huge lake he was now looking at was reminiscent of Lake Kariba, which he'd led trips on for several years before a serendipitous encounter with a group of field scientists from MuTron International, who'd hired him as a guide and consultant on studying predatorial behavior in the bush. Two months later he received a very generous offer in the mail, along with an NDA, to do the same thing on a new project being developed in the South Pacific.

Playing both a very real guide and a fictional character for wealthy Western vacationers was more than a bit odd to Bello, but the generous compensation far outstripped any reservations and the level of rudeness he found himself subjected to. They'd given him a one-month training course coaching him on how to manage clients like Peyton, as well as keep the party moving along on key plot points for their vacation. It was absurd, but like many things about him, his plan was pragmatic: work the gig as long as possible, make as much money as he could off the Chinese and save every penny. In just the past year alone he'd tucked away a sizable amount. At 32, he still had plenty of time to marry and raise a family if he wanted, by his reckoning.

For now, he was young, single, and witnessing an incredible moment in history: the return of the dinosaurs.

"What do you see out there, Bemba?" Peyton asked, stepping up alongside.

Bello grinned. It was something he excelled at. Even around assholes like Peyton. *Bemba* was something of a two-way joke. Peyton had overheard the word when Bello had been having a conversation with Doyle about his home country, and had confused it with the name of a corrupt Finance minister then making the news from a nearby country. So, Peyton thought casting Bello as 'Bemba' in his group was a not-so-subtle way of putting him in his place. Peyton was a big advocate of pecking order and reminding everyone – with rare exceptions – of his perceived top place in it.

However, the ironic truth was simpler: 'Bemba' was Bello's ethnic group and language.

It was like calling an American Lenape Indian speaking Lenape a 'Lenape'.

"Something incredible, 'Sir' Roxton," he replied. He had been eyeing the two Tyrannosaurs lurking at the edge of the jungle canopy while running the classic Lotka–Volterra predator-prey model through his head. Mainly out of sheer habit. Most of what he'd observed here didn't adhere cleanly to any mathematics model. Real life seldom did, past a certain point at least.

Peyton chuckled, rubbing his chin with one hand while cradling the big game rifle with the other. Then he clapped Bello on the shoulder.

"You can say that again, fella."

He checked the action on the rifle, making sure the chamber was clear. Putting on his best John Wayne squint, he pointed and said: "Just how close do you think you can get us to that Brontosaurus herd?"

Bello drove them along a strand of trees that led out toward the lake, still a couple hundred yards away from the Brontosaurs. He knew full well what Peyton was looking to do, but he wasn't going to make it easy for him or anyone in his party. It was a fine line between delivering the goods and skewing a distasteful job, one he'd been tested on many times with some of his less savory clients back in Zambia. Part of the trick was to keep smiling and look like you were doing the best job possible.

The Brontosaurs were just slightly downwind from group – Bello had been noting the tops of the trees swaying slightly in the tepid late morning air – but didn't appear to show any signs of apprehension at their approach.

He stopped the Jeep at the last of the trees and putting the gear shift in neutral, pulled up the parking brake and waited. He gave a quick scan with his binoculars. Though for all appearances a standard pair of vintage 10x40 German Zeiss army-issue, these were outfitted with an augmented reality overlay that showed Bello not just the visible dinosaurs, but any hidden or concealed ones as well. Every dinosaur had an embedded tag with GPS info. The overlay also showed a graduated boundary indicating the safety zone of how far the dinosaurs could approach before the safety protocols kicked in. Green was clear – the area where the dinosaurs could roam freely - then the shades went to yellow, orange, then bright red. They were parked just outside the red zone. Any dinosaur managing to get to the red zones would be immobilized by the implant. Likewise, the vehicles were outfitted with a subsonic alarm system that would scramble the hearing of any dinosaur that came within ten yards. One thing they learned - particularly with the predators – was that they had an incredibly acute sense of hearing. And smell.

Even the massive *Brontosaurs* had repeatedly shied off during all their field tests.

The Land Rovers pulled up behind them but only Charles Banyon and the Blodgetts got out.

Peyton clambered out and walked around to the driver's side of the Jeep, using the hood as an elbow rest and taking a preliminary look down the barrel of his rifle.

"So, what kind of 'scientist' walks around with a Thompson?" Roger Blodgett was saying to Banyon as they walked up.

"The kind that knows how to take care of himself in the field, not like that nitwit college professor playing Indiana Jones!" Banyon replied, grinning.

"Like the kind of man you only wish *you* could be," Suzie Blodgett chimed in, the edge of her lip rising in a sneer.

Roger shot her a venomous look and his right hand curled into a fist, but as always, that was as far as it went. Despite his wildly imaginative fantasies throughout the fifteen acrimonious years of their marriage of standing up to his wife and giving her a good verbal (if not physical) whipping, Roger was at heart, a coward. And his wife knew it. He might spend endless nights downstairs in the rec-room at their 3,000 square-foot house in suburban Atlanta getting blitzed and talking up a storm about how he was going to show her this and that, or do something outrageous to show her what an undervalued, incredible guy he was, but none of that was yet to have ever crystalized into reality. Roger Blodgett was a card-carrying member of that tribe of *big-talkers* and *no-walkers*. 'All bark and no balls', as his wife was known to point out, often in front of their friends at their regular back-yard BBQs or predictable rotation of holiday parties.

Except, Roger Blodgett had convinced himself that this time – this trip to the Lost World of Kharamu – was going to be his shining moment. He was utterly positive of it. An opportunity to unveil to the world the inner man-of-action waiting patiently within himself after all these years. And to show Suzie too: partly out of vanity, partly out of the misplaced residual affection he felt for her after so many years together, partly out of a desperate need to validate himself in a way his 401k and benefit package never could.

As they came up to the Jeep, Peyton shouldered his rifle and turning, reached out with one beefy arm and pulled Suzie Blodgett to his side.

"Ah, my dear Lady Roxton!" he said, not bothering with any sort of faux English accent. Next to him Bello winced, just. It was liking watching John Wayne play Genghis Khan in 'The Conqueror".

"Sir John Orville!" she replied, wriggling her nose like he was her plaything.

Banyon glanced at Roger with a 'you're going to take that?' look.

Roger snorted and walked past them, pointedly ignoring his wife, while fingering the .45 at his hip. Despite everything he felt relaxed, confident. *And that hot little Indian scientist? Maybe she would like a little bed time with a man of action! That would show my little Suzie!*

"Incredible! This place truly is a lost world!" he blurted out, remembering some of the recommended lines from his script. "Is the first camp just beyond that herd of dinosaurs?" he asked, turning to Bello. According to the 'loose script' their goal for the first day was to make camp by mid-afternoon, then head toward the eastern mountains first thing in the morning.

"Yes sir, *Professor*," Bello replied, not missing the irony that *he* was the real professor here. "We may want to skirt around them to the south." He nodded to his right. "That copse of trees there is a good viewing spot, if you want to take photos."

"Yes, yes, of course!" Blodgett replied, puffing his chest up, "Professor, um, Summerlee and I would certainly like a closer look at these, er, remarkable creatures. I understand the plants we're interested in were sighted over there in the mountains to the east, yes?" He sounded like a third-rate actor reading a script at an audition.

"Correct," Bello answered, stepping up to his cue. "Near one of the streams coming out of the peaks there. But I'm obliged to warn you – as I did back at the falls – that dinosaurs aren't the only thing known to be dangerous here on Kharamu. The last party that came here searching for that fabled plant never returned."

"Then we shall be the first!" Mr. Banyon announced, lifting his chin up.

Bello looked over at the Tyrannosaurs and suppressed a shudder. *And maybe the last, if those safety protocols aren't as good as they're claiming,* he thought.

A little over twenty minutes later, disaster struck.

Due to the topography and the necessity of the dinosaurs to have multiple access points to the lake, while also being able to get the visitors near enough to them to have what MuTron marketing called a 'close-contact' experience, there were 'hot-zone' areas that had to be crossed by the convoys. In this case, there were only three plotted out throughout the course of their expedition.

The most important thing was to make sure the area was clear of dinosaurs in both directions, particularly of any predator species. Bello had been through this many times in his field training, as well as how to handle any contingencies. The biggest threat, however, were from the smaller, swifter species. Contrary to Hollywood misconceptions, Utahraptors weren't capable of running as fast as Cheetahs (nor were they clever pack hunters, like in Jurassic Park, but more solitary predators like eagles and hawks) but they certainly could outrun a man on foot, averaging 25 to 30 miles per hour, with occasional bursts of an additional few miles an hour when after a prey. And of course, the variable physicality of each animal had to be taken into account, or 'individual mileage may vary' as Bello had quipped to the MuTron field instructor, who had stared back at him, stone-faced.

There had been a darker side to the equation as well.

It had only been hinted at, and picked up through various comments such as the "Beta X" trials and "Trauma Induction Studies", but Bello had a hunch that a lot of the data MuTron had on dinosaur speeds, eating habits, and so on, had been cultivated from live test subjects.

Human test subjects.

The crossing, through a dried stream bed, should have been straightforward. It had been checked by one of the recon parties the day before and had been run hundreds of times during the training simulations.

But reality, as Bello was well aware, was a temperamental mistress.

A fluke squall had passed through in the early hours of the morning and turned the stream bed wetter than usual. And while according to the surveillance cameras it appeared the same, it wasn't. A large herd of *Ankylosaurs* had trampled through it, turning the soil into a soupy mud that appeared dry after a few hours of tropical morning sun.

But that was only on the surface.

There were no dinosaurs in range when Bello drove the Jeep out of the safe range and across the 'hot' zone, but halfway across the tires sunk down six inches and the vehicle became mired. The Land Rover behind them – driven by the same 'dock hand' who had been flirting with Dr. Banaji back at the village - made the mistake of trying to accelerate past and instead fishtailed and became mired as well. From the back seat, the Blodgetts and the Banyons peered out. The driver of the second Land Rover prudently backed off at a safe distance.

The first thing Bello did was take the binoculars slung around his neck and scan both directions. That was basic protocol. There was nothing to the south except for a bunch of *Ankylosaurs* grazing around half a mile away, with a few *Compsognathus* or 'Compys' darting in and about. Directly ahead toward the lake were the Brontosaurs. Neither seemed to take interest in the vehicles.

Bello then alternated putting the Jeep into reverse and first gear, trying to get some traction, but it only resulted in sinking them further.

"Stay here," he said to Peyton, but to his surprise Peyton shook his head and jumped out instead.

"I'll push, you drive," the billionaire said, heading to the back of the Jeep. Since swearing off the meds the day before, he realized he was feeling like a new man. Full of vigor. Energy.

Shouts accompanied them as the other porters scrambled out to help manhandle the Land Rover forward as well. Neither the Blodgetts or Banyons made any effort to get out.

If nothing else, Peyton was at least physically strong. Digging his boots into the muck, he gave the Jeep a solid heave and with Bello gunning the engine, the vehicle lurched forward a couple feet. Mud flew.

The Jeep sunk down again with a wet *sklorking* sound, halfway up to the wheel wells.

Bello cursed under his breath and glanced to the trees ahead of them. The safe zone was at least eighty yards away.

God damn it! This never happened in the simulations before! Never!

A voice spoke up in his earpiece. This time it was Farnsworth himself. Though somewhat delicate in appearance, the Programming Director had a surprisingly deep voice: "Bello, you need to get your passengers out of the vehicles and escorted over to the safe zone. Let the porters deal with the vehicles, all right?"

He sounded calm, but there was an edge to his voice Bello didn't like.

"What's up?"

"Probably nothing, but the *Brontosaurs* are looking a little agitated. Don't loiter."

"What about the fail-safe devices in the vehicles?"

Silence.

Bello glanced over at the lake and saw that the enormous sauropods indeed looked agitated, their tails whipping back and forth. They'd stopped eating and were trumpeting back and forth with their odd, nasal-sounding honks. Behind he saw the driver – an ex-Disney theme park operator named Jamie Evans (who like many of the porters had also been swept in with Farnsworth) - also jump out and open the back door of the Rover. It sounded like a heated argument was going on. Suzie Blodgett was yelling at Evans, who was jabbing his finger toward the second Land Rover idling back in the safe zone.

Peyton now had rivulets of sweat describing lines through his dirt covered face, making him look like some sort of bizarre animal. Bello motioned for him to stop pushing and put the Jeep in neutral.

"Evans!" he shouted. "Get them back to the other vehicle, now!" He motioned to the other porters. "Help me get the Jeep across first. We can worry about the Land Rover second!" He turned to Peyton. "Ah, Sir Roxton, you should join the others. Be patient. We'll find a better crossing area."

Peyton shook his head. "Hell no, Bembo! I ain't here to watch from the damn sidelines!" He gripped the back of the Jeep again as four of the men came over and joined him.

Then all heads turned as the ground shook and the sauropods trumpeted. They were marching straight at them.

Fast.

Farnsworth piped up again in Bello's earpiece. "Uh, Joseph? Now would be a very good time to get your party back into the safe zone!"

Bello snatched up his binoculars and saw what looked like a wall of dinosaurs coming at them. Something was wrong – he'd never seen the *Brontosaurs* acting like this. Even worse, three *Tyrannosaurs* were pursuing them.

OFF THE COAST OF KHARAMU

The ex *Bureau Veritas* semi-submersible boat had been the Vietnamese commando's idea.

A French-built, 54-foot long craft built of fiberglass and wood, it had originally been designed for a Greek tourist company for visiting shallow wrecks and ruins in the northern Mediterranean. The company had gone bust with many others during the Greek financial crisis years back and this particular asset had bounced around, serving alternately as a drug runner (and retrieval) vessel in the Caribbean, a spy boat in the Philippines, and more recently a renewed – and highly unsuccessful - effort by a handful of North Koreans to abduct Japanese women.

The latter effort had ended when the submersible became entangled in an impossibly dense school of jellyfish and ran aground, a victim, ironically, of global warming. Shortly after it was picked up at an auction by a relative of Taylan's ex-girlfriend, then taken back to Vietnam where it languished at a dock for over a year.

Tuan and Lanh had bought it and had it refurbished for another contract that fell through when Gorimov's call had come. It was quickly decided it was the perfect means to get to the island undetected, as the boat's low profile was perfectly suited to avoid radar detection and after painting its original bright yellow to sea-green camouflage pattern, all but undetectable except to the sharpest observer.

From there it had been a matter of getting it transported to a location within reasonable range of the island. The brothers had also recruited ten more members from their old elite 126 Naval Commando Regiment, including two military hackers, a demolitions expert they'd known in the army and a female sharpshooter named Dinh Thi Nguyet.

The weather off the east coast of the island had picked up and was a little choppy, but was deemed the best approach after reviewing the maps and documents provided by the German. Most of the perimeter of the island was protected by remote cameras and security drones, but the southeast shore had a blind spot created by three steep islets that were inaccessible.

It was a dangerous place to land, with powerful currents and jagged cliffs, but a quick analysis had revealed a short strip of beach just past the largest of the islets, near a spot where the cliffs could be rappelled. The sub was equipped with an advanced 3D Multibeam scanning sonar and was maneuverable enough that Tuan thought they could risk it. From there it was a half-mile jaunt down to the generator plants at the south of the island.

The trouble began when they narrowly missed getting intercepted by a couple of high-speed Chinese patrol boats that appeared unexpectedly, forcing them to cut their engines and lose a good hour and forty-five minutes drifting away from their destination until the patrol had disappeared over the horizon.

The next setback occurred on their approach, when a sudden cross current slewed the submersible into an outcropping near the largest islet, damaging the hull enough to cause a leak. There was a jarring crunch that sent all of them tumbling about in the narrow hull, followed by a hiss of ruptured pipes. The hull was already fatigued from years of neglect and in short order, they took on water.

Lanh, who was piloting the boat, did exactly what he'd been trained to do in similar situations during covert missions: rammed the throttles forward, went in obliquely at the thin stretch of beach and hoped for the best.

The vessel ran aground a dozen feet from the shore, canting precariously on the shelf that formed the beach. Hatches were thrown open and the Vietnamese commandos clambered out with a silent efficiency Gorimov found impressive.

All the Vietnamese – now in their early thirties – had served together in the 126th Naval Commando Brigade, considered one of the most elite units in the Vietnamese People's Ground Forces. Created fifty years previously out of the cauldron of the Vietnam War, its members had a usually high level of *esprit de corps* and in recent years adopted the slogan "More than 1", which meant: *any individual can work one, two, 'n' times better than himself.* In practice that resulted in its members regularly achieving intense levels of endurance, such as swimming 15 – 20 kilometers in the ocean, drifting at sea for days, and with their sharpshooter, Dinh, training herself to destroy a target with one or two shots during field exercises when her commanding officer couldn't do it in four.

Now retired and struggling to find work in a post-recession world, the Nguyets and their fellow commandos had turned to mercenary work for supplemental income. This job would be their highest paying ever. Two brothers had already discussed how they might cut out the Russians altogether, expanding into a more lucrative market.

First things first, however, and they had to get the mysterious plant, which Gorimov was tightly secretive about.

"Can it be fixed?" Gorimov asked, once they were assembled on the beach. He was standing in a half-soaked military surplus uniform, one of the blue-and-green camo ones the Vietnamese had supplied.

Tuan was directing the unloading of the rappelling gear. Like the rest of the commandos, he was lightly armed, eschewing the heavy tactical outfits favored by most modern special forces, though the gear and weapons were all standard issue Russian: NRS-2 Combat knives, Serdyukov SR1M semi-automatic pistols with 18-round magazines, and AKM assault rifles. The latter – an updated version of the classic AK-47 – was still considered far more reliable in the field than some of the newer weapons. Each member (including the Russians) also wore a military issue machete, rigorously sharpened.

Lanh, who was standing next to Gorimov, shrugged. "Maybe. We'll have to leave two of our team behind to repair it, unless you have a better way off this island?"

Gorimov looked at the commandos, then at Vlad and Oleg, who were staring up at the cliff nearby, wearing nearly identical frowns. He wasn't overly excited about the additional hands Tuan and Lanh had brought along, and by his reckoning, *two less gooks* to deal with suited him just fine.

Although Vlad and Oleg weren't exactly inspiring his confidence right then. The former was still a little green around the gills from the boat ride over here – he'd spent most of the trip in the bow of the cramped sub puking his guts up in a plastic pail – while Oleg sat beside him making dire predictions about the whole operation. The only reason he kept them along was that they were intensely loyal to him. And distantly related.

"Do whatever you can to fix the sub. We'll look for another way, but I like my ass covered with both hands, yes?"

Lanh didn't reply, but stared off into space. He flicked his eyes to his brother, over by the growing pile of equipment. Tuan met his gaze and it was as if an entire shorthand dialogue occurred between them in one glance. Tuan's nod was barely perceptible.

Gorimov acted as if he didn't catch it, making a point of rubbing his chin while looking up at the cliff. He fished a pack of cigarettes out of his pocket and checking to see they were still dry, lit one up.

"Now we get some exercise!"

Even the agile Vietnamese were soaked in sweat by the time they reached the top. The ascent was trickier than it first appeared. Halfway up Vlad had taken a near fatal plunge when the root he had been grasping at pulled out, sending him tumbling down with a yell. Only one of the lines snaring his leg had saved him, though he'd dangled precariously upside down for a good ten minutes while they worked out how to secure him.

When Gorimov slid back down to assist, he noted the broken root was partially cut through – one a commando had paused on shortly before. The expression that crossed his face right then was as cold and merciless as any executioner's.

When they assembled at the top it was mid-afternoon.

Putting aside any thoughts of settling accounts for the moment, Gorimov called Tuan and Lanh aside for a quick talk, squatting on a small rock basin filled with loamy soil and surrounded by large ferns. A hundred feet below the surf boomed and hissed around the islets.

Gorimov had collected a bunch of rocks and arranged them to approximate their key objectives, while drawing a crude outline of the island in the dirt using a stick.

"Now we split into two parties," he said, gesturing with his first two fingers to make his point. "Both of you will take six commandos to the southern compound here, hacking into their security network and shutting down the security systems, then use your demo man to blow the generators sky high. At 3 a.m., as we discussed. To create maximum chaos and confusion." Gorimov tapped the little pile of rocks he made to the eastern outline of the island. "I take

Vlad and Oleg and the second group to secure the plants which are here, at the base of the mountains. Tonight. You keep your sharpshooter, but I'll need your other hacker, and last two commandos. Once the plants are secure, I send them with two commandos back to here, while I lead the rest to the second prize. Which we take soon as generators are blown. All goes well, we leave here tomorrow morning."

"Second prize?" Tuan said, eyes narrowing. It was the first mention of this.

"Yes. The main compound. Where the dinosaur breeding facility is. The DNA. This way we double our profits and get to retire fat happy old men. Yes?"

The brothers exchanged looks.

Tuan shook his head. "No good. One of us goes with you. To deal with Taylan." When Gorimov shrugged, he pressed on, "Besides, how can you possibly find this plant in the middle of the jungle, in the middle of the night?"

"That's the easy part," Gorimov grinned, patting his breast pocket. "GPS tracker. My contact here left it by the plant we need. Take us right to it. No problem."

"But how do you know what it looks like? There are probably thousands of plant varieties here."

Gorimov tapped his bald cranium. "That part is right here."

Lanh was frowning. "You forgot one thing."

Gorimov raised his brows: *now what?*

"The dinosaurs," Lanh responded. "What do we do about the dinosaurs?"

Gorimov didn't hesitate.

"We kill them. And anything – or anyone else – that gets in our way? Understood?"

After a brief discussion, Lanh agreed to lead the group tackling the generator facilities. Being the older of the two, Tuan insisted on first crack at Taylan, if possible, and they decided it was most likely he'd be with Peyton's party looking for the plant or if not, back at command center.

Gorimov indicated there was a rough trail they could follow down to the old hospital and animal husbandry complex. More importantly, according to his sources it was lightly guarded. The plan was to get there in early evening to make a thorough reconnaissance, then hole up until 3 a.m. The trick was to identify the security cams not just at the perimeter, but the ones set up throughout the island.

Gorimov had assured them approaching the compounds wouldn't be a serious issue. Not with the Mutron International uniforms the German had provided them with.

CAPTIVE

Wang had no idea how long he had been out.

He came to in an eruption of consciousness, like a diver breaching the surface of a deep, still black lake after pushing way past his limits underwater.

Wang sat up straight, saw stars swim before his eyes, then the pain hit: a red-rimmed throb that seemed to encase his entire skull in agony, starting from his jaw. He immediately collapsed back into a prone position again, the back of his head cracking on damp concrete.

The pain was nearly blinding. For a few moments, he squeezed his eyes shut and focused on breathing.

Several other things asserted themselves in short order – the rank, cloying stench of mold, the methodical drip of water, the maddening itch of rough rope binding his wrists and ankles. An odd, scissoring sound he couldn't quite place.

When the agony in his head settled down to a steady thrum, he ever-so-carefully eased his eyes open.

The room was a large storage chamber of sorts, accessed by a heavy steel door, the kind with heavy bolts one saw in old ship bulkheads. Anemic light filtered in from grilled ventilation pipes in the ceiling. Rotting wooden crates were stacked everywhere, while against one wall was floor to ceiling racks filled with heavy, oblong objects he couldn't quite identify.

A few feet away from him lay a crumpled figure, breathing raggedly. Tao.

Prisoners, he thought. *We're prisoners in some moldering dungeon in this damn complex. We'll never get out of here.*

And what the hell is that damn scissoring sound? It's making me crazy!

Wang was distracted by a movement in his peripheral vision – a blob coming down from the air vent over his head. His first thought was that it was some sort of hideously large bumble bee. Then he saw the splayed legs.

It was a particularly vicious-looking Orb-weaver spider. Dropping directly at his head.

Wang's eyes went wide as his instincts rammed all throttles forward.

Overriding all pain, he jackknifed to his left side, hampered by the ropes binding his wrists and ankles. He felt a crunch and stinging sensation on his cheek, sending a bright needle of pain to his eye.

Then he saw them.

The spiders.
Hundreds of them.

Wang hissed in terror. He didn't have an issue with arachnids – or even insects for that matter – when they were at a *distance*. But the thought of any such non-human or animal creature actually *touching* him sent his entire nervous system into blind red panic.

Even as he stared, one of the things did a hideous scuttle then jumped at his head.

Wang screamed as he twisted, half-rolled toward his feet. Pincers scrabbled through his hair. The ropes bit painfully into his wrists as he convulsed in horror, his gorge rising as he rolled over several of the spiders with a series of hideous popping sounds.

Still screaming, he managed to get into an awkward position on his knees and elbows.

"Tao!" he yelled through clenched teeth. "Get up!"

Tao stirred in response, then after a pause screamed incoherently.

Wang felt the icicles of panic seep out from the nape of his neck, sending goose bumps rippling along his arms and scalp. The damn spiders were everywhere like a living carpet, with their undulating, questing legs and relentless, malicious sets of eyes fixing him with their venomous gaze – he could practically sense their alien anatomies processing, assessing him: *intruder! Bite! Attack!*

Never one who had ever given more than a cursory thought towards arachnids – including the one Tao had seen back in the tunnel – he found himself overwhelmed with fear and loathing of the things.

Further thought was interrupted as Tao, in a burst of panicked energy, somehow catapulted himself up into an upright position. He was screaming in big, high-pitched whoops. Hobbled by the rope binding his ankles he described a series of spinning hops, which sent him crashing into the massive wall racks.

The result was impressive.

Corroded by decades of rot, the racks all-but exploded, sending their cargo flying in all directions. The ringing cacophony of metal was deafening, like hundreds of barbells ricocheting off each other at once. Even as the first one clipped Wang's foot, sending him tumbling atop a bunch of them, he grasped what they were: brass canon projectiles. Huge ones – six or eight-inch shells for the original Japanese batteries.

Of course! This must have been the main magazine for the fortifications!

With that came another unsettling thought: how was it the shells weren't exploding?

Wang yelped as another shell glanced off his thigh and went tumbling away, but the result couldn't have been crazier than anything he could have imagined moments before: the massive shells were flattening the spiders in every direction.

The clanging of metal went on for a minute or two more. Miraculously, none of the old munitions detonated.

In the dim light, he saw something else that sparked his hope – the jagged metal post that had snapped when the shelves collapsed. Carefully (after flicking one spider off his knee, with a shudder), he worked his way over to it. His head was hammering not just from his jaw but from his ears now as well, the ringing echoing on as if trapped in his skull.

Ignoring it, he placed his wrists around the jagged post and began sawing back and forth.

It was hard work, made more difficult by the post swaying back and forth, but he was able to steady it with his knees and soon enough the rope frayed and broke. Gasping in relief, he freed his ankles, taking a moment to brush a few more errant spiders off (including one trapped in his hair) and stomping them into oblivion.

"Tao!? Are you okay?"

Nearby his friend, lying in a collapsed pile of rusted shells, let out a moan.

"My head hurts," Tao mumbled. *"Shen me!"*

What crap!

Wang picked his way carefully over and tried to help his friend up.

Tao stumbled, and Wang saw that his friend had split his head open. A ragged gash ran up the side of his forehead into his hairline, sending rivulets of blood past his eye and cheek. He must have hit one of the shells when he fell. It was bleeding a lot, but the wound was clean and best as he could tell, not very deep.

This, oddly, was something he was better equipped to deal with. Taking off his shirt – and wiping off as much of the mold and spider remains as possible – he tore a broad strip off the back. He bent down, his face close to Tao's.

"It's not too bad, but it's bleeding pretty good. Hold still while I bind it up!" When Tao whimpered in protest, Wang did something instinctive – he reached over and pinched his friend's earlobe.

"Ouch!"

"That's better!" Wang replied. He tried to remember the protocol for treating head wounds. He held up three fingers. "How many?"

"Sixty-five," Tao murmured, as a tiny smile curled the side of his mouth.

"You jerk!

"Now find a spot on the wall behind me, and focus!"

Tao cried out again as Wang went to work, but then he clenched his teeth and fixed his gaze on the moldering remains of some Japanese military sign posted to the wall.

Wang used the second strip to clean out the wound best as possible, then wrapped the other tightly around Tao's head.

"It hurts! You put a tourniquet around my brain!"

"Probably do you some good," Wang quipped. "Let's get out of this place. Too many spiders!"

It took the better part of five minutes to get the steel door open, which gave Wang time to consider several other questions, mainly focused on the true nature of their captor.

Ghosts don't usually skewer men with swords, drop-kick programmers and lock them up in abandoned armories, best as I know! So, who is he? There's no way he could be an original solider – that would make him close to 90! That man looked in his mid-50s! Impossible!

With a wretched screech, the door opened.

And whoever he is, he has the strength of ten men, if this door is any indication.

Outside was a low-ceilinged hallway, obscured in darkness. As Wang helped his friend through, his head brushed a heavy spider web and he almost screamed.

Which way?

Wang's parents – his father a civil engineer and his mother an airport customs agent - hadn't raised him to be indecisive. And besides, he was the one responsible for getting them into this jam to begin with.

He glanced up and down the corridor, then remembered the smartphone in his pocket. It was gone. So was everything else. Whoever their captor was, he knew enough to empty their pockets. Like so many things in life, it came down to a 50/50 decision: left, or right?

The rough-hewn corridor went on for a bit in both directions, but the one on the right described a bend thirty or so yards down while the one on the left disappeared into darkness.

Right it was, then.

Clasping Tao's hand, he said, "Come on. Let's get the hell out of here."

The corridor went past several vacant chambers, some lit by slit vents high up on the walls. From outside came the mixed scents of ocean brine and vegetation. The tantalizing reminder of the outside world being so close gave him renewed hope. After another ninety-degree turn it went on for twenty yards, then went upwards in a series of debris strewn steps. The amber bars of light suggested they were very close to getting outside.

Yes!

They'd gone about half that distance when Tao stumbled on a pile of rotting sticks and stuck his hand through what appeared to be a wall of stringy moss to steady himself. Instead, his arm shot right through and with a scream, fell into a narrow, concealed alcove.

Wang caught him just in time, yanking him back.

Sweeping the moss aside he saw nothing but a rough, concrete wall.

"It's nothing," he said, peering in. "Come on let's—"

"Look," Tao interrupted, having recovered somewhat. He was pointing to a bunch of rotted slats in the ceiling. To one side was a hanging vine that appeared well-handled.

Without thinking, he tugged at it.

"I bet—"

"—*duck*!"

Wang, whose attention had been drawn to a set of three evenly spaced pencil-sized holes at chest height in the opposite wall, reacted instinctively. Shoving Tao away with both hands, he hit the deck. There was a barely perceptible cough as something whisked overhead. A second later came the clatter of *glacettes* ricocheting off the opposite wall, hard enough to send concrete chips flying.

Tao cried out and staggered backwards, but kept his balance.

Wang didn't move for a moment, focused instead at the needle-sharp projectile that had skittered to a rest near his hand. Its tip was dipped in a purplish-blue substance he figured was some sort of poison.

He got slowly to his feet, brushing dirt and mold off his arms. Glancing about, he spotted a three-foot branch amongst the debris on the floor and snatched it up.

"Stay put," he said. Leaning in carefully, he used the stick to prod at the rotted boards. There was a rustle, then the boards came tumbling down, pushed by something heavier that uncoiled in the small space.

Wang jumped back, brandishing the stick.

It was a climbing rope.

Still not convinced, he thrust the stick up into the opening and batted it around.

Nothing.

Wang and Tao looked at each other. Tao raised his eyebrows. Wang shrugged.

Whatever was up there, it was important enough to set a deadly booby trap for.

Looking up into it he could see there was some sort of low-ceilinged chamber. The rope was secured to a cross bar. He gave it a tentative tug. It held.

"I'm going up."

"Why!?" Tao whispered. "Let's just get out of here! My head's killing me!"

"I know. Give me a few minutes. If something happens, just go!"

Tao's brow furrowed with worry. With blood still seeping out of the makeshift bandage, Wang decided his friend was one sad looking customer. He stepped over and in a rare moment of physical affection, patted his friend's shoulder.

"Don't worry. I'll be right back."

The small chamber must have been some sort of low level gun bunker originally, guarding one of the rear entrances along the ridge that dipped down into the bay. The oblong slot was almost completely overgrown, though here and there he could just make out the remains of a trail – a secret entrance, perhaps?

He was more interested in the room itself, however, which was someone's living quarters. Japanese - at glance - if the woven reed mat bedding and impeccable orderliness of everything was any indicator. The furnishings were crudely, if efficiently fashioned; it's resident clearly some sort of castaway working with salvaged and found materials.

Aside from the bedding, there were a bunch of old munitions chests, several oil lanterns made from steel lighting cages, a crude chair and a desk assembled from random wooden slats. Similarly, there was a hand-built armoire that reached almost to the top of the low ceiling. On the opposite side was a *zazen* meditation bench carved in burnished mahogany, set on another woven mat before a *Shinzen* shrine containing a collection of personal objects and dominated by a water-stained parchment tacked to the wall, displaying several oversized Japanese characters painted with a coarse paintbrush.

In front of it was a mount holding a worn wooden paddle and set behind that, several military-style *katana* swords in simple sheaths. The center holder was empty, suggesting it's occupant was elsewhere. With that brought the memory of Mr. Zhang's gruesome death, making Wang shudder.

Next to the shrine was a collection of several antique military rifles (including one at the top with a scope) mounted on the wall that Wang guessed were Japanese. They appeared to be well oiled and taken care of. On the crate underneath them on a soiled cloth was arranged three pistols, one which was disassembled, its bullets lined up neatly next to it.

Wang let his eyes wander around the space, taking it all in, dozens of questions causing him to unconsciously screw up one side of his face in disbelief.

To all indications, it appeared to be the quarters of a Japanese survivalist, presumably one that was a member of the original forces occupying the island during the Second World War, only -again - that didn't make any sense. Even if the man was a soldier that had been, say, sixteen or seventeen at the time, that would now make him in his late 80s, which didn't reconcile with the man who had quite energetically dispatched his supervisor or had been showing up like an elusive ghost around the complex.

Could their ghost have had a son?

That was certainly more plausible, but how? With who?

Wang's eye settled on a small photograph nestled amongst the items on the shrine. Stepping over carefully, he bent over and peered at it.

And gasped.

Impossible!

THE NUTS AND BOLTS, AS IT WERE

The three archeologists were speechless for a moment.

The sprawling facility before the metal landing they found themselves on looked more like a Hollywood FX studio or modern museum than a working laboratory. A study in grey and brown tones accented by striking cobalt-blue and orange equipment lights, the entire place appeared to have been dreamed up by a Restoration Hardware-obsessed designer with an eye toward ultra-sleek high-tech. Here and there the eye caught glimpses of lacquered brass and satin chrome, the glitter of lasers and dials amongst pools of bright fixtures, while up-lights lent the overhead ductwork and gantries a cavernous feel.

The broad opposite wall was decorated with stylized versions of various dinosaurs executed in different shades of embossed metal, as if an inspirational reminder to staff milling around below. Muted voices of Chinese and English wafted up, accompanied by the methodical dialogue of machinery and computers.

What really drew their attention, however were the dinosaurs.

Mainly hatchlings and infants, though larger specimens in holding cages could be seen through glass windows to the left. For Taylan and his two colleagues, it was difficult to decide what to look at first. Despite all the flash, however, it was hard for him not to feel like a proverbial kid in a candy store. Next to him, Audrey and Roma were equally enthralled – Audrey's eyes were wide and bright with excitement, while Roma had a trace of a smile tugging at the corners of her mouth.

Mr. Luo stole a barely perceptible glance to assess his guests, and was pleased at what he saw. He also sensed Miss Grey studying him, but was discreet enough not to acknowledge her here. Instead, he waited patiently for an acknowledgement.

"I'll be bloody double gobsmacked," Audrey said in a quiet voice.

"Count me 'gobsmacked'," Roma added.

Taylan just grunted.

Mr. Luo waited a minute longer, a barely perceptible smile touching his lips. When no-one said anything further, he gestured toward the stair.

"Shall we?"

The first section they visited was a semi-circular elevated work area where the DNA sequencing was handled. Most of the scientists here were Chinese and southeast Asian, though Taylan noted a few who looked English and one or two who might have been Arabic or Israeli.

With the oversized, HD monitors and uplit workstations, the scientists looked like they were on the bridge of some futuristic starship. A group was clustered around one station, caught up in a heated discussion over a pair of 3-dimensional helix strands rotating on the screen. Mr. Luo indicated they should stay well back.

"Genetic engineering is delicate work," he said quietly. "They're creating a new sequence based on known characteristics of an existing Styracaceous against a newly discovered variant in Mongolia."

Standing next to him, Miss Grey added helpfully: "Here on Kharamu, we not only feature many of the better-known dinosaur species, but have produced the more exotic ones as well."

Mr. Luo flicked his eyes toward her in annoyance.

Roma was studying something on the corner of the screen. "What is the new species you discovered?" she asked.

Mr. Luo drew up a smile. "I'm afraid I can't divulge any specific details at this time. Suffice to say, this is our primary think tank – the 'brains' of the operation as it were – that drives our entire asset generation."

"Is that what you refer to the dinosaurs as . . . *assets*?" Audrey replied. From the measured tone of her delivery, Taylan knew she was getting wound up.

Unfazed, Mr. Luo smiled. "Yes. That is *exactly* what they are. We're not here to assign sentimental value to the creatures that have been created here. That would result in all sorts of complications. The only sentiments we wish to achieve is with our clients, who pay generously for the privilege."

"No doubt," Audrey shot right back, "but it's a little depressing that you've made one of the most significant scientific breakthroughs of the 21st century and are treating it like a new line of Louis Vuitton handbags available only to the very elite. They're living creatures, for bloody sake, they deserve a little more respect than that!"

Mr. Luo's smile compressed into a thin line. "May I remind you, Miss Adams, you've been brought here by one of our guests to evaluate the validity of our assets, not present us your private opinions of how we treat them. This is an elite vacation paradise, not the SPCA International."

Audrey's right eyebrow shot up but before she could respond, Roma interjected: "Fair enough, Mr. Luo. But you haven't really given us anything concrete to evaluate thus far and unless you present us with something other than what *Doctor* Taylan would no doubt refer to as a 'dog-and-pony' show at a distance, we won't have much to report to your client. At least not *favorably*."

Touché, Taylan thought. *She just managed to eloquently slap him in the face.*

The smile was instantly back on Mr. Luo's face.

"But of course, Doctor Banaji!" he replied, with just the slightest inclination of his head. "Normally we would show you the incubation stations next, but since you seem interested in something a little more tactile, why don't we go to the hatchlings chamber." He glanced toward the glass windows off to their left and an expression approaching relief appeared on his face. "Ah! I see our Science Group Director, Roger Burroughs, is in there now. He's quite good with particulars and can answer many of your questions."

Taylan snorted. "Roger Burroughs? As in the rogue geneticist who was expelled from Oxford?"

Mr. Luo paused. "I'm not concerned with Mr. Burroughs' past issues with that esteemed academic establishment. What I *can* tell you, is that he has a stellar track record with MuTron International and it has been his 'rogue' approach that has led to the incredible breakthroughs we've made here."

"At what cost?" Audrey interjected.

This time it was Mr. Luo who raised his brow. "There is always a 'cost', Dr. Adams, that accompanies every great scientific breakthrough. Look at Curie, Einstein, Oppenheimer."

Taylan couldn't resist a little jibe, "But one could argue they weren't playing God with extinct life-forms."

"No, but they wound up playing God with human lives, no?"

Taylan didn't respond. He was already working his way down to a few conclusions, the first being that their host was getting rattled and that their tour was already on much more confrontational ground than it was no doubt intended. The whole presentation felt edgy and forced. The second was the dog-and-pony show they were being given, which already didn't add up in his mind.

He realized Audrey was studying him out of the corner of her eye. He couldn't quite read the look, but it wasn't a convinced one.

"Well," she said to Mr. Luo, "shall we have a look at what your rogue geneticist God has been up to?"

That got another brittle smile in return.

"Miss Grey, can you lead the way?"

The Hatchlings Chamber was easily fifteen degrees warmer than the main lab. Near the double set of doors that acted as an environmental airlock was a series of circular hatching tables with overhead heat lamps. Automated robotic arms with padded calipers were rotating the dinosaur eggs at regular intervals. Further down were a series of various-sized holding pens while the far end had examining tables and industrial-looking cabinets with medical supplies.

As they entered, Taylan noted with some disappointment that none of the eggs appeared to be near hatching, but the groups' attention was distracted by four lab-assistants in lab coats manhandling a brightly feathered raptor onto a stainless-steel examination table.

It appeared to be a *Zhenyuanlong*, a species of dromaeosaurid dinosaur from the early Cretaceous period. With its striking iridescent blue, green and teal plumage, it resembled more of a homicidal macaw with a lizard-like mouth rimmed with sharp teeth instead of a beak. About the size of a condor, it also sported white feathers around its neck and chest, while its tail had a fan of yellow and rusty brown feathers. There was a hint of bright green and blue on its crest, while the delicate fan of feathers ridging its lower legs gave way to the pronounced, deadly sickle toe on each foot. The golden-hued eyes were half closed from the sedatives it had been given, though it still gave out an agitated, trilling call intermittently.

The three anthropologists were all but ready to bolt over and see the creature up close, but just then a man appeared, blocking their path.

"Ah, Dr. Roger Burroughs!" Mr. Luo announced.

Audrey Adams, who was in front, nearly ran in to him. When she caught the penetrating – seemingly lifeless – hooded eyes of Roger Burroughs boring into her own, she couldn't help but shrink back. Even Taylan felt his hackles go up. Crossing paths with Burroughs was like coming up against an efficiently built cyborg.

If eyes are the windows of the soul, Taylan mused, *then this man has had his completely extinguished.*

Next to him he sensed Roma stiffen as well.

A smile appeared on Burroughs' chiseled features with an eerie suddenness, as if the brain behind it was compensating after an inappropriate lag.

"Ah, the esteemed archeologists have arrived!" he said, in a measured – and to Taylan - suspiciously pleasant voice. The voice of an impeccably mannered gentleman; one who was about to run you through with the family sword he was just showing off.

"Come to see *real* dinosaurs?" he added.

"Yes," Taylan said, stepping up alongside Audrey. "We're naturally quite curious how you achieved this."

Burroughs put his hands in the pockets of his lab coat and let out a professorial '*hmpf*'. The impenetrable blue eyes gazed momentarily into the distance.

Then he indicated a windowed door to their left.

"Please," he said. When he noticed them hesitating he added, "Don't worry, you'll have plenty of time to see the *Zhenyuanlong* up close shortly. They have to draw blood and insert the tracking tag. But first I have a remarkable story to tell you."

In contrast to the orderly appearance of the man, Burroughs' office looked like a tornado had just struck.

Stacks of printouts were everywhere, scattered amongst various scale models of dinosaurs, bones, and dioramas. File cabinets were overflowing, shelves were overstuffed with papers, and to one side was an oversized smart board crowded with calculations that Burroughs hastily stepped over to and snatching up a remote, flicked off.

With another remote he activated a widescreen monitor opposite his desk. A splash screen appeared, with a 3D version of the MuTron International logo on it. Burroughs clicked through a few screens until he came to one with a common-looking version of a chicken on it, with call-out insets on its legs, arms, beak and tail.

"The first steps," he explained, "involved working with a chicken, much as the legendary Jack Horner proposed in his paper, *How to Build a Dinosaur*. We at least now know birds were descended from at least one kind of dinosaur – the velociraptors. We tinkered with hindering the IHH, or 'Indian Hedgehog' gene in chicken embryos, to alter the development of things like the beak, wings, tails and of course legs. The tails were the trickiest, as they were the most altered part of the anatomy after so many millions of years."

The next slide had an animation of the chicken slowly morphing into a horrifying, Frankenstein version of one.

"It took a good two years to finally arrive at our first 'dino-chicken'. Bit of a hideous-looking thing, wouldn't you say?"

"*Crikey!*" Audrey said.

He flicked the remote again and now a silhouetted version of a velociraptor appeared, doing a turntable rotation in space. "A remarkable breakthrough, no doubt, but not unpredicted. But our objective wasn't just to re-create a single species of dinosaurs, but a whole variety of them. No small task, I'm sure you'll agree. And I'm sure we wouldn't have been able to at all, if it hadn't been for two fortuitous events, one in science and the other in archeology. With the former, I refer to the invention of the Hayton-Kress lattice light-sheet microscope, and the latter, the discovery of partially intact DNA in the medullary bone of a pregnant Tyrannosaurus Rex in a remote part of Northern Canada."

Burroughs waited a moment, head half-cocked toward his guests, to let the enormity of what he had just said sink in.

The three archeologists were speechless. It was Roma who spoke first.

"I've never heard of a Hayton-Kress lattice light-sheet microscope, but what exactly do you mean 'partially intact DNA' from a pregnant Tyrannosaurus Rex? The last I heard there's never been any DNA older than a few hundred thousand years. But 65 Million? Seriously?"

Burroughs looked amused. "Yes, seriously. That's where the Hayton-Kress microscope comes into play."

Taylan cut in, "Ah, you're saying you have a functioning Hayton-Kress microscope? I thought that was only theoretical."

That got a soft chuckle from Burroughs.

"We're well past the realm of the theoretical here, if you haven't noticed, Dr. Taylan."

"I'd say you're well past the realm of a lot of things," Taylan shot back. "But how on earth did you come by a working Hayton-Kress microscope?"

"Just what is this microscope?" Roma interjected.

"One of the most remarkable inventions of the 21st century," Burroughs replied, his brow rising just slightly. He jabbed at the remote and a new slide appeared, this one showing an ungainly unit that was closer to a CRT scanner than any conventional microscope. Near to it was a TV-sized curved screen monitor with a sleek keyboard and mouse.

"It's still years away from the marketplace, but we have an operational prototype that has performed far better than expected."

He turned to Roma. "It's similar to an electron microscope, except it has nearly double the resolution and more importantly, it generates 3D point-cloud data. It was originally designed to view living organic data in real-time, but we found an even better use for it: we discovered it was capable of detecting the latticework of DNA structures in fossilized cells – and with an additional proprietary software module we developed for it – reconstructing the decayed or missing pieces with an incredible degree of accuracy."

"That sounds . . . quite remarkable," Roma said. She looked equally impressed and skeptical. "How exactly do you reconstruct 'missing pieces'?"

"We found the resolution revealed incredible details in key specimens." Burroughs clicked the remote again and a spectacular animation of a partial DNA double helix, followed by a series of highlighted call-outs 'retrieving' missing parts of the nucleotides from other strands, resulting in a 'finished' strand. Burroughs let out a gentle chuckle. "Not quite as simple as it looks I'm afraid, which I'm sure you'll understand was created with considerable artistic license. In reality, it was over a year of trial and error, countless setbacks and mistakes, before we refined the process and began getting usable results."

"So, you managed to recreate DNA strands of a T-Rex from the Cretaceous Period? And nobody knows about this?" Taylan was having a tough time with this, it simply didn't add up. Or did it?

"Oh, we did much better than that," Burroughs purred. "We applied it to other species as well. You see, while the line of raptors and the T-Rex were descended from birds – not the other way around - the other species of dinosaurs are from a completely different branch all together. It was exhausting work – combing through remains of eggs, finding tantalizing fragments here and there, but eventually a comprehensive database resolved itself; a gnome map of the dinosaur world, as it were. In 3D, thanks to Hayton-Kress."

The last animation on the screen went from a single, feathered raptor, to 26 distinct species of dinosaurs.

"You've created *26 distinct species of dinosaurs?*" Audrey asked, incredulous.

Burroughs glanced over at Mr. Luo, who nodded. "More than that, actually. That animation is months old. And we took liberties where necessary."

"*More* than that?" Roma chimed in. "And none of this has been released to the scientific world? I find that hard to believe. The value of the IP must be in the tens of billions."

Mr. Luo spoke up, "Eventually, we will reveal our efforts to the rest of the world. But we must proceed cautiously. Once the cat is out of the bag, as they say, it will become very difficult to control."

"Why not just cash out now?" Taylan asked. "Sell the entire operation to the highest bidder. You'd be set for life."

"Ah, the American way - always thinks of money, first," Mr. Luo said. "But yes, eventually we would sell off the technology. But right now, we have excellent earning potential with a very discriminating – and highly lucrative – client base. Which again (I must remind you) is the purpose of your visit. All the wildest claims are only so much paper tigers unless we get the endorsement of qualified archeologists such as yourself."

"Well, we'd really have to go over your white papers before commenting on the validity of your research. And so far, we haven't examined any of your specimens directly. Computer animations only go so far, yes?"

Taylan noticed something else as well. Burroughs was gazing at Mr. Luo with a look utterly devoid of expression, as if he were clinically contemplating any number of ways he might put the CEO on the dissecting table.

Not completely devoid of emotion, he realized, there was a brief flair of anger in the eyes, just before Burroughs looked away and quietly turned off the display screen. He noticed Miss Grey had caught it too. For a moment, she looked panicked.

The congenial smile was back on Burroughs' face, however, as he addressed the archeologists. "Yes, well, you haven't seen one of our specimens up close. I believe it's time to remedy that! If you'll follow me?"

The *Zhenyuanlong* was still on the examination table, its golden eye half-lidded with sedation, its body rising and falling in shallow breaths. One assistant had just drawn blood and was dropping the syringe into a sealable plastic bag as they came out.

It was Audrey who ran up to the table first, causing the assistants to defensively put themselves between her and the table, until Mr. Luo waved them off and gave them an affirmative nod.

Two of them – both wearing gloves and masks - remained holding the raptor secure by the head and legs. The table was equipped with straps, though they hung to the sides.

Audrey pulled up short, hands raised, like a kid getting ready to touch their first present on Christmas morning. Across the table, a Chinese female assistant produced a pair of latex gloves and dangled them in front of Audrey's eyes.

"Oh yes, of course!" she said, putting them on. "May I?" she asked the man to her right, then without waiting for an answer, ran her hand over the bristly feathers of the thing's flank, closing her eyes as if in ecstasy.

"*Wow*," was all she could say. The feathers trailing the creature's leg were fine – delicate, actually, though firm to the touch. The bottom of the legs was scaly, the inner toe ending in the classic sickle-shaped claw, while the iridescent outer feathers of the arms and tail were more dazzling than any bird's she had ever seen. Around the neck the brace of white feathers was almost downy, while the bright blue-tinged crest was as sporty as any punk's moussed-up haircut. The head of the thing was its most sobering feature, with its reptilian snout and needle-like row of teeth jutting out under the delicate upper lip.

"I never believed I would ever touch a living, breathing raptor before. Utterly incredible!"

It felt like touching a bird, and it *didn't*. Despite their fine appearance, the feathers weren't really soft in any way, but almost hard. And oily. It was like touching an utterly alien being – or the embodiment of a mythical, exotic Chinese creature, which, she supposed, wasn't that far off. The vicious appearance of the head only enhanced the effect. She noted the musculature of the leg and upper arms, the way its clawed fingers twitched with her touch.

"How old is this one?" she asked, half turning back to Burroughs.

"Young adult," he replied. "They mature quite rapidly."

Roma had found a pair of gloves and had come around to the other side of the table, bending to examine the face. Her expression was equally amazed.

"Incredible," she said, lightly touching the area around its snout. "The eye – of course it would be a raptor's eye. And look at the scales here . . . flat, like a crocodile. They must be extremely sensitive."

Only Taylan didn't seem inclined to touch the thing. His brow was furrowed in thought. Something was troubling about the whole set up to him, including Burroughs' song-and-dance presentation.

For that reason, he had no desire to touch the thing at all. Something in the creature's behavior wasn't quite right. In fact, it reminded him of a time while examining a . . .

"Audrey?" he said, putting his hand on her shoulder and drawing her back. "I don't think you should—"

There was a scream and thump as with no warning, the *Zhenyuanlong* twisted and leapt up with the speed of a striking snake. Just as quickly its jaws snapped on Roma's hand. There wasn't time to register the crunch of bones before the thing darted right and scrabbled up and over the assistant who had been holding it down earlier.

The result was instantly catastrophic.

The raptor's claws tore the man's upper chest, neck and face to ribbons; blood flew, a shredded eyeball was ripped out, whole divots of flesh disappeared. He didn't even have time to react. There was a grunt and a feeble grab as he instinctively attempted to stop the creature, then it was already gone, leaping onto the stainless-steel counter behind him.

He staggered a couple of steps, then collapsed.

One of the assistants turned and fled, three of them tried to corner the thing, which landed with a bone-jarring *thud* as its legs gave out on the slippery surface, sending it caroming into the tiled backsplash.

"Oh," Roma said, looking at her mangled hand in shock, as if it belonged to someone else.

Taylan patted himself for something to subdue the thing with, then remembered all his gear (including the pistol, Bowie knife and machete) was back at the hotel where they'd unloaded. At the time, it hadn't seemed wise to show up at the facility fully armed.

Audrey ducked down and grabbed one of the loose securing straps, which were made of heavy-duty nylon. Taylan grabbed the nearest thing, which turned out to be a shallow stainless-steel pan.

None too soon, the raptor scrabbled to its feet and let out a wet hiss that made Taylan think of a small Komodo dragon. Its head and neck feathers stood on end in a fear/attack response. One of the assistants already had a syringe in one hand – a sedative presumably – while the other two attempted to confuse the thing by waving their hands and shouting.

No one paid attention as Mr. Luo and Miss Grey discreetly (but quickly) made for the safety of Burroughs' office while Burroughs himself stepped gingerly over to the side of one of the lab tables.

The raptor let out another hiss and catapulted off the counter, this time landing just between two of the assistants and bolting past them, too quick to follow. Seeing it was bee-lining toward Roma (who was still staring at her hand – which was freely dripping blood – in shock), Taylan jumped to intervene.

He did the only thing he could: he whacked the thing upside the head with the steel pan.

The result was nearly comical.

The raptor came to a screeching halt and shook its head vigorously, blinking, in a close approximation of a Warner Brothers cartoon. Taylan clocked it again, but it was only a glancing blow. The creature drew back its head much faster than he would have believed possible and countered by snatching the tray in its jaws a moment later, wrenching it out of his grip with a violent twist of its neck. It shook it back and forth several times before spitting it out, sending the pan clattering across the tiled floor.

Then it crouched down on its haunches and hissed, teeth bared and winged arms fanning out.

Taylan went into a boxer's stance, spotting one of the assistants creeping up from behind, the kind of tensile net used to subdue wild game in his hands. Taylan couldn't deny a certain irony in the situation he found himself in: a paleontologist finally meets the living example of something he'd only seen fossilized remains of his entire life, and all he wanted to do was knock the thing's damn brains out.

He was also simultaneously determined and terrified – there was something undeniable about it that triggered the most basic atavistic fear: man vs. deadly predator. And he'd just witnessed what it'd done to another human being in a few short seconds.

The thing prepared to leap at him. Taylan's eyes widened, the knuckles on his fist going white.

Before the thing could launch itself, however, there was a loud *crack* right near its head, causing it to jump sideways.

Standing with the examining table between her and the *Zhenyuanlong,* Audrey had the nylon strap wrapped around her hand, with a good five feet of it trailing like a lion-tamer's whip.

Hissing, the creature whipped around to face this new threat.

Undaunted, Audrey gave the strap a second shake, then cracked it again. The raptor snapped at it, then leapt up onto the table, winged arms and tail flaring like an angry rooster. The effect was even more terrifying with the blood and gore staining its teeth and feathers.

Behind it, two assistants pounced, throwing the net over it.

Almost.

He brought it down over most of the thing's body – but missed the head. The raptor twisted – again with fantastically fast reflexes – it's sickle claw punching through the netting and opening the one assistant's chest to the bone, slicing through coat and shirt in an instant.

Audrey grabbed the loose end of the strap with her free hand and was about to wrap it around the raptor's neck to subdue it when there was a whistle and thunk in the air before her.

The creature's head flew off and rolled, the machete in Burroughs' hand clanging off the table top with the finality of an executioner's bell.

A stunned silence followed, broken only by the choking gurgle of the injured assistant on the floor and the slump of the other one wounded in the chest sliding down to his knees. The headless raptor spasmed on the examination table, one leg tapping feebly at the stainless-steel before going still. The coppery smell of blood momentarily filled the room.

Taylan ran over to Roma, who was still clutching her dripping hand, shaking uncontrollably.

"Hold still," he said. "Let me look."

The palm and fingers were perforated in several places, but nothing appeared broken. The raptor's bite probably wasn't as powerful as many people assumed, though the damage was bad enough. More concerning to him was the risk of infection, not to mention whatever enzymes or pathogens the thing's bite carried. It wasn't exactly the neighborhood dog.

He snatched a bunch of paper towels off a dispenser above the counter and wrapped it judiciously.

"How bad is it?" Roma asked in a trembling voice.

"You'll live," Taylan responded dryly. "But you're going to need stiches. And antibiotics. This'll be a good one to tell the grandchildren someday."

"Bloody hell," Audrey said nearby, stooping to tend to the assistant wounded in the chest. "Lie still," she ordered, forcing the man to stay on his back. The wound was deep and ragged. She hoped they had a competent hospital facility. The man would require surgery, not to mention quite a few stitches.

Burroughs dropped the machete with a clang as Mr. Luo and Miss Grey emerged from his office.

"Are you mad? Do I have to remind you what those things cost!?" Mr. Luo said, straightening the lapels on his jacket and looking like he'd been forced to step back into a particularly unpleasant stockholders meeting.

"May I remind you we have plenty more?" Burroughs replied, unfazed. He turned to the female lab assistant, ignoring all the staff outside the windows who had stopped working and were staring. "Call the EMT unit," he said. When she nodded but stood there, obviously in shock, he prompted: "*Quickly.*"

Another of the assistants shooed Audrey aside and used his lab coat as a makeshift compress to his colleague's chest. Audrey joined Taylan at Roma's side, taking her arm and bending it so her hand was up by her shoulder. "Keep it elevated. Above your heart. And we need to keep pressure on it." She put both her hands on the wrapping. Blood spots blossomed out in several places.

She turned to Burroughs, glaring. "What the bloody hell!? Don't you have any idea how to properly sedate these creatures!?"

"It was," Burroughs bristled. Just slightly. The slight testiness to his voice suggested he didn't care much for being questioned by women. "I assure you, all the protocols are rigorously followed."

"You might just want to rethink those a little," Taylan said, eyeing the carnage. The EMT unit had arrived and were coming in through the airlock doors.

"This is unacceptable!" Mr. Luo shouted, at no one in particular. Miss Grey was keeping well back, eyeing the corpse of the raptor as if it might yet come back to life and attack her.

Burroughs seemed unaffected by the bloodbath and violence that had just occurred around him. "We'll have to revisit the sedative dosage again. That shouldn't have happened."

Taylan was shocked by the man's indifference. He nodded toward the dead assistant being loaded onto the stretcher. "That would get this entire operation shut down in America," he said, offhandedly.

"It's a good thing we're in China then, isn't it?" Burroughs replied.

"...A WRETECHED SOUL, BRUISED WITH ADVERSITY."

Half an hour later, Roger Burroughs stood in his office, alone.

"I'm better than you, aren't I?" he said to the empty room.

He'd listened to Luo Pan Wei's vicious reprimand with measured calm, contemplating several times through the CEO's rants if he should just simply kill him if only to put an end to his ceaseless jabbering. He'd never been particularly fond of the Chinese – or any Asians for that matter – but the opportunity at MuTron had been simply too timely to pass up.

The man was an officious little slant-eyed prick, he thought, w*ho believes money and appearances are a kind of God-like armor that elevates him into a superior plane of existence! And he thinks he can talk to me like some misbehaving, mewling little schoolboy? He has no idea how he was just a ghostly whisper away from death just now!*

Burroughs' fist was still clenched around the capped syringe he kept in his lab coat pocket, the one filled with pure *pumiliotoxin 251D* from the Columbian poison dart frog, *Phyllobates terribilis*. It was his secret last-ditch defense in case he ever faced a situation like the one earlier.

During the CEO's little tirade, however, he'd kept his thumb on the cap, idly musing how enjoyable it would be to plunge the needle through the man's jugular, savor the surprise, then the fleeting expression of horror as poison raced through his system, shutting down everything with merciless ease within minutes – too swift to take any countermeasures, but slow enough for him to register what was happening.

It would have been delightful, but cheating himself out of his bigger mission.

Burroughs chuckled softly to himself as he paused by his desk, near the drawer with the framed photo that had lain face-down in it for three months now. As he neared the desk, his lips dropped down into a frown and his eyes focused on a point far beyond the confines of the room.

"Yes, I'm so much better than you," he repeated softly, not to the person whose face was in the photo on the drawer, nor Mr. Luo or any of the staff of MuTron but to the person who had been moldering in his grave for decades.

His father.

Ian Patrick Burroughs had been a design engineer with British Rail in Birmingham, making his name with several innovative patents during the recovery years after World War II. As much a relentless perfectionist as he was an innovator, he also excelled at what his eldest son thought of (but never spoke aloud) as "Jekyll & Hyde" syndrome: utterly charming and gracious in public, at home he was diabolically strict and prone to violent outbursts. Occasionally directed at his wife, Evelyn, but as he grew older, increasingly at his eldest son. Roger and his brother Tom might be sent to bed without supper for such a minor infraction as using the wrong fork at dinner, or find themselves at the wrong end of a leather belt for simply entering the sanctity of their father's workshop in the basement of their modest suburban house.

Even more damaging was the relentless psychological beatings. In the Burroughs' household, nothing was ever good enough, perfect enough, worked hard enough at. In this, Roger's mother was equally complicit. When the elder Burroughs dropped dead of a heart attack (riding home from work on one of his beloved trains, ironically), she stepped up to the role of lead critic and disciplinarian. Almost immediately the ghost of Ian Burroughs became lionized to the level of an almighty God, an unreachable gold standard by which young Roger would be measured against at every opportunity.

Tut-tut! Your father would be disappointed! Your father would have done that so much better! Tsk! Perhaps someday, you might do something half as accomplished! And of course, the classic: *"If your father was here . . ."*

If Roger brought home an excellent grade on a science project, it would be dismissed as something his father would have already done at a much younger age. If it was a trophy for a track meet, it was scoffed at as something his father had several of.

So early on in his teenage years, Roger Burroughs – who had never a particularly strong reservoir of empathy or emotions – developed an armor around himself, an iron-shod façade that masked the thin ghost of humanity in his heart, effectively suffocating it.

Life went on. Burroughs went to college, excelled at his studies, married a young, suitable woman who bore him a suitable son. He became an excellent, if somewhat unspirited, pianist. Graduating top of his class, he went on to earn an advanced degree in genetics, a burgeoning field in the 1980s where he saw enormous potential, and opportunity.

He also discovered he had an aptitude for taking risks, partially from his father's inventive streak, but also because of his complete lack of fear. He and Grant Taylan shared that in common, if for different reasons. However, Burroughs lacked one thing the Paleontologist didn't: an internal moral compass. Whether it was cheating, stealing someone else's ideas or plans, or throwing someone under the bus to further his way up the ladder, Roger Burroughs did it with no hesitation whatsoever.

His pioneering, if unorthodox, inroads into the field of genetic recombination that drew him back into the attention of his Alma Mater, Oxford, and a coveted tenure. For a time, it appeared his life was following an enviable arc of academic success.

Then it all unraveled.

It was his utter disregard for university protocols that created the first cracks in this perfect picture. Vicious interdepartmental jealousies and rivalries seeped in, creating more fissures. There were several incidents, including an accident at the lab where one of his students came in contact with a deadly retrovirus generated by one of the genetic re-combination tests. That and another student died within minutes. The inquiry revealed even worse things: Burroughs had circumvented several safety protocols, and there were mounting suspicions several of his more spectacular claims had been fudged. Burroughs stellar career began to spoil under a cloud of suspicion.

On the home front things were coming apart as well.

His wife, Olivia, had exhibited signs of severe mental disorder. Always an obsessive-compulsive, she had displayed even more aberrant behavior, like getting up at two in the morning to layout dinner settings for a party still two days away, filling the shelves of their library with unlimited tchotchke's (always Victorian-themed houses and figurines) and locking herself in her sewing room for days, talking politics with her collection of porcelain dolls.

Their son, Caleb – entering his middle teens at the time - got into all sorts of trouble as well.

Bright, intelligent, preternaturally good-looking (taking his mother's side) with the type of reckless, windswept hair and attitude only certain privileged English boys seemed to possess, he was the proverbial apple of his father's eye.

For all his rebelliousness and contradictions, Burroughs was convinced he had taken all the necessary steps to ensure his son would eventually step up and fulfill his shoes; his protégé, his successor.

Until the night the message appeared on his personal, encrypted smart phone. Three months previous.

It was from one of his few remaining friends back in England, Anne Hutchins, an old neighbor from the house in West Bromwich:

Roger – attempted to leave several messages on the phone # I have, but to no avail. Terribly sorry to tell you this, but the police stopped by today regarding Caleb. Please phone the Metropolitan Police Department as soon as possible. The number is:"

It was just as bad as he imagined.

Caleb had been found dead in his apartment in Birmingham, sitting in front of the television set, after administering a generous amount of heroin to himself. Based on the levels, the coroner was positive it was an intentional overdose.

A wretched soul, bruised with adversity, he'd thought at the time, thinking Shakespeare somehow apropos of how he thought of his son.

And in no small way, of himself as well: a tragic character.

Burroughs told no one of this at MuTron, nor did he return or make any arrangements for a funeral. His son had opted to abandon him, let whatever should happen to his corpse happen. What little essence of humanity – and arguably his sanity – that remained in him, it died that day. That was also the day Burroughs struck on a new plan for the dinosaurs he was developing on Kharamu, one that would have been at distinct odds from the corporate mission statement.

This new direction would involve elevating their full potential and unleashing it on humanity. Or at least the entire population of the island.

They were in for a very, *very* big surprise.

A while later, he stood by one of the holding cages, staring at the security code override box that controlled all the locks. It could be set to operate on a timer in the event the facility was abandoned, and they wanted to free the animals.

"Well, that's it then," he said, a ghost of a smile gracing his lips as he set the timers on all the cages of the new species. "Let's see what you can really do, all right?" he added in a gentle, fatherly voice.

"THIS ISN'T HAPPENING!"

"Bello, I'm going to—" Farnsworth began again, when the transmission was cut off. Bello glanced about wildly. The Brontosaurs were mounting what was now turning into a full charge. Or their version of it. It was more like a wall of buildings that had grown legs and was coming at you.

Behind them the Tyrannosaurs had been joined by several other, smaller theropods. Ones that Bello had never seen before.

The three archeologists would have recognized them – they were *Deltadromeus*, a mid-sized T. rex with slender legs and fully articulated arms. Sporting an aggressive array of upright spines along its back and drastic body stripes, they simply *looked* dangerous.

And as their name implied, which meant "Delta Runner", they were *fast*.

What in the hell!?

He fumbled with his earpiece, but there was nothing but static.

Like it or not, he was on his own for the moment. He calculated distances. If they could get the Jeep and at least one of the Land Rovers all the way to the safe zone on the other side, they could leave the other one to go for help. They were already about two-thirds of the way across, so it made sense for the bulk of the party to keep going. Although the vehicles were equipped with their own built-in safety devices, he had a feeling they didn't want to test their reliability against the 60-ton sauropods bearing down on them.

"Evans!" he shouted toward the Land Rover. "Get the guests across now! Help me get the Jeep and Rover across. Then take half the porters back and hold tight 'til the way is clear!!"

Despite the brevity of the situation, both the Blodgetts and the Banyons looked put out, and it wasn't until Bello did his two-finger whistle – one that didn't offer any argument, that they began to grudgingly get moving. Except for Mrs. Banyon – when she stood looking down at the mud like she was being asked to step into raw sewage, one porter unceremoniously whisked her up and simply carried her across. They were only beaten by Jeff Doyle, who, without any prompting, tore past them and up to the safety of the tree line ahead of everyone else.

Peyton jumped in like he was having the time of his life.

With the extra muscle, they were able to manhandle the Jeep up onto dryer ground, where Bello gunned it up into the tree line, before running back and directing the crew on the first Land Rover.

"Mr. Peyton, your help is much appreciated, but I must insist you guide your party to safety and let us handle this," Bello said.

"Nonsense!" Peyton said, wiping his forehead and shoving his hat back on his head. "I'm not paying to—"

Bello's hand clamped him on the shoulder, cutting him off. This was a different Bello than Peyton had seen before – one hard as iron. "This isn't a discussion, Mr. Peyton," he said, in a no-nonsense voice. "I'll cover you, but you need to get out of the way. *Now*."

Peyton took a second look at the oncoming dinosaurs and decided he'd done enough heroics for the moment. "Sure, Bembo . . . sure. I'll give you fellas some . . . backing cover. Come on everyone! You heard the man – get some pep in your step!"

The ground shook and the closing Brontosaurs trumpeted. Bello estimated they had only three or four minutes before the herd was on them.

"Move it!" he hollered.

Three more porters joined him to put their backs into moving the Land Rover, while Bello steered with his left hand through the open door, using his right hand to gun the gas pedal. After a precious minute, the vehicle began to lurch forward. They'd made it half a dozen yards when Bello heard shouting followed by the *crack* of a rifle shot. Raising his head, he saw something alarming – several of the *Deltadromeus* had abandoned chasing the Brontosaurs and were making a bee-line straight at them.

Several more gun-shots followed.

Even worse, Bello saw that Evans - either out of panic or confusion – was working with the remaining porters attempting to get the second Land Rover to their side, instead of back to safety.

"Back!" he shouted against the din of gunfire, but it was fruitless.

There was an exceptionally loud bang, followed by two others – Peyton's Weatherby – and the lead *Deltadromeus'* lower jaw shattered in a spray of teeth and blood, then came the clatter of the Thompson submachine gun, which stitched the theropod along the leg and tail.

And missed the one behind it.

Bello had been in one or two bad scrapes in his safari days, including one close call with an ill-tempered lion, but those had been a cakewalk compared to this.

The jaws were a deadly maw crammed with pointed teeth. He even noted the pale pink lining and thick tongue, the heavier scales forming its lips and its bright, golden-yellow eye. The sight of the monstrosity bounding at him made his bladder feel hot and squishy.

He had time to think: *God that thing is fast*, and then it was upon him.

Using the hood of the Jeep to steady his aim, Peyton was so excited he *pulled* the trigger instead of *squeezing* it, causing the first shot to go high and wide. The rifle felt like a mule kicking him in the shoulder, but his wind was up. Working the bolt, he chambered another round and this time, remembered to hold his breath and lead a little . . . *bang!* The rifle bucked again, this time rewarding him with a satisfying splatter of gore as the running theropod – scarcely sixty yards away as it charged Bello and the first Land Rover – took a direct hit in its jaw.

Behind him, Blodgett squeezed off a few ineffectual rounds with his carbine, mainly due to the fact he'd only fired it on the range and never out in the field, let alone at a moving target. Next to Blodgett, Charles Banyon was fumbling with the Thompson, his hands panicked and trembling as the events unfolded with uncanny speed. Like the others, he'd been focused on the charging Brontosaurs and the Tyrannosaurs pursuing them, not really processing that the smaller *Deltadromeus* had charged ahead after easier pickings – them.

When Blodgett knocked his hand aside with an annoyed, "Here, give me that!" and grabbed the machinegun out of his hands, he didn't even resist.

Blodgett was irked at seeing Peyton get off the successful shot and his inability with the M-1 Carbine.

What the hell is Banyon's problem!? he thought, distracted by the fumbling next to him. Then he smiled.

The Thompson felt heavy and powerful in his hands, 11 pounds of deadly purpose waiting to do its job. He realized he was grinning as he worked the slide, an honest-to-God erection rising in his pants as he held it at his hip, gangster-style, and let her rip.

I bet Suzie is watching me now! She'll be begging for a taste of 'Little Rog' afterwards too!

The bullets spraying across the stream bed before him – just missing Bello and finishing the *Deltadromeus* that Peyton had already shot.

"Harrr!" Blodgett shouted, showing his teeth and feeling like a kid again, back when he and his friends used to play Sgt. Rock and Easy Company in the field behind the house in North Carolina.

Only this time, it was for real!

He paused, raised the gun slightly, and stepping forward to get a clearer shot, took aim toward the next theropod coming in. Not bothering to check the ground, his foot went partially into a spongy spot of the soil.

He lurched forward, his overweight (and uncoordinated) body twisting, reflexively pulling the trigger as he did.

Twenty yards off to his right, Jeff Doyle was kneeling by one of the outermost trees, the Springfield 30-06 rifle at his shoulder. He had just put two rounds in the *Deltadromeus* that was past the other two, that was racing toward the second Rover with the porters trying to muscle it forward.

Damn idiots! he thought, hearing Peyton and Blodgett behind him. He wasn't a hundred percent sure how effect the fail-safe measures with the dinosaurs were, which was why he had elected to post himself near a tree he recognized he could climb quickly if he had to.

For all of his recklessness, he was arguably the best qualified to handle firearms: as a teenager Doyle had been heavily involved in competition target shooting. Also, he didn't trust Blodgett and Banyon, which was why he had picked a spot a few yards back of their position.

It was a terrifying situation by any measure. The charging theropods were bad enough, but he certainly didn't want to be in the path of the charging

Brontosaurs. They made the biggest elephant he'd ever seen look *puny*. They were charging down the corridor, long necks extended forward, stiffened tails straight back, flattening everything in their path.

The primordialness of the scene wasn't lost on him, yet Jeff Doyle was not a man overburdened by imagination, sentiment or second-guessing. The rifle in his hands had triggered a side of him he hadn't felt in years: a surety of purpose.

One of those purposes at the moment was to kill, something he could be quite good at.

Still, the attacking theropods presented all sorts of logistical problems, including the way, he realized, they ran somewhat like pheasant: not in a straight line.

It's almost like they know they're being tracked, he thought, but that's impossible. He recalled hearing the things only had a brain the size of a pea.

He took careful aim and shot the far theropod through the eye, sending it tumbling to the ground in a hissing screech.

Good thing I insisted on the Leupold Scope. Damn thing is amazing.

He scanned the remaining *Deltadromeus*, and choosing the third one closing in on Joseph Bello, took aim.

That was when he became aware of the whickering sound of bullets chopping away the tops of the low bushes immediately to his left.

What the—?

"Bello, I'm going to—"

Farnsworth was cut off as the COMM link went dead.

"What the fuck just happened! You can you tell me exactly what the fuck just happened!?" he yelled at the assistant whose shoulder he was leaning over. He turned to her partner, a young Chinese woman from Bejing University, who shook her head, wide-eyed, even as she tapped furiously at the keyboard.

Farnsworth stood up straight, and addressed the entire control room, which was more like a small-sized television production studio, very similar in decor to the lab facilities with its dark walls and ceiling, bright ultra HD monitors and architectural table lamps and seating. Unlike the lab, though, the staff here was only six people, not including Farnsworth, and while they had run through all sorts of simulations and training in the past, they'd never suffered a complete audio communications cut.

There were two rows of workstations, but Farnsworth was looking at the huge composite screen on the main wall. Its resolution and high-dynamic range was so sharp it was like looking out a window into the real world, instead of on a cave wall fifty-feet under rock and concrete. It was set up so the central real estate was taken up by the primary camera, while to both sides secondary feeds – there were thirty in all total – were organized to give a supporting narration to what was happening in the field.

Farnsworth gestured at the big screen.

How did things go wrong so fast!? It was a simple crossing! It was supposed to be a minor tension point in the narrative! What the hell were those Theropods doing there? They were still in beta testing and not supposed to be out in the field at all!

The script had only called for three Tyrannosaurs and the herd of Brontosaurs, getting caught in a squeeze play with the Ankylosaurs at the far end of the corridor. Peyton and his crew were supposed to have an opportunity to knock off a couple of them, then head off to their first camp. The real excitement wasn't scheduled to kick in until the following day.

Now this.

It was, in a way mesmerizing. The staff around him was acting in a panic – shrill voices in Chinese were shouting back and forth.

Isolated in the control room, Farnsworth felt like he was watching one of his old Disney rides devolve into a horror movie.

Was it possible he was about to watch Bello, Evans and most of the porters get killed!?

"Code red!" he shouted. "Code red! Where's the fucking button!?"

Cliché as it appeared, there was indeed an emergency override button in case events went catastrophic. What Farnsworth didn't know, was that it hadn't been wired up yet.

He lifted the plastic cover next to his own workstation and thumbed the red button.

Nothing happened.

Then all the screens and lights went dead.

THE PROBLEM WITH INITIATIVE

Lanh had no intention of following the 'plan' they'd hashed out with Gorimov including waiting to take out the substation. In fact, as he and his brother had worked it all out earlier, it was critical they do everything to disrupt the Russians and keep them off-balance.

They made remarkably good time, arriving at the substation and husbandry complex without incident. The regularly cleared trails were easy to follow and they didn't run into any security patrols, unless there wasn't any need for them.

Or maybe they're just sloppy, or underpaid. Or both, Lanh figured. He didn't have a high opinion of the Chinese when it came to these things.

They were quite shocked at the lax level of security when they arrived, in the oppressive balminess of the tropical afternoon. Which was exactly what they were counting on. Lanh knew from his training that as a rule, people tended to be at their lowest emotionally and physically at three in the morning and three in the afternoon. It was nearly four already, which – as one of the Americans he met once said – was close enough for government work.

From a perch in a tree set twenty yards in from the compound, Lanh studied the layout with a pair of binoculars. With him was Dinh, cradling the one non-Russian made weapon in their group, a .308 Remington 700 with a Swarovski Z8i scope and tactical stock.

The main building, housing the husbandry facilities, was an ugly 70s concrete block, steel and glass affair designed by some miserable soul who must have hated architect school. Painted in a half-hearted attempt at camouflage, it had a simple lobby entrance on the west side, while the west side had loading docks and outdoor pens, some large enough to hold an elephant, if it didn't need to move around too much.

Separate from that was a second, smaller concrete building, that from appearances, was probably constructed by the Japanese during World War II. The roofed addition housing the transformers made it obvious this was the generator plant and their secondary target. The first was to hack into the computer network and put their communications into chaos. The two brothers decided it was a safe bet there was a secondary or battery back-up system to the power grid. At a glance, it looked like the island was being powered by a 1930s powerplant, though Lanh noted through the binoculars the transformers were newly built Chinese models.

The two buildings were surrounded by a fenced-in compound, with two guard towers built out of aluminum struts with corrugated roofs. It was accessed by a gate and entry building. Three of the MuTron liveried vehicles sat in the parking area, along with a small shuttle bus and a Toyota pick-up.

Lanh spotted six guards, one at the thatched-roof entry building, two in each of the crude guard towers, one patrolling the roof of the husbandry building and two more walking the grounds in a predictable pattern. Five of them looked bored and listless at their duties. The one in the left guard tower appeared to be the most alert. It would be difficult to take him out without attracting the attention of the other.

Difficult, but not impossible.

He also figured there would be more inside. Based on the Russian's intel – if it was reliable - few, though. Gorimov's source in the compound claimed the island's high level of isolation and secrecy gave them a fair amount of security, plus the blanket protection of mainland China. Not to mention the dinosaurs themselves. The staff on the island would know the limits of safe zones – but an unfamiliar intruder wouldn't.

He didn't think they'd be much of a problem. According to Gorimov, they hadn't succeeded in creating anything larger than dogs, though much more vicious. The large holding pens gave him some pause, however. What if they *had* gotten them as big as elephants? Either way, their DNA would be worth millions.

He glanced over at Dinh.

He sometimes fantasized about her, though she was more like a sister to him and his brother. A saner version of a sister, anyhow, than their real one back in New York. Who always seemed to get them roped into some lunacy or another.

Dinh wasn't overly attractive, but she had a cute, compact fierceness he found an intriguing contrast to the high maintenance *femme fatale* types he always hooked up with. She was dangerous.

Probably cut my balls off if I ever made a move at her, he figured. But he liked the way, after so many years, they were able to communicate volumes without speaking a word aloud.

Would make for some interesting sex!

He realized she was staring at him, unblinking, as if reading his thoughts. Lanh nodded toward the compound to distract himself. And her.

They would need to create a diversion, on the ground. Get the two sentries in the towers focused on that, and not each other. And get whoever was handling the security cams distracted as well – but not enough to raise the alarm. Something that wouldn't be out of place on the island. According to their intel they would need passes to get access to the inside, something that would have been impossible to duplicate or get a hold of in such a short window.

Then they would have to move fast.

Dinh followed Lanh's gaze and pointed to the guard pacing the roof and raised one finger. Then she pointed at the guard towers and raised two and three fingers respectively.

The three guards didn't know it, but they were already dead.

Lanh gave her a nod of agreement and slipped down through the branches.

The Sulfur-crested Cockatoo turned out to be relatively easy to capture. The birds were unaccustomed to people and the hacker on the team – a quiet man named Bao – had a natural affinity for them. As they approached the compound he was able to walk right up to one they spotted on a low branch and pet it.

That had immediately given Lanh an idea how to solve their distraction issue. "Cover its head," he ordered Bao.

The guard in the screened-in entry hut didn't know what to make of it at first. In fact, he was annoyed. The battery-operated clock on his desk registered 4:04 when the commotion began down the path – what sounded like a bunch of breaking branches, followed by laughter.

He was tired, hot, and just wanted to get through the last part of the action movie he was watching on his handheld, and now *this*.

Let the perimeter guard deal with it, he decided, one eye still on the movie.

Then there was a loud screech that had him jumping to his feet.

What the hell!?

He was about to tap the intercom to alert inner security when he saw something white flash out of the trees in a beat of panicked wings.

The cockatoo shot up into the sky, losing a few feathers in its haste.

Then he saw the two men dressed in nothing but their undershorts staggering up the roadway, arms around each other's shoulders, mumbling some old Chinese sailor's ditty.

The guard let out a chuckle and stepped out of the hut.

God damn laborers! They look like the new Southeast Asians we've been getting in lately. Figures.

They'd had a couple of incidents previously, but nothing like this one. *Worse than a couple of drunk monkeys.*

He took a couple of steps, shaking his head. Then out of habit, he glanced up at the guard tower to his left.

Odd. No-one there!

Puzzled, he glanced up toward the other tower and saw that guard was gone as well. For a moment he felt the first threads of alarm.

Then he smiled.

Aside from the recent deaths he heard about, nothing exciting had happened here in the past two years. Except for the practical jokes that got played from time to time out of sheer boredom. It was a set-up. It had to be!

He turned back just as the two men staggered up to him, laughing and smiling. Instinctively, his hand went to the 9mm at his hip.

One of the two men – Lanh - disengaged himself with a laugh and, stepping lightly as a (drunken?) ballerina, fell into the guard, pushing him under the view of the security cam mounted on the guard hut.

"Hey—" he said, unaware that Lanh had reached behind and snatched the combat knife taped to his back. There was a brief struggle followed by a grunt; the Chinese guard sagged inside of his hut, the knife embedded nearly to the hilt in his jawline.

Working quickly and avoiding the blood trickling out of the wound, Lanh stripped down the guard as the other commando joined him.

"Check for internal cameras."

There was only one – in the upper corner. The second commando went up to it and smiling, snapped it off its mount.

Inside the main entrance at the reception desk, the young Chinese man sitting behind it looked up as the sliding glass doors opened as Lanh - wearing the Guard's ID tag - approached.

That was odd to him, as the outside security never came into the husbandry facilities. Even odder, he realized the man was one of the new South Asians. He stood up, indignant.

"I am sorry, but there's no admittance—"

His eye fell on the streak of fresh blood on the collar. Before he could finish his sentence the barrel of the dead guard's 9mm was pressed up against his forehead.

"Where is the control room?" Lanh asked.

There were only two Chinese IT men working the security cameras and servers, and neither looked ready to trade their lives for their jobs. They all but wet their pants when they looked up to see the business end of the pistol aimed at their heads. Lanh was tempted to shoot both of them just out of contempt, but decided it wasn't worth wasting the ammo.

Mao would roll in his grave if he saw this new generation, he thought.

He was able to shut down the security cam feeds which, as he guessed, were also monitored at the main facility. A brief interrogation told him what he needed, including how many staff were at the facility, how many of the dinosaurs were in the field, and a guide map issued to all employees. Minutes later, after tying the two men up – along with the receptionist, he went outside and signaled the rest of his team.

"Quick!" he said, as Bao settled himself into one workstation. He produced a flash drive from one of his pockets and slipped it into the USB port. "We can completely shut down the generator plant from here. No need to waste time blowing it up." He laid down a slip of paper with the various passwords and logins needed to access the main frame. At least they hadn't upgraded to one of the new fingerprint systems, he thought, fingering the blood-stained commando knife at his hip. If they had, and if the IT personnel had made things difficult, things would have gotten messy.

"How long?" he asked Bao.

The hacker leaned back and cracked his knuckles like a maestro. "Just a few minutes. This is going to be *easy*."

Lanh nodded. He'd sent two men to reconnoiter the husbandry labs to see if there was anything of value. As a safety protocol, the dinosaur cages were on their own separate locking system from the rest of the island's systems, just in case of a major power outage. Dinh was in one of the guard towers, keeping company with one of the three guards she'd picked off while Lanh had been doing his charade.

Lanh parked himself in at the second security station while Bao went to work. This one had two HD monitors, each split into six screens that were the live feeds for the internal facility cams.

One camera showed the two commandos he'd sent hunkered down on a catwalk along a line of cages. On the floor below several lab workers were going about their tasks, oblivious. The space was enormous – perhaps 150 cages on two floors – with overhead gantrys and skylights. Unlike the spotless, hi-tech atmosphere of the main complex on the other side of the island, this place had the down and dirty charm of a mass breeding facility. With it was the smell: an overwhelming fetid mix of urine, shit, blood and lizard. And of course, methane. The planteaters were nothing if copious farters.

Lanh glanced over at Bao as the hacker chuckled.

"Ready for this?" Bao said. He held one finger up in an air of mock drama, savoring the moment.

Lanh nodded. He wondered if all hackers were like this.

Bao hit the enter key.

"May hell be unleashed!" he joked.

It was.

Over in the main facility the two commandos looked at each other as the overhead lights cut out. A moment later red back-up lights came on, along with a white strobe accompanied by a droning but insistent *de-weeeep de-weeep!*

From within the holding pens came agitated sounds down on the floor, the half-dozen workers didn't seem overly disturbed by this, as if it were a common occurrence. Instead, they filed in an orderly way towards the exits.

The one commando sat back on his haunches, relieved it would be that much easier to search the facility. They hadn't expected everyone to simply clear out. This thought was disrupted by a chorus of heavy clicks as the holding pen locks along each side disengaged, followed by the unmistakable sound of doors sliding back.

It was minutes before the regular feeding time.

Again, the commandos looked at each other, this time with dawning horror. With a scrabbling of claws and a series of chittering, almost purring sounds, a bunch of brightly feathered (and fierce-looking) creatures clambered out onto the deck before them. The nearest one – the size of a dog – straightened its tail, leaned forward and let out a distinct reptilian hiss, pulling its lips to reveal a mouthful of dreadfully sharp teeth.

Neither man had ever seen anything like it. Both raised their AK-47s and fired.

Down below came the first screams.

"What in the hell did you do!?" Lanh yelled.

Bao held his hands up. On a separate display to his right, a series of flashing animations on the floorplan graphics indicated all the holding cells were opening. The main screen on which he had been working had shown a series of scrambled pixels and gone black.

"I don't know! This shouldn't be happening! You said the cages were on a separate power grid! Why are they opening?"

Lanh's face went dark as the implications sank in.

"Fuck," he said. "Let's get out of here."

Up in the guard tower, Dinh whirled around as the muffled sounds of gunfire and screams came from the main building. Leaning over the wood parapet, she caught the attention of the two commandos who had been lounging by the entrance and made a quick spinning gesture with her hand: *what?*

Both men shrugged, but unshouldered their weapons, raising their heads to look in through the main doors.

Dinh's first thought was: Lanh!

She'd never breathed a word about her feelings toward him, which were a raw, school-girl's passion beneath an opaque glass façade. Partly it was a brutal upbringing with a household of brothers under a career military father, part of it was ingrained cultural reticence. Perhaps, even more heartbreaking, was that she didn't know how to begin to articulate these feelings toward the object of them. It didn't help that Lanh was equally clueless in this department.

Regardless, her first instinct was as a soldier.

She raised her rifle, scanned the perimeter of the buildings, then looked past the scope as she saw half a dozen workers in MuTron lab uniforms go sprinting pell-mell out the back, obviously in a panic. They were pursued a few seconds later by the most bizarre – and terrifying – creatures Dinh had ever laid eyes upon.

In the lead was a brilliantly colored dinosaur about half the size of a T-Rex known as *Lythronax Argestes* . . . or 'Gore King'. The reddish-orange and black markings suggested a tiger. With a battery of teeth.

Even as it charged down the nearest worker (who was letting out a shrill scream) a blue-feathered velociraptor darted past and pounced, seizing one out-flung hand and snapping its jaws on it. Yanked off-balance, the man stumbled, attempting to yank the shredded remains of his hand loose. His agony was short-lived; the *Lythronax* clamped its mouth over his head and with a sickening wrench, bit it clean off.

Several more raced around and ganged up on the next closest worker, who was making an ill-conceived attempt to scramble up a tree. He didn't get more than six feet off the ground before one raptor latched onto his calf, sinking its teeth in. A second raptor, using its long fingers and hind claws like log-man, scrabbled up the tree trunk and grabbed his upper thigh, one hand batting the other raptor's head almost comically. The weight of the two creatures was too much and they brought him down in a flurry of snapping branches. They were quickly joined by another, falling into a brutal feeding frenzy.

Dinh didn't fire. Ammo was limited and not worth using on anything not a direct threat.

Lanh!

The thought of one of those things sinking its teeth into him made a cold, hard knot on her gut. With a flick of her thumb she turned the safety off and scanned the exits. There was a yell and the front doors slammed open – there he was!

Lanh bolted out with Bao hot on his tails. The commandos by the guard house dropped to their knees in a defense fire mode, but Lanh made a quick chopping gesture with his free hand: run!

Crack!

He glanced over his shoulder as the first creature chasing him stumbled, then tried to stand up again, as if not processing the fact that the left side of its head had been blown out with the exit of Dinh's bullet. The raptor behind it dodged to one side, only to catch a bullet in the side of the neck. Lanh sprinted down the trail when he saw the vehicles off to the left, changing his course immediately. Bao followed but veered off toward the MuTron vehicles.

Lanh was nothing if not a quick thinker. Spotting the open window of the pick-up cab, he barked a single order at his hacker and made a beeline for it.

Dinh let off another shot, winging a third raptor in the snout, causing him to pause and shake his head, almost like a dog stung by a wasp.

Crack.

The fourth shot took it in the eye.

Dinh looked over the rifle. There were three more rounds in the clip, and dozens more dinosaurs of all kinds coming out of the building. Some were as small as chickens, a few as large as the *Lythronax* that had run out the back. Not all were predators and from the commotion erupting from within (and now outside) the building, not all were attacking humans – they were attacking each other as well.

None of this made sense to her. The plan had been to only shut down the computer systems – not to release the dinosaurs. But it was all happening too fast.

Dinosaurs seemed to be everywhere in a chaotic free-for-all. She couldn't tell which ones might pursue Lanh and Bao, each other, or simply run for it. At least half a dozen were attacking the pick-up, or running over the top of it. She wasn't even sure they'd made it inside the cab.

Of the other commandos, one had been overrun and trampled, another had disappeared into the bush. She had no idea what had happened to the rest. Tactical awareness had simply disintegrated.

She turned as the floor under her gave a slight shake. Eyes widening, she looked in horror as three scaly claws pushed the trapdoor open. She slung the rifle over her shoulder and drew her sidearm.

The trapdoor popped up before she could jump over and stomp on it. A brightly feathered thing with a mouthful of serrated teeth chittered at her. Up close, there was something about the combination of bird and reptile struck her as instantly repulsive; and aberration in the world as she knew it.

Whether it was simply curious or hungry Dinh didn't bother to consider. She opened fire at point-blank range, putting five rounds into its head before she realized what she was doing. Its head obliterated, the creature tumbled down to the ground below, where a passing raptor the size of a horse snatched it up in its teeth.

Dinh stepped back as horrified by the creatures themselves as much as another realization: she was on the verge of panic.

More of the things were climbing up the sides of the tower, and even as she backed up, a bat-winged dinosaur with four long tail feathers – a *Yi Qi* – landed on the rail and chittered angrily at her, spreading its wings. It was quickly joined by several others. The largest glared at her and hissed. Her thoughts rippling with panic, she debated whether she should just put her gun in her mouth and pull the trigger. Dinh Thi Nguyet, veteran sharpshooter with 58 kills in over two dozen combat situations in six different countries, completely lost it.

She turned around and clambering up onto the rail, jumped.

Lanh had made it inside the pick-up. Barely. With several of the raptors almost on him, he'd whipped around and leveling the AK-47, let out a controlled burst sweeping from left to right. Feathers, blood and gore flew. He felt seized by primordial killing urge, an irrational urge to keep killing and killing until no bullets were left. There was still the machete.

Instead, Bao's shout got through and turning to wrench the cab door open, Lanh threw the gun in and piled in after it. No sooner did he slam the door shut than a larger raptor slammed into it, denting the metal and starring the window. Bao climbed in from the other side.

The keys! The keys!

Lanh hurriedly went through the motions of checking the visor, under the seat, and was reaching for the glove compartment when he realized Bao was jabbing him in the shoulder.

"What!?" he shouted.

Bao pointed to the ignition, where the keys were dangling.

Of course! On a remote island like this they wouldn't be much concerned with car thieves!

The pick-up roared to life as he turned the ignition and floored the gas pedal. A second later he was fishtailing out in reverse – just as the raptor attempted to ram them again. Instead, the dinosaur clipped the front hood and tumbled away. Lanh resisted a sudden urge to put the truck in first and try and run the damn thing over. Instead, he spun the wheel around and took off toward the building.

Regardless what was happening, he was still compelled to go back, if only for Dinh. Glancing over at the tower, he couldn't see her, but saw half a dozen feathered raptors climbing all over it.

"Where are you going!?" Bao yelled.

"We have to go back!" Lanh hissed back. "We just can't leave them!"

"They're dead!"

Lanh never cared much for the hacker. He was an expert in the world he was familiar with; gigabytes, code cracking, data streams, ransomware and viruses. But in the real world, he always put himself first. And faced with any physical threat, he folded right up.

"Then we're dead too," Lanh replied, hitting the gas.

Coming up on the entrance, he nearly collided with a young *Ankylosaurus* charging by, the spikes along its body scraping divots out of the side of the truck as he went past. There was no sign of any commandos as he skidded to a stop next to the guard tower, only the chaos of hundreds of (juvenile) dinosaurs running rampant.

"We have to get out of here!" Bao said, his voice now shrill. To make his point, a large raptor landed in the bed of the truck with a *thud*, then tilted its head about, as if puzzled by this unfamiliar environment.

This was followed by a second *thud*, as a dinosaur landed nearly square on top of it from above. Simultaneously the passenger side window shattered as something tried to scrabble inside. Bao's head jerked to one side as he pulled his sidearm and fired. Lanh reached over, then saw to his horror what was happening in the back of truck.

Jumping without thinking was an utterly alien concept to Dinh, who had made a lifetime habit of calculating and planning everything meticulously.

All that discipline flew out the window when she saw all those homicidal-looking raptors joining her in the guard tower.

Now here she was, flailing through the air, dropping twenty feet to what would certainly be broken bones, or worse.

Even as she fell, however, she saw the pick-up skid to a stop right under her, then – it all happened too fast to process – something large jumped up into the bed. She instinctively bent her legs and put her hands out . . .

. . . and slammed onto the back of the rusty feathered raptor, snapping its spine with a sickening *crack* as she fell off to one side, her left shoulder first hitting the grooved metal bed painfully, then her head whacking off the wheel well hard enough to split the skin on her scalp. The rifle dug into her back but she rolled forward, onto her stomach, instead of backward.

Even so when she tried to sit up, stars swam across her vision and the world around her slewed. Blood ran down the side of her face as she tried to push herself away from the writhing, snapping raptor in its death throes.

A larger head appeared over the side of the pick-up, a *Lythronax* drawn by the blood and the convulsions of the dying raptor. At first, Dinh thought it was going to simply go for the dinosaur, then she saw its bright, gold-flecked predator's eyes lock onto her head.

That moment was another first for her - cold, unreasoning fear: not of death, but of being *eaten alive*. Just as the massive jaws came at her she twisted sideways and kicked the raptor's convulsing head upwards, into its mouth.

Then, mercifully, Lanh floored the truck and they took off, the raptor snatched out of the back like so much finger food from a passing caterer.

Lanh headed north, racing ahead of the unleashed dinosaurs, weaving along the rutted jungle roadway at breakneck speed. It wasn't until he thought they were safely out of range – roughly three miles – that he pulled over to check on his passengers.

He tugged Bao's shoulder. The hackers lifeless head lolled limply toward him and Lanh saw that the right half of the face had been torn off.

As he fought down his rising gorge he heard a light tapping on the cab's rear window. Craning about he saw Dinh's shell-shocked face smeared in blood.

A CLOSE CONNECTION

Wang felt like all the air had been kicked out of his lungs. He'd heard his grandfather often joke about what a small world it was – even with 1.35 billion Chinese in it – but the reality of that bit of wisdom had been lost on him until now.

He knew the face in the photo, even if it was a much younger version of her: his *great-grandmother*.

It was a face he knew well – she had been a much-talked about beauty in the family, and her hand-tinted portrait had hung proudly in his grandparents, and later his parent's, house. The story was that her husband, an older man named Chou Zin, had been killed while working on the Manchurian railroad during the Japanese occupation, and that brokenhearted, she had never remarried. And yet, how was it possible that her portrait had ended up in the possession of some deranged Japanese survivalist on a remote island in the South China Sea?

A deep furrow creased Wang's brow. It made little sense . . . except, did it? Could this Japanese soldier somehow be her son? How could that be, if he was Japanese (and best as Wang could tell, the offspring of one of the soldiers on the island, though that part he hadn't quite puzzled out either.

Was it possible this was simply another woman who looked remarkably identical to his grandmother?

Looking at the time-worn image, he realized it *was* her. It had the same photographers mark and was an exact miniature of the portrait in his parent's house. Which raised another question – why hadn't he ever seen any pictures of his great-grandfather? He'd always assumed it was because they might be a heartbreaking reminder to his great-grandmother.

Was there another explanation?

Wang let his gaze wander around the chamber, taking in its oddness: the makeshift belongings, the weapons, the feral, unbathed coppery smell of someone who had been living here a long, long time. The answer seemed to be here, present but illusive . . .

"Wang?"

Tao's voice swam up from above, tight and urgent.

"What is it?" Wang asked.

"I saw something down the tunnel. I think it's him!"

Wang lifted the rifle he had retrieved from the room above, but wasn't quite sure how effective it would be, having never fired a real weapon before in his life. Fired plenty of them in his many years of playing Call of Duty and other first-person shooters, but that was pretty much it. He wasn't even one hundred percent sure the ammo he'd found in the locker was the correct caliber, though it seemed to fit.

One thing that was quickly apparent, though, was that whatever was coming down the corridor toward them was, it *wasn't* human.

Out of the gloom emerged a ferocious predator's face: a larger version of the same *Zhenyuanlong* that had wreaked havoc in the lab earlier, its pupils appearing to glow through some odd trick of the light. A bloody shred of flesh was hanging from its teeth.

Wang glanced up at the debris-strewn steps.

"Come on!"

As they reached the top of the stairs, they were startled to find the old Japanese soldier blocking their way, sword drawn.

If Wang had seen him in time he might have hesitated – and probably been killed right there and then. Instead, the rifle held horizontal before him, he plowed right into the man's shins. Grimacing in pain, the soldier was knocked aside as the sword strike went into a wobbly arc, missing his head by millimeters.

Wang barely registered what happened. He bolted down the trail he was on, dimly aware that he was somewhere along the back ridge of the complex. After sixty yards he came out into a circular clearing where an anti-aircraft gun had once been installed. Only the rusted, overgrown base remained. It took him a moment to realize that Tao was no longer behind him.

"Tao?" he gasped, between breaths. He was just beginning to grasp how far out of shape he'd gotten at his new job.

Nothing. The jungle was quiet.

Then there came the crashing of someone – or something approaching. Fast.

Wang raised the rifle to his shoulder, this time remembering to run the bolt and chamber a round.

Closer.

Wang's finger curled around the trigger.

Tao appeared so abruptly, Wang nearly shot him out of reflex.

"*Shen me!*" he exclaimed, lowering the gun. "I almost shot you!"

Bleeding from a dozen scratches, Tao looked about wildly, not saying anything.

"Hey, what's—?"

Tao jerked forward as something erupted out of the leaves behind him, its jaws clamping down hard on the back of his neck, its tapered claws grasping his shoulders like that of an intimate lover. There was a dry *pop* as the vertebrae snapped. Tao's head bent unnaturally to one side, then he was lifted off his feet and shaken viciously, blood drops spraying in all directions, including across Wang's face.

Wang stumbled backwards, unsure what to do next. Nothing in his job training or experience had trained him for anything like this.

Shoot? Run? Scream?

The raptor dropped Tao's body and glared at him, as if challenging him. Then it leaned forward on its haunches, brightly colored feathers fanning outwards in agitation, and hissed at him. The size and proximity of the thing, its fetid breath – and the inherent violence in every feature of its body – triggered an icicle-tinged response in every nerve of his body. He felt his testicles shrivel.

Defiantly, Tao raised the rifle and pulled the trigger.

Nothing happened.

The thing hunched even lower, preparing to spring.

From its rear quarter came a cry – more of a primal '*argghhhh!*' than a traditional '*bonzai!*' yell – as the Japanese soldier dashed out of the overgrowth, katana raised, and with one swift strike, chopped the creature's head clean off.

There was a heavy thud as it landed in the soft earth, the creature's claws clenching convulsively. The body took a tentative step forward, then collapsed half onto Tao, blood arcing out of its severed artery.

Wang stood there dumbfounded, the rifle now pointed at the Japanese soldier.

Something inexplicable and unspoken passed between the two men as they stared at each other.

The gun in Wang's hand jerked as the misfired old round finally went off, the loud *crack* violating the heavy air of the clearing.

The soldier's eyes flared, his brow knitted in surprise. He staggered back a step. The sword dropped as his hands went to the tattered clothes covering his abdomen, where bright blood blossomed.

Wang was horrified, despite the fact the man had nearly killed him minutes before.

"*Kuso,*" the soldier hissed, dropping to his knees. Wang ran over to him.

"*Qingkuang!*" he blurted: *what shit!* - unwittingly echoing the Japanese sentiment.

Even more odd, the man put his hand on Wang's shoulder, in an almost fatherly way.

Any other person might have folded right there and then: Wang had just escaped a nightmare prison, seen his best friend killed, a dinosaur beheaded and had just shot another man with a gun. Instead, he knelt, instinctively pulling the man's arm around his own shoulders in a classic gesture.

"I'm sorry, I need to get you to someplace safe," he said, speaking in Mandarin. Not that he had any idea where any safe place might be anymore.

"My room, now," the soldier replied quietly, speaking perfect Mandarin. Then: "My *katana*. Bring my *katana*."

HE SHOULDN'T HAVE GOTTEN IN THE WAY!

Jeff Doyle's torso jerked as the .45 caliber slugs cut through him from left to right, pulverizing most of his internal organs in one sweep. The rifle tumbled out of his hands as he let out an agonized grunt, then he toppled face first into the dry grass.

Banyon was staring in slack-jawed shock, unable to process that his colleague had just killed another man – from behind no less.

"What the hell did you just do!?" he shouted, in a high-pitched voice, hands shaking together as if he were about to start clapping. "You . . . you just *killed* him, for Christ's sakes!"

Blodgett's response wasn't encouraging, nor did his eyes look quite sane. He let out a short laugh. "Ha! Well maybe the little punk shouldn't have gotten in the way! Hahaha!"

There was no time for Banyon to formulate an answer. Everything was happening all at once. The herd of Brontosaurs was charging down on them, even the nearby trees shaking and swaying. One of the *Deltadromeus* snatched a porter in its jaws and veered away, the man screaming shrilly at the top of his lungs as his shoulder was chewed and crushed. Evans – who had jumped into the stranded Land Rover in a last-ditch effort to escape the theropods – glanced up in time to see a massive brontosaur foot descending on him. A moment later his scream was stifled by the muffled *crump* of imploding metal and glass as the vehicle was smashed flat by the stampeding titan.

Bello rolled to one side, unable to believe the massive predator that had just been about to seize him was now a writhing mess on the ground, its lower jaw shot off. Then it too was half crushed by a stampeding Brontosaur, which narrowly missed pulverizing Bello as well.

Another of the porters made a sprint for the cover of the trees, only to be struck aside by the whip-crack of a passing Brontosaurs tail. He fell face-first into mud of the stream-bed, only to have his head squashed flat by a second, smaller Brontosaur trailing its parent.

Bello was jerked up to his feet and looked up at the grinning, sweating face of Peyton.

"Hey there, Bembo! We can't be losing our only competent guide!" He looked oblivious to the danger around him. In fact, Bello realized, Peyton looked like he was enjoying himself.

He manhandled the African into the passenger seat of the Land Rover, then jumped behind the wheel himself.

"Don't worry, I'll handle this!" He turned the engine over, threw the vehicle into gear, then slammed on the brakes as a Brontosaurus leg the size of an oak tree stomped the ground in front of them, nearly clipping the front hood.

"Whoa there!" he yelled, hitting the gas and fishtailing around it. Then the back leg of the sauropod clipped the roof, crumpling the rear quarter and knocking the Land Rover onto two wheels. The last *Deltadromeus* raced past them, filling the tilting windscreen for a moment, before the vehicle landed back on all four wheels with a jarring thud. Miraculously the way before them was clear and Peyton put the pedal to the floor. They rode up the low incline into the trees, where after 20 yards or so Bello came enough to his senses to yell at Peyton to stop.

Peyton was flushed. His lips back in a wild grin.

"God-damn that beat the living heck out of any stockholder meeting!" he said, smacking the wheel with his palm.

They'd passed the Jeep where Blodgett and Banyon had caught up to the two women and got out. Miss Banyon was in hysterics while Suzie Blodgett stood next to her, hand on her forehead, shaking her head in either disbelief or disgust, or perhaps both.

"Mr. Peyton, we need to find somewhere safe to get to," Bello said, looking over the stream bed. Only two of the porters had survived, and they were running back into the trees on the other side. Even as he watched, the surviving *Deltadromeus* – impossibly – bolted into the woods after them.

That meant something catastrophic had occurred with the failsafe mechanisms. Even worse, over where the lake was, an adult T. rex had emerged out of the jungle and was sniffing in their direction. Bello felt his pulse was jack-hammering away.

Peyton stood looking over at the carnage, frowning, as if the reality of their situation was finally sinking in. He hadn't missed what had happened with Blodgett and Jeff Doyle, either.

"Yeah, reckon we ought to do that," he said, followed by an odd, barking laugh. "Har! This thing has turned into one balls-out shit-fest, now hasn't it, Bembo?"

Bello studied him a moment, trying to decide whether Peyton was still a member of the sane party or had gone full over and joined the Loony Tunes bloc. It was a close call.

Was his entire party gone? Just like that?

He'd seen people mauled by predators in the bush before, and seen one kid die horribly from a black mamba bite after attempting to put on his boots without checking, but nothing approaching this.

For the first time since his employment with MuTron he was seriously questioning the sanity of his own thinking. All of it had been predicated on the level of control he'd observed since arriving on Kharamu. At the moment, it was quite clear that had been an illusion.

Joseph Bello was well acquainted with catastrophic (and often ironic) results brought on by men making bad decisions – he just never considered he'd be one of them.

Still, control had to start somewhere. And right now, the key to survival was safety in numbers.

"What about Mr. Doyle?" he asked, spotting the face-down body nearby.

"He ate something that didn't agree with him," Peyton said, oddly. When he didn't elaborate, Bello said, "We should get up to higher ground. There's an access road we can catch a hundred or so yards south of here. It'll take us to the ridge on the eastern side of the island. Most of the predator dinosaurs will avoid it."

Actually, he knew nothing of the sort. But it seemed prudent to start somewhere. Down toward the lake the Tyrannosaurus was heading in their direction.

"Come on people, you heard the man!" Peyton yelled, shouldering his rifle. "We're moving out!"

"Do you see it? I don't see it!" Oleg, complained, swatting again at a mosquito on his neck. "Do they have malaria here? I bet they do. I feel sick already."

"Shut up and keep looking!" Vlad replied, not bothering to indulge his friend's complaints. The oppressive heat and humidity was maddening. Even Gorimov was on edge. They'd arrived to find the GPO emitter up in a tree nowhere near any plants. Gorimov had told them to fan out and look for a plant which he'd described to each of them by whispering in their ears.

Only the Vietnamese commandos seemed unfazed.

Fuckers are enjoying this, Vlad thought, then grinned to himself. Not for long though. Gorimov had plans for them. That didn't involve getting off this island. Ever.

"Hey, check this out!" Oleg, said. He was bending over a strange-looking plant, one with radiant petaled flowers and thick leaves. Vlad thought there was something repulsive about it.

"That's not it, you stupid idiot! Don't you remember what Igor told us? It's a—" he cut himself off, aware he had just about revealed the secret within earshot of the commandos. "—never mind. Just keep looking!"

Oleg was intrigued by the plant however, its odd, misfit appearance triggering a sympathetic chord in himself. He was about to turn away when, impulsively, he reached into his satchel and pulling out a large plastic bag, bent over and grabbed the plant by the stem and pulled it out of the soft earth. He had just wrapped it around the roots and was tying it off with a rubber band when he felt a sharp sting in the fleshy part of his hand between the thumb and forefinger.

"*Derr`mo!*" he snapped: *Shit!* Jerking his hand away, he caught a brief glimpse of an aggressive-colored, furry spider being flung off into the bushes. He checked the plant but saw nothing else on it.

"You okay?" Vlad asked, annoyed.

"Something bit me! A spider I think."

"Maybe you should ask Igor to come over here to kiss it and make it better!" Vlad replied.

"Fuck-you!" Oleg said, shaking his hand violently. It felt like it had been stung by a wasp. He stuffed the plant into his satchel and pushed the other plants around again, this time using just his booted toe.

"Fuck-you, too!" Vlad shot back, then added: *"Girlie man!"*

Oleg swung about, fist raised.

Gorimov emerged from the foliage and pointed to a brilliantly flowered plant next to the one Oleg had just taken out of the ground.

"What's *that*!?"

"What's *what*?" Oleg replied, puzzled.

"That, you stupid idiot!" Gorimov's stubby finger jabbed toward the plant.

"It's a plant."

Gorimov glared at him and pushed past, pausing long enough to cuff Oleg upside the head.

"Fucking smartass! That's *the* plant!" Then he glanced sideways, realizing he'd spoken too loud. Stepping over carefully, Gorimov plucked the plant out of the ground and stashed it in his own satchel.

Tuan and his commandos were bivouacked nearby, having cleared out an encampment for the night. He'd feigned nonchalance when Gorimov told them to stay put while he went to look for the plant. The plan had been simple, and as he knew from years of experience, simple was best.

Wait until the Russians looked off-guard – just as they were about to turn in for a few hours would probably be the most unexpected moment – then kill all three. Tuan was considering leaving it all to their hacker, who went by the old French Vietnamese slur 'Dinky Dau'. Unlike the other hacker in the unit, Dinky Dau knew plenty about killing and was an expert at doing it brutally quick.

Not only that, but he *enjoyed* it.

Of all the team members, Tuan valued – and feared – him the most. It was like having an unstable, loaded weapon around: you better know exactly where it was at all times.

There was also something repulsive about Dinky Dau, with his broad, frog-like features and perpetually damp lips. He'd been the one who had relentlessly tracked Taylan down in London and navigated their escape out of the country afterward. Tuan often wondered if he would be forced to kill him one day, and sometimes, even *if* he could kill him. It wouldn't be easy.

For safety reasons, the group had set up portable seats surrounded by an outside perimeter of strategically cut branches, hung carefully with tiny bells. Tuan clambered up into the nook of a tree and checked his shortwave again. He hadn't heard from Lanh in nearly two hours, and that wasn't good. Taking out the generator plant and sabotaging the computer network should have been relatively easy.

This little situation would be tricky, even with Dinky Dau. The two Russian sidekicks would probably be relatively simple to take out but Gorimov was another matter. There'd been plenty of stories about him through the grapevine, and no shortage of corpses of those who had underestimated him.

Lanh had told Dinky Dau to focus only on him.

Gorimov pulled Oleg and Vlad in close to him like a football huddle.

"Okay, boys. We got the plant. Next, we go to the main facility, grab what we can out of their lab, then get the hell off this shithole island, yes? But first we have to deal with these slant-eyed gooks. Best time I think is just when we are about to turn in . . ." He glanced at his watch. "In another two hours. What's the matter Oleg? You look like you eat rotten fish or something!"

He squeezed Oleg's shoulder to make his point.

Oleg shook his head. "I don't feel so good. Something bit me, spider I think."

Gorimov snorted, "Ach, poor little *bubi*. Pull it together. We got work to do!"

"THAT'S NOT POSSIBLE!"

"Bloody fuck!" Audrey said. "That *Zhenyuanlong* did a number on her, didn't it? Pissier than a dingo with a fire-poker up its bum."

"You could say that," Taylan agreed. "The doctor in the infirmary was competent. She'll be fine."

Audrey gave him a sharp look. "You really don't know jack shit about women, Grant Taylan," she said, more to herself. The two of them were in the back seat of a Range Rover now barreling toward the meetup point with Peyton's group. The suspension system was getting a full workout on the ruts and grooves of the crude roadway. In the front seat was a New Guinea driver with a safari hat. Next to him was one of MuTron's security team, an AK-47 cradled in his lap.

Taylan raised one hand in mock dismissal.

"How long to the rendezvous point?" he asked the driver, gripping the handle above the door to keep his head from slamming into the roof. The driver seemed to be driving faster than necessary, though Taylan and Audrey hadn't been given any specifics. Taylan suspected Mr. Luo wanted them out of the facility as expediently as possible after the incident in the lab. Audrey had peppered him with all sorts of questions about their security protocols before Miss Grey intervened and smoothly escorted them to the field prep room for late arriving guests.

"Dr. Banaji is receiving absolutely the best care possible!" she'd said brightly, as if Roma had suffered nothing more than a skinned knee. "We have Rhys, one of our best drivers, waiting outside to run you over to the rendezvous point with Mr. Peyton, whom I understand is eagerly awaiting your arrival. Mr. Luo has already had a detailed conversation with Mr. Peyton over the unfortunate incident in the lab, so we would appreciate it if you didn't bring up the issue further. Rest assured, we take this very seriously, but all will be well!"

Audrey had been incredulous, her eyes flaring wide with anger, but Taylan had hustled her out of there just as her mouth opened. He knew Miss Grey was lying through her teeth, but there was no point belaboring it, he figured.

Now, better or for worse, they were heading off to catch their first glimpse of the dinosaurs in the field. Despite his reservations and all the red flags that had popped up so far, Taylan felt flush with excitement.

He looked over at Audrey. She was momentarily focused at a point beyond the horizon, tendrils of hair whipping around her head from the breeze coming through the open window. Yet again, he couldn't deny she was a strikingly attractive woman. Did she even remember what had happened – or almost happened – the other night? Did she care? After all these years, he still couldn't figure her out, other than that she continued to be a ball of contradictions and mixed messages. He tended to favor women who were straightforward and uncomplicated. Of course, that criteria had worked out fabulously with his last girlfriend. Certified psycho, that one. Somewhere out there on the planet, hopefully a long, long way away, her brothers were still out there looking for him.

Yet, here they were. As if some strange string of fate kept pulling them together. Was it a sign? A signal from some higher power above? He looked at the bold cast of her profile, the arched brow. The finely drawn upper lip. What was on her mind right at the moment? From the slight flair of her nostrils, he suspected she was thinking about dinosaurs too.

Then, sensing his gaze upon her, she glanced back at him. To his surprise her hand reached over and gave his a light squeeze.

"That's not possible," Rhys said, braking the Land Rover to an abrupt stop. They were near the crossing where most of Peyton's party had met their end. Dozens of Compys were picking over the remains in the sweltering afternoon sun, along with hordes of flies. Taylor leaned forward and took in the flattened wreckage of the Land Rover, what was left of the body parts. The carnage was so brutal and fresh, it had all their attention riveted.

Taylan had seen plenty of people die, but never anything like this. It was butchery. Despite his horror, his analytical side kicked on. He noted the path the remaining vehicles had taken to the other side. Just in from the tree line the Jeep was still there, though there was no sign of the second Land Rover.

Taylan had a bunch of questions, but settled on the obvious one: "What's 'not possible' about any of this?"

Rhys pointed into the forest opposite woods where several large Utah raptors were disappearing.

"That," he said. "There's safety protocols. Especially on the vehicles. Those dinosaurs shouldn't be where they are."

"Guess they missed the memo," Taylor said.

No-one laughed. Audrey looked around, as if something was nagging at her.

There was an abrupt *squawk* as the guide in the passenger seat tried the dashboard radio. Nothing came through but static. He thumbed the *send* button several times, with the same result.

"Rhys?" the man said in a tight voice. "Comms are out. That's *never* happened before. What do we do?"

Rhys looked over the scene a moment, then tapped the other man on the shoulder. "We need to check it out. You come with me." He turned around at Taylan and Audrey, his eyes as hard as marbles. "Both of you stay here. Do *not* exit the vehicle for any reason, understood?"

"I don't think that's a good idea," Audrey said. She'd been on a safari or two herself.

Rhys stared at her a second, but didn't reply.

"Come on," he said, swinging the door open.

The two men didn't go far – perhaps ten yards. The guide stood with his AK-47 ready, the safety off.

Rhys had a cold feeling in the pit of his stomach. None of his training had prepared him for this. In fact, he realized, it had never come up at all. They'd always been assured there were double-redundant failsafe systems in place guaranteed to make sure this would never happen.

Yet here they were.

From all appearances, most of the party they were sent to meet had been slaughtered.

He fingered the .45 holstered at his hip as he counted the bodies, including the remains of Enrico over by the tree line. He estimated at least six were unaccounted for.

"Okay, that's enough."

A heavy thud made him whip around, drawing his gun. Then, for the first time since being an infant, his bladder let go.

Taylan was so focused on watching the two men it took a moment to register that Audrey was gripping his wrist hard enough to break the skin with her nails.

"Um, Grant?" she said, teeth clenched.

"Yes?"

"They're *behind* us."

"What do you mean, 'behind us'?"

"Exactly what I said."

Taylan felt the hairs at the nape of his neck stiffen, already sensing whatever it was, it was probably bad.

He slowly craned his neck around to where she was looking, back through the rear right side of the Land Rover. It seemed impossible they had missed it, but there it was:

A *T. rex*.

It was roughly 20 yards away, stretched forward in a classic ambush stance: massive legs bent, five-foot long head down low, tail straight out. Its battery of fangs was half-concealed under its upper lip, its nostrils flared. Twelve feet high at the hip, its dappled hide covered around the upper back with a scattering of coarse proto-feathers, it was nine tons of killing machine waiting to launch.

Its merciless golden-flecked eye was staring – Taylan was convinced – right through the glass and right into his own.

"*Fuck*," he said, under his breath.

Then he saw there was not one, but *two* of them. A smaller one – presumably the male – was another ten yards off to their right. Due to the way the road curved on their approach, and the density of the jungle forest (and wild shapes cast by the vines), it wasn't hard to see why they missed them, despite their massive size.

He'd never guessed that a creature that big could stay motionless like that.

Not for long. With terrifying swiftness, it charged.

Unlike the classic scene in Jurassic Park, this *T. rex* didn't announce itself with an ear-splitting roar. The ground shook, but not as much as he expected. It came right at them.

Instinct said to get the hell out of there and run, but all Taylan and Audrey could do was sit there and pray.

At first Taylan thought the thing was going to smash into them like a battery ram.

It didn't – instead one titanic foot went over the top and landed squarely on the front hood, imploding it. The vehicle snapped up quickly enough that Taylan and Audrey banged their heads on the roof, the sunlight blotted out by its massive body.

Before their world went helter-skelter, Taylan glimpsed the guide out front dropping down into a firing position and letting the AK-47 go full auto.

Then the *T. rex* did roar, or rather, an incredibly loud, wet gurgling hiss like that of a super-sized Komodo dragon. Many of the guide's bullets must have hit home, but it didn't stop the Tyrannosaur's charge. The thing took two more steps and snatched man and machine gun in one snap. There was a brief scream followed by a bursting gurgle, then the *Tyrannosaur* veered to the left, knocking Rhys aside.

A moment later the second *T. rex* was there, its jaws clamping onto Rhys' leg.

Inside the vehicle, Taylan instinctively looked away as Rhys was half-gobbled in a rapid one-two motion. Bones snapped. Rhys screamed at the top of his lungs. He didn't stop as he was carried away, partially eaten, as the two *Tyrannosaurs* moved off to the edge of the trees to finish their catch.

Audrey bent down between her legs and threw up.

A stunned silence followed, broken only by the ticking of something broken in the destroyed engine compartment and the hideous sounds of flesh being torn apart. After an eternity of minutes Rhys stopped screaming.

Taylan looked warily around, trying to assess their situation. The Land Rover was finished. But there was still the abandoned Jeep on the other side of the creek bed. The question was, how to get to it with the two Tyrannosaurs nearby, and of course, if it still was usable.

And there was a more pressing question: how many more predators were in the area, roaming free? And how long before they smelled them out. They couldn't stay in the Land Rover forever. Already the air was getting suffocating, worsened by the rancid fumes of vomit.

Taylan tried to think.

What did they really know about *Tyrannosaurus rex*? Not much, beyond a lot of academic supposition. Some computer simulations claimed they could probably be outrun by a human, but it was easy enough to make claims from the safety of a remote location as opposed to sitting sixty or so yards from the real thing ripping apart a human being.

Would it seek another prey while in the midst of eating? The general rule of predators said no: it would mean risking a definite meal for a probable. Taylan knew predators tended not to hunt more than they needed. But what if all rules of nature were off in this isolated environment?

Right at that moment, Taylan would have liked to ask Mr. Luo a few choice questions, then strangle him.

That and a quarter will buy you a cup of coffee, his dad used to say.

Think! Think!

What could they use? He twisted around and looked at what was in the storage compartment. Nothing but a bunch of nylon ropes, some tools, and a couple of large cans of . . . what? It took a moment for the label to register.

They were large spray cans attached to a gun-like apparatus.

The label on the can said "ZECON -47"

"Audrey? Audrey? Are you okay?" He squeezed her shoulder.

She didn't respond for a few seconds, simply sitting there with her eyes squeezed shut. Then she wiped her mouth with the back of her hand and looked at him.

"Well, you don't see that happen every day," she said. Her complexion had gone ash-white.

"No. But we have to get the hell out of here. My best guess is that that Jeep over there may be our best shot. Unless you have a better idea."

"Fresh out, I'm afraid. Do you think it works? Why did they leave it?"

"No way of knowing. It's possible they thought it was safer to all stay in one vehicle, and the Land Rover would be a logical choice."

Audrey seemed to get some of her color back. "Hmm. Something's wrong with that *Tyrannosaur* – it must be injured."

Taylan peered through the cracked windshield. Sure enough, the larger *T. rex* was making odd, twisting motions of its head, hissing in distress.

Which brought back another bit of advice from Taylan's father, from back when they used to go hunting in Pennsylvania: if a bear comes at you and you can't drop it with one shot, don't take it. Otherwise you just end up with a pissed-off bear. And don't count on getting a second shot.

Looks like our guide never had that advice, he thought.

Which made things more complicated.

Taylan grabbed the can of ZECON-47 and studied the warning on the label, written right under the clear graphic symbol of a dinosaur with the universal red circle and slash over it. Then he grabbed the thinnest rope.

"Okay, Audrey. Here's how we're going to do this . . ."

"WE ARE IN FULL LOCK-DOWN, MR. LUO"

Byron Farnsworth brought his fist down again on the red button, and again, nothing happened. To the further dismay of his staff, he started jumping up and down like a five-year-old throwing a temper tantrum.

"Fuck-fuck-fuck-fuck-fuck!" he screamed, his face turning a threatening shade of maroon. "Doesn't anything fucking work around here!? God-damn fucking Chinese garbage!"

The staff did what they always did during one of their supervisor's frequent meltdowns: they stayed very still and didn't say a word.

Except for one assistant, who raised her hand tentatively.

"Yes!? What!?" Farnsworth screamed, focusing his full wrath at her like a homing beacon.

She pointed to the handset next to the red button.

Fuming, Farnsworth picked up the phone. A moment later Mr. Luo's suspiciously even voice came back at him.

"What is it, Mr. Farnsworth?"

Farnsworth's features twisted – with eerie swiftness – into a caricature of theatrical calm. "So sorry to bother you, Mr. Luo, but it seems we have a little problem."

"So, I understand," came the terse reply.

"Do you?"

"Enough of the histrionics, Mr. Farnsworth," Mr. Luo said, in a tone that was like a hard slap on the face. "I suggest you focus on making every effort to re-establish contact with Mr. Peyton's party. An IT team is on its way now."

Before Farnsworth could respond, the line went dead.

"Well that's great!" he said, staring at the handset. "That's just A-fucking great!"

Upstairs Mr. Luo looked at the garbled 3D holographic display table and frowned. He had just ended a conference call with the mainland when everything went to hell. *Hackers*, he realized immediately, *but how? And who?* Their systems had all sorts of firewalls and hi-level encryptions in place, and the entire MuTron hi-speed LAN was completely isolated from external access. They'd run it through all sorts of rigorous trials to make sure no-one from the outside could access their data and even if they could, make any sense of it.

So, it was an internal job. 'Protocol 1' required shut down and reboot of all communications and computer systems. The remaining protocols were systematically more comprehensive until 'Protocol F', which entailed immediate evacuation of the entire island.

And with it, the death knoll for MuTron International. Along with Mr. Luo's career, and life, probably.

He'd already been riding it tight to the knife's edge for some time now, and had often wondered himself how long it would be before he simply broke. He'd been in the middle of reviewing the safety protocols – just in case – when the systems went down. There was an independent back-up line hard-wired to a battery satellite hookup if all else failed, but that was only to be used as a final resort.

His thumb went to his mouth and he began to nibble obsessively at the nail. When he stopped a little smear of blood was on his upper lip.

Four minutes later he had all his chief company officers assembled in the main conference room. As Chief Technical Director, Greg Xióng was getting the worst of it. After getting the broad strokes in his usual cutting tones he came straight to the point.

"How long before we can get the systems back on line?"

Xióng looked flummoxed. "Sir, you haven't been listening to me. I don't know if we *can* ever get the systems back on line. This was a retro-virus that morphed into a back-door virus that allowed the hack to gain the deepest levels of our database and insert a *third* virus, a worm. I've never seen anything like it. It makes the *Mirai*, *Tiny Banker Trojan* and *Lucky* viruses combined look like child's play."

"What about our entire back up system? The Double Redundancy you crowed so much about?"

Xióng was pale. "Sir, we never implemented it. *You* were the one who denied us the budget. I've brought it up at every meeting that—"

"I didn't ask for excuses, did I!? DID I!!?!" Mr. Luo screamed in a shrill, wavering voice. He snatched up the security protocol printouts he'd brought with him and waved them in the air accusingly.

His staff stared back at him, shocked. Except for Roger Burroughs, who looked bored by the entire proceedings.

Nancy Wú put on a brittle smile. "I'm sorry, Mr. Luo, but I really must advise you that at this point, activating Protocol 7 would be the most prudent course of action. May I remind you, we are already in full lock-down, Mr. Luo."

Mr. Luo turned the power of his gaze on her.

"I thank you for your input, Miss Wú," he hissed, "and I'll be sure to put a note of it in the company do-gooder log, along with a bright gold star next to it! In the meantime, I would be greatly appreciative if you could stop acting like a Western, defeatist cunt and start doing your fucking job! That would give me no-end of great relief!"

He shot out the cuffs and adjusted his sleeves as if he'd just announced something profound. His smile widened. "There! Now let's get to work, yes? I have a shareholders meeting on the mainland tomorrow!"

A stunned silence followed, except for a soft chuckle from Mr. Burroughs. He was inspecting his fingernails thoughtfully.

"Do you find this all amusing, Mr. Burroughs?" Mr. Luo asked, his tone icy.

"Indeed, I do, Mr. Luo, indeed I do."

"Perhaps you'll find it less amusing that you're *fired*. I'll call security, and have you escorted off the premises!"

"I doubt that," Mr. Burroughs said, softly. He glanced at his watch. "As of five minutes ago, I believe you'll find your security has had its hands quite full."

"Well, I'll call my private bodyguard then! The rest of you get to work!" Mr. Luo threw aside the papers he had held knotted up in his hand and stormed out of the room.

Burroughs chuckled. The silence stretched out. There was no 'private bodyguard' – everyone knew that. The lights dimmed and came back up again.

After a minute, Burroughs stood up. "Well then," he said, looking at no-one in particular, "I believe I have a few things to tend to. I wish you luck."

Miss Grey, Greg Xióng and Nancy Wú sat in silence. The lights dimmed, then came back up again.

Nancy Wú's expression remained frozen in place. She'd dealt with all levels of abuse – or thought she had – but this was well past anything before. Past her own breaking point, she was both alarmed and pleased to discover. *Cunt!? He had called her a cunt!?*

She stood up. "*I'm* activating Protocol 7. Screw this," she said. She briefly considered whether she should head down to her quarters and get her personal things, then decided the best course of action was to get the hell off the island as quickly as possible. Marching over to the control console, she was so preoccupied it wasn't until she was reaching for the red 'Emergency Evac' switch that she realized Miss Grey had beaten her to the punch.

The lights dimmed again and stayed there while the red evac lights came on, filling the complex with their pulsing glow. A non-urgent, but persistent droning alarm kicked in with it, followed immediately by a Chinese woman's soothing, yet insistent voice: "Protocol 7 has been activated. Please evacuate the facility in an orderly fashion . . . Xiéyì 7: Qǐng shūsàn. . . Protocol 7 has been activated . . ." It sounded as if she was selling luxury spa treatments - for a limited time only.

From down the hall where the lobby was, came the tinkle of breaking glass, followed by a shriek.

Nancy Wú almost touched hands with Miss Grey, who was staring at her over the top of her librarian's glasses with a look that was a mix of both fear and excitement.

"Us girls have to stick together," she said.

"Get away from me, you freak!" Nancy Wú screeched, shoving Miss Grey aside. She took two steps past the glass-walled entrance and froze, seeing the apparition that was scrabbling up the stairway toward her. It was a *Guanlong wucaii*, an ostrich-sized raptor with a bright red crest and a long, feathered tail. A second one was bounding up the stair behind the first, ribbons of blood coming from its mouth.

Back pedaling, hands flapping in front of her as if she could wave the dinosaurs away, she let out a sound that was more of a squawk than a scream. She backed straight into an equally shocked Miss Grey, then spun around and grabbed her. The only thing she could think of was to save herself.

"You!" she said, then swung Miss Grey around in a clumsy pirouette and tried to throw her at the first creature.

Hormone treatments and sexual surgery aside, Miss Grey still had the blocky strength of her former self and her nearly anorexic opponent was no match for her. Following through with her momentum, Miss Grey swung Nancy Wú back around, and right into the striking jaws of the raptor.

There was a hideous chomp as the *Guanlong wucaii* turned its head sideways and bit down, seizing Nancy Wú's head in its jaws. Its teeth tore huge divots out of her scalp as the jaws snapped several times in rapid succession, then shook her viciously like a rag doll, her eyes going glassy as her nervous system acquiesced to the overwhelming trauma. The second raptor caught up and bit down on one flailing forearm, tearing it off with one sideways wrench.

Miss Grey saw no more. She turned and fled past a panicked Greg Xióng, who was indecisively trying to run in three directions at once. The last she saw of him, he was trying to hide under the conference table as the raptor clamped onto his foot.

Miss Grey took the elevator down to the basement level, with a vague plan to get down to the submarine pens and perhaps escape onto one of the small speed boats moored there. That plan derailed when two floors down, the lights flickered, and the elevator bumped to an ungainly halt.

Miss Grey closed her eyes, hands holding the sides of her head.

How many things can go wrong in one day? she asked herself. *In fact, how is any of this happening? I've done all the right things, made all the right moves, got out of a dead end (and sexually suppressed) lifestyle back in China, made the long-awaited transition . . . landed a successful career at a bright star in the bio-tech and entertainment industry. . . and was even enjoying unbridled and deliciously perverse sex with the CEO . . . and now this!? I'm doomed to get eaten alive by a bunch of nightmare dinosaurs!?*

Why!??

A small smile traced her lips.

For all her frustrations, uncertainties, fear and anger at life, self-pity had never been Miss Grey's indulgences, either as a man or as a woman, and she realized with a growing cold certainty it wasn't going to save her now.

She'd always been on her own – she saw that with stark clarity now – and now, more than ever, she would have to rely on her wits. And willpower.

The former she wasn't completely sure about. The latter she was, absolutely.

She pulled at the elevator doors.

Burroughs headed back to his office, judiciously avoiding the main corridors. Not that he was overly concerned about his safety. He did, however, have a compelling desire to get back to his secret stash of 30-year-old Balvenie, that had set him back over a grand. He'd paid too much because of the import, of course, but not much. His best scotch was back in England, thanks to the ultra-strict regulations on carrying alcohol on flights since 9-11.

The lab was a slaughterhouse, but he didn't see any dinosaurs except for three infant Compys nibbling over the remains of one of his assistants – Mike Cho best as he could tell – and as they seemed preoccupied and on the far side of the facility he paid them no mind.

At a glance, he estimated half the staff had made it out, which he found mildly disappointing.

Still, there was the prospect of the final refuge of his office and bottle of vintage scotch to look forward to. And, of course, the loaded Webley .38 hidden in the bottom drawer of his desk. Fortunately, as a precaution, he'd insisted the entire lab be on its own power grid with a separate generator back-up system. That argument he'd won: the company's most critical assets were here in the lab, after all.

Locking the door behind him, Burroughs went over first to the shelf behind his desk where he turned on a vintage Kardon HK670 Receiver, then queued up Tchaikovsky's "String Quartets one through three", one of the better recordings by Yuri Yurov, Mikhail Milman and the Borodin Quartet on the turntable.

The plan was simple: enjoy an excellent glass of Harman scotch, listen through an entire album of his favorite music, then blow his brains out.

He'd even prepared a brief note, inspired by the great George Eastman:

To my fellow colleagues, my work is done.
-Roger Burroughs

Not that anyone would be around to read it. Roger Burroughs had set up a plan for that, too. MuTron International would go out with a bang.

Luo Pan Wei stood by the picture window in his office, surveying his domain. From this angle nothing looked untoward, except for the unusual amount of activity around the docks and the trawler. One just had to ignore the pulsing red emergency light behind him and the incessant drone from the speaker:

"Protocol 7 has been activated. Please evacuate . . ."

Mr. Luo smiled to himself, flirting briefly with his next scenario in his mind – rebuilding MuTron International from the ground up, with an entirely new branding of course. Maybe even a new name.

Yes, a new name, absolutely. Something hip and eco-friendly, without being too hip and eco-friendly. Something that would magnetically draw the new generation of neurotic, ridiculously self-important and brand-obsessed youth of the world! It would have to be bigger than 'save the planet' . . . save the galaxy? Save the universe? UR1? No . . . perhaps something about how every person is an integral part of the cosmos . . . a future-sustaining critical part!

Mr. Luo knew it would need work, careful thought and attention with a touch of bravado mixed with ample sincerity and grass-roots earnestness. But the wheels were turning, and that was the most important thing.

He slipped the slim Barretta back into the holster under his armpit. When Miss Grey had come pounding on his office door earlier it had been necessary to make it clear any previous 'relationship' they'd had was to be considered terminated. The Beretta had been quite useful in pointing out that any plans for the future didn't involve her, which pleased him in a twisted way.

Good riddance. Although he'd discovered new levels of unbridled, 'perverse' sex with Miss Grey – particularly their roleplay games where she was his doctor – it was a release to leave her behind. Her continued presence was an irresistible temptation and worse, forced him to question facets of his own personality and image he found repulsive in others.

In short, she was bad for his self-esteem.

His hand – the one with the cuticles nibbled to the point of bleeding – absently caressed the leather attaché case holding the back-up data drives and DNA samples. From the back of his office a private stair led up to the roof where his helicopter was warming up.

Her crest-fallen look at the glass door had been sad . . . and pathetic.

Weak.

But that was all about to fade out behind him.

Soon . . . soon, he thought, *a new future will open up to me. Even better than this one!*

AN INCREDIBLE TALE

As Wang manhandled the injured Japanese soldier back to the bunker complex, he was convinced any moment another of the creatures would leap out of nowhere and tear them to shreds. He resigned himself to the grim fact there was little he could do about it and by all indications, there was probably few if any remaining safe places left on the island.

For his part, the old man didn't complain once, though it was evident he was in a great deal of agony. His deeply tanned skin had gone a few shades paler and his already fierce features were immobile as granite.

Several times they heard screams in the distance, but miraculously, they made it back to the complex without encountering anything worse than the incessant mosquitos and flies.

By the time they made it back to the alcove where the hidden room was, Wang was drenched with sweat and filled with the bone-draining exhaustion one only gets after running on pure adrenaline for hours. He couldn't even remember the last time he'd eaten.

Breakfast? That felt like weeks ago.

Still, there was nothing to it but to do what he had to.

"I can take you to the infirmary," he said to the old man, speaking Mandarin. "They have good doctors, everything to get you patched up!"

The soldier shook his head dismissively and pointed one finger: up.

The question was, *how?*

As if reading his thoughts, the old man took the loose end of the rope and handed it to him. "Wrap this around me. Then you go and pull me up. Hurry! Not much time!"

Five minutes later he had laid the old man onto the makeshift bed. The air was more stifling than ever in the confined space. By this point, his complexion had gone a pasty, ashen hue Wang didn't care for.

The old man ripped open his shirt – the fabric was in such bad shape it simply tore – revealing an ugly hole in his midsection. He motioned impatiently at a military style box with a faded symbol Wang recognized immediately: a red cross. He fetched it and set it down alongside the cot.

"Is it bad?" Wang asked, realizing how stupid he sounded. "What should I do? Tell me how to help you!"

The old man struggled with the lid, so Wang opened it for him.

"Compress," the soldier said. There was a whole variety of tissue packs – new ones, much to Wang's surprise. Then he realized they all had Chinese writing on them.

The infirmary! Of course! He must have raided the infirmary over the previous months, perhaps even years!

He held up one that was a thick, four-inch square bandage and when the man nodded, tore it open.

"Should I cover it with Sulfa powder, or something?" Wang asked, struggling to recall what he knew about these things, which was primarily from old war movies.

The old man shook his head, instead pointing over to a battered iron teapot and a cracked cup next to it. Wang was perplexed. He knew the Japanese were even more fanatical about their tea then the Chinese, but this hardly seemed the time. Shrugging, he brought the two items over.

To his shock, the old man took the tea pot and poured what was in it right into the bullet hole, his teeth grimacing with the effort. Then he poured a cup from it and slugged it back like a shot. Only after this did he permit Wang to apply the bandage, instructing him to secure it with medical tape.

With this done he seemed to have regained some of his color, though his breathing was labored in a way Wang thought was a bad sign.

"Now what?" Wang asked after a few minutes.

"We wait," the old man whispered, his eyes now closed. "It may be too late, but then it has been too late for me for a long time."

Wang looked around at the room, avoiding what he knew he must eventually ask.

Instead, he asked another question: "What's your name?"

A few breaths passed.

"*Tetsuro Kuzikawa*," he finally said, then speaking again in fluent Mandarin, added, "Once known as 'the ghost'."

"You mean 'the ghost' as in the ghost that has been haunting these tunnels?" Wang's laugh came out as a bark. "You don't seem much like a ghost now!"

That brought a faint chuckle to Kuzikawa's lips. "No, I mean 'the ghost' as in the best sniper in my unit."

"Which unit is that?"

"Remnants of the 5th Division of the Japanese Imperial Army. Most went to Okinawa, I ended up here with a bunch of other wounded soldiers. I am the last one, and will continue fighting until I die."

Wang blinked, unable to process the implications of all this. If Kuzikawa was part of the original garrison, he would have to be in his 90s. The man in front of him couldn't be older than 50 or 60. And then there was the . . .

His speculations were cut off as the Kuzikawa gripped his arm with surprising strength and pulled him closer.

"There isn't much time," Kuzikawa said. "I think it's too late for the tea to work. Listen carefully."

Wang surprised himself by interrupting, "Not until you tell me why my great-grandmother's photo is over here!"

Kuzikawa let out a grunt. "*Your* great-grandmother? Shu Yuan?" He closed his eyes a moment and switching to Japanese, said under his breath: "*Shiranu ga hotoke.*"

Not knowing is Buddha.

"Yes! Shu Yuan! My father said her nickname was 'shoe laces!'" Wang blurted out.

Kuzikawa's eyes opened and he stared long and hard at Wang.

"Shu Yuan was my wife. Back in Manchuria, before I was reassigned to the Pacific. Then you *are* my great-grandson! Somehow, I knew. I see the echo of her face in yours."

Wang blinked several times, trying to digest all of this. It seemed way too fantastic. *This man . . . his great-grandfather? A Japanese sniper? How could he not of known this? How hadn't this ever been mentioned before?*

Easy! Another voice spoke up in his mind. One that sounded suspiciously like his (dead) friend Tao. *You never thought it odd that nothing was ever spoken at all about your great-grandfather? No photos? The polite redirects whenever the topic came up?*

A man you never thought really existed.

Even worse: a man about to die from his own hand!

Wang was seized by an overwhelming urge to scream, stand up, and simply run out of there.

Instead he leaned forward.

"Explain," he said.

Kuzikawa spoke.

He didn't go into details about his time in Manchuria, other than to mention that while stationed as a guard on the railroad there for seven years he perfected his ability to shoot targets at incredible distances. It was also there, while stationed in Shenyang, that he met the young local woman who would become Wang's paternal great-grandmother.

Kuzikawa didn't mince words, but it was apparent he was quite taken with her, that it was an illicit union, and that it was a major heartbreak for both when, in 1943, he received transfer orders to the Pacific where the tide was tipping drastically against the Japanese Imperial forces.

Wounded in New Guinea during a strafing attack at the Wewak airfield, he was evacuated and after a month in the hospital was temporarily stationed with the now 'backwater' garrison at Kharamu – a rare fortune at that point in the campaign – where he could recuperate before rejoining his unit.

That opportunity never came. Instead, the situation deteriorated rapidly as the island was cut off and forgotten, left to fend for itself.

One by one the garrison fell to disease and starvation. The promised evacuation ships never arrived, nor did orders to surrender. When an Australian unit showed up finally in 1947 to round up the survivors only a dozen soldiers were left out of 247. The survivors had deteriorated to various levels of insanity and malnutrition.

Kuzikawa was in the best shape of any of them – having come from an old Japanese military family that had ingrained in him a strict code of rigid self-discipline worked in his favor. That alone wouldn't have saved him, what did was sheer accident: stumbling across a peculiar-looking plant while foraging in the foothills to the east of the island.

It had been another solider with him that discovered it – yanking it out of the ground with maniacal glee and devouring several of the thick, rubbery leaves. Something about it looked particularly juicy and appetizing. Within minutes he was writhing on the ground in his death throes, bloody foam erupting from his mouth, while still clutching the half-eaten plant in one skeletal hand.

Kuzikawa stood by, mesmerized, then was struck by an idea. While stationed in New Guinea a local native he had hired as a guide showed him how to live off various plant species in the area. Kuzikawa was forward-thinking that way – always investigating his surroundings and picking up bits of information that might prove critical to his survival. In that way, he always treated those around him firmly but fairly – unlike many of his fellow soldiers, most of whom he considered little better than prison thugs.

He'd looked at the pulpy, white roots of the plant and recalled the simple trick that the guide had shown him with a very similar-looking, poisonous plant.

Make tea from the root.

He did. The result was amazing.

Kuzikawa didn't elaborate on what happened after that, though Wang surmised from the few comments he did make that he wasn't particularly forthcoming with his fellow soldiers about his incredible discovery. It was more than just aristocratic snobbery, it seemed, but more like a sense of cultural outrage at what the garrison survivors were doing.

Instead, he withdrew into the depths of the jungle, falling deeper into his shell as a survivalist. He hoarded and hid as much of the remaining supplies from the bunker complex as possible – mainly ammunition and uniforms – and when the Australians showed up in '47 he kept to the shadows until they left.

His existence went on quiet, methodical, until the Germans showed up with their pharmaceutical company in the 70s, threatening to destroy everything.

And take away the source of his longevity.

The plant had proven to have not only incredible curative and nutritional properties – it had proven to stop and reverse the aging process itself. Perhaps not completely, but Kuzikawa was convinced he could live long past a hundred; plenty of time to contemplate and meditate on the nature of life. He'd seen enough of the brutality of man and paid the price of heartbreak.

He dealt with the Germans quickly and efficiently.

Wang shuddered as he recalled the strange quasi-religious altar he and Tao had stumbled onto and the remains of whom he suspected were those same Germans. Which led to all sorts of other disturbing questions about the man lying in front of him.

Wang may not have seen a whole lot of the world, but it didn't take much of a leap to grasp that wasn't the work of a sane man. Not by a long shot. Then again, he couldn't fathom what living in such conditions as an isolated survivalist could do to a man's mind. Especially over decades. Perhaps he didn't want to know what kind of man his grandfather had become. The aristocrat soldier turned savage killer. He'd seen the sword bursting through his late supervisor's chest with his own eyes.

A strained cough brought him out of his speculations.

Kuzikawa was staring at him, as if reading his thoughts. He reached out with one trembling finger and tapped the teapot.

"This time, maybe too late to work. For me. But not for you! Drink it. And take what's left in the box over there." He then pointed to one gun mounted up on the wall, a heavy, military bolt-action with a scope. The scope had each end covered with a piece of cloth held in place by a thin string.

"Bring that over!"

Wang wasn't sure he wanted to do that, but he did anyhow. The rifle felt heavy and deadly in his hands. When he brought it back to the cot Kuzikawa had lifted the sword and was holding it across his chest.

He pointed to the rifle.

"Mauser K98k. With ZF39 4X scope. A gift from an old friend. Take it. There is ammo over there too." He held up the sword, which Wang realized had a subtly better designed sheath than any military ones he'd ever seen. "This is the most important thing. My grandfather's – from Edo era. An original *Honjo Masamune*. Tested at *five,* I was told."

"Five what?"

"Five bodies. In one stroke with *Ryu Guruma* - a hip cut. It's the finest workmanship and very rare. Use it with respect. And honor."

He coughed again, and this time a trickle of blood came with it.

"Go! Get off this island."

"I don't understand," Wang said. "This plant – the tea. Shouldn't it . . . fix you?"

Kuzikawa shook his head. "Not this time, I think. Too much damage. Now go!"

Wang felt rooted to the spot. Whatever this man had become – deranged or not – he was a missing link in his family. It ran against his nature to simply abandon him.

From under the cot Kuzikawa pulled out a long knife and laid it across his abdomen. Wang shook his head and gathered up the rifle and sword, along with a leather military belt with cartridge packs and a canvas carryall that was once standard issue with Japanese soldiers. This one looked ratty but was still holding together. Wang stuffed the dried root tea into it and then as an afterthought, snatched up the photo of his grandmother and placed it next to Kuzikawa's head.

Kuzikawa's eyes were half-closed and glazed with pain. But he touched the teapot.

"Drink."

Wang refilled the cup and downed it in one gulp.

Nothing.

As he stepped over to the exit way he paused and turned. He wanted to say something profound or meaningful, but nothing came.

"*Zàihuì,*" he said.

"*Genki de,*" Kuzikawa said quietly.

As Wang stood at the bottom of the passageway he realized it was already evening. He also realized, with a start, that he felt amazingly refreshed and energized. Ready to take on anything, in fact.

The question was, which was the best way to go?

Back into the complex, of course. There were boats down in the old submarine pens.

A NARROW ESCAPE

"*Now!*" Taylan yelled.

Audrey bolted to the right toward the Jeep while Taylan ran at a 90-degree oblique angle from her – toward the *Tyrannosaurs*. It was an insane, if gutsy move. He had no idea how effective the ZECON-47 would be, but he had to buy Audrey enough time to start the Jeep, or failing that, get up into the trees.

But to do that, he needed both *Tyrannosaurs* to come after him.

The rope was slung across his shoulder, one can of ZECON-47 knotted at the end of it. He'd briefly considered running to grab the guide's gun, but it was too close to the one *Tyrannosaur* and it was too risky. Plus, it would probably slow him down.

He immediately got the attention of the smaller *T. rex*. 'Smaller' was a relative word – the damn thing was still sixteen-feet high. It wheeled about, gore dripping from its jaws, and fixed Taylan with its basilisk eye. The larger one was now sweeping its snout in the reeds by the dried-up creek, as if trying to wipe its nose, while thumping around in circles.

Still shouting, Taylan ran as hard and fast as he could. Like it or not, he was about to put the computer simulation claims to the test.

Only the fact that the second *Tyrannosaur* hesitated – perhaps from a reluctance to leave its latest kill (which it was still working on) – saved Taylan. Once the thing was underway, it proved the simulators wrong.

Taylan ran across the drying mud of the creek, which fortunately slowed the *T. rex* as much as it did him, then was bounding through the tall grass, letting the bound-up can of ZECON-47 pay out behind him. He prayed it wouldn't snag on a loose rock or branch and trip him up. Either way, there was no time to second-guess matters.

The ground shook as the dinosaur charged.

The red can bounced and dragged behind him, the effect even better than he could have anticipated - the *T. rex* went after it like a cat chasing a ball of string. Except this 'cat' was evolution's ultimate killing machine, weighing in at nine tons and stinking of rotten meat.

He could only pray Audrey was being successful.

As he closed on the nearest trees, near to where a cloud of flies buzzed around the remains of Jeff Doyle, in fact, he sensed the *Tyrannosaur* was closing in on him. A quick glance back confirmed the worst: the creature was only ten feet back. He was three meters away from being eaten alive.

Without breaking stride, he reached over his shoulder and gave the rope a quick jerk with a flick of his wrist. The bright colored can shot up into the air. With a hissing roar, the *Tyrannosaurs* snapped at it.

And missed.

"Fuck!" Taylan said under his breath.

He would never outrun the thing to safety.

He spun around and flicked the rope upward again, his blood freezing at the terrifying behemoth coming at him.

At first, he thought the T-Rex would ignore the can and simply go for him instead, tearing him up in its savage maw. The Tyrannosaur was coming in head low, in a classic predator pursuit mode.

The can ricocheted off its snout. One massive foot stomped down and the creature stopped, snapping at it with uncanny speed.

There was a muffled *pop* as the can exploded in its teeth.

The effect was nearly instantaneous. The spray was intended as just that – a mace-like squirt to stun an attacker. Not an entire mouthful of the stuff.

The *Tyrannosaur* stopped dead in its tracks. It tried to let out a hissing roar, but it came out as a strangled choke. The nerve agent both stunned and was incredibly painful. The *T. rex* swung its head side-to-side violently, as if it could shake off the effect. Saliva dripped out of its mouth in ropey gobs, its glands losing control. It gagged and coughed, then to Taylan's surprise, dove forward face first into the ground with a heavy *thud*, driving its snout into the dirt.

Taylan ran, now making a looping path toward the Jeep.

Audrey still hadn't gotten it started but was still stubbornly working at it. The engine was turning over, but not catching. The larger T-Rex had stopped in its circles and had cocked its head. Blood was leaking from a dozen bullet holes in its head.

Taylan ran up to the Jeep.

"What the hell are you doing!? I told you to run if it wouldn't start!"

"Bloody bugger!" she replied, stubbornly turning the key again.

"Forget that," Taylan said. "Do you know how to pop the clutch?"

She looked at him, glaring. "Are you kidding? I'll pop *your* fucking clutch!"

Without hesitating she jumped out but kept her hand on the steering wheel, yanking it around so they could wheel the Jeep into a downhill position. Taylan ran behind the Jeep and put his shoulder into it. The two of them muscled the vehicle around until they were pointed at an oblique angle to the larger *Tyrannosaur*, who seemed to focus on them.

The Jeep was heavy, but both were running on adrenaline. Pushing hard, the vehicle began to roll down the gradual slope – toward the dried creek. Taylan prayed it would work before they got there.

At two-thirds of the way down he yelled "Do it!!!"

Audrey leapt into the driver's seat, put the shift into second gear with the clutch depressed, then a second later let it pop back while jamming the gas pedal with her other foot. Taylan saw with alarm that the *Tyrannosaur* was now coming at them. The second dinosaur seemed to be recovering – using its chin, it pushed backward and upward until the massive quads of its legs could engage, then sprang up.

The Jeep gave a lurch, hesitated, but nothing happened.

"Fuck!" Taylan yelled, shoving even harder until he thought his shoulder would snap. The *T. rex* let out its wet hissing roar and charged. The second one joined in.

"Come on, you bastard!" Audrey screamed.

"Agai—" Taylan shouted but Audrey was on it. She reengaged the clutch and the Jeep lurched again. Gratefully, the engine roared to life. Taylan vaulted into the back just as the dinosaur snapped at where his feet had been a second earlier. Dirt flew up and into the creature's face as Audrey floored the Jeep into a racing change as she looped to the left to avoid the creek bed, leaving the *Tyrannosaur* in a cloud of dust and exhaust smoke as they pulled away.

Taylan clambered forward into the passenger seat, snapping his fedora and jamming it back on his head. Without thinking he draped his free arm over the back of her seat.

"I'll take that as a *yes*."

Several of the smaller predators gave chase as she drove them along the crude road that went through the jungle, arcing northeast around the vast lake, but none caught up to them and gave up after bit.

"Where to?" she asked, the wind whipping her hair around her face. To the east the jungle infested mountains rose into the darkening, late afternoon blue sky, where the piled-up cumulus clouds were catching the setting sunlight like some old-fashioned postcard. Toward the north the mountain ridge dropped as it curved around to the west where the complex was. Driving across this exotic landscape, the day easing toward what promised to be a brilliant tropical sunset and savoring the momentary relief of escaping from what seemed like sure death, Taylan was just happy to be alive.

He said nothing for a minute, until he spotted the pickup truck racing along a converging road about a mile ahead of them.

"We should follow them," he said. "They seem to be in a hurry to get someplace. That may be the survivors of Peyton's party. Unless you have a better idea?"

"As good as any," Audrey replied. The Jeep picked up speed as she gunned the gas pedal.

"THE HONOR IS MINE, LORD ROXTON!"

Since arriving at the Camp A cave area that Bello decided would be safest for everyone for the moment, things had quickly taken a surreal turn. For one thing, he couldn't seem to convince them about the brevity of their situation. Almost immediately Peyton had attempted to build a firepit to cook their food on, until Bello warned him that even this far up out of the way, cooking anything would serve as a dangerous magnet for any predators. It was apparent that once they decided they were out of any perceived danger, they seemed to relax and convince themselves all would work out fine. It took Bello a bit to work this out and when he did, it came as an epiphany: *these people always had things work out for them.*

They had no concept otherwise.

Maybe, he decided, they thought they could simply pay someone to make things right, or bail them out, or call their lawyers or something.

The first indication came as they approached the foothills from the south, when Mrs. Banyon said from the back seat, "My, look at those mountains! They look simply beautiful! I would love to have a painting of them, dear! Promise me one, will you?"

Bello was driving the Land Rover, with Peyton riding shotgun again. He'd decided the Jeep with its open top was too vulnerable and they'd piled everything into the Rover. Peyton had leaned over and said confidentially to Bello, "Useless as tits on a boar hog! But don't worry, Lord Roxton will get everyone out of this fix – that's one thing he's an old hand at!"

The sun was just beginning to set as they arrived up at the caves, and Bello took inventory of what equipment they had. It wasn't much – at least half the supplies were destroyed with the other vehicle, but enough to last the night. They had enough weapons and ammo, if Peyton's party kept their heads, at least. But that wasn't what had Bello worried the most.

What had happened?

He didn't think this was any momentary glitch. This was a catastrophic failure.

The logical move was to get everyone to the ship in the harbor. The question was: how? And when?

The route from the way they came was far too risky. All three *Tyrannosaurs* were back there somewhere. Not that the northern route would be much safer, with all the smaller therapods. Protocol wasn't specific, other than getting guests to safe and secure locale as quickly as possible. Camp A was supposed to be one of the 'safe' locations, but how safe was it? There'd never been a complete failure simulation, only layered contingencies.

From his watch, they only had an hour or so until sunset.

Many of the species had proven to be nocturnal, which at the time had been thought to be an excellent bonus thrill for their prospective guests. Now Bello was cursing whoever thought that should go through unaddressed. With all the wondrous technology the MuTron scientists had bragged about, one would have thought they'd come up with a foolproof way to shut the damn things down.

Or neutralize them.

At least they had several cans of the ZECON-47. He had a feeling they would get tested out before the night was through.

Bello clambered up into one tree, AK-47 slung over his shoulder, and broke out his binoculars.

From up here it looked like any other afternoon on the island. Almost.

The *Brontosaur* herds had scattered, along with the *Hadrosaurs*. The once orderly patterns were shot – nothing he could put an immediate finger to, but it was there nonetheless. Animals or dinosaurs, he'd observed, fell into certain predictable behaviors and postures once settled into an environment. What he saw now was agitation, organizational breakdown, chaos.

Too many variables had been introduced at once. That usually led to death. Extinction.

Not unlike our own group, he thought, with a grimace.

Which raised another troubling question. Bello was by nature a moral man, inclined to help those in his charge, no matter how irresponsible their actions might be. But he was having serious doubts about this group.

They might be past helping.

In which case, should he simply cut and run – save himself? His instincts were telling him all bets were off at this point. The communications channels were all dead and there was no indication search and rescue parties were being sent out. The only way to know for certain was to get over to either the command center, or the generator plant/husbandry facility at the south of the island.

Maybe there's a compromise solution, he decided. Have Peyton and his party stay here, while he went to get help. That had a certain amount of logic, flimsy as it was.

A darting movement caught his eye.

Down below was a Jeep, driving at high-speed toward a point just north of his position. Not just any Jeep – but the Jeep they'd abandoned!

Then he saw another vehicle, a truck, speeding along an access road southeast of the other vehicle.

He raised the glasses and after adjusting the focus, the first vehicle swam into view. His brows knitted together as he realized it was Doctor Taylan and Doctor Adams.

What the hell were they doing? And why were they driving around without any guides?

He got a bigger shock when he switched to the second vehicle, which was smashed up and covered with blood and gore. He couldn't tell much about the driver and passenger other than that they were wearing MuTron security camo uniforms.

What the hell?

Either way, he had to get to the two paleontologists – they would certainly know what was happening.

A minute later he dropped down and walked up to Peyton.

"Mr. Peyton?" Bello asked.

"*Lord Roxton*," Peyton corrected him.

"Yes, Lord Roxton, I mean. Look, sir, I've spotted someone in the area that may be of help, but I have to move quickly to catch them. In the meantime, I think it's safest if you and the party could remain here until I return. I trust you can take charge and look after everything?"

Peyton flashed a grin and clapped him on the back. "Of course, you can, Bello my boy! Of course, you can! That's what Roxtons were born and bred for! Isn't that right, my lady?"

Suzie Blodgett didn't look completely sold. In fact, she looked as nervous as a trapped animal, her eyes with a hint of pleading as she pulled up a smile and touched Bello lightly on the arm.

"Perhaps Mr. er, *Bembo* would like some company? I could use a little—"

"Nonsense!" Peyton interjected. To make his point he grabbed Suzie Blodgett by the arm, firmly. "She'll be just fine right here. Fine as paint . . ."

Bello didn't care for the gleam in Peyton's eye. It was a little maniacal.

"I'll bring help as soon as I can," Bello said, backing up slowly.

"Sure, you will, sure you will," Peyton said, raising his gun.

Bembo knew there wasn't time to unsling his own gun, and he was no physical match for Peyton. He also saw Roger Blodgett approaching, the Thompson cradled upward in the crook of his arm.

Instead, with the elegant speed of a disappearing ghost, he turned and vanished into the undergrowth.

Peyton shouldered the Weatherby and fired off a round, the boom deafening in an area where the trees crowded up to the caves, but even he knew it was a wild shot. When Blodgett raised the Thompson and worked the slide, Peyton pushed the barrel aside.

"Save your ammo, Professor. We have a long night ahead of us," he said in his Texas drawl, unaware he was talking like an actor in a 50s B-movie.

He turned and surveyed their encampment. They'd parked the Land Rover on the access road just below them. The caves, which Bello had advised against using – they were infested with a variety of snakes, spiders and various poisonous insects – were irregular crevices in the rocks, festooned with vines and drooping beards of moss.

Peyton wasn't entirely sure why he'd had the impulse to want to shoot Bello. He'd been having a lot of odd impulses since stopping his daily cocktail of anti-anxiety meds the night before, and the doctor did say he might have some odd side effects from the Provertica pills he'd been taking to stop his hair loss, but overall, he felt great. Better than he had in decades, actually.

He'd made a bargain with himself when he'd been preparing for this trip: no prescription drugs. Allen Peyton would face - and relish – this experience as a pure, undiluted version of himself. He felt, well, *unbridled*.

The camp looked good, he thought. The old-fashioned style canvas tents were set up, a firepit built and loaded with timber (despite Bello's adamant warnings – but what the hell did ol' Bembo know about surviving in the wild?)

Everyone knew the safest and foremost duty of any real man was to build a fire, Peyton told himself when the guide had spoken up. That was also the moment he started to have unpleasant little thoughts about the Zambian.

God-damn horny bush-bunny, doesn't think I've seen him sneaking looks at Lady Roxton on the sly. Thinks he's sly? Won't be too sly when I subtract his balls with handy Mr. K-bar knife here!

But that was all water under the bridge, now that Bello had run off like a little brown chicken.

That left Lady Roxton, the Summerlee's and the ever-annoying Professor Challenger, whom Peyton was also considering using for target practice. After they had a little fun going after some more dinosaurs, of course.

Peyton shouldered the Weatherby and grabbing Suzie by the arm again, led her back to the camp area. They at least had the small cooler with fresh meat in it, along with some Bavarian beers. Plus, Peyton had his own private bottle of single malt scotch, along with a hip flask of French VSOP brandy.

"Come on, it's been a long day! Time to rest our feet, get some chow on the fire, right folks?" Surprisingly, after all they'd been through (or *because* of it), the camp was just the sort of exotic, old movie fantasy he'd imagined. The jungle, the proximity of dinosaurs, the brilliant sunset tinged with salmon and orange hues. A few of the four-winged *Changyuraptors* glided overhead from tree to tree, exotically colored creatures that let out odd, squeaking calls.

"Oh lord, where am I supposed to use the bathroom?" Mrs. Banyon asked. "I have to go so badly!"

Mr. Banyon patted her on the shoulder, gently. "Now-now, dear, we set up the 'loo tent' over there by the tree, remember?"

"A tent?" she said, her expression both confused and incredulous. "You expect me to do my business in a *loo tent*!?"

"Well . . . we discussed this before we set out on the trip – about certain 'inconveniences' we would need to accept, yes?"

Mrs. Banyon took a few unsteady steps toward the small tent, then pulling the flap aside, stopped.

"Oh no, I couldn't possible do my business in *that*!"

Inside was a portable toilet on a folding stand. Next to it a heavy stick had been jammed into the peaty ground, a roll of toilet paper hanging off a nail that had been driven into it.

"It's either that or go in your underwear," Banyon replied sharply, his civility slipping. "Now get in there and go, goddamnit!"

Peyton stood nearby, frowning, but said nothing. He clapped Roger Blodgett on the shoulder. "C'mon, prof. Let's get that fire going and some chow cooked. Hell, I'm about as hungry as a Tijuana whore!"

Half an hour later the fire was going, with a half a dozen steaks cooking on the tripod grilling rack they'd packed. Citronella torches had been lit and positioned around the perimeter of the camp, to ward off the worst of the mosquitos and other insects. Beers had been distributed and Peyton had taken a few healthy swigs of his scotch, which he offered, but only Suzie and Roger Blodgett took him up on it.

The damp wood burned slowly and made huge clouds of smoke that whorled up through the overhanging branches, the smoldering wood mixed with the heady aroma of seared meat.

Enough to alert every predator within miles.

If anyone was traumatized over what had happened earlier in the day, they weren't talking about it. Suzie Blodgett was drinking quite a bit – she'd had two full glasses of the scotch before Peyton had taken it away – while Roger sat on a fallen log off to one side, sulking like a belligerent schoolboy.

"Do you think we're really safe up here, Peyton?" Steve Banyon asked, tipping back his beer. "I mean, those dinosaurs—"

He cut himself short as he realized Peyton was pointing his .45 Automatic at him.

"*Lord Roxton*," Peyton corrected him. "And you would do well to remember it."

Banyon gave an exasperated roll of his eyes. "Come on, Peyton, I think it's time we—"

The bang of the pistol going off was deafening. The top part of the bottle in Banyon's hand shattered. He dropped it like a hot potato.

"You're *hearing* me but you're not *listening*," Peyton said. "For a professor, you don't seem very smart."

Peyton fought down an incredible urge to take a second shot and plant a bullet right between the old man's eyes. He couldn't believe he'd been so accurate with the first one.

That's what happens when you get off the meds. You stop acting half asleep and get your chops back! See!?

Banyon's face had gone an ashy hue. His wife had her mouth fixed in an "O" of surprise, her overly made-up lips trembling.

"Are you listening *now*?"

Banyon shook his head rapidly.

"Good." Peyton stood up, taking a swig of the scotch. He looked down at Suzie Blodgett, who was glassy-eyed and in shock. "Lady Roxton, would you mind accompanying me to our tent? Doc Challenger here can take the first watch."

Suzie Blodgett fished up a brittle smile. "The honor would be mine, um, Lord Roxton," she replied.

Roger Blodgett stood up, frowning, "Hey, why do I have to—"

He too cut himself short as Peyton swung the gun toward his head. Peyton was grinning, his nostrils flared and his bloodshot eyes hard as marbles. Blodgett realized he was a hair-trigger away from getting his brains blown out. It felt like his balls were shriveling inside his khaki shorts. His knees felt about to buckle.

"Sorry, er, Lord Roxton," he stammered. "I can *definitely* take the first watch. And the second too, if you like!"

Peyton stood stock still for a moment. From the distance came a primeval roar, as if a reminder the danger wasn't just confined to their campsite. From somewhere overhead came the sonic calls of several passing bats, accompanied by the sing-song chorus of tree frogs.

Peyton debated whether to shoot his assistant, then decided it was better to wait. *I may want to save that fun little exercise for later*, he thought. He flicked the safety and jammed the pistol into his hip holster.

"Come," he said to Suzie Blodgett.

She felt terrified and excited at the same time. After all the pretense, there was a certain exhilarating thrill at the prospect of having sex with Peyton while her husband stood nearby, powerless. She was also extremely drunk, which shed her inhibitions considerably.

A naughty – and cruel – smile drew her lips apart. Not saying anything more, she grabbed Peyton's hand and gave it a squeeze, tracing the nail of her thumb along the inside of his palm suggestively.

"Heh!" Peyton said. He felt a burst of his old randy self.

Five minutes later there came a giggle and grunting sound from Peyton's tent. Banyon leaned forward, forearms on his thighs, staring into the fire as if it might provide some earth-shattering answer for their dilemma in its flames. Blodgett laid the Thompson across his lap, feeling emboldened by its weight. One finger caressed the muzzle brake gently, as if savoring its deadliness. He wondered what it would be like to put the gun on full auto and empty the entire magazine into the tent.

We'll see how tough you are then, 'Lord' Fuckwad. Maybe put a few rounds up your ass while I'm at it! With that came a cold, empty feeling in the pit of his stomach as it sunk in his boss was fucking his wife, ten yards away from him. He knew she hated him – despised him actually – yet what really surprised him was how bad it hurt. He had convinced himself in his fantasy episodes time and time again how tough he was, how he could walk away from their marriage in a heartbeat and find a woman who genuinely loved and respected him, who *saw* him for who he truly was.

Across from him the Banyons sat quietly, as if any conversation might acknowledge his shame.

He was considering going for a short walk to stretch his legs, when a darting movement out of the corner of his eye distracted him, followed by a trilling sound.

It was a *Compsognathus*: a small, two-legged dinosaur about the size of a hen, with mottled bright green skin accented by darker green stripes. Unlike the other dinosaurs in its class, it had no feathers, though its oversized eyes gave it a somewhat cute appearance.

The compy hopped up onto the log next to Blodgett and cocked its head at him, letting out its trilling call as if asking him a question.

Blodgett was more amused than alarmed, holding out his hand the way he would toward any small animal. The creature sniffed his fingers, which still had traces of grease from the steaks they'd eaten. Even the Banyons seemed amused: Charles cracked a little smile and Ethel raised her brows, lips pursing.

"Ooh, isn't he adorable?" she said. "Charles? Don't you think he's adorable?"

Roger Blodgett snickered. "These things are kind of cool, no?"

"Yes, I suppose they are," Mr. Banyon agreed, looking around as a few more of the little dinosaurs came out of the underbrush, talking to each other in their peculiar trilling dialogue.

Blodgett felt a sharp, bolting pain.

"Hey!" he said, instinctively yanking his hand back. To his surprise – and horror – the first joint of his forefinger was *gone*, bitten clean off. He looked at the compy in horror as the thing swallowed it down in one rapid gulp. "What the *hell!!?*" he screamed. "Charles – did you see that!? The thing bit my damned finger off!" Enraged, he swatted it aside as hard as he could.

The creature let out a shrill squawk and half-tumbled away, but nimbly regained its feet. Another of the things jumped up in its place, giving the first one a warning nip as it bounded past it.

Several jumped all over Mrs. Banyon, attacking her head as if fascinated by her coiffed hairdo. Mr. Banyon tried to bat them away but several nipped and bit at his fingers. Blodgett smashed the nearest one with the butt of his Thompson, pulverizing its neck. Finally remembering the can of ZECON-47 Bello had left, he snatched it up and gave the nearest compys a good squirt. The effect was instantaneous. Letting out high-pitched titters, they abruptly scattered and vanished into the undergrowth.

Blodgett grinned and nodded, for the moment ignoring the blood streaming out of his severed finger. "Showed those little fuckers," he said.

Then he was aware it had grown deathly quiet, except for the crackle and snap of the fire and the animal-like grunts coming from Peyton's tent.

From nearby came a heavy *thud.*

"What was that?" Mr. Banyon whispered. "It sounded like a—"

Thud.

Banyon's face went taught. He and his wife half-turned in unison as the rank smell of spoiled meat permeated the campsite, blended with an undertone of that dry reptilian skin odor.

Eighteen feet over the top of their heads the branches rustled as the massive snout of a Tyrannosaurus Rex appeared, nostrils flaring, the pebbled rim of its lips pulling up just slightly to reveal more of its battery of ten-inch long serrated teeth.

Mrs. Banyon turned back, trembling all over like a leaf, as if staring in some other direction would simply make it go away. Charles Banyon craned his neck upward until his vertebra popped, oblivious to the dark stain spreading at the crotch of his khaki shorts. Blodgett sat slack-jawed, eyes bulging in their sockets.

The *Tyrannosaurus rex* stepped forward, its gigantic foot squashing the meat cooler flat as it leaned down toward the fire, sniffing, but wary. The six-foot long massive head was only a yard away from Blodgett, close enough to bite his head off in one nip.

Blodgett felt like his muscles had been injected with Novocain – the proximity of such a deadly and terrifying predator simply shut his systems down. All he could do was stare at the teeth and whimper. The gold-rimmed eye sizing him up was as merciless and glaring as a bald eagles', and twice the size.

Only one word entered his mind: *lunch.*

The air was cut by a shrill cry from Peyton's tent. In his wildest dreams, it had never occurred to Blodgett that he'd be saved by his wife's over-melodramatic orgasms.

The *Tyrannosaur's* head swiveled at this unexpected sound. Curious, it sidetracked the fire (and nearly flattening the Banyons in the process) and in two swift steps crossed the distance. With a fluid grace that didn't seem possible in such a titanic creature, it bent down and tore off the top of the tent with its teeth in one motion.

Stark naked, Suzie Blodgett was straddling Peyton on his cot like a racehorse and was so caught up in her orgasm there was a delayed moment before she registered her audience. She didn't see the *T. rex* towering over her at first. Instead she let out an *eek!* and covered her breasts with one arm.

She looked straight at her husband first, then her eyes traveled upward. The flickering firelight made the *Tyrannosaur* look more diabolical than ever: a prehistoric leviathan from hell. Then it occurred to her to run.

She didn't get very far. Unstraddling herself with a shriek, she made it roughly four steps before the *T. rex* struck, its jaws engulfing her from the waist up in one gruesome *chomp.* Her last muffled scream was lost in the snap of broken bones as she was snatched up in the air.

Peyton was screaming as well; he scrambled out of his cot – oblivious to his nakedness – and stood up, one arm over his head as if to ward off the dinosaur. The *T. rex* shook its head viciously side-to-side, biting Suzie Blodgett's torso clean in half. Blood and organs flew. Peyton found himself spattered head to toe, a torn loop of intestine landing across his shoulder like a grotesque bandolier.

Mrs. Banyon found her voice then, a high-pitched cry that come more of a whooping *yeek! Yeek!*

Peyton, who was inches away from becoming snack number two, was spared as the *Tyrannosaur* swung about, the shredded remains of Suzie Blodgett in its jaws, its tail snapping off branches and leaves as it did.

The underside of the tail swatted Peyton aside, knocking him flat.

"No-no-no!" whimpered Mr. Banyon, patting his wife as if he could placate her into staying quiet. Then he was tumbling into her as Roger Blodgett gave him a hefty shove toward the *T. rex.* The dinosaur took two swift steps, the last one pinning the couple down with its massive three-toed foot, mashing them together. Blodgett turned and ran for his life, trying to ignore the sounds of visceral butchery going on behind him.

He thought he was running toward the Land Rover but after a dozen yards realized he must have missed it in the dark. Instead, he ran toward the nearest – and biggest – tree and scaled it. About six feet up he paused in the nook of a giant branch, his breath coming in ragged gasps. It felt like every high-calorie dinner he'd ever eaten had caught up to him right at that moment. His heart was hammering in his chest and ominous white dots swam at the edge of his vision.

After a moment, it occurred to him he should climb higher, at least to get out of the reach of the *Tyrannosaur*, but with his adrenaline spent, it seemed all he could do was to raise a feeble hand and call it a day.

Movement out of the corner of his eye caught his attention. With a start, he realized there was a goose-sized creature sitting on the overhead branch only a foot away from him. It was one of the odd *Changyuraptors* they'd seen gliding from tree to tree earlier. Up close he saw that they weren't truly four-winged – the rear wings were actually legs with a wing-like fan of feathers along their sides.

He also realized there wasn't just one, but easily *thirty* of the things roosting in the tree with him. In the dying light, their eyes glittered.

They all seemed to be studying him. Hungrily.

He felt a lassitude overtake him. There was no place to go, no energy to run anymore.

Moments later the air was filled with the fluttering of wings and their peculiar squawking cries . . . and the screams of Roger Blodgett as he was torn apart and eaten alive.

"WHEN WOOD IS CHOPPED, WOODCHIPS WILL FLY."

Gorimov pretended to doze off. Nearby in their hammocks, Oleg and Vlad did as well, though Oleg was doing badly. He seemed to be in and out of delirium, and his hand had swollen up to twice its size, turning an unpleasant bluish-black around the area he had been bitten.

Vlad lay with his AK-47 cradled across his chest. Gorimov had one hand gripping his combat knife, which was hidden under his opposite armpit. He took deep, slow breaths, both to calm himself and to fool his enemy into thinking he was dozing. Bugs buzzed around his head, but most ignored him. The Russian gave off a vaguely unpleasant smell that was its own natural deterrent.

In the deepening shadows, a figure drew closer with nearly imperceptible movement, approaching from behind Gorimov's left shoulder. Nearby, the other Vietnamese appeared to be relaxing around their temporary camp. Two of the commandos were talking in soft tones, punctuating their conversation with light laughter – cultivating an atmosphere of calm, though closer inspection would have revealed each one had a hand on their weapon and that the eyes of their 'napping' colleague's eyes were only half-closed.

Dinky Dau glided forward with utmost care, his motions suggestive of a stalking predator.

From far off came the hissing roar of one of the dinosaurs, followed by what could have been either the scream of a human or the screech of a parrot.

Around the camp, and the three Russians, the air seemed to grow heavier and still, as if imbued with dreadful anticipation. Except for the whine of mosquitoes, even the insects had grown hushed.

From over Gorimov's shoulder appeared a gleaming eye, and the dull glint of a razor-sharp machete. With the speed of a striking reptile, Dinky Dau made his move.

Even though Gorimov had been anticipating this, it was the smell that gave him away. To the Russians, the Vietnamese had a body odor that was a combination of fish and oranges (to the Vietnamese the Russians smelled of things far worse). If Dinky Dau was a merciless predator, Gorimov was an equally merciless survivor.

The machete came down – and passed through empty air where Gorimov's neck had been a second before: the Russian snap rolled in his makeshift hammock toward the commando, smashing into his shins. Not missing a beat, Dinky Dau went into a front roll and catapulted himself back on to his feet, the machete already swinging again. For all his ungainly appearance, though, Gorimov was surprisingly quick. He was on his feet and leaping under the swing before it came down, slamming the Vietnamese up against the mossy tree the hammock had been hanging from, one hand on Dinky Dau's throat and the other plunging the knife toward his gut.

Dinky Dau's left hand caught the wrist holding the knife just as the blade pierced the first half-inch of his stomach. He tried to angle the machete inward to jab at his opponent while raising his knee up between them to stop Gorimov's forward momentum. Though much smaller, Dinky Dau's was a bundle of steel muscle, honed by decades of martial training. Realizing the machete was useless at such close quarters, he released it and struck a lightning-fast palm heel blow at Gorimov's temple. Gorimov twisted his head slightly as it came in and the blow cuffed his ear. Still, it was hard enough to make him see stars and ease off his knife thrust as Dinky Dau twisted his body and shoved forward with his knee. Hooking his other leg behind Gorimov's knee, the Vietnamese kicked off the tree and the two went tumbling into the ferns.

Shouts came as the other commandos grabbed their guns and moved in.

Vlad had been prepared too. He rolled out of his hammock firing, keeping a low profile and sweeping from left to right. Two of the commandos fell while a third – the back-up hacker – was clipped in the leg and rolled away, groaning. Tuan ducked behind a tree just as the bullets reached him.

Oleg tried to stand up and instead collapsed in a heap, sweat pouring down his face in rivulets.

Gorimov and Dinky Dau rolled through the damp foliage, locked in a life-and-death struggle. Gorimov was a brute of a man, strong as a bear, but the Vietnamese was like a steel trap, his legs locked around the Russian's hips. After dropping the machete he'd twisted his wrist in Gorimov's grip, activating a spring-loaded blade strapped to the inside of his forearm. He'd already sliced open the Russian's scalp with a quick jab, just missing the eye. In return, he'd caught another jab, this one in the ribs.

Still rolling back and forth, neither seemed to get the advantage. Then, coming out of a roll on top of his opponent, Dinky Dau slammed his forehead into Gorimov's nose, breaking it. Blood poured out immediately.

Instead of stunning him, however, it resulted in an incredible burst of rage. Swinging the Vietnamese sideways, Gorimov somehow got his feet under him and in a fit of raw strength, stood up, Dinky Dau still locked around him like a homicidal koala bear.

Gorimov roared like an animal and charged forward, smashing through branches and vines. He crashed through ten feet until he drove Dinky Dau into a tree with the force of a runaway truck, impaling him on the stub of a broken limb so hard it went through the back of his neck and came out next to his Adam's apple. A second branch punched through his left side, skewering his kidney and liver.

Gorimov stepped back, panting, blood from his nose and scalp pouring down his face in rivulets. A bullet whickered near his head, forcing him to duck and dive for his AK-47, which still lay propped near his hammock.

"Vlad, you O.K.?" he shouted, working the slide on the assault rifle and flicking the safety off.

"Okay!" Vlad shouted back from where he was hiding behind a tree nearby. "Commandos not so good!"

Even as he spoke, one was sneaking up behind him. Lanh was keeping well back, realizing he was out numbered.

A single gunshot rang out. The commando's head snapped back, the bullet coming up through his chin and exiting the back of his head, sending his cap flying along with part of his brains. A few feet away Oleg slumped back down, pistol in his hand.

"Ha! Only one left!" Vlad shouted, then dropped to his knees. He had a rough idea where Tuan was, but was smart enough not to expose himself.

Gorimov let out a grunt. "I'm coming to get you, little fucker, and rip you to fucking pieces!"

He picked up a large rock and tossed it to the left, then made his way to the right toward the camp.

Tuan thought quickly. He was outnumbered three to one – best he knew – and from the distance heard a vehicle approaching.

That should be my brother, with the rest of the commandos, he thought. He wasn't afraid of the Russians – he was smart. His training had drilled into him that teamwork was always critical for success, not personal glory.

Tuan inched backwards.

Lanh was finally making good time. The pickup was bumping and shaking along the rough road, but was at least holding together. Glancing over at Dinh he felt a rush of exultation: death, quick-thinking and narrow escapes – it was like old times. When it came to him and his brother, his mother had always told him he was the lucky one.

You have the aura of good fortune about you, she'd often said, but only when Tuan was out of earshot.

Racing along in the growing dusk, he hoped his brother had been successful.

They were just approaching a crude bridge over a culvert when he caught a flash of movement from the left. Something huge burst out of the jungle. Even as he swung the wheel hard to avoid it, he had the terrible feeling his luck was about to run out.

There was the crumple of metal and shattering glass as they were broadsided.

It was like being hit by a locomotive.

The truck tumbled and went airborne, then abruptly flipped and flew down into the stream bed, wheels up.

The *T. rex* that had run into them barely checked its stride. It was completely focused on the intoxicating, irresistible smell of cooking meat up on the mountain.

The impact of the truck was buffered by the thick vines and vegetation edging the stream. Even so the cab was nearly mashed flat when they landed. The thunder of footsteps from the disappearing *Tyrannosaur* faded away. For the space of a few minutes, there was only the soft ticking of the engine and sing-song trickle of the stream.

Then came the sound of another vehicle coming up the road.

"We must have lost them," Audrey said as the scenery changed from tall grass into thickly forested jungle. In the darkening light, trees and shadows and trees took on fantastic shapes – not a difficult leap considering what was now running loose on the island. A mile back they had to brake to a screeching halt when two *Ankylosaurs* ambled across the road.

"Look there!" she said as they continued, driving at a breakneck speed. A mile or so ahead they caught the unmistakable shape of a *Tyrannosaur* crossing ahead. At twenty-feet high it was hard to miss.

They crossed the culvert, the few broken branches and torn vines where the pickup truck had catapulted through all but invisible in the growing dark.

The road continued northward, ramping up toward the foothills and the stream bed where Gorimov and the commandos had set their camp. Audrey downshifted as they went up a steep incline, the road becoming more approximate than literal. The Jeep was nothing if sturdy, fortunately.

Just as they got to the top, a strange figure stepped out of the woods.

Taylan recognized Tuan immediately. Tuan's eyes went wide, first with surprise, then rage. Taylan was just reaching over to tell Audrey to hit the gas when the Vietnamese raised his AK-47 and fired at them, fully automatic.

Taylan acted instinctively. He jammed his left foot over Audrey's while wrenching the steering wheel to the left, causing them to career off the road and into the bushes. A few bullets clipped the windscreen, but most missed them, pulverizing the back end of the Jeep instead. They rammed into a tree, Audrey smacking her head on the oversized steering wheel, Taylan twisting himself painfully as his shoulder hit the metal dashboard.

A branch snapped.

Taylan glanced up, squinting, to see Tuan standing alongside them, the assault rifle raised to finish them off.

He was grinning.

"After all these miles, here we finally are," he said.

"Seriously?" Taylan replied. "Your sister is insane, you know that? Do you have any idea what *really* happened?"

Tuan's expression remained opaque. "I'm not here for explanations, Grant Taylan. I'm just here to kill you."

Even as he pulled the trigger, there came a loud *crack!* Tuan's head jerked as part of his scalp and brain blew out sideways. His eyes rolled back as he crumbled to his knees, the front of the Ak-47 driving down into the soft earth. It gave a muffled pop as it misfired.

Audrey sat up, blinking, blood running from a gash above her left eyebrow. "What the—?"

Igor Gorimov emerged from the bushes, pistol in hand. He too was grinning.

"Nobody gets to kill you, Grant Taylan, except *me*. That's my job!"

Gorimov stepped back to survey his handiwork. With Vlad's help, he'd just finishing staking and binding Taylan to the ground where the camp was. Audrey had been trussed up thoroughly, except for her legs. Apparently Gorimov wanted her walking wherever he was taking her.

It was now dusk, with several of the four-winged *Changyuraptors* flying from tree to tree overhead. In another circumstance, Taylan would have found them fascinating. In his current situation, he was wondering how long it would be before they decided he was a buffet dinner.

"So, no traditional bullet-in-the-skull for me, then?" he asked.

Gorimov chuckled. He looked ghastly with the dried blood all over his face.

"No, no my friend, what's the fun in that?"

Taylan glanced around at the bodies of the dead commandos the Russians had dragged and left around the camp, presumably as bait.

"You're getting sloppy, Igor. Not a hard man to track down. My employer won't be happy, and he has a long reach." The words sounded lame to his own ears. But it was worth a shot, at least.

Gorimov stepped over and squatted next to him. "Really? Would your 'employer' happen to be Allen Peyton the third?"

Taylan squinted one eye. "You know him?"

"Hmmpf. For such a smart guy, you're not so smart!"

"You keep saying that."

"You haven't figured it out yet, have you?"

"Figured out what?"

"*Peyton.* Who the fuck do you think I was selling the *Tarbosaurus bataar* skeletons to in New York? How do you think I knew to come here?"

"Jesus." Taylan banged the back of his head in the dirt.

"You bloody cocksucker!" Audrey said.

"Ha! Maybe I let you suck on mine!" Gorimov said.

"As if anyone could ever find it," she shot back. It was a juvenile response, but it hit home. Gorimov's lips took on a compressed, prunish look. He nodded to Vlad, who backhanded her. She dropped her head, but through the tangle of her hair her eyes were murderous.

"That doesn't make a lot of sense, Igor," Taylan said, trying to redirect the Russian. "Why would he pay me to come here? He offered to bank roll my research, after all."

"Did he 'show you the money first', as you Americans say? No? Because you are an idiot, Doctor Taylan. Peyton didn't just come here for a 'role play' vacation. His goal is to get his hands on what will be the biggest breakthrough in genetics in the 21st Century! And guess what? *You* are about to become food for that 'genetic breakthrough'! How about them oranges, eh?"

Taylan struggled against his bonds. He would have loved nothing more right at that moment than to wrap his hands around the Russian's neck and throttle him. Nearby, Vlad fingered his assault rifle, as if sensing his intention.

Taylan was mentally kicking himself. The whole thing had been off-kilter from the get-go, a set-up designed to keep him off-balance at every turn. Starting with Gorimov's 'convenient' appearance at the top of the Palisades cliffs that day. He tried to remain focused. He had to get as much information out of the Russian as possible.

I have no idea how, Taylan said to himself, *but I will catch up and make them pay, dearly. Starting with that hit to Audrey.*

"It's 'apples', you mental midget, not 'oranges'! Oh, and you're just going to waltz off this island, in what? Your rowboat?" he said, aloud, "And how did you get here anyway? Fly in with those fat arms of yours?"

Gorimov smiled again, but it fell far short of his eyes. "Very funny, Grant. For a man about to die in a nasty way. No, I came here in a sub, with some Vietnamese friends of yours. As you can see," he gestured around, "the climate here didn't agree with them too well. And to answer your question, dummy, I plan to leave here on Mr. Luo Pan's yacht. I understand he keeps it in the old submarine pen near the harbor. Only first class from now on, for me . . ." he nodded toward Audrey, "and my new bitch!"

He stood up. Without the hacker, getting the data out of the MuTron computers at the facility would be problematic, but he didn't think getting the DNA samples would be. There was still Dinh and Lanh to deal with, but he'd deal with them the same way he'd dealt with the others: in bullets.

"All right, Vlad. Time to go."

"What about Oleg?"

"What about him? He's as good as dead. Unless you're in a mood to carry him?"

Vlad shrugged. "No. He's always been bad luck."

"Fine. Let's go. We have roughly three miles to cover and a lot of dinosaurs between us and getting off this fucking island. Goodbye, Doctor Taylan."

Vlad hauled Audrey to her feet, who struggled with him until he put the gun to her temple.

"Behave," he said.

Taylan craned his head around, and catching Audrey's eye, winked. It was false bravado, but it was all he had at the moment.

She tried to draw up a smile, but it was a weak one. She looked like the fight was out of her, and that was more dispiriting to him than anything.

Within a few minutes their footsteps faded, leaving him alone with the dead bodies and buzzing flies. The jungle was alive tonight: he could pick up all sorts of sounds, including the roars and cries off in the distance.

Closer to him came the rustle of branches and patter of tiny feet.

It only took a few minutes for the first dinosaurs to arrive.

They were the brightly-colored *Tianyulong*, hopping excitedly around the clearing, their bright golden eyes looking *hungry*.

THE CALL OF REVENGE

Dinh came to with a moan, the tinkle of broken glass around her as she shifted her weight.

From the corner of her eye she caught movement. Blinking slowly and turning her head, she saw that Lanh was shaking his head slightly, as if trying to wake up.

It took her a moment to realize she'd blacked out during the impact. Her shoulder and neck were aching from where she'd instinctively twisted it sideways as they hit, but best she could tell she hadn't suffered any serious injuries. That in itself was amazing, considering the condition of the cab.

The windows were all shattered, with ferns and branches sticking in at all angles. Unfastening her seatbelt, she slid to the roof of the cab, reaching over and rubbing Lanh's shoulder.

"Lanh! We made it!" she whispered, in Vietnamese. "Are you all right? Let's get out of here."

Lanh's head kept shaking.

"*What!?*" she said, leaning forward.

Abruptly his head snapped to one side, and she saw the *Zhenyuanlong* raptor that was half-inside the driver's window, chewing apart the other side of his face. Lanh's right eye, glazed in death, looked past her into nothingness.

For the first time in her life, Dinh screamed.

The raptor hissed at her, and as if challenged, lunged further in, trying to get past Lanh and get at her. Its gore-covered jaws snapped and bit.

Still screaming, Dinh pulled up her machete and in the close confines, jabbed at it. After a few futile tries, she finally let the thing grab it in its teeth. With a twist of her wrist, she rammed it forward and jerked upward, severing the raptor's upper palette and snout.

It screeched and pulled out backwards.

Dinh kicked the passenger door open and clambered out, finding herself knee-deep in ferns. The mutilated raptor stood up, still screeching in pain. Remembering her sidearm, Dinh drew it and fired over the pickup, hitting it in the head several times until it dropped. Another raptor leapt up onto the truck's undercarriage, hissing, and she shot that one too.

She could hear more in the jungle around her and felt all her survival instincts kick in. There was no time to worry about Lanh – he was already dead. She had to retrieve as many weapons and ammo as possible and get moving.

Meet up with Tuan. Complete the objective. Get off this island.

And if the opportunity presented: exact revenge.

She reached in and snapped off the ID tag Lanh always wore around his neck, as a keepsake, avoiding looking at the ruins of his head. A tear gathered at one eye – only one, and she quickly blinked it away.

The sniper rifle had a gouge in the polymer stock, but otherwise looked intact. There'd be no way to know if the scope was out of adjustment until she used it. Before she left she did something unusual: she dabbed her finger in Lanh's blood and smeared it on her cheeks and the tip of her nose.

Whatever lives she claimed going forward would be his too.

Joseph Bello sprinted as nimbly as he could, getting away from Peyton and his lunatic party. One thing was abundantly clear: all bets were off here on out. He had only one mission going forward, and that was to get off the island at all costs. MuTron International could go fuck itself, if it hadn't already.

He headed northwest, toward the service road that led to the second camp, the one that was highly doubtful Peyton and his group would ever get to. There were supplies cached there, including weapons and ammo, but only if you knew where to look.

He was also keenly aware of the fact he was unarmed (aside from his machete) and running through a jungle crawling with all sorts of prehistoric predators.

He tried to piece together what he'd learned from the previous run-throughs.

Only certain species hunted at night. Trees weren't necessarily safe havens. But open areas were riskier. The larger predators favored the game trails and watering areas. Keep your eyes and ears alert. And of course, your nose.

Not a lot to go on, he decided. He would have killed for a can of the ZECON-47.

At least you have the machete. Plenty of people have been stuck in worse situations with less.

He decided to at least stick to the road. If any help was coming, it would be from there, and trying to travel through the jungled areas at night was pointless. He'd only end up lost. Or worse.

And crazy as it sounded, he decided sticking to the middle of the road was the safest bet. Anything could ambush him from the thick foliage on either side – but at least he would have time to react.

As he made his way along, he realized the island was spookier than ever. The wilds of Africa were at least something he understood. This place felt utterly alien. Primordial.

Of *course,* it was! There were creatures extinct a millennia before the dawn of man running loose. And from all indications, all the fail-safes on the island had broken down. Rescue parties should have been out in full force. At the very least, the helicopter should be out searching for Peyton's team. *An African guide might be considered expendable,* he thought grimly, *but a billionaire investor?*

Something had gone terribly wrong.

Gunshots came from ahead, in the distance.

Semi-automatic fire. From the direction of the second camp. Overhead the first stars were winking in the sky.

Instinctively, he ran at a loping base, hunkered down. If there were guns, there were people. Hopefully MuTron security.

He'd gone about fifty yards when he heard the distinct patter of feet following him, quickly. Risking a glance backward, he saw three ostrich-sized raptors – young Utahraptors he figured, gaining fast.

Shit!

Bello went into a full sprint.

He was a naturally agile runner, and the fact that he was never a smoker helped. On the other hand, the older-style work boots they were forced to wear as part of the 'Expedition Dress Code' did not.

He knew they could get up to 25 miles-per-hour for short bursts – maybe ten or fifteen seconds – which was about five more than he was capable of.

Terror lent speed to his feet.

Still, they continued to gain on him. Relentlessly.

The gap closed: twenty yards. Fifteen.

Fucking kids! he thought, somewhat irrationally.

Bello scanned the area ahead of him for options, but it was incredibly challenging to focus when one was running for one's life.

Then he saw it.

To the right in a small clearing was a herd of *Parasaurolophus* - crested, duck-billed herbivores roughly sixteen-feet high - dozing in the early evening heat, resting in a protective circle.

Bello cut off the road and darted right through the center of them. He ducked under the largest and gave it a hard slap for good measure.

The creature let out an alarmed honk and snapped around just as the first *Utahraptor* arrived, leaping through the air like a deranged kangaroo. It was met in mid-jump by the herbivore's whipping tail, sending it catapulting sideways in a tangle of limbs. A second *Parasaurolophus* stomped on it with its hind foot, crushing the raptor's lower spine.

The second raptor leapt onto it, slashing with its front claws as it clambered up on the herbivore's back, the creature wailing in pain.

Bello didn't see what followed, as the third *Utahraptor* skirted the herd and continued after him, possibly sensing an easier meal.

His breath was coming in ragged gasps as he leapt and bounded through tall grass and bushes, somehow managing not to get tripped up. He ran straight through a huge spiderweb without breaking stride, barely registering the brightly-colored arachnid as big as his hand scrambling up his chest and tumbling over his shoulder.

The third raptor wasn't giving up.

Once his foot hit the oiled dirt of the roadway, Bello wheeled about and drew his machete. The creature bounded through the air at him, claws splayed in anticipation, hind legs tucked up.

To pin me down, he thought.

Again, Bello went on instinct. Raising his left arm to protect himself, he dodged sideways and swung with all his might above the thing's feet at its throat.

The blade was razor-sharp; it sliced off the raptor's right fingers, feathers, and went through the side of its throat so cleanly he wasn't sure if he'd even done any severe damage. The raptor stumbled as it landed, then whipped about alarmingly fast. It tried to hiss, but what came out was a gurgling gasp. Bello saw the ugly, crescent-shaped wound open and gouts of blood spill out over its feathered neck. Even so, the raptor made a flailing attempt to attack him again. Even dying it wouldn't quit.

He made it quick and merciful.

Taylan knew he was down to minutes. After feeding on the dead bodies, the *Tianyulong* had taken several tentative nips at his legs, as if assuring themselves he was unable to defend himself. One leapt up onto his chest, its nails digging at him through his shirt.

He forced himself to stay perfectly still.

The creature bent forward taking a few tentative sniffs. He could clearly see its rows of fine, needle-sharp teeth and the glimmer of light off its iridescent feathers. It struck him as a beautiful, terrifying creature.

That was looking to eat him.

The *Tianyulong* took another step forward, both feet squarely on his chest. It leaned down, its body tensing, pulled its head back slightly . . . and struck.

Taylan was quicker.

He snapped his head sideways, the dinosaur's teeth just grazing his cheek, then twisted and bit.

He caught part of its neck in his front teeth. The *Tianyulong* screeched and tried to bite him back, its taloned wing scratching his face, but Taylan's wind was up. He bit down hard as the thing's clawed feet raked his chest and shirt, then, even as it squirmed and cried in pain, he snapped his head sideways and spat it out, its momentum rolling it away.

To his dismay, several more hopped up to take its place, then abruptly scattered as a heavily feathered *Utahraptor* stepped into the clearing, flapping its winged forearms and hissing left and right, making him think of a diabolical 6-foot high goose.

Gritting his bloodstained teeth, Taylan's eyes widened in terror.

The clatter of gunfire ripped through the air.

The *Utahraptor* jerked as a dozen bullets hit its neck and head with the sickening *thwip thwip* of metal punching into flesh. Blood and feathers flew. The raptor spun and fell, its head decimated. It tried to stand up on its hind legs, once, then collapsed.

From Taylan's right, a figure emerged out of the jungle, the AK-47 held shoulder high.

Joseph Bello!

Taylan let his head drop back, spitting bits of *Tianyulong* out.

"They're just superficial, but the risk of infection is high," Bello said. "That should kill it for the moment though."

183

Taylan's teeth were still clenched from the sting of hydrogen peroxide from the first aid kit, one of the many things Bello had retrieved from the campsite supply cache.

"Infection is going to be the least of our worries," Taylan replied, rubbing his wrists where the bindings had chafed them. "Any word on what's happened? Dr. Adams and I were trying to hook up with you and Peyton's group when everything went to hell. Our guides are dead. It appears the much-touted 'safety protocols' have gone by the board, and all communications are out. Oh, and my old friend Igor has popped up, along with a bunch of Vietnamese commandos. From the looks of this camp, they weren't here for just a friendly social call."

He didn't think it prudent to mention Peyton's connection with the Russians just yet, until he had a better handle on which side of the fence Bello's interests lay, so he gave him an edited account of what had happened with Gorimov and how he'd run off back to the complex with Vlad in tow.

Bello nodded.

"I left Peyton and his group up by the caves southeast of here. I don't think they stand much of a chance." He summarized what had happened up at the caves.

"I don't understand," Taylan said. "We found the remains of the 'expedition' and figured out there were survivors. We were trying to track you down when we crossed paths with the Russians. They took Dr. Adams. What exactly the hell is going on, Bello?"

"I'm not sure. Something catastrophic. Those bodies are Southeast Asian military. The fact that no search and rescue parties have been sent out is a bad sign. There were protocols for emergency events like this. It appears there's been a complete breakdown. The best bet would be to get to the main complex and find out just what. I believe that's the safest place."

Remembering what happened in the lab, Taylan had his doubts about that. But that was where Gorimov was taking Audrey. And where Roma still was, presumably.

"Agreed," he said. He hefted the AK-47 Bello had given him. "Was this one of MuTron's official 'safety protocols'?"

Bello grinned. "No. Well, the guns are at least – from the armory. Chinese manufacture. Old surplus. But still the best gun ever made. I buried a cache along with medical supplies and a few food rations near each camp. Just in case. Old trick I used to do in the bush."

"*Hmpf,*" Taylan grunted. "You may be the first person I've met here who plans ahead."

He stood up and slung one of the knapsacks Bellow had retrieved over his shoulder. It had half a dozen extra clips, bottled water and some beef jerky. He'd already taken a K-bar knife out and strapped it to his belt.

"What's the quickest way to get there?"

THIS WAY, PLEASE

The incessant voice continued to politely urge on from the hidden speakers: "Protocol 7 has been activated. Please evacuate the facility in an orderly fashion . . . Xiéyì 7: Qǐng shūsàn. . ."

Miss Grey ran down the corridor, feeling like she was caught in one long, unending nightmare. The elevator ride had been brief, fortunately, as she tried to ignore the bloody hand smears on the inside of the door and what she was quite positive was someone's hand lying over in the corner in a pool of blood.

The corridor was something out of a horror movie: blood smears here and there, a spatter on the ceiling, a crumpled figure in a lab coat with most of its face chewed off. Bloody footprints – mostly three-toed, were everywhere. It looked like a blood-thirsty stampede had passed through. There wasn't any alarm – just the polite woman's voice – but the strobing emergency lights were nerve-wracking enough.

Her first thought was to get to the trawler, but that would mean exiting the complex and trying to cross open ground all the way to the dock. That left the second alternative, the old submarine pen where Luo Pan Wei's private yacht was kept.

It was off limits to everyone except Mr. Pan's private guards. Provided, of course, they hadn't left in it themselves.

Still, it was her best bet.

She continued running down the corridor, cursing her shoes, then stopped as she heard a woman scream. She looked up at the door nearest her and saw the entrance to the infirmary.

Of course! Dr. Banaji!

She'd all but forgotten about her.

Through the door she could see Roma was atop one of the stainless-steel cabinets, trying to kick away one of the *Zhenyuanlong* raptors with her feet. The creature was on the counter, hissing and snapping at her. The only thing keeping it from getting her foot in its teeth was that it kept slipping and falling on the polished counter surface, its scaled feet unable to get any traction.

Miss Grey looked about and quickly spotted a mop and bucket leaning near the door, presumably left from the clean-up earlier. Another of the lab workers had succumbed to their injuries after the lab accident.

"Ahh! *Help!*" Roma screamed.

185

The raptor scrabbled again, flapping its winged arms ineffectually.

Not hesitating, Miss Grey snatched the mop. Bolting across the room past the dead medical assistant lying half chewed next to an examination table, she shouted and rammed the *Zhenyuanlong* with the mop head, mashing it up against the backsplash.

The creature was nothing if nimble, though, and after the second blow it twisted around enough to grab a bundle of mop threads in its jaws, hissing and gnashing.

She tried to ram the raptors head flat, but it wrapped itself around the head, tearing and clawing viciously. It made her think of an enraged rooster mixed with an equally enraged cat. Seeing her thrusts were having no success at injuring the creature, she gripped the handle even harder, then whipped it around like a baseball bat, checking it after a three-quarter circle.

The *Zhenyuanlong* flew across the room in an ungainly tumble of feathers and claws, bouncing off the far wall.

It landed on its feet. Spitting out a few loose strands out of its mouth, with surprising speed it bolted immediately back at her, charging across the infirmary with its winged arms tucked close.

Miss Grey felt her skin break out in goose bumps, her eyes widening in atavistic fear. She backed up against a glass partition wall leading into a second room, then cried out as something smashed into that behind her. She half-glimpsed a young *Utahraptor* trying to bite its way through, doing little more than making a few starred cracks.

The *Zhenyuanlong* was only a dozen feet away when a loud *bang* filled the room.

Wang was standing in the doorway, the Mauser at his shoulder.

The shot missed, but it sent tile chips flying from where the bullet ricocheted off the floor inches near the raptors feet, and it certainly got its attention. Spinning about in a scrabble of claws, it focused in on this new threat.

Wang considered chambering another round, but immediately grasping his lack of training and the clunkiness of the bolt-action, opted to toss it and draw the sword instead.

With that weapon, his instincts were more of use. Grabbing the hilt in both hands, he brought it down in an overhead blow just as the raptor ran up to him.

The blade was as true as his grandfather claimed.

It was like the creature had been struck by a razorblade: its head, neck and upper shoulder fell cleanly away while the rest of its body ran obliquely past his leg, before caroming into the counter behind him and collapsing.

He was still standing in shock when Roma shrieked, pointing to the doorway at his back. Wang spun about as another *Utahraptor* attacked. He swung the sword, but the creature lunged first, knocking him down and sending the sword clattering away. A second later it pounced on him, talons slashing. The only thing that saved him from being eviscerated was his quick reflexes: before the clawed feet could pin him, he rolled up on his back, raising his feet to block its chest while grabbing its feathered forearms with his hands.

Even so, he wouldn't last more than a few seconds but for Miss Grey.

He didn't hear her pick up the Mauser and work the bolt, but she did. Instead of taking any chances she simply rammed the barrel into the thing's hissing mouth and pulled the trigger.

There was a muffled bang as the back of its head blew out.

"Are you okay?" Miss Grey asked Roma.

The door was secured, and the body dragged out into the hall, and they'd moved to an adjoining examination room where they didn't have to listen to the trapped raptor banging about. Wang leaned against the counter nearby, still giddy with shock. The katana had been cleaned off and was back in its scabbard at his hip. The bottled water he was guzzling shook in his grip.

Roma examined her heavily bandaged hand, which though scuffed, was fine.

"Yes, I think so," she replied. "They gave me a tranquilizer – it completely knocked me out. When I came to, that *Utahraptor* was eating the . . . the doctor's assistant. I tricked it into the other room, only to have that *Zhenyuanlong* come at me. My God, 24 hours ago I would have given everything in the world to see a living dinosaur. After this, I don't think I need see one of them again. *Ever.*"

Over the top of her glasses, Miss Grey laughed. It was a little edgy but genuine, which helped break the tension. Roma found herself chuckling too.

"Where's your friend Tao?" Miss Grey asked, turning to Wang. "You two are inseparable."

The stricken look that crossed Wang's features answered her question.

"I'm so sorry," she hastened to add.

Roma distracted her with a hand on her shoulder. "What's happened? Why is the place being evacuated?"

"I'm not really sure, but there seems to have been an attack on the facility– we've never had anything like it; a sophisticated hacker that brought down all the systems."

"*All* the systems?" Wang asked.

"Apparently it was a 'retro-virus that morphed into a back-door virus that allowed the hacker to gain the deepest levels of our database and insert a *third* virus, a worm'. According to CTO Xióng, at least."

"That's not possible! Even in a worse-case scenario, they could shut down the entire system and restore it from scratch. There was a double redundancy back-up!"

Miss Grey shook her head. "No, there *wasn't*. There was supposed to be, but it was never implemented."

Wang went pale. "That means . . ."

"Yes, that means all safety protocols are gone. The dinosaurs are loose. *All* of them."

"What about Dr. Taylan, and Dr. Adams? Peyton's party?" Roma asked.

Miss Grey shook her head. "They were out in the field when it happened. It's unlikely they would survive. Even if they did, there's nothing we can do to help them."

"*Nothing?*" Roma replied, her voice rising in anger. "Aren't there any rescue parties? Isn't *anyone* in charge?"

"No," Miss Grey said. "There simply isn't. If you want to live, we have to find a way out of here as quickly as possible. Now."

"The *trawler*?" Wang asked. "According to the evacuation protocol, that's how we're supposed to evacuate the island."

"I was thinking the submarine pen," said Miss Grey. "Mr. Pan's yacht is there."

"Where's Mr. Pan?" Roma asked.

"He's already left."

"He's *already* left? What the bloody hell kind of operation is this?"

"One I believe I'm sorry I ever took a job with," Wang interjected. He heard smashing glass from the other room where the raptor was trapped. "I don't think we should stay here much longer."

Could be worse, he thought, *at least I'm stuck with two hot ladies! Or one definite at least, the other is, well . . . he had to admit, was oddly attractive. Maybe Tao had a point?*

Regardless, this wasn't any time to ponder such questions. Something else was nagging at him.

"We're supposed to get to the trawler," he said "That's the evacuation protocol."

"Too dangerous," Miss Grey said, "We'd have to get down to the beach and cross half way around the bay on foot. The submarine pen would be safer."

"No, it wouldn't," Wang replied.

"Why not?" Roma asked.

"The access stairway is right near the main lab. If all the security and coms are down, you don't want to go anywhere near that place. But I've got a better idea."

Miss Grey raised her brows, "What?"

"The hangar. It's right down the hall. There's a dune buggy there. It was abandoned in the 70s when the pharmaceutical company was here. Tao and I had been working on it as a side project for a year now. We did the exterior restoration and paid one of the mechanics to handle the engine work. I could have us out to the docks in no time."

Miss Grey looked annoyed. "How do you know the guards haven't taken it?"

Wang chuckled and reached into his pocket. "That's easy – I have the only keys!"

The vast hangar was empty of any personnel. The main doors had been left partially open – it appeared the guards and crew had taken off in the maintenance vehicles in a haste.

"It's over here!"

The buggy had been stored in the corner, covered with a tarp. They'd only taken it for a couple of trial spins around the hangar, not sure when – if ever – they'd get permission or even an opportunity to take it outside.

Wang yanked the tarp aside. The buggy was a classic 1971 Volkswagen Beach Buggy, with iridescent teal-blue paint and loopy contours that suggested California sand dunes and Pacific-blue skies.

"Wow," Miss Grey said, clearly impressed. She'd never seen anything like it outside an old movie. "I had no idea we had anything like that here."

"Oh, there's all kinds of things around here you probably had no idea about," Wang said, unable to resist a little bravado.

"Like that Japanese sword? And that antique rifle? Where on earth did you get those?" Roma asked. "From the prop store?"

"Yes, *do tell*," Miss Grey interjected, arching an eyebrow.

"Uh, that's a long story," he replied, looking Roma in the eye. "And a very strange one. Maybe I can explain it to you sometime."

"Yes, *maybe*," she replied.

Blushing, Wang placed his rifle in the back seat, and after a moments consideration, slid the sword in next to his left leg in the driver's seat. Whatever happened, he wanted it right where he could grab it.

"Come on, get in!"

Miss Grey jumped into the passenger seat without hesitation, leaving Roma – to Wang's chagrin – to climb into the back.

He primed the choke three times, then turned the key and fired it up. The engine roared to life with a plume of blue-grey exhaust smoke out the tailpipes. Wang gunned the engine, which was when he saw something large come wandering through the hangar door.

Grant Taylan might have recognized it: it was a young *Tarbosaurus bataar*. A slightly smaller, Asian version of the *Tyrannosaur*, with dramatic, tiger-like stripes along the length of its body. The same species whose remains Gorimov had stolen off him.

The Tarbosaurus paused, looking around the hangar, and immediately zeroed in on the Dune Buggy and its occupants.

With a sinking feeling in his gut, Wang had time to think: how many more dinosaurs did they make here?

It let out a hissing roar and charged.

"ONE SHOT AT YOUR NUTS, POOFTER!"

Audrey tried not to think what might be happening to Grant Taylan.

Gorimov was dragging her along like a tethered dog, one end of the rope gripped firmly in his one hand, while the other held an AK-47. Vlad trailed behind them, watching their backs for any dinosaurs.

Somehow, she'd exchanged one nightmare for another.

Not that she'd never been in any narrow scrapes before. There'd been the corrupt Egyptian officials who'd held her and her guide in jail illegally for a week after she'd exposed them for selling priceless artifacts on the black market (for a couple days there was talk about selling her to some Libyan sex-slave traders, which fortunately never happened) and the three drunken lumberjacks that had appeared out of nowhere in the Saskatchewan Province while scouting a remote discovery of a rare *Ankylosaurus* species. They'd tried to gang rape her until she stuck one of them in the balls with a Bowie knife and slashed one of the other's chest wide open. The third had tried to shoot her but fortunately was too drunk to aim properly – even so, there'd been a few harrowing minutes when he'd pursued her through the woods, exacerbated by a pack of wild wolves that picked up the chase after she'd lost him. She'd spent two nights in a tree before she could escape.

And of course, there'd been all those years in the Australian bush camping with her brothers, who had no shortage of pranks to toughen her up with: scorpions and brown recluse spiders in the boot, snake in the sleeping bag, all sorts of amusing things.

But she'd thought all those rough times in the field were well behind her.

How the bloody hell had she gotten from a swanky set-up in London to this?

That's an easy one: Grant Taylan. *Surprised?*

But this – this was one for the books. She was hot, sweaty, riddled with mosquito bites, trussed up like a chicken and being dragged along by a deranged Russian.

The real question was: how quickly can I get out of this?

They'd got about a mile and a half down the road when they ran into trouble.

A herd of *Styracaceous* came charging out of the jungle, spooked by a group of marauding predators. With their enormous frill spiked with horns and curved nose-horn, they resembled a much more aggressive version of the Triceratops. A little larger than a black rhino, they came charging across the road in a thunder, followed by several *Deltadromeus*, a swift-running theropod with teal stripes and black spikes running along its upper spine.

The theropods leapt and capered past as they pursued the herbivores, focusing on a smaller one trailing the herd. The *Styrcosaurus'* brayed in distress, and it was only Gorimov's quick reflexes that prevented them from being trampled.

He got them backed up against a heavy date palm when one of the *Deltadromeus*, a younger one that has been trailing the adults, landed right in front of them. Bowed down, its three-foot long head swaying before them, it was a terrifying sight.

Just as Gorimov was about to fire, Audrey saw her chance. Jerking sideways and throwing off the Russian's aim, she gave Vlad a swift kick in the ass, pushing him in front of the creature. It snapped with the speed of a snake, its jaws clamping down on Vlad's assault rifle and tearing it out of his grip, biting off his left arm from the elbow with it.

Vlad screamed. A second later the *Deltadromeus* struck again, snatching Vlad up in its jaws and shaking him around. Bones snapped.

Gorimov fired – missing the creature wildly as his gun arced from Audrey yanking on the rope. Cursing, he yanked back, and Audrey narrowly missed getting stomped by the *Deltadromeus'* three-toed foot. She had time to marvel at the amazing agility of the thing, then she was reversing her tumble to avoid the other foot as it came down.

This time Gorimov aimed straight at its neck – heedless to Vlad's flailing limbs – and pumped the rest of the 30-round clip into it.

The creature whipped sideways – mortally wounded – then writhing on the ground, Vlad still clenched in its jaws, died.

Audrey found herself jerked to her feet . . . but not before she traced a figure on the ground with her finger. Gorimov's face was red with fury.

"Fucking *bitch!*" he snarled. "Maybe I should shoot you now!"

Undaunted, she glared right back and spat at him, "Fuck-you, I'd just like one shot at your balls, poofter!"

Gorimov considered this for a moment, then whacked her in the head with the stock of the gun.

Audrey's eyes rolled up and she collapsed.

Gorimov replaced the AK-47s clip with a fresh one, then squatted next to Audrey's prone body, waiting until he was sure the dinosaurs were gone. The scavengers were already arriving when, shouldering the paleontologist over his shoulder in a fireman's carry, he headed down the road.

A mile behind, Taylan and Bello were following the same road, staying dead center to avoid getting ambushed. Cursing the hot, sultry weather, Taylan would have given anything to be driving the Jeep, but a quick survey made it clear the vehicle wasn't going anywhere without major mechanical work, and time was wasting.

Bello assured him it was only three miles to the complex, and fairly easy going. Taylan was all for bolting straight ahead, but Bello advised they keep it at a brisk walk. "Unless you've lived in this climate a good many years, you'll only wear yourself right out. Conserve your energy. You're going to need it – for either the Russians or the dinosaurs, or both. Besides, they're on foot too, they won't get too far ahead."

Even so after a few hundred yards Taylan was soaked with sweat. The heat was oppressive, the humidity tangible. It felt like walking through a continuous hot, wet blanket. At least Bello's cache had included bottled water and insecticide.

"What in the hell ever led you to this place?" Taylan asked. He was following Bello's cue and keeping the AK-47 at a ready position across his chest. He knew his way around a pistol and had grown up hunting with traditional bolt-action rifles, but this was something altogether new to him. It felt both oddly calming to be carrying a military assault rifle and vaguely ridiculous; like an adult version of playing army. Except the stakes here were deadly.

"Long story, but I had a good career as a safari guide back in Zambia. Until MuTron International came along with a lucrative offer. It seemed *very* lucrative at the time. Right now, it doesn't seem like it was worth a penny of it. I'd take a pack of starved lions over this."

"A pack of starved lions, *and* a herd of stampeding elephants," Taylan replied.

"Yes, that too," Bello agreed. He flashed a grin. "What about you? No doubt MuTron made you a tempting offer too, one I bet you couldn't resist. Sorry now?"

Taylan considered that.

"Not really, terrible as it is, it's definitely a *tactile* experience, even if arguably an artificial, man-made one. The 'dinosaurs' here may or may not be acting the way their original counterparts did – probably not, as this is all a fabricated environment, manipulated as a tourist attraction. It'd be sort of like going to a zoo and expecting to understand the species behavior in the wild, from species created in a laboratory. Still, it's a quantum leap from prying petrified bones out of bedrock and trying to guess how they functioned and looked. It's a brilliant opportunity, however horrible the price."

"And what about Dr. Adams? Do you think she feels the same right now?"

Taylan chuckled. "She might be having second thoughts. But she's never been good at expressing doubt in front of anybody."

"Ahh, you speak as if you're fond of her. Is that so?"

"She kind of grows on you. And don't underestimate her ability to look after herself. Gorimov may end up very sorry before too long."

"Hmm, sounds like a handful. I would like to be with such a woman like that someday."

Taylan smiled. Something felt right about being with Bello, like meeting up with an old friend.

A few minutes passed in silence, except for the sounds of the jungle; the sing-song chorus of tree frogs and crickets, the occasional far off sound of something roaring.

"So, you're not afraid right now, of this?" Bello asked, after a space.

"No," Taylan replied, matter-of-factly.

"Well, you should be."

It was ten minutes later when they came up on the spot where the Russians had met with the dinosaurs.

They smelled it first; the coppery aroma of fresh blood, accompanied by the buzzing of flies and chittering of scavengers. Bello picked up on it immediately, putting a hand on Taylan's shoulder to stop him. The day was sliding into that golden hour where the shadows were drawing out, casting the scene into a more spectral light.

Before them a bunch of *Compys* were picking over the corpse of the *Deltadromeus*. So far, however, no larger predators had arrived.

Bello looked carefully over the ground, then at the jungle on both sides, where the bushes tall grass was flattened. It looked like an army of bulldozers had plowed through. The large, circular shaped imprints mixed with equally large three-toed ones confirmed it.

Taylan surveyed the area, saw the severed arm and shoulder near the gaping mouth of the therapod.

His first thought was: *Audrey!*

Then he saw it was clearly a man's arm, with its blunt, hairy fingers and developed muscles. It wasn't Gorimov's, he could tell at a glance. Which meant it was Vlad. There were no other signs, until he spotted the arrow drawn in the dirt.

"We should move," Bello said. "The bigger predators will be here soon."

Taylan nodded. The scene only underscored to him how quickly things go disastrously wrong on this island.

"Yes," he said. "We're wasting time."

A mile and a half behind them, Dinh had just discovered the remains of her fellow commandos at the camp. When she came to the half-eaten body of Tuan, she paused, crouching over it, and though her lips trembled just slightly, she said nothing. Her eyes went as opaque and cold as a doll's.

***

Alan Peyton abruptly sat up, roused by something rustling nearby.

The expedition! We were ambushed! were the first thoughts through his head. He felt strange – a hot, compressed sensation around the upper left part of his skull – and yet exhilarated at the same time. He was Sir Roxton, after all, and this was the part where he had to find Lady Olivia . . . has she been kidnapped by a cannibal tribe? To be sacrificed to the dinosaur God?

He stood up out of the wreckage of his tent, ignoring the *Compys* that were picking at what looked suspiciously like the remains of a woman's head. He pulled off something wet and ropy from his shoulder and cast it *aside*.

Damn snake! he thought, then looking at the *Compys*: *Small potatoes! Now where's my rifle?*

He spotted the Weatherby nearby and snatched it up. The clip was still full, and he had two extra clips in his belt.

"Now the adventure begins!" he said aloud, stepping right past the pulverized remains of the Banyons without looking down. He headed straight toward the Land Rover, a mild grin on his face, oblivious to his blood-streaked features.

SO CLOSE AND YET...

Wang jammed the gas pedal down and for a moment the Volkswagen was like an over-eager teenager trying to get out of the house after being locked-up way too long: the wheels spun on the concrete flooring, screeching and sending up plumes of bluish smoke and burnt rubber. Then the tires found traction and finally they were off like a rocket, fishtailing as he steered them into a looping arc around the perimeter of the hangar.

His objective was simple: lure the *Tarbosaurus* away from the entrance so they could escape. He was fairly positive the buggy was faster than the dinosaur, the operative word being *fairly*. The question was how smart the creature was.

Being a predator, with a few million years of genetic programming, he had to assume it had some level of cunning.

In full pursuit mode, the *Tarbosaurus* was unnervingly fast, huge, and relentless.

It bounded over a work table, landing atop a palette of new Dell computer monitors, which buckled under its weight. Even as the boxes imploded it leapt off making a bee-line toward them with its head down low, tail slightly raised at the back as a counter-balance. The savage rim of teeth under its upper lip gave it a terrifying, *grinning* appearance.

Miss Grey gasped as Wang took the buggy around the perimeter of the space, like a mouse racing along the baseboard of a large room.

The therapod adjusted its course to intercept, which Wang was hoping for. Its path would lead it past the decrepit Ki-67 Bomber. Strangely, he had a moment of realizing all those years of playing computer games had been useful for at least one thing: his reflexive ability to analyze angles and speeds, and compensate on the fly.

"Hang on!" he shouted as he put the buggy into a skidding fishtail. The *Tarbosaurus* came racing past the parked bomber and tried to stop, skidding sideways on the polished concrete instead. It shot past them, snapping, and slammed into a workbench, sending tools flying in all directions in a cacophony of metal.

The therapod was nothing if agile, however, and it scrambled back to its feet faster than Wang would have thought possible. In the backseat Roma was equally amazed, from her wide-eyed expression. Using its chin instead of its tiny arms for leverage, it jumped upright and resumed the chase.

Wang recovered and accelerated, taking a diagonal course under the derelict bomber, yelling "Duck!" as they passed too near one of the static propeller blades, clipping it with the roll-bar and sending it flying.

Undaunted, the *Tarbosaurus* bolted over the top of the aircraft, its weight causing the rust-eaten landing gear to collapse. It at least bought them a few precious seconds as he veered back toward the open hangar door.

It was enough.

They shot out onto the level area that had once been a runway, lined by 8-foot high Kunai grass that might host all sorts of things. The runway was still mostly dirt, with a trail about a hundred yards down between a copse of giant mahogany trees that led to the bay and fishing village. As they raced down toward it Wang risked a glance back and saw the *Tarbosaurus* was still in pursuit, even though it was falling behind.

Miss Grey shrieked and jerked the steering wheel to the right as three red-crested *Guanlong* darted out of nowhere. As Wang whipped his head back around they missed two, but the third had its back end caught under the tires and there was a sickening thud as they ran it over, the dinosaur screeching in agony.

Then they were veering toward the canopied entrance to the trail. The trail wasn't meant for vehicles per se, or at least speeding ones, and there was fifty yards of bone jarring moments as they ran over tree roots and ruts, hard enough to nearly bounce them out of the vehicle.

They came out onto the connecting road circling the bay. The ship was still docked, with all its lights on, with lines of MuTron employees still on the main wharf, disembarking under mist-shrouded lamps that were just beginning to flicker on.

Wang felt the first glimmer of hope; it was a quarter-mile to the town, and less than a hundred yards to the dock. It was just feasible he might save the day – and these two ladies – in the bargain.

Twenty yards down another *Tarbosaurus* burst out of the trees, nearly toppling the dune buggy.

Both women screamed.

The snapping jaws missed Roma's head by inches, the impact sending the buggy canted up onto the two right wheels. For a few precarious seconds, they continued that way down the road, the jury out whether or not they would roll right over.

Then Wang shifted his weight sideways and nudged the steering wheel just enough to bring them back down, the buggy's spongy suspension absorbing the worst of the teeth-clacking impact. With a slight skid, he got them heading again toward the village at full speed. Looking up at the rearview mirror he saw the *Tarbosaurus* was chasing after them. Even worse: as he looked ahead again, the larger of the two *Tyrannosaurs* stepped out into the middle of the street.

He slammed on the brakes and fishtailed them to a stop.

They were trapped.

31. A FAILED ESCAPE AND A FEW CHOICE WORDS

Luo Pan Wei paused for one last look as he was about to climb into the waiting helicopter. The sun was disappearing into a fiery display to the west amidst a cauldron of layered clouds, while the velvety gloom of evening seemed to rise out of the east; an apropos (and in his mind, *momentary*) visual metaphor for the world he had built here.

The Lost World of Kharamu.

It had been a dream – a wonderful dream – that had, for a time, become a reality, through the relentless and imaginative application of my will.

And what was built once could be built again. Better. More refined.

I am, after all, a God of sorts, he thought, not for the first time, *am I not? It feels good!*

He glanced at his watch and estimated they could be back at the mainland within two hours, plenty of time for him to formulate his next move. Perhaps a couple weeks of R&R in Thailand to decompress.

He clambered into the back seat, stowed the cases and closing the door, he took a moment to relish the soft leather upholstery and air-conditioning. Buckling in, he leaned forward and signaled the pilot to take off.

With a gentle lurch, they lifted off into the evening air, the island and all its horrors falling quickly away from them.

As they rose and headed north, Mr. Luo realized for the first time there was an envelope taped to the back of the passenger seat in front of him. Puzzled, he reached forward and tore it off.

Inside was a note on MuTron International stationary.

On it, in Burroughs' unmistakably neat, block writing, it said:

"By the pricking of my thumbs, something wicked this way comes."
I bid you adieu, old friend.
-RB

Below that it said:

P.S. open the door under your seat for a sample of my private work, as promised.

Puzzled, Mr. Luo bent down between his knees and peered under the seat. There was an oblong metal door to a medical container with bio-hazard symbols stored there. He had a vague notion that it must be Burroughs' experimental DNA samples. He knew he had been working on a variety of new strains for the second developmental cycle – the proposed 'Phase II' as it were – that had been anticipated as something of a surprise.

Of course!

He slid the case partly out and flipped the latches. Should he wait? Burroughs always knew he wasn't the patient type when it came to results. Smiling in anticipation, he popped the lid open.

And frowned.

It took a moment to register what he was looking at.

Nothing. The case was empty.

Frowning, he pulled it all the way out.

It was only seconds after that he realized it wasn't what was *in* the case, it was what was *behind* it. The case had formed a perfect seal for the storage compartment, at least for the large, prehistoric insects that must have been frantic to escape: foot-long centipedes and spike-covered ancestors of the giant cave spider. The vibration of the helicopter engines must have agitated them intensely. At least half were dead or dying from attacking each other . . . but plenty more were full of life. Even as he watched, a giant centipede writhed up his pantleg in a helix, while a fourteen-inch spider scurried out, its venom-tinged pincers quivering in agitation.

Mr. Luo screamed, his fingers clawing frantically at his seatbelt.

Not that there was anywhere to go – they were climbing past a thousand feet over open ocean.

He tried to bat the centipede away, but the creature only wrapped itself around his forearm instead, then shot up toward his neck. Mr. Luo screamed even louder as the pincers went through the shoulder of his suit-jacket and right through his shirt. The pain was excruciating.

Now the pilot was looking back over his shoulder in wide-eyed horror, as a half-dozen pie-sized spiders scurried up over the seats, their leathery bodies the size of his fist. He tried to veer the copter to one side, as if that could somehow throw them off, but the creatures were spreading out all over the inside of the cabin.

Mr. Luo tore at the centipede as something covered in spikes tried to squeeze up inside his pant leg, then bit him painfully in the soft tissues of his ankle.

Unbuckling his seatbelt with trembling fingers, the pilot kicked open his door and simply jumped, leaving his passenger still clawing away in his seat.

The helicopter described an ungainly loop in the sky, accelerating as it arced down toward the expanse of the South China Sea. The muffled screams from within the cabin went with it, heard by no-one, not even the pilot plummeting to his own death a thousand feet below.

A minute later there was a *thwump* and explosion as the copter impacted, sending parts skimming and flying in every direction.

Except for the insects, Mr. Luo died very much alone.

***

Gorimov was bathed in oily sweat as he finally entered the complex, from the same back entrance Wang had exited hours earlier. He had a general idea where he was headed, as Peyton had sent him a rough layout of the complex drawn from memory – most specifically, where the manufacturing laboratory was. As Peyton had put it in their last conversation: "What the hell do I care about a bunch of skeletons if I can lay my hands on the living, breathing son-of-a-bitches? You get me that DNA, Igor, and I'll triple what I was going to pay you before."

Gorimov had other plans (and potentially higher bidders), but first things first. If he kept his eye on the eight-ball he could come out this a very rich man *and* one with a feisty little *bychit* to break in.

Or if she proved too much trouble, simply sell her. He had plenty of eager clients in *all* sorts of markets.

Surprisingly, he hadn't seen too many dinosaurs after the run-in with the *Deltadromeus* other than a few swift-running *Compys* and one moment where he'd hidden behind a tree while three *Zhenyuanlong* went tearing up the road past them, possibly heading for the kill site he'd left behind.

Inside the complex was much cooler, even without the air-conditioning on.

Over his shoulder Audrey forced her body to remain limp. She'd come roughly halfway to the compound, but despite her throbbing head, figured out what was happening (and for once) while keeping her mouth shut. Survival instinct overrode everything. Instead, she focused on leaving little signs wherever she could. Just in case – and she forced herself not to let go of this idea – that someone (Taylan in particular) was following.

A bent twig there, a wrapper out of her breast pocket there. When they reached the entrance to the complex she even plucked out a few hairs and hung them from a branch while Gorimov was focused on navigating the stairs down.

The next time, she sensed, might be her last opportunity. If not to escape, then to at least inflict some lasting damage on Gorimov.

After that last blow to the skull, however, she realized she was having some doubts on her ability to deliver on that score. For the first time in her life, she had cracks in her self-confidence.

He didn't even flinch, she thought, *and nearly split my skull open.* But he's also human. Which means he will screw up at some point. Patience.

Her chance came about ten minutes later.

***

Bello and Taylan stood for a moment at a spot where the trail forked. To the left it wound down toward the inside of the bay, the left followed the ridge they'd been on.

"Which way?" Taylan asked.

"Either gets us there. The left one will take us to the elevator entrance. The right, I believe, is one of the unused back entrances. Quicker but there's a rabbit-warren of abandoned tunnels we could get lost in. The left route is safer."

About six feet in on the trail to the right Taylan spotted something on the ground.

He stepped over and picked it up. It was the top half of a 'Tim Tam' wrapper. Original chocolate flavor.

"They went this way," he said, smiling.

"You recognize that?" Bello asked.

"Only one person I know is a junkie for these," Taylan replied.

Bello bent down on his haunches and checked the ground.

"It's a clear trail, besides. Your Russian is not subtle."

"No-one will ever accuse Gorimov of being that," Taylan agreed.

As it was, they were closer on Gorimov's heels than they thought. The Russian might have had incredible endurance, but he was walking in 90-degree temperatures with a hundred and twenty pounds slung over one shoulder, and a laden knapsack over the other. Their main advantage, however, was that Gorimov wouldn't know he was being followed. At least by Taylan and Bello.

When they got to the stairs they found the strands of blond hair Audrey had left, confirming any question whether they'd followed the right path.

They paused briefly by the alcove while Bello glanced upward, sensing something.

Taylan raised his brows, but Bello gave a dismissive shake of his head. "Someone's been up there recently, but not Gorimov, I think. We should keep moving."

Gorimov found the lab quickly. Even from the outside, one could hear the muffled crescendos of Tchaikovsky through the closed doors of Burroughs' office. The lab itself was a slaughterhouse, the air heavy with the coppery scent of blood and death. Not much of the bodies remained. Gorimov stopped, looking around, then zeroed in on Burroughs' office.

He tried the office door and found it locked. Depositing Audrey on the floor (after a cursory check of her eyelids and pinching her ear, to which she let out a convincing moan), he unslung his assault rifle and smashed the glass. Inside he could see Burroughs, who was sitting at his desk, his back to the door, one hand describing graceful motions through the air as if conducting. The hand continued as if oblivious to the forced entry.

Undaunted, Gorimov went in like he always did – like he owned the place. He walked up to Burroughs, the AK-47 leveled at his head. When he didn't get an immediate response, he worked the action, to announce himself.

After a minute, the music dropped abruptly in volume, as if by a hidden remote.

"So good to have company," Burroughs said, without turning around.

"I've come for DNA samples," Gorimov said, getting right to the point. He leveled the AK-47 at the back of Burroughs' head. "Tell me where they are and maybe I don't kill you."

That elicited a soft chuckle. Burroughs dropped his hand and swiveled around. He looked as relaxed as a man conducting yet-another interview for a job position.

"Why, that's quite generous of you," Burroughs said, smiling with a tilt of his head, crow's feet appearing at the corners of his eyes. The eyes themselves, however, remained as empty and vacant as any assassin's.

Gorimov saw that right away. His finger tightened ever-so-slightly on the trigger. At the same time, his lip trembled, and a tear ran down his reddened cheek.

"Ah, *Pyotr Ilyich!*" he said, unable to contain himself. The mournful threads from the Borodin String Quartet seemed to float around the room.

Burroughs took a sip of the scotch in his hand. "Yes," he said quietly. "It's quite beautiful music, is it not? Excellent music to die to."

The Webley .38 was lying in the open drawer next to him, but from where he was standing, Gorimov couldn't see that. Nor could he see the small controller device sitting in Burroughs' lap.

Gorimov smiled back, fishing out a cigarette from the rumpled pack in his breast pocket and lighting it up.

"You're not going to tell me where the samples are?"

"Of course not," Burroughs replied.

"Pity then, as you are about to die."

Burroughs continued to smile. "Well, we all do, we all do," he said, gently placing the scotch on his desk. "But it's not often one gets the opportunity to play God, at least I can make that claim. Can you?"

"No, I get to play executioner," Gorimov said, pulling the trigger.

Burroughs' hand never made it to the Webley, perhaps he didn't care. But his other hand pressed the remote a split second before the 7.62mm bullets blew apart his skull.

The gunfire was ear-splitting in the confined space; empty shell cases tinkled across the smooth concrete floor as the acrid stink of gunpowder filled the air, mingling with cigarette smoke. The turntable and receiver were shot up as well, silenced forever.

Gorimov shook his head, then frowned as he saw the device in Burroughs' lap. He recognized it immediately, even from a distance: a Volchek T87 timer.

Used to remotely activate explosives.

He darted around the desk and looked down at the digital read-out.

"Shit!" he said, bolting for the door. He paused as he saw Audrey was no longer there and repeated to himself: "Shit!"

Then he ran for the outer door as fast as he could.

A moment later Audrey emerged from behind one of the examining tables outside Burroughs' office and peered in. Her head was throbbing, and she felt like she might have a concussion, but she was at least able to stand.

What had Gorimov wanted? And how did he know to come in here?

It was, she suspected, something she'd spotted in the locked refrigeration unit next to where she'd been hiding.

She glanced around the office, avoiding the grisly remains of MuTron's Chief Science Officer. Her gaze rested in the timer in his lap. Then on the Webley. And the heavy-looking syringe next to it – the one that reminded her of a tranquilizer dart.

She grabbed them and checking the gun to make sure it was loaded, ran out.

As Taylan and Bello crossed the hangar, the setting sun cast its last rays through the main doors, bathing the vast space in golden light. It would have been a perfect Kodak moment, except for the blinking evacuation lights in the corners and the still persistent message of the female voice, urging them to follow Protocol 7 and evacuate.

Bello held up his hand as they caught a movement from the other end. A figure emerged, jogging along the wall to where the safari motorcycles were parked. These were modern Kawasaki dirt bikes, probably used for security to get around quickly. Only two remained, along with a vintage military BMW with a sidecar.

Taylan recognized the figure immediately: Gorimov!

But why was he running so fast? And where the hell was Audrey?

Gorimov slung his AK-47 over his shoulder and jumped onto one of the dirt bikes, starting after a couple of aggressive kicks, then peeling out with a screech of rubber.

Taylan pointed to the other dirt bike. "Follow him," he told Bello, "I have to find Audrey."

He trotted toward the open door Gorimov had come out of while Bello jogged over and fired up the second dirt bike. A few seconds later Bello was gone, out the hangar doors with a trail of exhaust floating in the air behind.

Taylan had just gotten to the door when a figure flew right into him, sending the two of them sprawling on the concrete floor. He found himself on his back with Audrey right on top of him, her face inches from his own.

"Uh, I was just looking for you," he said. It was another of those surprise moments of intimacy between them where he had a sudden urge to kiss her.

That seems to keep happening lately, he thought.

"You found me," she said back, her own eyes going momentarily half-closed. Then, they went wide.

"We have to go. *Now!*" she said, jumping up to her feet and picking up the Webley revolver she'd dropped. "This place is about to blow sky high!"

"What!?" Taylan replied, sitting up on his elbows.

To make her point a thunderous bang went off inside the complex, followed by several more. The ground shook. Debris rained down from overhead.

Taylan didn't need any more motivation, he grabbed Audrey just as several feathered raptors and *Compys* came sprinting out of the same door she'd exited, racing past them without a second glance. A bigger explosion followed, hard enough to cause them to lose their footing. A chair-sized chunk of rock fell mere feet away from them, sending shards whizzing in all directions.

"Come!" Taylan shouted, jumping to his feet and dragging Audrey with him. A fireball shot out of the entry door, sending a crisped raptor flying out ahead of it.

Playing dodge and weave with several other chunks of rock coming down, they made it to the old BMW and sidecar. Taylan handed her his assault rifle as she clambered in to the sidecar.

 Straddling the motorcycle, he turned the ignition switch and rammed his heel down on the kick-starter several times. The engine let out several rumbles but refused to start up.

Audrey made a face. "Grant!?" she yelled above the din. "*Anytime* now?"

Taylan rammed his heel down again, this time determined to break the damn thing off if nothing else.

The bike responded with a burbling roar. Gunning the throttle, they took off hard enough to snap Audrey's head back, then veered them around another chunk of falling debris, the awkward gyro effect of the sidecar causing it to rise off the ground. Another explosion sent the rusted propeller of the Tony fighter spinning just over their heads as Taylan turned to the left, forcing the sidecar tire to drop with a *thud*.

They burst out into the dying rays of the day, just as one of the hangar doors buckled and fell in a groan of bending metal.

As they tore down the old runway, between the coconut palms lining the south edge he spotted the Portuguese trawler still at the dock, its lights now full on. Above the din of the explosions came the forlorn call of the ship's horn, signaling that they were ready to disembark.

DEATH FROM EVERY DIRECTION

Wang froze for a moment, torn by indecision. It would be hard to fault him – two eight-ton apex predators were blocking his path, while behind him a secondary apex predator had him boxed in. On either side were rows of dilapidated buildings.

Nothing in his life had prepared him for this moment.

Except his game-fast reflexes.

Glancing left and right he gauged each of the buildings: to the bay side was a fish and tackle shop, to the left a café, with a large open window and rolled-up reed awnings.

He wrenched the wheel to the left, just as the larger of the two Tyrannosaurs charged.

"Hold on!" he shouted, then drove them through the front of the café.

The roll-bar on the front bumper protected them from the worst of it. That and the fact the building was of lightweight construction. They drove into the main room, pulverizing tables, while the front end of the café partially collapsed behind them. Wang didn't think they could drive through the main counter – *that* was too solidly constructed – so instead veered left out onto the side patio, scattering more tables. A quick snap turn to the right drove them off the patio into underbrush toward the back of the building, where he drove them up a sandy embankment and around the backs of the buildings past a bunch of mangrove trees.

There were a few uncertain moments when it was questionable whether they were about to roll off the hill and crash the buggy, but Wang kept them upright until they were past the main buildings and down onto the main street.

A glance showed them what had happened: The *T. rex* had made a beeline at the *Tarbosaurus* – probably as it was the most immediate threat to its food supply – and the two were caught in a ferocious battle in the middle of the street. The second *T. rex* had joined it, tearing at the tail of the smaller therapod.

Wang was debating how he could get them back on the short roadway leading onto the wharf when the ground shook. A fiery plum rose up to the north where the complex was.

It was followed by another ground shake.

Seconds later the herd of *Ankylosaurs* burst through the buildings to their right. One of the armored herbivores came charging right at them, like some sort of medieval tank. Wang gunned the gas pedal and fishtailed them around just as the *Ankylosaur* caught up to them, just narrowly missing them with the oversized spikes jutting out from its sides.

Just as they accelerated away the massive club at the end of its tail swung and caught them sideways with the force of a battering ram.

The Volkswagen crumpled as it went tumbling, sending its three passengers catapulting out of the vehicle.

Four miles away Allen Peyton was racing down the dirt road when a petit figure dressed in MuTron camouflage fatigues stumbled out into the lane. He slammed on the brakes and skidded to a stop when he saw that it was an Asian woman.

He hesitated a moment, hand on the Weatherby in the seat next to him, until she dropped to one knee, clutching her arm. A wild thought ran through his brain: he'd never had an Asian before! He'd heard plenty, of course, business associates who'd bragged about the sexual exploits and submissiveness of such women.

Like that one Wall Street fella he'd met in New York – said he'd hooked up with a Korean woman and her three roommates, claimed they did the most incredible things! Not worthy of anything more than a little side-dish for a man of Lord Roxton's stature, of course! But since Mrs. Roxton was . . . was . . .

His mind skirted away from that thought as he focused his gaze on Dinh, who kept her gaze fixed on the ground before her.

Peyton got out of the Land Rover, one hand near the pistol at his hip (*can't be too careful with these slant-eyed fuckers!*), a little mischievous grin appearing under his moustache. Walking over, he stopped, towering, the dying sunlight casting the whole scene like some sort of metaphorical tableau: dominance of the west over the submissive east.

"Greetin's there, little lady," Peyton said, oblivious to the fact 'Lord Roxton' was speaking like a movie Texan. "You look like you could use a little hand. And, heh, I'm thinkin' maybe I could too!"

He felt a surprising twinge from his groin, and his grin grew larger. She looked like a little girl. He'd never done anything like *that* before.

Dinh slowly looked up with a slight smile of her own, doing a few fluttering blinks to disarm him further.

She struck like a snake.

Peyton was stunned by the agony in his groin. He looked down in horror to see the military knife buried up to the hilt at his crotch, then grunted as Dinh twisted it and yanked upward until it cut through his belt buckle.

Dinh said nothing as she stood up and yanked the knife free as Peyton collapsed and fell over. When he cried out she bent over and deftly cut his throat. She didn't know what she'd encounter when she'd heard the vehicle approaching, so she'd laid her rifle aside and put on a ruse with her knife tucked under her arm and her pistol behind in her belt.

Then she'd seen a towering Caucasian man covered in gore get out of the vehicle with his hand on his pistol and instinct had directed her from there.

Peyton half-rolled to his side and was still, blood burbling out of his severed jugular. She searched the body and took the money clip with the folded hundreds and the extra ammunition, noting the heavy shells. The body was too heavy for her to drag so she left it out for the scavengers.

After retrieving her rifle, she climbed into the still-idling Land Rover, made a quick check of the provisions and Peyton's rifle, then took off, skirting Peyton's body. She'd driven just over a mile when she heard the explosions and saw the mushrooming smoke to the northeast.

She had only one goal at this point: kill Gorimov.

***

Gorimov cut his dirt bike to the right as he came upon the Tarbosaurus at the end of the airfield, only to find himself with a *Tyrannosaurus rex* charging at him head-on. Bello wasn't so lucky – he tried to skirt around the other side and was instantly snatched up off the bike by the *Tarbosaurus*, which threw him up in the air like a toy before snapping him it its jaws. Gorimov glimpsed back and spotted Taylan on another motorcycle coming up on his tail, along with Dr. Adams sitting in the sidecar with an AK-47. Even as he spotted them she squeezed off several rounds in his direction. Behind them a pack of *Deltadromeus* had taken up pursuit.

"*Tchyo za ga'lima?*" he had time to spit out - *What the fuck?* – a moment before he veered right through the entrance of one of the pricier souvenir shops. Silver and diamond dinosaur-themed jewelry flew as display cases shattered. An authentic *Dilophosaurus* skull snapped off its mount and bounced off his shoulder as he plowed on, ducking as he steered between two support columns and driving right through the straw mat wall. The bike went sailing out onto a back porch, bounced once and then he jumped a gap, landing on the back patio of the hotel, fishtailing and smashing tables and chairs every which way.

Twenty yards to his right he saw he was coming up quick on the wharf leading out to the trawler.

The ship! He had to make the ship!

He had the plant stowed away in his knapsack. The DNA samples had been a wash, but he'd kept a slice of skin off the dead *Deltadromeus*. It would have to do. The plant was the most important thing. All he had to do was get it to the German.

He gunned the bike up onto the dock.

Wang came to half-trapped in the wreckage of the Volkswagen. The white agony telegraphing up his leg told him it was seriously injured - probably broken. Even worse, it was caught in the folded remains of the driver's seat. Near his head lay the sword, a foot beyond that, the rifle.

I'm getting out of here, he thought, snatching the katana in his hands, *even if I have to chop my own leg off.*

The buggy gave a groan as another *Ankylosaur* rumbled past it, its side-spikes raking the underside of the vehicle. The movement twisted his leg even further, eliciting a clenched-teeth scream out of him, but then his leg was free, and he was able to scramble away.

It took him a moment to orient himself. They'd driven just past the main wharf when they'd crashed, the buggy toppling over between two buildings where there was a slight rise in the beach surrounding the bay. Twenty feet ahead of him he saw Roma lying prone, her head and one arm in the water.

There was no sign of Miss Grey.

Even more confusing, there were tremendous explosions in the distance, with bits of debris falling all over the place.

Had a volcano erupted?

He checked his foot. It didn't *look* broken, though there was a nasty gash down one side of his shin. His shoe was gone. The ground continued to shake as more dinosaurs moved past, though they seemed to be heading south.

Slinging the rifle over his shoulder, he crawled down to Roma. At first, he thought she was dead. Then he saw her eyelids flutter and she let out a small cough.

"Hey! Dr. Banaji!" he said, touching her shoulder. "Are you okay?"

Slow-blinking, she propped herself up out of the warm bay water lapping around her, like someone who'd just come out of a serious bender.

"I'm not sure, I think—"

Wang twisted around to see a *Zhenyuanlong* come at him in a half-flying leap, winged arms outspread. He didn't have time to draw the sword, so he used the lacquered scabbard to bat it aside. The creature was only put off for a second, it scrambled on its feet and spread its wings again to attack.

Even as he raised his hand to defend himself there was a crunch in the sand followed by a whistle and a thunk; a large timber came down and crushed its head.

Miss Grey straightened up behind it, adjusting her glasses – which Wang noted had a drop of blood on the lens. Her suit was torn and dirt-smeared, but she looked alive and well. Then she glanced back and saw half a dozen more coming at them from the roadway.

"Duck!" yelled a woman's voice.

Then the air was filled with semi-automatic gunfire.

Taylan veered the motorcycle to the left to avoid the *Tyrannosaur* locked in a battle with the *Tarbosaurus*, noting Gorimov's gonzo trajectory through the gift ship as he ducked under a swinging tail. Driving a motorcycle with a sidecar at high speed, he realized, was utterly terrifying. Still, several things were apparent all at once: they were about to pass the wharf, there was a demolished dune-buggy about forty yards ahead to the right, and there were two bodies past the buggy along the beach line; one crawling toward the other.

Once past the wharf he braked to a stop, nearly ejecting Audrey out of her seat.

"Help them!" he yelled at Audrey – pointing to the people on the beach. There was no time to discuss. Thankfully, Audrey wasn't one for lengthy explanations in an emergency. She jumped out and he gunned the engine, aiming for the spot he estimated Gorimov would emerge.

He almost missed him – the Russian catapulted out of the embankment like some sort of deranged motocross racer: sand flying, front wheel spinning at an angle. Then he fishtailed, recovered, and shot down the wharf.

Snarling, Taylan was right on him. The dirt bike was highly maneuverable, but the military bike had ten times the horsepower. The two bikes described an ungainly double-helix down the rough shod decking for about sixty feet, then Taylan maneuvered up alongside and using the sidecar, rammed into him.

Weight-wise, the dirt bike was no match for the sidecar – the rear tire skidded out and Gorimov went sliding down the wharf, the planking shredding his pants and tearing up the skin on his left leg like a cheese grater.

Taylan skidded to a stop and jumping off his bike, ran over to the Russian. Gorimov was getting up, shaking his head like bulldog.

The setting was surreal: flaming debris continued to rain down around them, explosions erupting from the complex while back toward the town, the heads of the giant therapods could be seen battling it out. Further up on the ridge overlooking the bay, several *Brontosaurs* ambled along, the ground shaking even down by the water, heading toward the southern part of the island.

Taylan's wind was up. As he drew up before Gorimov, he felt his anger getting the better of him. Going into a half-crouch, he cocked his right fist and hit the Russian as hard as he could in the side of the face.

Gorimov rocked, even as Taylan hit him again – this time breaking his nose – yet to Taylan's amazement, stood up, blood streaming over his mouth. Even more to Taylan's amazement, Gorimov was grinning.

Taylan may not have been a prizefighter – but he was no slouch, either. A lifetime of clambering through cliffs and wielding hammers and handling rocks had honed his upper physique.

Gorimov's leg was ruined, his clothes in bloody tatters, he looked smashed and bruised. In short, he looked like he should be on a stretcher on the way to an ER.

And yet, he seemed to be enjoying himself.

"Ah! I see you have some good fight in you after all, Taylan!" Gorimov said, rubbing his jaw. "This time we do things the old way. I kill you with bare hands!"

An old childhood memory flashed across Taylan's thoughts: his father about to toss him back outside their old house in Cleveland one day, where the neighbor – a bigger kid named Marky Olson – was waiting after giving Taylan a sound beating. Taylan had come in bruised and beat up, talking about how one day he was going to show Mark a thing or two. "There are two types of people in this world," his father had said, crouching down on his haunches to look young Taylan in the eye, "People who *do*, and people who *talk* about doing. You'll never amount to anything if you're the latter. And one other thing: there'll always be another Marky Olson out there. You can either run or knock him out of your way."

Without waiting for a reply his dad swung the door open and pushed him through it.

Taylan snapped back to the present. Chin down, he looked at Gorimov from under his brows. Without another word, he charged.

Audrey bounded past the crumpled dune buggy, working the slide on the AK-47 as she topped the rise.

She took in several things simultaneously: a young Asian man hovering protectively over Dr. Roma Banaji, Miss Grey with a section of wood in her hands, and a bunch of feathered dinosaurs leaping in to attack them from her left.

Instinctively she dropped to one knee and opened-up with the assault rifle, raking from right to left and remembering to keep a strong hold on the front grip to keep the barrel from rising.

The result was instantaneous. Feathers and blood flew as she emptied the clip, the last three rounds going into the legs of the last raptor that was making a beeline at Miss Grey. The Marketing Director finished it off with her makeshift club.

Dropping the assault rifle, Audrey ran over to them.

"Dr. Banaji?" she said. "Fancy meeting you here!"

Roma stood up, her clothes half soaked, inspecting the muddied bandage on her hand.

"Yes well, I suppose I have a strange way of turning up in odd places."

"Who's this?" Audrey asked, nodding at Wang.

Miss Grey stepped over and put her free hand on his shoulder. "My hero," she said smiling. "Wang Chan, exceptional IT Professional!"

Audrey looked back and forth between them: one looking like a bloodied librarian, the other some sort of mix of fierce Mongol warrior and computer nerd. It occurred to her she probably wasn't exactly her photogenic best either at this point.

"Where's Doctor Taylan?" Roma asked, jarring Audrey's thoughts.

"Taking care of unfinished business, I suspect. We need to get out of here, quick," she replied, glancing about. She spotted an antique Tobin 'sea skiff' moored nearby – an old classic late 50s motorboat. It was tied off on one of the low floating docks that ran out from the land parallel to the main wharf. At the end of the wharf the trawler was already pulling away, the propellers churning up the water at its stern.

"Yes – everything's breaking down. I've never seen the dinosaurs acting this way," Miss Grey added.

"Systematic breakdown," Roma said. "Whatever behavioral structure they've developed – as artificial an environment as this is – it's collapsing. Fascinating. It may be similar to what happened at the original extinction event."

Audrey checked the Webley revolver she'd stuffed into her belt. "Fascinating or not, I suggest we get our bloody asses on that boat and get off it. *Now*."

Gorimov hunched down like a wrestler bracing for an assault, and just as Taylan was about to ram into him, ducked quickly and caught him on his shoulders. Taylan found himself lifted in the air and spun around like some TV Pro-Wrestling stunt, before Gorimov squatted again and slammed him down on the decking hard enough to knock the wind out of him. He jerked to one side as the Russian's foot came down full force where his head had been a moment before.

Taylan rolled away and got to his feet, drawing in air with a big, whooping gasp.

He barely had recovered though, when Gorimov was on him, hitting his chest right-left-right with his fists, sending Taylan staggering backwards. He ducked the fourth blow and came up with an uppercut that caught Gorimov in the belly, hard enough to make him gasp. But the Russian's eyes were focused on something back past Taylan's shoulder.

Taylan thought it was just a bad trick, but when he went in for a follow up punch Gorimov's reaction surprised him: he took the punch square on the chin and instead of defending himself, grabbed Taylan by the collar with both hands and spun him around like an aggressive dance partner, throwing him after a complete circle.

The next thing Taylan knew he was being hurled back down the wharf toward land, the momentum and Gorimov's incredible strength sending him tumbling, arms and legs akimbo. Over them something blotted out the dying light: Taylan looked up to see a boulder the size of a car coming straight down. He rolled away frantically as a whole section of the wharf disappeared in a shower of splinters and flying debris. Glancing back, he saw what Gorimov was originally reacting to – a *Tarbosaurus* cautiously making its way onto the wharf, head down as if sniffing the planking.

He spun around back toward Gorimov, who was now facing him with a fifteen-foot section of pulverized dock between them. Behind, ironically, was certain death at the jaws of an extinct creature that had brought both men here. Other chunks of rock continued to rain down around them, but Taylan was oblivious. He could take his chances and dive into the water, or finish what he started.

Gorimov stood with his arms at his sides, hands out: well?

Taylan stared right back him, his expression grim and merciless.

He backed up about ten steps, then running hard as he could, leapt across the gap.

He almost made it.

Audrey got the engine started on the Tobin while Wang undid the mooring lines. Miss Grey and Roma climbed in, situating themselves on the side seats while Wang shoved them off and jumped aboard, situating himself next to Miss Grey who was holding his sword and rifle. When a lone *Zhenyuanlong* came bounding down to the dock at them, Audrey calmly took out the Webley and shot it.

They were pulling out into the water when the boulder came down, smashing the dock, which gave them a waterside view of what was happening with Taylan and Gorimov. When Wang took his rifle and worked the bolt, Audrey, motioned for him to wait. Part of her wanted to gun the throttles and get as far as possible from the island and the falling debris, the other was compelled to help Taylan any way possible.

Either presented a nerve-wracking situation.

To make matters worse, she saw the *Tarbosaurus* step onto the wharf.

"Bloody hell, Grant," she said under her breath. "I hope you know what you're doing."

She angled the boat toward the south side of the dock. One hand steering, she pointed out Gorimov.

"Shoot that man, if you must."

Taylan fell six-inches short, grabbing instead one of the collapsed planks bent down from where the boulder had taken out the section of dock. Below him jagged planks of wood and twisted metal from the struts jutted out of the roiling water 15 feet below, waiting to impale him. Wood splinters dug into his hands and even as he hung there, legs flailing, one hand slipped off.

Gorimov appeared at the edge and squatted down, muscled forearms on his haunches.

"Here we are again," he said, grinning. "Somehow, I always on top, and you always about to drop to a messy death!" he laughed. "Pretty funny, yes?"

"Hilarious," Taylan hissed between clenched teeth. He didn't want to look down at what he was about to fall onto but couldn't help it. His heart was hammering in his chest.

"Yes – *hilarious*, as you say!" Gorimov agreed. "Taylan, Taylan. You've been such a pain in my poor fucking ass. You know that?"

Taylan was completely focused on the losing battle he was having trying to hold on to the plank.

This is going to hurt, he thought, his remaining hand sliding off.

A sudden pain flared in his wrist. Shocked, he looked up to see Gorimov gripping it with both hands. The Russian hauled him up.

Taylan couldn't believe it. Nor did he question it. Grabbing one of the intact planks with his free hand, he leveraged his leg up as Gorimov hauled him up to safety. Letting him go, the Russian took a step back. Taylan rolled onto the dock, most of the fight gone out of him for the moment.

"What the hell did you do that for?" he asked, his heart still hammering away in his chest.

Gorimov shrugged. "Truth is, the world is a more interesting place with you in it, Grant Tay—"

He was cut off as his chest jerked, a neat round hole appearing right near his heart. He looked down, brow furrowing as if puzzled, then his head snapped forward as another hole appeared above his left eye, the back of his skull blowing out along with a piece of his brain.

Igor Gorimov was dead before he hit the planks.

Audrey had maneuvered the boat up to the wharf, hoping it would offer some protection from the falling debris, though the boulder that had taken out the section of the dock didn't give her a lot of confidence. Jumping up on the foredeck, she secured the front deck line to a wooden access ladder and climbed up.

"I didn't shoot him!" Wang said again as they had approached. All four of them had watched Gorimov die.

Audrey knew that and knew she didn't like the implications either. It suggested a sniper someplace. She inched her head over the deck to see Taylan was now hiding behind one of the pylons roughly twelve feet away. Even as he glanced back at her there came a *thwip* as a bullet plucked at the wood near his feet. Nearby, Gorimov lay spread-eagled, blood pooling out around his head in a hideous halo.

Even worse, the *Tarbosaurus* was now ambling down the wharf toward them, the structure creaking and groaning, but holding up. Taylan may have had difficulty leaping a fifteen-foot span; *Tarbosaurus* could easily hop across it.

Taylan's eye's widened as he saw something even more shocking: out of the village emerged a *Tyrannosaur* – running right down the wharf, head low. He was awestruck: the charging twenty-foot tall dinosaur was an utterly terrifying sight: a ten-ton apex predator in full-out attack mode. The dock shook and sensing the approach, the *Tarbosaurus* wheeled, hissing, just as the *T. rex* struck.

It wasn't much of a battle. The *Tyrannosaur* bit down so hard and fast on the other theropod's head and upper neck there was a gruesome crunch, a spray of flying bone and blood. One chomp with 12,800 pounds of force pulverized the Tarbosaurus.

The T. rex shook its head, tearing the skull off the other creature.

Audrey felt a tap on her leg and glanced down to see Wang climb up alongside her, unslinging the Mauser. It seemed impossible to tell where the sniper much be, with so much smoke and debris. Past the brutal spectacle of the Tyrannosaur and its kill, several of the buildings in the makeshift Tiki village had caught fire and now burned fiercely.

Wang squeezed Audrey aside and brought the rifle up, using the deck for support. Putting his eye near the scope, he began a slow sweep from left to right along the shoreline. He had two things going for him: the German scope and his uncannily sharp eyesight.

Another *thwip* and *plink* as a bullet ricocheted off one of the fishing pails stacked next to the pylon.

Steady, Wang thought. The scope eased past the *Tyrannosaurs* foot, making it look like it was barely a yard in front of him. Something else had caught his eye though – a flicker.

A last ray of the setting sun behind him.

Off a scope. Of course!

He carefully pivoted the rifle back past the theropod.

There!

It wasn't hard to spot after all – the sniper was kneeling atop a Land Rover parked between two of the buildings, barely two hundred-yards away.

A woman. Dressed in military fatigues.

He didn't know much about windage and such, but there wasn't time. He put the cross-hairs on her head and letting his breath out slowly, gently squeezed the trigger.

The Mauser kicked against his shoulder.

Still looking through the scope, he saw the sniper drop and fall off the vehicle. He waited a moment, but saw no more movement.

Oh shit, I just shot a woman.

Then Audrey was tapping his shoulder and pointing down at the boat.

Still being cautious, Taylan ran to them in a crouch, pausing only to snag the satchel next to Gorimov's body.

Minutes later the Tobin arced out into the bay as the island fell into the half-gloom nautical twilight, lit by continuing explosions of the complex.

The *Tyrannosaurus rex* now stood before the gap in the wharf, rearing its head and letting out its hissing roar as if announcing its victory at the dying calamity of the island it was stranded on. Behind it the now fully engulfed village made a violent backdrop, a fiery finale to a primeval nightmare.

Grant Taylan stood in the cockpit of the Tobin craft as Audrey steered them out to the trawler, which had slowed to pick them up just before exiting the bay. The wind whipped her hair around her dirt-smeared face. The air before them smelled of brine and the ocean. Past the *Vazão* the stacked Cumulus clouds along the horizon were bathed in a brilliant nimbus as the day gave up its last, casting the calm surface of the ocean in gun-metal blue.

Taylan didn't say anything. No prophetic or witty quips were on his mind, just a mix of relief and disbelief of surviving another ordeal. Behind them Wang sat with Roma and Miss Grey, rumpled, shocked, but very much alive survivors.

Taylan glanced at Audrey, who sensing his gaze, looked directly back at him for a moment.

What was the message there? he wondered. Just relief? Desire?

Her gaze lingered before going back to keeping an eye on their approach.

He had a hunch it might be the latter.

BLOODY AMERICANS!

Evening had settled on the *Vazão*, accompanied by the sound of eight bells which signaled the first watch.

A brief argument had broken out with the senior management of MuTron International – now led by David Zhou – who were insisting on taking the best accommodations now that Peyton's party was unaccounted for, until Miss Grey stepped in and read everyone the riot act. A brief word in Mr. Zhou's ear turned him a shade paler and he backed off immediately. She'd also taken the captain aside and made it clear in no uncertain terms who was now in charge of the show, and who would deal with the officials once they made landfall back in China. Whatever trials had happened on the island to her, it was clear to Taylan (and everyone) she was now empowered in a way he wouldn't have suspected. He wouldn't be at all surprised if she wound up on top of this whole mess, if anything from MuTron and the Lost Island of Kharamu could be salvaged.

After getting cleaned up and a quick trip to the infirmary to have Roma's hand rebandaged, Wang's leg seen to and splinters removed from Taylan's, the five had met up in the salon for dinner. A buffet had been laid out for the senior employees while the junior ones had been relegated to steerage class.

A pall of shock and gloom hung in the room, with conversation minimal and hushed. The five of them sat at a table removed from the others. Taylan, Audrey and Roma still had their original cabins booked under Peyton, while Wang – at Miss Grey's insistence - was given the Bannon's while Miss Grey had opted for the opulent master cabin Peyton had used.

"What do you think will happen?" Taylan asked Miss Grey as they picked at their food.

Cleaned and showered, aside from bruises and scratches, there was little to tell outwardly what all of them had been through in the previous 24 hours. Which made their dinner all the more surreal.

"There'll have to be a formal investigation, of course," Miss Grey replied, sipping at a rather large Tahitian cocktail. "By the government. They may bring in another firm to rebuild off the technology – there were a few competitors that would die to get their hands on it – but either way it will all be hushed up. There'll be none of this in the news. Anyone who breaths a word of it will not only find it flatly denied, they will have legal action taken against them as per the NDA's. That goes for everyone here at this table, yes?"

"Of course," Roma replied, studying her glass of wine. "If I may speak for everyone here?"

Taylan took a hit off his scotch and made a noncommittal shrug.

"I'm quite capable of speaking for myself," Audrey interjected. Then after a pause where everyone looked at her, added, "Er, *yes*, I agree."

Wang had been silent. The deaths of Tao and his grandfather was weighing heavily on his mind. He still had no idea what he would do when they got back to China. A vacation, he hoped, though he would have to find new work immediately. First, he had to figure out how to deal with the sword and rifle. Miss Grey had promised to help with the paperwork, letting him claim them as 'props'. The brief exultation at saving the day had faded as the reality sunk in, though he couldn't help but steal glances at both Roma and Miss Grey, wondering who might first come to him in his dreams later.

"So, what exactly did you say to Mister Zhou to shut him up? He looked ready to have us all tossed overboard," Audrey asked.

In response, Miss Grey simply smiled.

Not getting any headway, Audrey turned to Roma. "And what about you, Miss Banaji? Still fancy hands-on study with extinct species?"

That got a blanched look in response. Audrey immediately followed with: "Er, sorry, bad choice in words."

Roma managed a little laugh. "Yes, an understatement. But I believe I've been inspired to improve on my approach to Systematic Extinction."

"And you, Mr. Wang?" Audrey asked.

Wang continued to pick at his food. Shortly after they'd gotten out of the sickbay, Taylan had pulled him aside and queried him about the contents of Gorimov's satchel. The withered plant, he'd explained – without mentioning the plant leaves in his own satchel - were an unusual but not particularly remarkable variety. The moleskin notebook, however, proved much more interesting. "Totally Old School," Wang had said as they'd gone through it in Taylan's cabin. It included a bunch of encoded entries and passwords-usernames, but not to any accounts that made sense. Except for one. 763W33#2993TARBO8473. Wang thought the numbers were gibberish, but Taylan recognized immediately what they were. It was the address of a self-storage company in Manhattan followed by a room/container label and the four-digit pin. He'd used the place himself a couple times. He had a hunch he might locate a few interesting things there.

"I have no idea," Wang finally said, though that wasn't exactly true. Miss Grey had mentioned something else to him. A plan she had in mind to take to the MuTron board of directors when they got back.

Conversation fell off after that. Kharamu was falling away in the distance and the lull of the ships' engines below was like a balm.

After dinner Taylan had gone over to the bar with Audrey and Roma. Miss Grey had followed Wang shortly after he'd excused himself, but Taylan wasn't sure if there was anything to be made of that. Either way, it wasn't his business.

At the bar, he felt enormously tired, but also *over*-tired. It was one of those states where he wanted to prolong it just a bit further, if only to better relish the feeling of dropping asleep in his bed.

Roma had made small talk, but she looked haggard and after a glass of wine, wished both a good night and left.

Taylan ordered two more glasses of scotch and handed one to Audrey as they walked out onto the rear deck, looking back from the aft rail. Kharamu was still giving off a distant glow on the horizon. It seemed impossible they were here again, on the ship, intact, after what had just happened. *How many were dead? Was anyone still alive back there? And poor Bello.* Taylan had looked on in horror as the Tarbosaurus had snatched him up like a piece of candy.

That's your beloved dinosaurs for you. Never forget it.

After a minute of drinking in silence, Audrey turned to him. Her blue eyes were hard, like she was looking for a battle.

"What is your bloody deal, anyway?"

Taylan's brow furrowed. "What do you mean?"

"What do I mean? I mean with *women*. You're always after such daft, air-head eye candy."

Taylan was stunned. He'd been expecting her to unload about what happened back on the island. This was completely out of left field. Typically Audrey.

"The hell I do," he said, annoyed.

Audrey rolled her eyes. "Oh, come off it, you're always going after those pretty-faced bimbos with vast amount of gaseous matter between their ears! Confess!"

Now Taylan felt his temper rising. "I do not! Name one."

"Opal? The actress from 'Which way is Up?'"

"That was just a date!"

"For three bloody months?"

Taylan was taken aback. Then the penny dropped. He chuckled.

"You're jealous," he said, quietly.

She cocked her head at him. "Seriously?"

"Seriously," he echoed. Then tossing his scotch over the rail, he snatched her in his arms and gave her a kiss on the lips.

She broke off and slapped him hard on the face, staring at him with a look of ... *what? Anger? Lust? Love?*

Just as he thought she was going to turn and walk away she lifted her chin, "Bloody Americans!" she said, then tossing her drink over as well, stepped forward and taking his head in both her hands, kissed him back.

Several hours later, Taylan woke up.

He wasn't sure why – at first, he put it down to simple over-exhaustion and nerves. They were sprawled across the double bed, the sheets akimbo. From the porthole windows moonlight reflecting off the ocean sent dappled reflections dancing around the room.

It was one of those utterly serene, peaceful moments; the kind cast into a hyperdetailed relief one only truly experiences after surviving a particularly grueling, deadly experience. Several things imprinted themselves on his awareness: the warmth of Audrey's naked body next to his, the twist of the sheet revealing one small but wonderfully-shaped breast, sweeping away down towards her hips where a tantalizing tuft of her pubic hair was just visible. There was the slight citrus smell of shampoo from her hair, the hint of lemon oil from the furniture, the compact luxury of the wood cabinetry and furnishings of the stateroom.

In that much, he had to give it to Peyton: it was like waking up in wonderful mid-century dream, one where the good guys won, and the monsters were defeated.

Taylan took a slow breath and let it out. He felt battered and exhausted, but also basking in the afterglow of sex. Looking over, he traced a finger along the side of Audrey's head, pushing an errant strand of hair away from her cheek. She stirred, nuzzling his hand. The corner of her mouth twitched in a hint of a smile in her sleep.

London seemed like a million miles – and years – away. How the hell had they gotten from there to here?

The room was a mess – clothes tossed every which way. Audrey's purse was on the nightstand where she'd dropped it right after pulling him into the room. Her bra hung off the little lamp next to it. He could see that his own underwear draped over the vintage radio on the writing desk. One of his shoes lay on the corner of the bed. It looked like they'd undressed in the middle of a tornado.

Taylan decided he had to get up and take a leak. Like their original counterparts, the staterooms used a common bathroom instead of private ones. There were two in the stern compartments for the passenger's exclusive use.

He plucked his underwear off the radio and slipping into them, stepped quietly over to the door.

Later, he realized the faint whiff of cigarette smoke from beyond the door should have been a tip off. At the moment, however, he was still half-asleep and having made it onto the ship (and into Audrey's arms) at such long odds, let his guard down.

His initial thought was that – as if in a sort of bizarre reply – it was Roma standing in the hallway in front of him. With the hall lights turned low for the evening, the person before him was dimly lit, and roughly the same height. That impression quickly vanished as she took a step towards him, revealing the icily beautiful features of his ex-girlfriend.

Yen.

He was also aware that there was a rather large butcher knife in her right hand. In her left was a cigarette, held between her straightened first two fingers in that odd, feminine affectation of hers.

From the various butts strewn on the floor, she must have been standing there for some time.

Her smile had a cruel turn to it.

"Aren't you going to invite me in?" she whispered.

Taylan shook his head.

"No."

He made to slam the door in her face, but Yen was faster. She came at him so quickly with the knife, he had no choice but to grab her wrist with his free hand to stop it from entering his chest.

They tumbled backwards into the room. Though only five-three, Yen was as fierce and vicious as an enraged cat – whatever she lacked in muscle weight she made up for in speed and a dizzying level of agility.

Taylan got one slice to his ribs and another that narrowly missed his jugular before he was able to toss her, sending her crashing into the bureau. She bounced back, knife held up, then her eyes went to Audrey, who was still out cold on the bed.

"Her!?" Yen hissed "I bet you were fucking her the whole time we were dating! *Weren't you!?*"

Taylan knew there was no point in answering. If there was a point of reasoning with this woman, it was way in the distant past. If it was ever even there.

The only thing on his mind now was either to disable her, or failing that, kill her if necessary. He felt his heart hammering in his chest, his system flooding with adrenaline he would have thought exhausted after the last twenty-four hours.

Yen launched herself at him, the knife flashing in the dim light.

Taylan feinted to one side, then jumped to the other, his right fist coming up at her head.

It might have worked.

His foot landed on Audrey's silk panties and shot out from under him and Taylan landed on his ass. Yen stumbled but again – like a cat – landed nimbly and was on him in a second, the tip of the knife missing his head by a hair as he jerked it away.

He was able to grab her wrist again with his left hand but was forced to fend her off with his right as she hammered him with punches and then clawed at his eyes. He tried to grab her fingers, but she countered by grabbing the knife with both hands and put every ounce of her strength into driving it through his left eye.

The feral rage in her face and disheveled hair made him think of some sort of savage demon. Worse, despite his strength, she had better leverage and was a split second from driving the blade through his cranium.

"Die!" she hissed.

Taylan realized he was about to do just that.

Just as suddenly her body jerked, her manic eyes flaring even wider. The blade stopped a half inch from his eyeball. As if whisked away, the rage in her glare winked out, the eyes taking on a faraway look to some infinite point past his shoulder.

Her body went stiff.

Taylan looked on in puzzled horror as she convulsed once more, then fell to one side. He looked up to see Audrey, completely naked, crouched down behind her. Then he saw the heavy-duty needle sticking out of Yen's neck.

Audrey looked equal parts mortified and angry.

Taylan propped himself up and pressed his fingers to the other side of Yen's neck. There was no pulse.

"I-I picked it up in Burroughs' lab. I thought it was a tranquilizer of some kind."

Pushing Yen aside, Taylan got to his feet and helped Audrey up.

"I'd say it was a little more than a tranquilizer. Punched her clock on a dime. She's dead."

"Oh shit." Audrey put her fingers to her temples as she huddled into Taylan's arms. "Now what?"

Taylan glanced down at the body. He was giddy with relief. But this was a whole other dilemma. Chinese authorities frowned on murder, justified or not.

"All right. Here's what we're going to do . . ."

THE LOST WORLD OF KHARAMU, 0800 HOURS.

The sun was coming up, giving the already fetid jungle an instant extra ten degrees of heat. Next to the Tahitian Chestnut tree, a figure curled up in a fetal position stirred and groaned, half-covered by low nipa palms. Around it several Compys picked over remains of the bodies, while nearby several Hadrosaurs grazed on ferns and bushes, their golden brown mottled skin glistening in the damp morning air.

A cough came from the figure, causing several Compys to scatter, though the large Hadrosaurs were unperturbed.

Vlad rolled over onto his back, looking up and the snatches of sky between the canopy of leaves. He couldn't believe he was alive. All he remembered was waking up in the middle of the night, wracked with thirst, and nibbling on the root of the plant he'd found the day before, as it at least had some moisture. He'd gone in and out of consciousness several times after that, once ravenously hungry and eating at least half the root.

Then nothing.

Until now.

Another rustle from behind him caught his attention. He tried to reach for the machete at his hip but was too weak. All he could do was stay there and look up at the sky.

Another rustle, followed by the distinct sound of a footstep near his head.

A shadow fell over his face.

Looking up, he saw it was an Asian woman, her right eye covered in a makeshift bloody bandage. Smaller pieces of the shattered scope were still embedded around her face, but she was confident she would live, though probably lose her right eye.

Her face was merciless.

"Who did you kill?" she asked in badly accented English.

Vlad closed his eyes slowly.

This trip sucks, he thought. "No one," he whispered aloud. He feebly lifted his hand, which seemed to weigh a ton. Surprisingly, he could move his fingers. "Spider bite" he added. "I thought I was dead."

Dinh studied him a minute longer, reaching a decision. *If he cut his hair and shaved off the scraggly beard and had a decent bath, he might do.*

"Not yet," she said, squatting down to help him up. Then she said three words she'd never said to anyone in her life: "I need you."

EPILOGUE: ONE YEAR LATER.

From the top of the Palisades cliffs, the vast expanse of the Hudson River Valley settling into evening was breathtaking.

Across the river the last rays of the sun touched the waterfront of Wyvern Falls, while the river itself had momentarily turned gunmetal blue, making the barge churning northward toward World's End appear it was navigating through liquid mercury.

One of the logs on the fire popped, sending a cascade of sparks skyward. Technically, it was illegal to set a campfire in this section of NY State Park, but it had been raining lately and Taylan didn't think anyone was going to call them on it.

"I've never seen anything quite like this," Roma said, taking a sip of her beer. Dressed in black sportswear with a scuba-style windbreaker, Taylan thought she looked sharp and fresh. And a hell of a lot more interesting than the landscape before them, magnificent as it was.

He was sitting next to her on a log, a dozen feet from a three-hundred foot drop to the rocks below. Not far, in fact, from a hair-raising fall he had taken just over a year previous, courtesy of a certain Russian now lying dead half way around the planet.

"It *is* something," he agreed.

"So, you're going to show me this 'groundbreaking' find down the cliff-face tomorrow morning?"

"That's the plan," Taylan said, taking a pull off his own beer. He'd brought along a six-pack of Newberg Pale Ale, from a local microbrewery.

"No daring exploits this time. Promise? You need to be in one piece for the wedding."

"I'll do my best," he said, looking off across the river.

"Having second thoughts?"

"No."

He was, however, contemplating what a strange and convoluted world it was.

After Audrey had made a quick end to Yen's murderous rampage he'd decided the best solution was to toss the syringe out the porthole window and bring Miss Grey in to handle the damage control. She'd done it with ruthless efficiency.

For a price.

In exchange for a free pass Audrey was going to use Chinese assistants and Chinese fabricated dinosaurs on the new program she was going to take back to London for the Natural History Museum. Two MuTron employees had shown up and Yen's body was carted away. Audrey had been mortified, but when she spoke up Miss Grey had simply held up one finger.

They'd made it back to London, but their relationship didn't last more than a month. Taylan suspected it had something to do with that final battle in the cabin, but it may have simply been the reality that their personalities brought out the absolute worse in each other. In the end it was Audrey who pulled the plug, walking out of his hotel room after yet another argument over dinner. In a way it seemed appropriate – Taylan figured that made them even.

He'd returned to the states sullen, but not completely down. There'd been the matter of Gorimov's storage room, which yielded not just another *Tarbosaurus* skeleton, but a treasure trove of other contraband dinosaur remains, including several unknown specimens intact in amber. The bonus was a strong box with enough cash to keep Taylan solvent for a good many years. Not the windfall promised by Peyton, perhaps, but Taylan figured too much money would be an anathema to his well-being.

Then over Thanksgiving, Roma had shown up in New York en route to a paleontology conference in D.C. and they'd met up for dinner at Fraunces Tavern down in the financial district. Taylan had suspected her visit wasn't entirely business, but despite a flirtatious stroll along the lower Manhattan waterfront, didn't put much weight on it.

Until he'd gotten a call the day before New Year's.

He'd offered to meet her in Manhattan again. This time she'd shown up at his doorstep with a vintage bottle of Krug and two glasses. She didn't leave for a week.

From there things had progressed with a natural smoothness Taylan didn't think was conceivable. Roma Banaji, he discovered, was quite a lot of fun to spend time with. Unlike Audrey, her personality was like a cool drink of water to his. Six months later, he still couldn't get enough of her, whether it was debating the accuracies of the dinosaur species they'd encountered on Kharamu or spur-of-the-moment lovemaking sessions anywhere from his truck to his campus office.

When he'd popped the question one night, while in bed, it hadn't required much guesswork. She 'officially' moved in with him a week later.

Her family was relieved.

"Mmmm," what are you thinking?" she asked, her eyes flashing in the firelight.

Taylan chuckled. In his hand was the broken tooth of the *Tarbosaurus* that had landed near them that day. Audrey had retrieved it and later sent to him as a keepsake. It'd come with a note: *Reminder: in case Dr. Grant Taylan gets too cocky – he was almost somebody's lunch.*

It had become a reminder of a lot of things, but mostly of how terribly wrong things could go so quickly and yet . . . be horrifically amazing. A paradox. Oddly, it didn't make him think of Audrey, but of Bello. Snatched out of life in an instant.

He forced himself back into the moment. Something he'd gotten even better at.

"I was thinking of a dirty joke."

She touched his hand with her fingers. "I love those. Actually, I was thinking of something dirty too. Not a joke, though."

"You don't say?"

"I *do* say."

She leaned over and gave him a nip on the ear, followed by the teasing caress of her tongue. He felt his groin stiffen in response. When it came to sex, he'd discovered, Roma didn't seem to have any inhibitions. At all.

"Now enough talk, Doctor," she said. She stood up and giving him a flirtatious over-the-shoulder look, disappeared into the tent.

Taylan stood up and stretched.

Always the quiet ones, he thought.

It was going to be a long night.

THE END

NOTES FOR THE CURIOUS

First, I would like to thank several people who helped pull this tale off: my wife, Tomiko, and her incredible patience at being my first critic and beta-reader. Dana White for tipping me off about a certain locally manufactured motor yacht and John Wunderlich for his helpful tips on riding motorcycles with sidecars, though the hardcore bikers will chuckle at 'adjustments' I made to reality. Gary Lucas at Severed Press for enabling a story idea fermenting since my childhood to become a reality. My friend, Yangyang Wang, for his helpful advice on how to swear properly in Mandarin. Also, the folks at the American Museum of Natural History in NYC and the Natural History Museum in Kensington, London. When it comes to riveting, graphic dinosaur displays, the Brits really take the cake, especially those gore-stained animatronic raptors and that life-sized T-Rex that *moves*. But that exhibit of the Titanosaur at the AMNH was stupefying in scale and is an irrevocable demonstration of how little we do know about these giants that roamed the earth a millennia ago.

Apologies to Londoners - some liberties were taken with the geography along the Thames to facilitate the story line, though All Hallows Lane is very real. And yes, I was inspired by a London taxi driver who was an elderly Asian man with a nearly incomprehensible Cockney accent, but I did understand enough to keep me laughing all the way from Heathrow to Russell Square.

Although some may think the events in Mumbai are a little over-the-top, I can assure you, they are not. Although not pursued by a bunch of gun-toting Vietnamese, I did survive a catastrophic monsoon there that flooded the entire city and managed to escape after many days in a series of events that seemed right out of an Indiana Jones movie, and in many ways, was far, far worse than the events depicted here. The Mumbai Marriott is pretty much as described, or at least was, and is a wonderful hotel to stay at. Special thanks to the liquor store down the street who provided me with a fine bottle of Chivas for "medicinal" purposes during the crisis – it's possible the alcohol staved off the worst of the mosquitos that were a nonstop assault. That's the only explanation I have for not contracting Dengue & Malaria, as I had absolutely no immunizations.

Kharamu is entirely fictional, so don't look to book your vacation there anytime soon. It was inspired by my own trip to Malaysia & Singapore during July, in a season I would definitely not recommend visiting the tropics. I thought they *must* be joking when they said, "more than 100% humidity". They were not.

Also, thanks, of course, to Michael Crichton, who inspired new generations of dinosaur lovers and took what was a fringe topic and turned into something mainstream and accessible. I seriously doubt I'll ever experience the gobsmacked, dumbfounded exuberance I had walking out of the theater after that first Jurassic Park movie. A lot has changed in the decades since that movie, and I've tried to integrate those new discoveries where possible. For those interested, here's some of the sources I referenced for recent updates in dinosaur discoveries:

1. Lida Xing China University of Geosciences, Beijin/ Ryan McKellar Royal Saskatchewan Museum, Regina, Canada
2. John Ruben, Professor of Zoology at Oregon State University
3. Mary Schwitzer, North Carolina State University in Raleigh: T Rex DNA:
    http://www.smithsonianmag.com/science-nature/dinosaur-shocker-115306469/?page=1
4. Jack Horner – the very real paleontologist behind Sam Neill's character in Jurassic Park: https://www.washingtonpost.com/national/health-science/paleontologist-jack-horner-is-hard-at-work-trying-to-turn-a-chicken-into-a-dinosaur/2014/11/10/cb35e46e-4e59-11e4-babe-e91da079cb8a_story.html
5. Extinction theories:
    http://www.ucmp.berkeley.edu/diapsids/extinctheory.html
    www.sciencedaily.com/releases/2010/02/100209183335.htm
    http://www.businessinsider.com/lisa-randall-thinks-dark-matter-killed-the-dinosaurs-2015-11 http://www.iflscience.com/space/dinosaur-extinction-may-have-been-caused-interstellar-cloud/
6. Behavior: http://www.ucmp.berkeley.edu/fosrec/ScotchmoorDino.html
7. Size issue:
    http://phenomena.nationalgeographic.com/2013/02/25/dinosaur-reproduction-not-ancient-gravity-made-sauropods-super-sized/

There's plenty more, if you start digging, and it's a constantly evolving landscape. There's compelling developments that dinosaurs will be brought back in our lifetime, most likely through genetic manipulation of birds. Of course, this begs the deeper question, which is *should* we be attempting such a thing, and what are the consequences?

On that note, I hope you enjoyed the tale.

Best,

Robert J. Stava

Robert Stava is a writer, art director & musician currently living along the Hudson River, not far apparently, from that strange village of Wyvern Falls where so many of his tales are set. His wife Tomiko Magario is a professional ballet dancer & teacher in NYC. An ex "Mad Man" and NYC musician, Stava is also an avid mountain biker and holds a 2nd Degree Black Belt in Karate. When it comes to writing, his firm belief in "nothing beats hands-on experience" has landed him in the ER several times over the years, much to his wife's chagrin. These days when not holed up in his attic overlooking the river knocking out horror stories, he can be found poking around old ruins and cemeteries in the area.

His short horror stories have appeared in various anthologies in the U.S and U.K. "Nightmare from World's End" - his fourth novel set in Wyvern Falls – was published in late 2106 by Severed Press. "Lost World of Kharamu" is his first foray into the world of dinosaurs. His next novel, "Neptune's Reckoning" is a Science Fiction/Horror tale set out in Montauk, NY, and is due out from Severed Press in late 2018.

His first book, "Combat Recon" – a pictorial history of his great uncle's experiences as a 5th Air Force combat photographer in the SW Pacific during WWII – was published as hardcover in 2007.

SEVEREDPRESS

 facebook.com/severedpress
 twitter.com/severedpress

CHECK OUT OTHER GREAT DINOSAUR THRILLERS

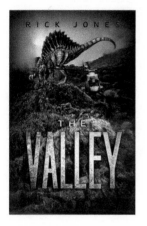

THE VALLEY
by Rick Jones

In a dystopian future, a self-contained valley in Argentina serves as the 'far arena' for those convicted of a crime. Inside the Valley: carnivorous dinosaurs generated from preserved DNA. The goal: cross the Valley to get to the Gates of Freedom. The chance of survival: no one has ever completed the journey. Convicted of crimes with little or no merit, Ben Peyton and others must battle their way across fields filled with the world's deadliest apex predators in order to reach salvation. All the while the journey is caught on cameras and broadcast to the world as a reality show, the deaths and killings real, the macabre appetite of the audience needing to be satiated as Ben Peyton leads his team to escape not only from a legal system that's more interested in entertainment than in justice, but also from the predators of the Valley.

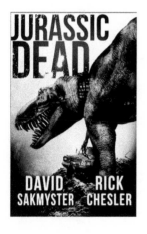

JURASSIC DEAD
by Rick Chesler & David Sakmyster

An Antarctic research team hoping to study microbial organisms in an underground lake discovers something far more amazing: perfectly preserved dinosaur corpses. After one thaws and wakes ravenously hungry, it becomes apparent that death, like life, will find a way.
Environmental activist Alex Ramirez, son of the expedition's paleontologist, came to Antarctica to defend the organisms from extinction, but soon learns that it is the human race that needs protecting.

SEVEREDPRESS

 facebook.com/severedpress
 twitter.com/severedpress

CHECK OUT OTHER GREAT DINOSAUR THRILLERS

WRITTEN IN STONE
by David Rhodes

Charles Dawson is trapped 100 million years in the past. Trying to survive from day to day in a world of dinosaurs he devises a plan to change his fate. As he begins to write messages in the soft mud of a nearby stream, he can only hope they will be found by someone who can stop his time travel. Professor Ron Fontana and Professor Ray Taggit, scientists with opposing views, each discover the fossilized messages. While attempting to save Charles, Professor Fontana, his daughter Lauren and their friend Danny are forced to join Taggit and his group of mercenaries. Taggit does not intend to rescue Charles Dawson, but to force Dawson to travel back in time to gather samples for Taggit's fame and fortune. As the two groups jump through time they find they must work together to make it back alive as this fast-paced thriller climaxes at the very moment the age of dinosaurs is ending.

HARD TIME
by Alex Laybourne

Rookie officer Peter Malone and his heavily armed team are sent on a deadly mission to extract a dangerous criminal from a classified prison world. A Kruger Correctional facility where only the hardest, most vicious criminals are sent to fend for themselves, never to return.

But when the team come face to face with ancient beasts from a lost world, their mission is changed. The new objective: Survive.

SEVEREDPRESS

f facebook.com/severedpress
🐦 twitter.com/severedpress

CHECK OUT OTHER GREAT DINOSAUR THRILLERS

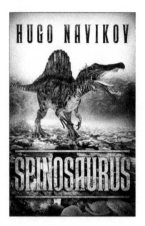

SPINOSAURUS
by Hugo Navikov

Brett Russell is a hunter of the rarest game. His targets are cryptids, animals denied by science. But they are well known by those living on the edges of civilization, where monsters attack and devour their animals and children and lay ruin to their shantytowns.

When a shadowy organization sends Brett to the Congo in search of the legendary dinosaur cryptid Kasai Rex, he will face much more than a terrifying monster from the past. Spinosaurus is a dinosaur thriller packed with intrigue, action and giant prehistoric predators.

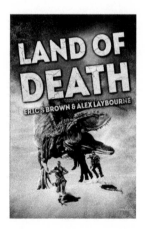

LAND OF DEATH
by Eric S Brown & Alex Laybourne

A group of American soldiers, fleeing an organized attack on their base camp in the Middle East, encounter a storm unlike anything they've seen before. When the storm subsides, they wake up to find themselves no longer in the desert and perhaps not even on Earth. The jungle they've been deposited in is a place ruled by prehistoric creatures long extinct. Each day is a struggle to survive as their ammo begins to run low and virtually everything they encounter, in this land they've been hurled into, is a deadly threat.

CPSIA information can be obtained
at www.ICGtesting.com
Printed in the USA
FSHW010449090119
54892FS